DANGEROUS WATERS

Twenty-year-old Phoebe Dymond, a trained herbalist and midwife, boards the packet ship *Providence* bound for Jamaica and an arranged marriage. Incidents on board provoke clashes between Phoebe and the ship's surgeon, Jowan Crossley, but their professional antagonism turns to mutual respect and a deepening attraction neither dare acknowledge. Arriving in Kingston after a skirmish with a French privateer, they find the town in the grip of a slave revolt. Terrifying events on the plantation of which she will be mistress force Phoebe to relinquish all hope of the happiness she had glimpsed, but fate has one more trick to play...

DANGEROUS WATERS

DANGEROUS WATERS

by

Jane Jackson

Magna Large Print Books
Long Preston, North Yorkshire,
BD23 4ND, England.

British Library Cataloguing in Publication Data.

Jackson, Jane
    Dangerous waters.

    A catalogue record of this book is
    available from the British Library

    ISBN   978-0-7505-2674-6

First published in Great Britain in 2006 by Robert Hale Limited

Copyright © Jane Jackson 2006

Cover illustration © Len Thurston by arrangement with
P.W.A. International Ltd.

The right of Jane Jackson to be identified as the author of this work
has been asserted by her in accordance with the Copyright, Designs
and Patents Act, 1988

Published in Large Print 2007 by arrangement with
Robert Hale Ltd.

Magna Large Print is an imprint of Library Magna Books Ltd.

Printed and bound in Great Britain by
T.J. (International) Ltd., Cornwall, PL28 8RW

00322076

Chapter One

The bitter pungency of herbs and brandy stung the back of Phoebe's nose as she poured the dark liquid carefully from basin to jug. She tipped the thick mush into a second bowl lined with muslin then, gathering up the cloth, squeezed the remaining liquid from what was left of the elder flowers, peppermint and yarrow that had been steeping for two weeks above the warmth of the kitchen range.

Shaking the mush from the cloth into a third bowl, already half full, she set it aside. Later she would spread it on her herb garden to nourish the soil and strengthen the new shoots. First the tincture must be poured into the waiting row of small brown bottles.

The winter had been cold and wet with easterly gales from the Channel. Howling along the streets that ran parallel to Falmouth's inner harbour, the wind had sliced like a blade through coats and shawls, spreading epidemics of colds and influenza. Spring should have brought relief. Instead, the warm moisture-laden air had acted like a smothering blanket. Phoebe had never known so many cases of bronchitis, and the herb cupboard had never been so bare. She was dispensing remedies faster than she could replace them.

Tipping the last drops from the jug, she corked the bottles tightly. The labels waited, secured beneath a small stone mortar. She had written them the previous evening. Uncle George had been out at a supper party. So while Mrs Lynas and Mary gossiped comfortably in the kitchen, she had sat alone by the fire in the drawing-room with her notebooks and her memories.

She had known for a while that change was coming. It was inevitable. And fear of the future feathered like cold breath across the back of her neck.

She picked up the mortar, its stone bowl cool and smooth beneath her fingers. It had been one of Aunt Sarah's favourites. She pictured her aunt's beloved face furrowed in concentration, then softening into a smile at the first cry of a healthy newborn baby.

Though Phoebe experienced that same satisfaction at a safe delivery, hers was still tinged with amazement, awe and relief. This was not surprising given the contrast between her aunt's long experience and the brevity of her own. Yet despite the fact that she was only twenty years of age and as yet unmarried, women once delivered by her aunt now asked for 'Sarah's girl' to attend them. To Phoebe this was a source of great pride. And a constant reminder of the debt she owed her aunt.

Inhaling the scents of melted beeswax and lavender, of thyme, winter-green and marigold, she felt a sharp stab of loss. Then, hearing her uncle in the passage, she realized from his purposeful tread towards the kitchen that the post-boy had brought a letter. Would it be the news he hoped for? The prospect of another prolonged stay in London filled her with dread.

She just had time to compose herself before the door swung open. Seeing his downcast expression Phoebe's tension eased.

'Ah, there you are. Well, my cousin has replied.' Her uncle waved the sheet of paper in his fingers. As she glimpsed the crossed and re-crossed lines, Phoebe swallowed. 'I daresay you will not be surprised to learn,' he continued, glancing at her from under thick wiry brows, 'that Amelia has declined to present you for a second season.'

A tremor ran down Phoebe's legs, making her knees feel oddly weak. But well schooled in hiding her feelings she ensured her relief did not show on her face. 'How is Mrs Winnan?' she enquired politely.

'Well enough. However, she's made it plain–' He broke off at the sound of footsteps on the back stairs. The latch rattled up and the house-maid whirled in.

'Oh, beg pardon, Captain, I didn't know you was–'

'It's all right, Mary.' Quickly, Phoebe untied the apron covering her high-waisted gown of lavender muslin and hung it on the back of the scullery door. 'Leave everything on the table. When Mrs Lynas gets back tell her I'll make sure it's all cleared away before she needs to start lunch.' She tugged down close fitting sleeves she had pushed up her forearms to avoid splashes on her cuffs. 'Shall we go through to the morning-room, Uncle?'

A fire burned in the grate; dancing flames throwing warmth and cheer into the high-ceilinged room. Phoebe welcomed both. For though the tall

9

window faced east it was still only April and the mid-morning sunlight held little heat.

As her uncle closed the door with a firmness that betrayed his frustration, Phoebe crossed to a Queen Anne chair upholstered in worn green damask and sat down, folding her hands in her lap. Since her aunt's death she had hoped something might happen that would allow her to remain here in the only home she could remember. In fact something had: though she didn't think her uncle was aware of the offer made in his name. In any case as far as she was concerned the price was too high. So what now?

'I was a sad disappointment to her.' Phoebe pulled a rueful face.

George Oakes slumped into a chair opposite, heaving another sigh as he rubbed his face with his free hand. 'I think we're all agreed on that.'

Phoebe braced herself. 'What exactly does she say?' Her uncle had not been himself for over a week, lurching between frowning preoccupation and false heartiness. She suspected his abstraction was in some way connected to her future, and if he didn't tell her soon she would have to ask. Though she dreaded change, not knowing was even worse. But this must be dealt with first.

He sighed, pursing his lips as he scanned the letter. 'She found your lack of enthusiasm deeply hurtful. She also considers that for a young female with so little to recommend her you demonstrated an astonishing lack of gratitude for the opportunities she had gone to such trouble to arrange.'

Phoebe bent her head and tucked a feathery tendril behind her ear. Her hair had been yet another cause of friction. All the rage in London when she had been there the previous year, the new style had only just reached Cornwall. In Falmouth and Flushing, fashion-conscious young women sported hair cropped into a helmet of curls over the top and sides with the back left long to be dressed in loops or ringlets.

Phoebe's quiet but unyielding refusal to have her thick tresses cut into a style that required hours of attention from a personal maid had further infuriated cousin Amelia who considered it a personal attack on her own fashion-sense.

Rather than submit to the scissors, Phoebe twisted her hair into a coil high on her crown during the day, and for evening arranged it in a fall of glossy black curls. 'I'm sorry, Uncle. I should have been more appreciative. I know it was very kind of her and that everything she did was with the best of intentions but – it was – I felt–' *bullied*. Phoebe shrugged helplessly. 'I felt exactly like a cow being paraded at the market.'

Shock and the briefest spasm of a smile were instantly smothered by irritation. 'For heaven's sake, girl! Good God, no wonder Amelia found you impossible.' His vehemence surprised Phoebe. 'You *know* that's the way these things are done. How else would well-brought-up young women meet future husbands if not at properly supervised social events? That's the whole point of all those parties, suppers and dances. And it worked. You attracted the attentions of not just one, but two gentlemen. That was what upset Amelia so much. You received two proposals. And you declined them both.' He shook his head and waved the letter. 'She still hasn't got over it.'

'I'm sorry,' Phoebe repeated. She had wanted to please Uncle George and Cousin Amelia by doing what was expected of her. Yet she had been haunted by Aunt Sarah's face.

Both gentlemen had been excellent dancers, and had kept her amused with conversation and flattery during their frequent encounters at the various balls, parties and suppers. Each in turn after talking at length about his property and his many acquaintances and preferred pastimes, had quizzed her about her own interests.

She had seen no reason to dissemble. If she were truly honest with herself she had perhaps been guilty of unbecoming pride at her involvement in work so important and so satisfying. She had assumed – hoped – they would understand. But on each occasion she had watched her escort's surprise harden into disapproval. When both gentlemen had declared her occupation 'totally unsuitable' and made it clear that if she wished to further the relationship she could not possibly expect to continue such activities, she had known marrying either of them was out of the question.

'Please,' she had begged her uncle who, between voyages, had visited in the hope of being asked for her hand. 'Please don't ask me to accept. It would be a betrayal of everything Aunt Sarah taught me. She called my talent a blessed gift from God. Giving it up would be like – like losing a limb. How could I be happy? I have the knowledge and ability to alleviate suffering yet they would forbid me to use it. How could any man who would demand such a sacrifice be the right husband for me? To marry such a man would be–' She searched wildly for a suitable analogy. 'It would be like punishing me for a crime I haven't committed.'

Taken aback by her distress her uncle had tried to calm her. 'Now, now.' He flapped his hands, shifting uncomfortably. 'There's no need for that. Don't take on so. I only thought – and I am bound to point out that if *both* gentlemen who offered for you made the same stipulation, then you must see that it will not be easy to find another who thinks differently.'

'Not in London perhaps,' Phoebe agreed, her heart still thudding against her ribs. 'Clearly gentlemen from outside Cornwall are more conservative in their outlook. It's very plain they would be happier with a bride willing to devote herself exclusively to running a home and rearing children. Believe me, Uncle, I do not intend any criticism, but such a life is not for me. I was raised differently. You and Aunt Sarah were far more liberal. Did you not encourage her in her work?'

Wry and fond, George Oakes's snort of laughter echoed his expression. 'Encourage? She never needed that. No, I married Sarah knowing she must and would do what she was born to. With me away at sea so much of the time it was good for her to have an interest, especially once the boys were out of leading strings and growing away. But–'

'Please, Uncle George, believe me, I could not be happy with anything less.' As the conversation replayed itself in her head, Phoebe watched her uncle re-read the letter.

'Oh well.' Blowing out a breath he pushed a large scarred hand through his cropped hair, now streaked with silver though he was only fifty-four. 'There's no point in raking over dead coals. But the fact is' – he cleared his throat, averting his gaze from hers as she waited – 'the fact is, and I'm sure you must have realized this yourself, things can't just drift on the way they have. It's almost two years now since we lost–' He looked away for a moment. 'I daresay it was harder for you than it was for the boys. They were already away at sea. And from the day you came to us you spent more time with your aunt than we ever did. That's not to say I don't miss her. I do. I think of her every day. But–'

'But it's nearly two years,' Phoebe repeated quietly, letting him know she understood what he meant even if he could not bring himself to put it into words. Just before Christmas she had begun to hear his name linked with increasing frequency to those of two very different but equally deter-mined widows.

These murmurs had coincided with her uncle's acceptance of an increasing number of invitations to the parties, suppers and balls that were so much a feature of a packet captain's life ashore. As a senior captain on the Lisbon run his round trips lasted less than a month. His relatively short absences were the only reason she had been able to remain in the house with only the cook and maid for company without the situation giving rise to gossip.

As he nodded, she read in his gaze shame, defiance, and a plea for understanding. Then he raised the letter, shaking it. 'If only you could have– Two proposals, *two.*' He shook his head. 'No wonder Amelia – still, what's done can't be undone. But we have to think about your future.'

'And yours,' she said gently.

'What?' Clearly startled, he frowned. 'How did...? Who...? What are you talking about?'

Phoebe took a deep breath. 'When I was down in the town yesterday I met Mrs Tonkin. She left me in no doubt that there is a strong attachment between you. She also gave me to understand that when you both feel the time is right to marry she would be happy for me to continue living here. And she is sure I would be pleased to repay that generosity by assuming the role of nanny and governess to her three children. Unpaid, naturally.'

'She what?' George Oakes spluttered, flushing. 'But I never – mean I haven't– She actually said– Well! Good God!'

'I have to tell you, Uncle, much though I appreciate the offer, I would not be able to accept. The thought of spending all day looking after her appalling children–'

'Phoebe!' A flush darkened his weather-beaten face. 'Still, I take your point. They are a bit of a handful. Though that's hardly surprising when you remember how long they've been without a father's discipline and guidance. Martha's done her best since Henry died.' As Phoebe's brows climbed, he raked his hair again. 'All right, she's not as firm with them as she might be. But you would soon–'

'No, Uncle,' Phoebe was quietly firm.

He met her gaze. 'No. You're right. You deserve better than that: and better than those two in London. You do have a gift, girl. I don't know about such things. But Sarah did, God rest her. I miss her something awful, Phoebe. Lord knows I'd do anything to have her back.' His gesture held both anger and helplessness. 'I don't expect you to understand. How could you? But the thing is – you see, I–' His chin jutted defiantly but his gaze pleaded for understanding. 'I don't want to spend the rest of my life alone.'

His understanding and his confession brought a lump to Phoebe's throat. Fifteen years ago she had come to this house, to this family, an orphan. Aunt Sarah had gradually taken the place of a mother she could no longer picture. Uncle George had welcomed her, provided for her. That she had been of less importance to him than his two sons, who treated her with the same careless affection they might have bestowed upon a stray kitten, was perfectly understandable. He had always been kind, and this was the only home she could remember. But it was beginning to look as if she had outstayed her welcome. She forced a smile.

'If you have found happiness again, Uncle George, then I'm glad for you. Naturally you will want – when – I mean, how soon would you like me to leave?'

'Dear life, Phoebe! I'm not about to throw you into the street. For Heaven's sake! Do you really think me so shabby?'

16

'No, of course not. I'm sorry, I didn't mean– I certainly didn't intend to–'

'Yes, well, enough said. We'll talk later.' He cleared his throat. 'Now, about dinner tonight. I've invited two guests. Mrs Bishop–'

'Not Mrs Tonkin?' Phoebe asked in surprise.

He shook his head, and his face twisted briefly, half embarrassed half ashamed. 'Martha is a good woman, and I'm fond of her. But there was never any question – I don't know where she got the idea. Truth is, you're right about those children.' He shuddered. 'I couldn't be doing with all that again, not at my time of life. No, it's Carina – Mrs Bishop – who's coming tonight.' He seemed to find his neckcloth suddenly tight and loosened it with a forefinger. 'As you know, she never had children. She told me she used to consider it a great sorrow. But since she – since we – got to know each other' – he cleared his throat again – 'her thoughts on the matter have changed.'

Astonished, then touched as once again colour darkened his complexion, Phoebe was intrigued.

'Carina says,' he went on, losing the struggle to contain both astonishment and pride, 'that without other demands or distractions in her life, she's free to devote herself entirely to my comfort. Now then, what do you think of that?'

Her uncle's delight told Phoebe that this was an extremely shrewd woman. Carina Bishop would be aware that William and Joshua, Uncle George's two sons, both in their early twenties and established in the Packet service, were courting. Both would soon marry and set up their own homes thus removing them permanently from the house.

17

She would also be aware that Sarah had often stayed through the night with a woman in labour, or at the bedside of a sick child until the crisis passed. Returning home at daybreak Sarah would, if George were home from sea, join him for breakfast where they would talk over the night's events. Sometimes after he had left for whatever his day held, she retired to bed to catch up on missed sleep. But often there were other clients to see, or remedies to be made. Sarah had shared her time and her energy between her family and those who sought her help.

So with that one statement Carina Bishop had transformed her barrenness – something once perceived as a failure – into an advantage. Also, without a word of criticism against her predecessor she had made it clear that, for her, total fulfilment lay in devoting herself solely to the care of a husband.

After two years' grieving, Uncle George had stopped looking back and was beginning to look forward. Who could blame him for being tempted by such an offer? Phoebe couldn't. She moistened dry lips.

'You mentioned two guests, Uncle. Who is the other?'

'Oh yes.' He cleared his throat again. 'His name's Quintrell, Mr William Quintrell.'

'Is he new to the service?' Phoebe enquired. 'I don't recall hearing his name before.'

Rising from his chair George Oakes turned away. Crushing his cousin's letter into a ball, he tossed it onto the fire. Phoebe watched the flames lick, then flare brightly as the paper blackened

18

and fell into ash. 'He's not a packet man. He owns a sugar plantation in Jamaica. Built it up from almost nothing so I understand. It's doing very well now, very well. He's been out there over thirty years. I first met him about ten years ago when I was on the West Indies run. But he's not in the best of health. That's why he's come back to Cornwall. Well, one of the reasons. Stroke of luck meeting up with him again. In fact, it couldn't have happened at a more – yes, well, I'm sure you'll like him. A very interesting man.'

Phoebe suspected he'd started to say something different but changed his mind. On his way to the door he glanced back.

'Tell Mrs Lynas to do something special for dinner.'

Phoebe smiled. 'Of course.' As he went out she stood perfectly still and drew a slow deep breath. So there it was. Uncle George was going to remarry. And Carina Bishop, with exquisite tact, had made it clear she did not wish to share married life, or her new home, with an indigent relative.

Returning to the kitchen Phoebe wondered why William Quintrell had been invited to join what was, after all, a family celebration. Still, an additional guest would make an even number at table and ensure conversation remained general. Considering the past hour that was something to be grateful for.

Chapter Two

Phoebe sat with her hands out of sight in her lap, the starched white napkin crushed in her fists. Trained by Aunt Sarah never to betray fear or anxiety – for a woman in labour or the mother of an ill child needed to feel reassured, to have confidence in the person helping her – Phoebe maintained her expression of polite interest and somehow kept a smile on her lips.

The meal over which Mrs Lynas had taken such pains had been a great success. Mrs Bishop and Mr Quintrell had both praised the salmon with shrimp sauce, the chicken vol-au-vent, ham garnished with broccoli, and roast fillet of veal all served with a selection of vegetables. The cabinet pudding, lemon cream, rhubarb tart and meringues had also been greeted with exclamations of pleasure.

Phoebe had forced herself to eat, taking tiny amounts from a selection of dishes, anxious that her loss of appetite should not attract notice or comment. Swallowing had required real effort and now the food lay heavily in her stomach. Only pride and stubborn determination kept her back straight and her smile intact.

Watching Carina Bishop lay her fingertips lightly, possessively, on Uncle George's arm as she murmured something to William Quintrell, and seeing her uncle's normally taciturn expression soften in open adoration Phoebe felt anew the shock of betrayal. And under that the first stirring of fear. Mentally she slammed a door on it. Not now, not yet. If she allowed herself to dwell even for a moment on– *No. Concentrate.*

She could not blame her uncle; she didn't *blame* Carina Bishop. Even William Quintrell seemed a pleasant enough man, if somewhat overindulgent in his drinking. What cut so deep was the realization that they had arranged it all between them. Her future had been discussed and planned in considerable detail without her knowledge. Everyone except her had sat down to dinner already knowing what was intended.

Couldn't Uncle George have given her a hint, a clue? Had he feared rebellion? Feared delay or disruption to his future with Mrs Bishop? Did he not know her better than that? How could he imagine, after all his kindness to her, that she would stand in the way of his happiness. But for him to do this...

'Well now, Miss Dymond,' William Quintrell's jovial tones broke into thoughts she was glad to escape, 'I have no difficulty at all understanding why your uncle speaks so highly of you. I daresay this evening's news came as a bit of a shock. In truth I'm astonished at my own good fortune. I hadn't expected the matter settled so swiftly. But meeting your uncle again – well, it has all worked out most satisfactorily. Yes, indeed.' He turned the stem of his wineglass, clearly expecting it to be refilled.

'Would you care for a little more wine, Mr Quintrell?' Carina Bishop enquired. The frac-

21

tional lift of her dark brows signalled her surprise at Phoebe for neglecting her role as hostess. 'George?'

Phoebe watched her uncle start, then jump to his feet. Refilling his guest's glass, he paused beside Carina who demurred. He glanced briefly, anxiously, at Phoebe. She gave her head a single brief shake, afraid to accept: afraid the tremor in her hand would reveal the depth of her distress. Topping up his own glass he replaced the bottle on the sideboard and resumed his seat.

William Quintrell drank deeply, released a gusty sigh of satisfaction and addressed her again. 'I admire your style, my dear. That I do. I must say I wouldn't have been surprised at a few tears or even an attack of the vapours.'

He would never know. None of them would ever know what it was costing her to deny them such a spectacle.

Carina Bishop clicked her tongue, saving Phoebe from the need to respond. 'For shame, Mr Quintrell. You do Phoebe an injustice. She is made of sterner stuff. And, of course, she is very sensible of the compliment you are paying her.'

'Isn't that just what I'm saying?' He turned to Phoebe once more. 'To be mistress of a sugar plantation requires very particular capabilities.' He leaned forward, enveloping her in warm, wine-tainted breath. 'I've heard all about your skill with herbs and such like. And George here tells me you're not afraid of hard work. Not that you'll be expected to do anything that might soil those pretty hands. The slaves see to all that. There were a dozen taking care of the house before I left. But if you want more then more you shall have.' He beamed, making an expansive gesture. 'Just remember to keep them on a tight rein. It wouldn't do to let them get the better of you. But from what I've heard you've got more sense than to allow anything like that.'

Phoebe glanced at her uncle. Already flushed from good food and wine his colour deepened. He avoided her gaze.

'You'll be an ideal wife for my son,' William Quintrell stated. 'You're exactly what he needs.' He emptied his glass.

Somehow Phoebe managed to hold her smile in place as she silently dipped her head in a gesture she hoped might be construed as modesty. Already her shock was being crushed beneath helpless resignation.

She had told her uncle she could not accept as a husband any man unwilling to allow her to continue her work. Carina Bishop, her uncle's intended, did not want her included in their new household. A match between herself and Rupert Quintrell resolved both problems at a stroke. It was the perfect solution. Most marriages were the result of family discussion and approval. It wasn't unheard of for the two people most concerned to be unfamiliar with each other.

Nor was there any other branch of the family to whom she could apply for asylum. Uncle George was her mother's sole remaining relative, and he was only a half-brother. Her father's family had disowned their wayward son when he contracted a marriage they deemed beneath him.

So if she was to travel to the other side of the

world to marry a total stranger, the responsibility was entirely hers for refusing to accept those earlier proposals. There was no doubt that this match offered far more in terms of wealth and status. And at least William Quintrell approved her skills rather than condemning them.

What would be his son's response? But with an ocean to cross first *would she live to meet him?* She swallowed hard as hysteria bubbled in her throat.

'If I had come back to England when Rupert first took over I would have spared myself a couple of bouts of fever. But I didn't like to leave him by himself. Not until I was sure he could cope.' William Quintrell's smile radiated pride. 'I needn't have worried. In the last couple of years he's expanded the cane fields and almost doubled the production of sugar, rum and molasses. I tell you, Miss Dymond, my son and I have built Grove Hill into an estate of consider-able importance. Oops, I nearly forgot.' He reached into his waistcoat pocket and drew out a miniature. 'Should have given you this earlier. There, that's Rupert. Handsome fellow, isn't he?'

The tiny painting was exquisite. Executed in finest detail it portrayed a fair-haired man with blue eyes beneath thick brows, a straight nose, jutting chin, and a sculpted mouth that curled up at one corner.

'He is indeed,' Phoebe agreed. But as she studied the smiling image the candlelight flick-ered, and the expression she had interpreted as amusement became sneering cynicism. Her skin tightened in a shiver and she caught her breath. She was being foolish, fanciful. It was just nerves.

Which was hardly surprising but *not* to be indulged.

'Do let me see.' Carina Bishop held out a slim white hand. 'Isn't it exciting? My dear, I imagine you can't wait to start packing. Such a wonderful opportunity.' Taking the miniature she glanced at it then smiled at the plantation owner. 'I see your son takes his looks from you, Mr Quintrell.'

'And you have dipped your tongue in the honey-pot, Mrs Bishop.' William Quintrell guffawed, his nose and cheeks crimson-veined and shiny.

'As we are all family – or soon will be' – Carina smiled around the table – 'I shall speak freely. Phoebe, I think I know how you must be feeling.'

'I beg leave to doubt that, ma'am,' Phoebe said softly.

'No, no.' Carina Bishop was determined. 'Were I in your place, I am sure I should be just as nervous. But I'm equally sure that as you think about it you will become ever more aware of the great advantages this match will bring you. Among those at this table it is no secret that the sad circumstances of your arrival into the care of your uncle and aunt mean you are without dowry or independence. Marriage to Mr Rupert Quintrell will instantly elevate you socially and in terms of your financial security. Am I not right, Mr Quintrell?'

'You are indeed, ma'am. She won't want for anything, I can promise you that.'

'And as the island is desperately short of doctors,' George Oakes began, his expression tinged with entreaty, 'I have no doubt–'

'Is it?' Phoebe's shock and dismay were

25

momentarily eclipsed by surprise. 'But why? I understood there is a naval hospital?'

'Oh, there is,' William Quintrell nodded grimly. 'But it's a known fact that the Admiralty staffs it with doctors too poorly qualified to be accepted at Haslar or Plymouth. And of those who survive the voyage out and the risk of yellow fever, at least half will develop too great an attachment to rum.'

'So you see, Phoebe,' Carina said brightly, 'your skills will be very much in demand if only on the plantation.'

Survive the voyage out. Phoebe tried to ignore the sickening surge of fear. She saw the plea in her uncle's gaze for her to *say something, anything.* Running the tip of her tongue between her dry lips she turned to their guest, seeking among the topics of conversation one with which she could identify.

'Mr Quintrell, you mentioned that your son had recently doubled production?'

Beneath his embroidered silk waistcoat, William Quintrell's chest swelled with pride. 'I did indeed, Miss Dymond.'

'I imagine he would have needed to employ more labour?'

'Employ?' William Quintrell grinned at his host. 'The lass has a fine way with words.' Shifting his gaze back to Phoebe he nodded. 'We – Rupert – has upwards of two hundred slaves now. But don't you fret about the revolt on Saint Domingue.' Though his smile was meant to be reassuring, its underlying anger tightened the skin on Phoebe's arms. 'The French managed that very badly, which I'm sure is no surprise.' He was scathing. 'But there's no trouble in Jamaica. Nor will there be. For if the slaves *were* foolish enough to try anything, the British soldiers and militiamen would very soon make them wish they had not. So don't you worry your pretty head. As for those other tales' – his dismissive gesture was at odds with the glitter in his eyes – 'Rupert made it very clear what would happen if he learned of such doings on *our* property. You may believe, my dear, my son is not a man to cross, and so the slaves know.'

Phoebe guessed he was referring to the articles that appeared at intervals in English newspapers hinting at devilish practices involving torch-lit dances in secret forest glades, poisonings, and tall poles crowned with dead birds appearing at roadsides.

The first time she read of such things she had asked her uncle what they signified. But declaring he knew no more than she did, nor did he wish to, he had changed the subject abruptly.

Later, Aunt Sarah had told her that before becoming a senior captain and transferring to the Lisbon run, Uncle George had made several voyages to Jamaica. One night, while his ship was anchored in Kingston harbour, the wind had carried the sound of drums, complex hypnotic rhythms that reached deep inside a man's head. The sound had upset and unsettled him. Nor was he the only one affected. The whole crew had been glad to leave.

'You set my mind at rest, sir,' she said politely. 'Would I be right in thinking that as well as male

27

slaves you also have women?'

His smile became fixed, and beneath the joviality Phoebe glimpsed a different, altogether harder man. 'Naturally. The strongest work alongside the men in the cane fields. Others do domestic work, look after livestock, tend the gardens, and,' he added, as an afterthought, 'raise their children of course.'

'Mr Quintrell, you must forgive Phoebe all her questions,' Carina Bishop broke in with a trilling laugh and a flashed glare across the table. 'Yet what a delight it is to see her interest already so deeply engaged.'

Ignoring her, Phoebe continued as if there had been no interruption. 'I ask, sir, because it occurs to me that whatever arrangements were in place for their welfare, or for treating sickness and injury, they must be hard pressed with such an increase in numbers.'

'*Welfare?*' William Quintrell repeated, bristling eyebrows signalling his incredulity. 'These are slaves, Miss Dymond. They certainly don't warrant–' He stopped, an arrested expression on his face. 'Then again – by Jove, you may have a point there. We've been lucky to get ten years out of each man. Some of them don't even last that long. There's no doubt that having to buy replacements eats into the profits.' He slapped the table, his good humour fully restored.

'Damme if your uncle wasn't right about you, my dear. You're as shrewd as you are pretty. You'll do very well for my boy.' His bloodshot eyes travelled from the top of her head to her waist. Concealed beneath the table, Phoebe's fingers tightened convulsively on her crumpled napkin. 'Yes,' he nodded. 'He's a lucky fellow.'

'Do tell us, Mr Quintrell' – Carina leaned forward slightly, her posture intimating fascination – 'were you born in Jamaica?'

'No, ma'am. Rupert was, of course. But I went out to Kingston in '56. My uncle was a merchant out there. He had no children so he sent for me. Wanted to keep the business in the family. When he died of the fever I took over. In five years I doubled our trade.'

'So what took you from trade into production?' George Oakes enquired.

William Quintrell gave a bark of laughter. 'Fate and good fortune. By the time I was thirty I owned three ships. One of the plantations I was buying from ran up huge debts in freight, shipping and sales charges. In the end I had to foreclose.' He shrugged. 'Still, it's an ill wind, as they say. Louise loved Grove Hill. My wife,' he explained, before Carina could ask. 'Pretty girl, and a wonderful hostess. Loved entertaining. Good thing really, as there's not much else for ladies to do, except increase the family of course.' He sighed, shaking his head. 'Though she wasn't much good at that, unfortunately. Lost four before she managed to produce Rupert. The next one killed her. Still, she'd done her duty and Grove Hill had an heir.' He roused himself, drained his wineglass, and beamed around the table. 'Did I tell you he's doubled the yields? He knows what he's about. No overseer would dare try any tricks on Rupert.'

'He certainly has an advantage over absentee

29

owners,' George Oakes said.

'They're mad,' William Quintrell stated. 'Leaving supervision of their estates in the hands of an attorney with ten or twenty plantations on his books? It's asking for trouble. Attorneys don't have time even to make regular visits let alone take a close interest. So the overseer is left to his own devices. Foolish.' He shook his head. 'Very foolish.'

'So how many owners actually live on their plantations, Mr Quintrell?' Carina enquired.

'On the largest estates, very few. And all of them send their children back to England to school.' Disapproval clouded his ruddy complexion. 'Waste of time and money. Boys can learn all they need to know from their fathers.'

'But what about girls?' Phoebe blurted, earning herself a frown from Carina.

William Quintrell's wiry brows rose in astonishment. 'What do girls need education for? They have slaves to do all the cleaning, cooking, needlework. Slaves look after the children, go to the markets and shops and tend the gardens. Their biggest concern is thinking up new ways to amuse themselves.'

Phoebe looked at her uncle. *He thought she would be happy with such a life?* She saw desperation in the glance he exchanged with Carina who turned smoothly to their guest.

'Indeed, it sounds a delightful existence, Mr Quintrell. Though I daresay those who desire more may find it?'

William Quintrell's surprise was laced with cynicism. *'More?'*

'Someone like dear Phoebe, for example,' Car-

30

ina explained. 'Who has been of such assistance to our local community.'

Watching William Quintrell's frown dissolve into an expansive smile it seemed to Phoebe that he appeared *relieved*. She could not imagine why. Unless he had misinterpreted what Carina meant.

'Oh, yes, of course,' he beamed. 'And I'm sure Miss Dymond's skills will be of great interest. But I confess I should be astonished if after a few months she does not feel drawn to a more relaxed and leisurely life.' He turned to Phoebe with a roguish smile. 'Especially once the babies start coming.'

Feeling heat flood her face Phoebe immediately lowered her gaze, not wanting to betray her discomfort at such a personal remark from a man she had met for the first time only two hours ago. She tried to make allowances. Perhaps ill health had made him more susceptible to the effects of the wine. Maybe Jamaican society was more relaxed and such topics of conversation were perfectly acceptable in mixed company. Besides, as the father of an only child, a son to whom he was clearly devoted, it was not to be wondered at that a grandchild, an heir to Grove Hill estate, would be very much on his mind.

'I'm not *against* education,' William Quintrell continued, oblivious to Phoebe's discomfort. 'A certain amount – being able to figure and so on – is damned useful. That's why I employed a tutor for Rupert.'

'What a very sensible idea.' Carina's smile poured admiration like cream.

31

William Quintrell nodded, proud and complacent. 'Well, I couldn't leave. And I didn't want to send the boy to England by himself. Not that he'd have gone. He overheard me talking about it to someone and got hold of the wrong end of the stick. Little devil ran away. Hid in the woods with one of the mulatto children. Nine years old he was.'

'My dear Mr Quintrell' – Carina's frown mingled disapproval and sympathy – 'you must have been beside yourself with anxiety. Children are so selfish. They have no conception of the worry they cause.'

Phoebe bit her tongue.

'Good God, I wasn't anxious.' His bark of laughter sent Carina's eyebrows towards her hairline and a spasm of irritation crossed her face. But like a summer cloud it passed swiftly leaving a puzzled smile. 'No, not at all. I knew he could take care of himself. And I soon discovered where he'd gone. Though it took me two days to find out. The children wouldn't tell. They were frightened of what he'd do to them if they said anything.' Pride lit William Quintrell's smile as he shook his head. 'Within a year he was riding the estate with me. On his fifteenth birthday I made him my overseer. He took to it like a duck to water.'

'What exactly does an overseer do?' Carina enquired.

'He supervises the two bookkeepers – gives them their orders for each day's work. They're called bookkeepers but they have nothing to do with figures. During crop season they divide their

32

time between the boiling house where the cane juice is turned into syrup and sugar, and the still house that produces the rum. Outside crop season they supervise the field Negroes and look after the keys for the stores.'

'Does your son have other responsibilities?'

Phoebe marvelled at Carina's display of absorbed interest.

'Oh yes. His next job is to take the daily roll call of slaves and make sure any claiming to be sick are not simply trying to evade work. Not that we have much trouble in that direction. Rupert won't stand for it. Then the rest of the day he's out riding over the estate making sure everything is as it should be. Of course, during crop he also has to keep checking the quality of sugar and rum as it's produced.'

Phoebe watched her uncle nodding thoughtfully. 'Sounds like a busy life and a heavy responsibility,' he murmured.

'Indeed it is,' William Quintrell nodded. 'But Rupert's more than equal to it. What he needs now is a wife: a steady sensible girl to smooth away a few of the rough edges.' Grinning at his host, he gestured with his free hand, the other tilting his empty wineglass. 'You know how it is with young men. They work hard and play hard. But it's time he put that behind him. Even he sees that now. So I don't want you thinking this is my idea, or that my son is being forced into anything against his will. Truth is,' he confided, 'I doubt there's a man born who could make Rupert do anything he didn't want to. A woman now' – he directed a waggish grin at Phoebe –

'that's a different thing altogether. Any sensible woman knows that you catch more flies with honey than with vinegar. He's a proud man, my son, and can be stubborn as a mule when the mood takes him. But you, my dear' – he patted Phoebe's arm – 'if you're even half the girl your uncle says you are, you'll have Rupert halterbroke within a month.'

As Carina gave her trilling laugh and clapped her hands together, and George Oakes nodded eagerly, Phoebe dropped her gaze to the miniature lying beside her plate and Rupert Quintrell's enigmatic smile.

'Well, Oakes,' William Quintrell announced, 'I see no purpose in delay. Now the matter's settled you might as well get the lass packed up and on her way. When does the next Jamaica packet sail?'

Phoebe's heart contracted as she glanced at her uncle who would not meet her gaze. *Surely he must know how afraid she was?* Perhaps he did. But he would not jeopardize his final chance of happiness. And in all fairness, why should he?

George Oakes cleared his throat. 'The end of next week.'

Chapter Three

Jowan Crossley drained his glass. The spirit burned his throat, matching his anger. But drinking prevented the escape of words he knew he would regret.

He looked across the table at his father. The remains of dinner had been quietly removed from the polished mahogany leaving only a crystal bowl of tulips and narcissi in the centre. His mother had retired to the drawing-room to weep slow silent tears over her embroidery.

'I'm astonished and disappointed in you, Jowan.' Leaning forward in his carver chair at the head of the table, Captain Richard Crossley cradled his brandy in an unsteady hand. 'With England at war and Ellis dead–' His voice broke and he stared hard into the glass, swirling the liquid then tossing it down his throat. Jowan saw him shudder and knew his father had not even tasted the fine old spirit. It simply deadened the pain. 'Your brother gave his life defending this country from the French. I should have thought honour and a sense of duty might demand some kind of response from you.'

'That's hardly fair–'

'I never have and never will understand your refusal to follow family tradition and join the Royal Navy,' his father continued, heedless of Jowan's attempt to reply. 'A long established and proud tradition, I may add.'

Jowan clenched his teeth. 'I thought I had explained my decision.' He kept his voice even, determined at least to appear calm. 'I don't know what other words to use, or how much more plainly I can speak. The reason I have not joined the navy is because I want to *save* life, not destroy it.' Meeting his father's red-rimmed glittering eyes, Jowan recognized in the purple-brown shadows beneath them too many sleepless nights and aching irreplaceable loss.

'Any man worth the name would be proud to defend his country.' Richard Crossley threw down the words like a challenge.

'As Ellis was,' Jowan nodded. 'The navy was his life, Father.' *His life and his death.* 'Ellis chose the sea: I chose medicine.'

'You are selfish.'

Aware that his father was reacting to the stress of battle and grief at losing his elder son, Jowan clung grimly to his temper. But he would no longer hold back what needed to be said.

'I'm not Ellis, Father. I cannot take his place, no matter how much you might wish it. Yet you are wrong to accuse me of not caring about the war. I qualified as a physician. But I took additional courses in surgery so that I would be able to treat the wounds of men injured in battle. We are both fighting the French, but in different ways. You are trying to take the ships and lives of the enemy's men. I am trying to preserve the lives of ours. Now, if you will excuse me.' Pushing back his chair Jowan started to rise.

'No, I have not finished.'

36

'With respect, Father, there is nothing more to be said.'

'On that subject perhaps.' Richard Crossley made a weary gesture, conceding defeat. 'However, there is another matter of equal importance I would raise with you.'

Reluctantly Jowan resumed his seat.

'Ellis—' His father swallowed audibly. 'Ellis is ... no longer with us. I will be returning to my ship very soon. The Mediterranean squadron has fought two major actions recently, and no doubt we will face more. Under the circumstances, and as you are now my heir, the question of your marriage—'

Jowan suppressed a sigh. 'We have already had this discussion, Father. You know my feelings.'

'Yes, but that was before—'

'I'm sorry. I know the Trevaylors are your close friends. And no doubt somewhere out there is a man for whom Celia would be the ideal wife. But it's not me.'

'Why not, for goodness' sake? What could you possibly have against her? She's pretty, and graceful. She has delightful manners, and can play the—'

'Indeed she is all those things. She may even have a brain beneath those copper curls.' Jowan's impatience spilled over. 'But during our few conversations it became painfully clear to me that we share no common interest.' He shrugged helplessly. 'How could I love such a—'

'Good God!' Richard Crossley's frustration erupted. 'What has *love* to do with anything? All that romantic nonsense is no way to choose a life partner. A decision of such magnitude needs solid foundations. Marriage should be based upon mutual respect, compatible backgrounds and suitable financial arrangements. There's time enough *after* the wedding for fondness to grow. That's how it was for your mother and me, and we have been very content.'

But have you been happy? Jowan knew he could not ask. When his parents were young, marriage was viewed a means of cementing family and political alliances or acquiring property. The only emotion allowed consideration was active dislike. That was the way it had always been, and for many still was. But not for him.

'If you found contentment in such an arrangement then I'm very pleased for you, Father. However, though Celia's background and dowry make her eminently eligible, her giggling would try the patience of a saint. I cannot claim that much tolerance.'

'Your flippancy does you no credit,' his father snapped. 'It's small wonder the poor girl becomes nervous if that's the way you–'

'Father, believe me, I am as unsuitable for her as she would be for me. But quite apart from the fact that we would make each other utterly miserable, this is not the right time for me to be contemplating marriage.'

'There's none better. With Ellis gone you are now my only child, my only son. Is it so unreasonable that I should wish to see my heir married with sons of his own to continue the family name? Your mother and I had hoped you and Celia might – and I know the Trevaylors too were very favourably disposed.'

Of course they were. Celia had been out in society for two seasons without receiving a single proposal. Jowan bit his tongue. Nothing would be gained by reminding his father of a fact he already knew.

'However, if the match is so abhorrent to you we will not mention it again. But that is no reason to reject the *concept* of marriage. Why, I can name at least half a dozen young women–'

'No, Father, you misunderstand.' Jowan took a deep breath. He had first considered the idea three months ago. When making enquiries he had been startled at the shortage and desperate need. But then had come news of Ellis's death. His own plans, still secret, had been shelved while he mastered his grief and took care of his mother until his father was able to get home.

But lately it had become all too clear that if he didn't get away soon he might never escape. And if he stayed he would suffocate: his own needs and plans crushed beneath the weight of his father's demands and expectations and his mother's loss.

'It's not *marriage* I'm against, Father, it's the timing.'

'For God's sake, boy. Speak plain, can't you? What are you talking about?'

Jowan tightened his jaw, silently self-mocking. He was twenty-six years old. Unmarried and childless he was in theory free to go where he wished and do as he pleased. Ellis, firstborn and dutiful, had been their father's pride and joy. Yet it had been to *him* – the renegade and disappointment – that both parents had clung during those terrible early days.

Devastated by their loss, isolated by their grief, Richard and Eleanor Crossley had found no comfort in each other. Jowan's training and familiarity with death had enabled him to distance himself emotionally from his father's desperate, white-faced suffering and the sight of his mother curled over in an agony of raw grief unrelieved by choking sobs. Nothing would ever fill the hole left in their lives by Ellis's death. But they would not be able to stop themselves hoping *he* might. It was an impossible responsibility. He had to go.

'I'm leaving Falmouth. I'm going to sea.'

Richard Crossley's jaw dropped. Jowan had never seen his father lost for words. Then a slow smile relaxed the strained, haggard face.

'My dear boy.' He slapped the table, his voice choked with emotion. 'You don't know how much this means – I never thought – and after all you'd said. I'm so proud of you. Just leave it to me. I'll get you warranted on to–'

'Father, wait,' Jowan interrupted gently, reluctant to spoil his father's pleasure, or shatter this rare moment of accord. But as usual his father had not let him finish, had not asked, had simply assumed. 'I'm not joining the navy.'

Richard Crossley's delight faded to frowning bewilderment. 'What do you mean, you're not – you just said...'

'I said I'm going to sea: but with the Packet Service, not the navy. I shall be sailing as surgeon aboard a packet ship.'

The morning after the dinner party Phoebe woke with a start to the sound of Mary's knock. Her night had been restless, her sleep filled with unsettling dreams.

'Well, you kept that some quiet, miss!' Mary half-scolded as she moved the candleholder, set down a cup of hot chocolate on Phoebe's nightstand, then bustled across to open the curtains.

'Kept what quiet?' Still dazed and disoriented Phoebe pushed herself up on the pillows.

'You, going off to Jamaica to get married. Dear life; gave us some shock when Captain told us. Come in the kitchen himself he did, not an hour ago. What with him and Mrs Bishop going to tie the knot as well, we shan't know ourselves. Like a dog with two tails he is, dear of him. Been some lonely he have since mistress went.' Mary sighed. 'Lovely she was. We do still miss her.' She rolled her eyes and gave a knowing nod. 'Be some changes now, there will. I'll fetch your hot water.' She bustled out.

Phoebe sipped her chocolate, cradling the cup in both hands as it clattered against her teeth. She understood why her uncle wanted to see her safely settled and her future secured. She thought she understood why William Quintrell considered her eminently suitable for life on a plantation and as a wife for his son. But what she did not understand was why a handsome young man who was heir to a wealthy and productive estate would accept as his bride a young woman he had never met. It intimated great faith in his father's judgement. Why not? William Quintrell had started out as a merchant working for his uncle, had increased that business to the point of owning three ships, had then made the transition into ownership of a

41

plantation that he had doubled in size.

And on reflection, was the situation so remarkable? Responsible for such large concern, and with his father now retired to England, what time or opportunity would Rupert Quintrell have for socializing and meeting a potential bride?

By the time she had drunk her chocolate she felt a little stronger and reached for the pencil and notebook on her nightstand. Sitting up in bed, her dark hair in its loose braid falling forward over one shoulder of her white cotton nightgown, she made a list of people she must see and jobs to be done before she left.

Her usually neat writing was erratic and spiky as the pencil trembled in her hand. This time yesterday morning she had been unaware of the momentous change planned for her. For an instant and with all her heart she wished she could turn the clock back. Immediately she saw Aunt Sarah clicking her tongue as she frowned. *Now, now, my bird. The good Lord don't give you a burden without He gives you the strength to carry it. So let's have no more foolishness.*

Besides, while she had gone about her day's business in blissful ignorance, it had already been discussed and decided. She, the person most concerned, had been the last to find out. But what if Cousin Amelia's letter had contained agreement instead of refusal? Would it have made a difference? Probably not. Why should a second season in London have met with any more success than her first? In any case the question was irrelevant. Amelia had refused, *as Uncle George must have expected her to*. Otherwise he would

42

never have finalized arrangements with William Quintrell.

Phoebe's eyes burned. The paper blurred. But she rubbed away the tears before they could fall. Panic still fluttered beneath her ribs. As her mind flew back over the previous evening she relived the shock of rejection. She fought both emotions, struggling to rationalize. Her uncle wasn't being deliberately unkind. He had suffered a terrible loss. Now, after a painful period of mourning he wanted to make a fresh start with a new wife. It was natural they should wish to be alone.

She had known some kind of change was inevitable. As she was only twenty and still in her uncle's care, it was he who controlled her future. But leaving the house was one thing; leaving Cornwall and everything that signified home and security – *to have to go to sea* – terror engulfed her. Millions of tiny needles prickled her skin and she gulped air. A wave of heat gathered strength inside her, surged and broke, dewing her with perspiration.

Shutting her eyes she exhaled slowly, deliberately; forcing herself to keep on breathing out even when there seemed to be no more air left in her lungs and her chest began to ache. Only when she could bear it no longer did she allow herself to inhale. As the prickling stopped so did the silent screaming that had filled her head.

Ships left Falmouth every day for destinations all over the world and returned safely. Her uncle and her two cousins had been making such voyages regularly for many years. Just because her mother – it didn't mean that *she*– Once again

Aunt Sarah's words filled her head. *Now, now, my bird … no more foolishness.*

It would be all right. She must think of it as an adventure. If Rupert Quintrell's nature were as pleasing as his image then they should get along very well together. She recalled the shiver that had taken her unawares while she was looking at his miniature. *It was simply the result of excitement, or a draught.* His father had spoken highly of him. *But then, a father would.* Refusing even to acknowledge, much less examine, the worm of doubt – for the matter was settled and she must make the best of it – she concentrated fiercely on her list.

An hour later, washed and dressed, she forced down a slice of bread and butter. Collecting her thick wool cloak from her bedroom she edged past the large trunk with leather straps and brass corners her uncle had brought down from the attic, and left the house.

Like Aunt Sarah, Lizzie Gendall had Romany blood. And like Aunt Sarah, Lizzie was a midwife and healer. Though Lizzie lived in Flushing and rarely left the village, the two women had been good friends for many years. When Phoebe had begun to learn the healing arts she had sometimes accompanied her aunt on visits across the river. Though initially unsettled by Lizzie's stony expression and taciturn manner, Phoebe had soon seen through to the kind heart beneath.

So, lost and desolate after Sarah's death it was to Lizzie that Phoebe fled. Sitting in the small kitchen as Lizzie moved between stove and table preparing salves and ointments, Phoebe had wept, rocking in her grief. When her tears were exhausted she had talked about life with her aunt, the funny moments, the successes, and the tragedies.

As always, Lizzie had said little, merely glancing up occasionally, her brown eyes gentle. Phoebe had returned home, soothed, grateful for Lizzie's parting words, 'Come when you've need.'

Though both were busy, every few weeks Phoebe would cross the river to spend an hour or two with Lizzie, and always left calmer and reassured.

Knowing she could not abandon the women who had been expecting her to attend them during their confinements without trying to make alternative provision for their care, it was to Lizzie she went.

The tide was low, the ferry a sturdy craft sailed by a gnarled old man who took her pennies, touched his cap, and with one hand on the tiller, the other controlling the single sail, skilfully guided the boat across the gently rippling blue-green water. After twenty minutes, during which Phoebe stared fixedly at her lap, they reached the other side. The ferryman flung a mooring rope to a boy waiting on the weed-fringed stone steps of a quay and turned to offer Phoebe a helping hand.

She rose, shaky with relief, as always pushing to the back of her mind the prospect of having to make the same journey back again. Inside her gloves her fingers ached from clinging to the flat wooden plank on which she had been sitting. Leaving the quay, she passed the bow windows of the milliner's shop where the Misses Polking-horne displayed hats and bonnets in the latest fashions.

Packet and naval officers thronged the cobbled street; many accompanied by elegantly dressed wives and daughters. Among them the men and women of the village went about their daily tasks. Passing the old Seven Stars tavern Phoebe turned up into High Street. The houses here were built on a bank overlooking the marshy creek that flowed down into the river at Fish Cross. Passing the post office to which the mail was brought from Falmouth, she opened the gate leading up to a small cob cottage.

Before she reached the front door, it opened and Lizzie emerged wearing a long cloak of brown wool. Now threaded with silver her once-dark hair was, as always, covered by a silk hand-kerchief tied at the nape of her neck. Carrying her ancient leather bag, she was clearly on her way to see a patient.

Seeing Phoebe she stopped, her bright gaze sharp. 'Trouble?'

Caught unawares by the succinct question, Phoebe hesitated, not sure how to answer.

Lizzie turned, opened her door again, and jerking her head to indicate Phoebe should follow, went back inside.

'I'm sorry,' Phoebe said, as Lizzie closed the door then dropped her bag on the scrubbed table. 'I won't keep you long.' In a few sentences she explained the reason for her visit. As she fell silent, Lizzie regarded her without speaking. Phoebe had once been shown a collection of butterflies. Brightly coloured and beautifully patterned, each one was fastened to the mount by a long shiny pin. She now knew exactly how that felt.

'Sarah would be proud of you.'

Phoebe's throat tightened.

'I'll go if I'm asked,' Lizzie said.

Phoebe's tense shoulders drooped in relief and gratitude. 'Thank you.'

After another hard stare Lizzie gave a curt nod. 'It won't be like you think, girl. But you'll come to no harm.'

Back in Falmouth news of her impending departure provoked mixed responses. Some of her clients reacted with dismay and anger. Despite her youth and inexperience they had trusted her. Now she was repaying them by leaving just when they might need her at any time.

Phoebe tried to reassure them they would be in excellent hands with Lizzie Gendall. Those familiar with Lizzie's name and reputation wondered why they hadn't asked for her in the first place, apparently forgetting their attachment to Sarah. Some who had lost babies at birth or in the weeks after refused to be comforted, calling her selfish.

She wanted to tell them that she too had been taken by surprise at the speed of events. But to do so would only invite questions and gossip. So she simply apologized for the lack of notice.

Fortunately, others she called on had, after their initial shock, wished her happy, thanking her for her care in the past and for making arrangements regarding their future welfare.

Time spent with them, recalling the arrival of much-loved offspring, or the miraculous properties of a linseed and mustard poultice, had made her feel less of a traitor. But having to see so many in so short a time meant that each evening she returned home exhausted.

Her next task was to decant the rest of the steeping herbs into bottles. While Mary worked her way through Phoebe's closet and chest of drawers – washing, ironing, brushing, pressing, checking hems and sewing on loose buttons – Phoebe spent several days restocking her medicine chest with tinctures, lotions, decoctions and ointments. Bags of dried herbs were packed with lengths of cheesecloth and muslin for poultices. Keeping busy ensured she had no time to think.

One afternoon towards the end of the week, with departure looming ever closer, Phoebe was busy in the kitchen when Mary returned from answering the front door bell.

'Mrs Bishop's here, miss, asking for the captain but he isn't back yet. I put her in the drawing-room. If you got too much to do I can tell her you're out.'

Phoebe scanned the clutter: empty bowls, pans scraped clean of melted lard and beeswax, and the row of little pots in which comfrey, elder leaf, and arnica ointments were solidifying as they cooled. This was the final batch. 'No. He shouldn't be long. I'll sit with her until he arrives.' As she spoke, Phoebe untied her apron, dropping it on the table, and rolled down her sleeves.

'Bring a tray of tea, shall I, miss?'

Phoebe nodded, raising both hands to her hair

to check that it was tidy. 'Yes, as soon as you can, Mary.' As she left the kitchen, Phoebe wondered if the tea was such a good idea after all. She had jumped at the suggestion as a way of filling the time until her uncle's return. The potential problems of acting as hostess to her uncle's intended, who might very well consider *she* had a greater right to the role, hadn't occurred to her. But it was too late now. Besides, Carina Bishop didn't live here yet. Opening the drawing-room door, Phoebe saw her uncle's wife-to-be standing beside the window.

Carina looked both elegant and fashionable in a short close-fitting long-sleeved jacket of bronze velvet worn over a round gown of spotted apricot muslin. A bronze velvet turban trimmed with gold braid and two feathers covered all but a strip of reddish-brown curls arranged above her forehead.

'Good afternoon, Mrs Bishop.'

Carina glanced round. 'Phoebe! Isn't this the most wonderful view? The harbour is always so busy; the sky and water never the same two days in a row.'

A vivid memory of her recent trip across the harbour, of being far closer to the water and other boats than she had ever wanted to be again, made Phoebe's skin crawl. 'Indeed,' she murmured with a shudder.

Turning from the window, Carina fingered one of the heavy curtains. 'Isn't it irritating how sunlight causes dark materials to fade? One is left with a most distressing striped effect that was never intended. Personally, I've always favoured paler shades. I find they lift the whole atmosphere of a room.'

Not sure if Carina was simply making an observation or criticizing Sarah's colour choice and housekeeping skills, Phoebe smiled politely and sat down.

Carina lowered herself gracefully into the chair opposite. 'I thought Mr Quintrell a most interesting man, didn't you? And what a fund of stories! It's such a shame his health has forced him to leave a place he's so clearly attached to. Still, one must look on the bright side. His loss will be your gain.' Glancing down at the chair arm, she brushed her gloved fingers across the padded damask. 'I've looked all over town for this shade and pattern, but none of the shops stocks it any longer. Do you know what would compliment a chair of this style quite beautifully? Peach velvet.' She flashed Phoebe a bright smile. 'I know you are going to be very happy in Jamaica. It's such a wonderful opportunity. The climate sounds positively idyllic. At least you won't have to put up with our biting east winds any more.'

'No,' Phoebe agreed. 'Jamaica has hurricanes.'

Carina looked momentarily startled. 'Really? Well, I'm sure they must be extremely rare. And if one did occur no doubt your husband would take every care to ensure you came to no harm.'

Phoebe stared at her, wondering how any man – even one as well thought of as Rupert Quintrell – might be expected to defy nature at its most powerful and destructive.

As she leaned forward, the older woman's expression was earnest. 'It would be most unusual if you were not a little apprehensive. But tormenting yourself with anxieties about things that might never happen is neither wise nor helpful, Phoebe.'

Don't patronize me, Phoebe wanted to shout, but good manners forbade it.

'You must think of it as a wonderful adventure,' Carina beamed.

Must I? 'Indeed,' Phoebe said, through gritted teeth, feeling the acid burn of anger beneath her breastbone. That she constantly sought to boost her confidence with those self-same words was one thing; to have them issued to her as an instruction from the person responsible for her being ejected from the only home she knew was something else entirely. She swallowed, trying hard to smother the bright flare of anger. Blaming Carina Bishop wouldn't change anything.

'I'm sure you're right,' she added dutifully. She wished her uncle would hurry up so that she could leave them together and get on with all she still had to do. But her guest's attention was already elsewhere.

It wasn't until Phoebe saw Carina's nose wrinkle as her searching gaze paused on the rug in front of the fireplace that everything suddenly fell into place. Carina Bishop's comments about the curtains and upholstery had not been mere idle conversation: she had been intimating the changes she intended to make. *Why? Why tell me?*

Everything would be different. All signs of Aunt Sarah would be removed. It would no longer be the house Phoebe had grown up in. How could her uncle allow such a thing? Yet how could he

51

live here with someone else surrounded by constant reminders of the past? Not that there was any possibility of his new wife allowing *that*. And who could blame her?

Phoebe fought her rioting emotions and struggled to make allowances. All three of them were moving on, starting a new life. But knowing that changes of every kind were a necessary part of this didn't make them any easier to bear. Carina need not have said anything. Was it nervousness that had prompted her remarks? Phoebe didn't think so. Yet what other reason could she have?

Just as Mary arrived with the tea, Phoebe heard the front door slam and her uncle's footsteps on the tiled floor of the hall.

'Bring another cup for the captain, Mary.'

'Yes, miss,' Mary made a brief curtsy and left, bobbing another as she passed her employer in the doorway.

'I'm sorry I'm late.' George Oakes beamed at Carina then turned to Phoebe. 'I've just come from the packet office. Your cabin is booked aboard the brigantine *Providence*. The packet's surgeon has kindly agreed to take responsibility for you during the voyage.'

Phoebe felt her eyes widen. It wasn't only the content of this announcement that suffused her with embarrassment, it was the fact that he had made it in front of someone else. Did her feelings no longer count for anything? She ran the tip of her tongue across her lips. They felt paper-dry.

'Uncle George, I'm sure you meant it for the best. But really, it wasn't necessary. I'm perfectly capable of looking after myself. I certainly have no wish to be thrust into the care of some stranger like – like an unwanted parcel.'

'My dear Phoebe,' Carina began. 'You must realize–'

'With respect, Mrs Bishop,' Phoebe said tightly, anger and mortification overriding her usual courtesy, 'this is between my uncle and me.' Turning from Carina's gasped 'Oh!' Phoebe faced him. 'May I ask how this arrangement came about?'

'It's common practice.' His expression reflected bewilderment and deepening irritation. 'The packet agent informs captains if any ladies are travelling without husband or female companion and have requested the protection of an escort. The reason this duty falls to the surgeon is that unless the ship sees action he has fewer demands on his time than do the ship's officers.'

'But I didn't make any such request,' Phoebe said. 'I wasn't even asked–'

'Why should you be?' her uncle demanded. 'You are not yet of age, Phoebe. I am still responsible for your safety and welfare. How could you imagine I would send you off on a voyage that will last many weeks without ensuring you have proper protection? Do you really think me so uncaring?'

Seeing the genuine hurt beneath his anger Phoebe ran to him and clasped his arm. 'No, no, of course I don't.' Yet hard though she tried she could not suppress a strong twinge of resentment. When he returned to sea after her aunt's death he had suffered no qualms about leaving her alone except for the cook and the housemaid. Nor, apparently, had the potential risks of her going about Falmouth alone while continuing her work occurred to him. And yet why *should* he have been concerned? Falmouth was a small town and he was well known, as were the other packet captains and commanders. That familiarity was her protection. Most of the townspeople were employed in some connection with the packet service: either serving as crew aboard the ships, or in businesses that supplied their needs. These covered everything from repairs to revictualling.

So, like her aunt before her, she had sometimes left her bed in the middle of the night, never doubting her safety as she accompanied an anxious husband home and stayed however long it took to deliver his child then care for his wife. She had visited the housebound and bedridden who relied on her poultices, ointments and infusions to ease their congested lungs and painful joints.

She was aware, just as her aunt had been, that to local doctors she was an irritant. They mocked herbal remedies, dismissing them as useless. Why they should be so derisive when all the evidence proved otherwise she had no idea. It wasn't as if she was any threat to their livelihood. Few of the people she visited could afford a doctor's fee.

If her uncle had considered her adult and independent enough to live alone at home, surely she could not need someone acting as her nursemaid while she was on board a ship? But once again she had been made to feel that *she* was in the wrong, as well as ungrateful.

'I think you owe Mrs Bishop an apology,' he

murmured. 'She has far more experience of the world than you do. She would have said exactly the same had you given her the chance.' He looked past Phoebe. 'Am I not right, my dear?'

'Indeed,' Carina nodded. 'But I understand that Phoebe has no desire for my opinion. I am not at all offended. Everything has happened very quickly, and we must make allowance for her youth.'

Phoebe clenched her teeth together. 'I'm obliged to you, ma'am.' She turned again to her uncle. 'Will someone have informed the surgeon of his additional duty?'

'You may rely on it.' He patted her hand. 'Stop fretting. You know how to behave. Anyone spending time in your company should consider himself fortunate. At least you will have interests in common,' he beamed. 'That should make conversation easier.'

Phoebe looked at him. He couldn't be serious. Did he really imagine a ship's surgeon would deign to discuss medical matters with a woman, especially one of her age – or rather her lack of it? But before she could think of a suitable response he patted her hand again then released it and gestured towards the door.

'No doubt you still have a host of things to do so I'm sure Mrs Bishop won't mind if you take your leave.'

Closing the door, Phoebe pressed her hands to her burning cheeks, wincing at her uncle's dismissal and the triumph in Carina Bishop's eyes.

Chapter Four

Gulls soared and swooped, shrieking and squab-
bling as they dived for scraps thrown overboard
from incoming fishing boats. Between the shores
of Flushing and Falmouth the wind-whipped
waters of the inner harbour were grey-green and
tipped with curls of white foam. Men were busy
aboard ships of all sizes, some newly arrived,
others preparing to leave. Between them punts,
jollyboats and cutters darted to and from quays
and jetties on both sides of the river, laden with
trunks, stores and passengers. Customs officers
were ferried from shore to ship and back again.

The wind carried shouts, snatches of song, the
groan of windlass and winch, and the crack of
unfurling canvas as it flapped in the stiff breeze
before being sheeted in.

Jowan's nostrils twitched at a sharp pungent
smell that cut through the reek of rotting fish,
seaweed, mud and sewage. Further along the
packet-ship's sides, seated on a plank suspended
by two ropes slung over the gunwale, a seaman
was hammering oakum between two planks. His
mate then painted on a thick coat of hot pitch to
make it waterproof.

Handing up the bulky leather bag containing
his medicines and instruments Jowan clambered
aboard the *Providence*. Glancing upward he saw
men balanced on ropes slung beneath the fore-

mast's main yard working on the sail bunched beneath it. Other men were replacing rungs on the ratlines that rose in a narrowing rope ladder from either side of the ship to the mainmast top.

Wood shavings pooled around the carpenter's feet as he turned up a spar, and the sailmaker and his mate wrestled with a billow of canvas.

As Jowan stepped onto the deck he was greeted by a short, almost square man wearing grubby canvas trousers and a faded salt-stained black jacket over a blue check shirt and red kerchief.

Clasping a short length of thick rope whipped with cord at both ends, he raised one hand to his hat brim in brief salute. 'Name's Hosking, sir. Arthur Hosking. I'm the bosun. You'll be the new surgeon. Mr Crossley, is it? Mr Burley said to expect you. Down below, he is.'

'Mr Burley?' Jowan enquired, picking up his bag.

'The sailing master, sir.'

Jowan wondered why the sailing master and not the captain waited to greet him. But before he could ask, the bosun turned away bellowing over his shoulder, 'Williams! Gilbert!'

At the bosun's shout, two barefoot men set down the cask they were carrying and straightened up. Both were clad in rags so filthy Jowan found it impossible to guess their original colour.

'Bosun?'

'Take the doctor's trunk down to his cabin and be smart about it.' He turned back, indicating the bag. 'Want 'em to take that as well, sir?'

'No, I'll bring it.'

With a nod the bosun turned away and stomped off down the deck towards two seamen snarling at

57

each other over a barrel. With lightning speed he laid the piece of rope across the shoulders of each and roared at them to get on with their work.

Jowan had wondered at the rope's purpose: now he knew.

On the forward part of the crowded deck men were rolling casks of fresh water and barrels hauled up from chandlers' boats to the hatches to be carried below.

Jowan followed his trunk to the companionway. In front of him the gaff from which the ship's fore and aft mainsail hung was lashed to the huge boom. This was tightly secured to prevent it swinging and sweeping the busy men from the deck into the sea. To his left stood the binnacle housing the compass, and behind it the huge wheel.

The ship moved restlessly as if she wished herself free of her anchor cables. Excitement rippled through him. He was joining a world very different from the one he knew. Though *Providence* would not sail for two days, his duties began right now.

The door to the captain's day cabin was wedged open. Light streamed in through stern windows beneath which banquette seating of crimson plush stretched in a shallow semicircle the width of the cabin. It illuminated a thickset man with receding hair tied back in a short pigtail. Leaning over a table covered with books, charts and ledgers, he wore a navy coat and blue breeches that seemed to suggest a uniform but lacked the elaborate gold braid and buttons of a naval officer.

'Mr Burley?' Jowan said.

The man looked up, a frown drawing his thick

brows together. 'Yes?' It was curt, impatient.

Jowan offered his hand. 'I'm the new surgeon. Crossley, Jowan Crossley.'

The master's narrowed gaze raked him from his bare head, serviceable brown frock coat, double-breasted waistcoat and buckskin breeches to his leather boots. The master's frown cleared. As he nodded Jowan sensed his relief. What had he expected?

'Glad to see you.' Burley's handshake was brief but firm. 'You've got some job on.' It sounded like a warning.

'Is Captain Deakin unwell?' Jowan enquired.

'So I understand from Andy.' As Jowan raised a questioning eyebrow Burley explained. 'Andy Gilbert: master's mate. Only a lad – well, twenty-one – but a born seaman, and brave with it.' Burley's expression changed becoming unreadable. 'We had a bad time voyage before last. We was chased twice *and* lost five men to fever. Captain Deakin got an infection of the lungs. He didn't sail last trip. Andy's been to visit him. Says he's still not recovered.' There was a brief pause. 'He was well enough to show Andy the plans though.'

'Plans?' Jowan enquired.

'Of this new house he's having built. Some big place it is.'

'Ah.' Jowan understood. It was common knowledge in the town that while retaining nominal command and all the financial advantages that went with it, an increasing number of captains were staying at home leaving their officers to sail the packet to her destination. No doubt Burley's

59

seafaring experience equalled that of his absent captain, and he had a mate competent to take the alternate watch. But looking at the deep frown lines and cluttered desk, Jowan guessed Burley was neither comfortable nor familiar with paperwork.

'Have you been told what your duties are?'

Jowan nodded. 'One of Mr Tierney's clerks gave me a list. I'd best get started.'

Riffling among the confusion of papers, Burley eventually found the sheet he sought and handed it across. 'List of victuals for the crew.'

Jowan scanned it. Bread, beer, beef, pork, pease and oatmeal, all supplied in barrels. Boring perhaps, but adequate.

'The rum's kept locked up. Hosking comes to me for the key.'

'Rum?' Jowan's brows climbed. 'I thought packets were dry.'

'We are, officially. But beer and water don't keep well at sea. I can't afford to have half the crew off with the squits and unable to work. So once the beer's run out they get half a pint of rum mixed with a quart of water twice a day. 'Tis a long way to Jamaica, Doctor, through dangerous waters. On the last two trips I lost a quarter of my crew through injuries, battle wounds and fever. Even with the dockyard dregs who've signed on to escape the press gangs, I'll still be short-handed.' Passing his large hand over a face seamed and roughened by decades of exposure to wind and sun he blew a gusty sigh. 'Anyhow, that's my problem. You'll have enough of your own.'

60

Nothing in Jowan's previous experience had prepared him for the demands and frustration of the next two days. Neither he nor his assistant, surgeon's mate Grigg, a wiry seaman in his mid-forties, slept more than four hours a night. There was too much to do.

Entering the fo'c'sle Jowan recoiled at the stench. Overall the area was thirty feet long and twenty-three feet wide. But parts of it were occupied by the galley caboose, the bosun and carpenter's stores, pump barrels, the foremast trunk, and the crew's sea chests. In the remaining space, twenty-two men had to live, eat and sleep. With no portholes or skylights in the deckhead the only sources of light or fresh air were the open hatches. What this space would be like in rough weather when those hatches were battened down did not bear thinking about.

Jowan recalled a passage from one of his medical books claiming that disease could be caused by *miasma* emitted from rotting and decayed matter. That being the case this stinking hellhole was a death trap. For though *Providence* was fitted with a urinal trough and a seat-of-ease in the angle of the bows beneath the bowsprit, reaching either in heavy seas would be a perilous journey. Jowan's nose told him that rather than risk being washed overboard, the men preferred to relieve themselves in a disgusting old steep tub in the corner.

'I want that cleaned out, and the bilge pumped and flushed through with sea water.'

'The ships downwind of us will love that,' Grigg muttered.

'Perhaps it will prompt them to take similar action,' Jowan responded.

Recognizing ominous signs of rat infestation he had Grigg put down poisoned oatcakes. Then he inspected the barrels containing the crew's food.

After nearly seven years' medical training and practice, few things had the power to turn his stomach. So when he prised the lid off a cask and saw in the stinking slimy liquid a pig's head with iron rings through its snout surrounded by tails and trotters he flinched briefly but reasoned that the men were used to it. However, after inspecting the rest of the barrels and checking the weight and number against the supply bill, he realized there was a discrepancy.

'That's right, sir,' Grigg nodded. 'Always is.'

'Why is that?' Jowan suspected he knew the reason. Grigg's reply confirmed it.

'Agent and chandler's perks, sir. Instead of supplying sixteen ounces to the pound they gives us fourteen, twelve, or even ten. They sells the difference and splits the profit.'

'Of course I'm aware of it,' Burley said, when Jowan confronted him. 'And there's not a damn thing I can do.'

'Then we must buy–'

'What with?' Burley cut in. 'The victualling allowance for each man is a shilling a day and that's all spent. I haven't got no more money.'

'What about the passengers? Surely their fare–'

'Their fares are paid direct to the captain who pays the packet agent a commission. I don't see a penny of it. The passengers supply their own food. Or they pay Mossop. The passenger's steward,' Burley explained, forestalling Jowan's question. 'He deals fair and straight. He'd be out of a job if he didn't. He keeps their provisions in his pantry and prepares their meals for them.' Burley rubbed his forehead. 'Captains make a handsome profit every trip, whether they sail or not. But it isn't like that for the officers. No bleddy wonder we carry stuff to do a bit of private trading. Couldn't make a living if we didn't.' Burley didn't even try to hide his bitterness.

'So while the captain remains at home watching his new house being built–'

'*I'm* responsible for sailing this ship to Barbados and Jamaica and delivering the mail. And if the weather and a half-raw crew wasn't enough, we got to outrun Frenchie warships and privateers who'd kill us soon as look at us. The only guns we're allowed are bow and stern chasers, a couple of nine-pounders and small arms. For that, Doctor, I get paid the same as you, not a brass farthing more. So 'tis no use asking me for money to buy more food for the crew. I haven't got it.'

Jowan's afternoon was acutely frustrating. The chandlers simply shrugged and referred him to the packet agent.

Edgar Tierney, a portly man whose immaculately tailored coat and breeches proclaimed his wealth and status, smiled blandly and shook his head.

'Mr Crossley–'

'Doctor,' Jowan corrected him. 'I am a physician as well as a surgeon.'

'Indeed? Then I cannot help but wonder why, with such qualifications, you would choose the

Packet Service over the Royal Navy. However, I will not enquire into matters you may prefer not to discuss.'

Jowan's hackles rose at Tierney's insinuation. But wise and wary enough not to respond he clamped down hard on his anger, raised one eyebrow, and waited.

The agent's fleshy mouth pursed in a smile, but his small eyes remained cold and hard. 'I was about to say – though I'm astonished such a reminder should be necessary – that you are, in fact, an *employee* of the Packet Service with a duty to care for the health of the men aboard your ship. I suggest you concentrate on that.'

'As short rations will directly affect the crew's health–'

'Don't fence with me, Dr Crossley.' Tierney cut him short. 'As a newcomer you have much to learn about the way things are done. If you wish to remain in the service you would be most unwise to involve yourself in matters that are not *directly* your concern. Acquiring a reputation for making trouble would do your career no good at all. Nor, I venture to suggest, would it reflect well on your father. Surely your family's recent bereavement is a heavy enough weight for him to bear? And now' – he glanced pointedly at an ornate gold watch pulled from a pocket in his patterned silk waistcoat – 'you will excuse me. I am a busy man, Doctor, with many demands on my time.' *And you are wasting it.* He did not say the words. His expression made it unnecessary.

Infuriated as much by his own helplessness as by the corrupt agent, Jowan curbed his tongue and his temper and left. Walking out of the office into the street he had a brainwave. Two hours later he climbed aboard *Providence* once more.

'Mr Hosking, could you spare two men?'

'God A'mighty,' Grigg gasped, peering over the side. 'That's never butter?'

'Bleddy 'ell,' the bosun breathed, gazing down into the jollyboat bobbing alongside, laden with casks.

'And flour, and jam, and molasses,' Jowan replied, as the barrels were hoisted up and carried below.

'Dear life, Doctor. How did you do it? You never made that bastard Tierney—'

'*Mr* Tierney.' Jowan corrected the bosun with heavy irony. He didn't attempt to hide his disgust and knew from the flicker in Hosking's gaze that the bosun had recognized it.

'Yes, sir,' Hosking said expressionlessly. 'But how in God's name did you get *him*—'

'I didn't. I went to the Quakers. They are very generous with charitable donations to worthy causes.'

'Old *Providence* a worthy cause?' The bosun shook his head in amazement. 'Never thought I'd see the day.' He darted a glance at Jowan, gave him a brief nod, and stomped away.

'Right,' Jowan turned to his assistant. 'I think it's time I took a look at the sick bay.' He had not yet had an opportunity to check the ship's medicine chest. But judging by what he had seen so far, he had little hope of finding anything useful. Thank God he had replenished his own.

Grigg blinked. 'Sick bay? We haven't got one, sir.'

'So what happens to men who are ill or wounded?'

Grigg shrugged. 'They either stays in their hammocks or they lie on the floor.'

Among the rats. Jowan ducked through the hatch, his brain already racing. If Burley had moved into the captain's stateroom, then the master's cabin would be free. Situated amidships between the crew and passenger quarters and directly opposite his own it would serve.

Phoebe stood at the sink in the kitchen gulping down a strong infusion of valerian and camomile. The few mouthfuls of bread and butter she had forced down lay heavy in a stomach that ached with tension. Her heartbeat pounded while she waited with desperate impatience for the herbal tea to take effect and relieve the dread and anxiety that were stretching her nerves to snapping point.

'We'll miss you awful.' Mrs Lynas wiped her brimming eyes with the corner of her apron. 'So don't you go thinking you'll be forgot, because you won't. Nothing against Mrs Bishop, but 't won't never be the same.' With a final sniff she drew a deep breath that made her starched bosom crackle. 'There's Captain out in the passage. Best get going, my 'andsome. You don't want to be late.'

Placing the empty cup in the sink, Phoebe dropped an impulsive kiss on Mrs Lynas's damp cheek. 'I'll write,' she promised in a husky whisper. Then straightening her spine she went to join her uncle.

Down at the quay, as her trunk and bag were stowed on the boat that was to carry her out to the packet, Phoebe turned to her uncle. Her throat ached and her mouth was as dry as yesterday's ashes.

'Goodbye, Uncle George. Thank you for everything.'

He seized her gloved hands, holding them against his chest. 'God speed, my dear. You need have no concerns about the *Providence*. She's a good strong ship.'

Phoebe swallowed painfully. 'I wish you and – and Carina very happy.'

'It's all for the best.' He pressed her fingers. 'Marriage will give you the status and security all women aspire to. You'll be mistress of a large estate: a lady of property. *And* you'll be able to carry on with your work. It will be a good life, you'll see. Better than you could have achieved here. That's not to say Rupert Quintrell isn't a very lucky man, for he is. Shall I come out to the packet with you? See you safely aboard?'

She shook her head quickly. 'No, Uncle. We've said our farewells. To do so all over again–' She tried to smile, but had to bite hard on her lower lip to stop it quivering.

'Of course, of course. Point taken. Well, then, I suppose that's that.' His hearty smile faltered and he cleared his throat loudly. 'Perhaps, if you have time, you'll write? I should like to hear how you go on.' He handed her down the stone steps and into the boat. 'Goodbye, my dear.'

Unable to speak, she mouthed goodbye, raising one hand as the boatman dipped his oars and pulled away from the quay.

Phoebe followed the steward – 'Call me Mossop, miss' – down the curving stairway. One hand clutched the rail so tightly her knuckles ached. With the other she held her skirts clear of the metal treads. To trip and fall now would wreck all her efforts to appear calm and poised. She had survived the boat trip across the choppy harbour and climbed her first rope ladder without anyone detecting how her head swam or her stomach churned. Her heart was still hammering painfully against her ribs and her legs had all the strength and support of wilted celery.

Crossing from the gunwale to the open hatch in Mossop's wake, she had glimpsed a plump, cheerful-looking man standing at the far rail gazing around him in keen interest. His coat and breeches were well cut if slightly old-fashioned, and his bushy grey wig proclaimed him a member of the learned professions. Assuming he was the surgeon and aware that, at this moment, polite conversation was beyond her, she had swiftly lowered her eyes.

The space at the bottom of the stairs seemed to Phoebe little bigger than the walk-in larder at home. *Only that wasn't her home any more.* Toward the back of it were two doors, both closed.

'This one here,' Mossop explained, pointing to the nearest, 'is the captain's sleeping cabin. But Mr Burley is using it, seeing Captain Deakin won't be aboard. Now through here—'

Feeling too wretched to care who Mr Burley might be or to wonder what had happened to the captain, Phoebe followed him into a short narrow passage with three more doors.

'This one on your left leads into the captain's saloon and day cabin. The one in the corner is the WC. There's another door into it from the saloon, so make sure you remember to lock them both. Then this one here is the armoury. Let's hope we don't see *that* opened this trip.' He opened the door to his right. 'This is the passengers' mess.'

Phoebe found herself in a room roughly eighteen feet by twelve. There were no portholes. Instead, the mess was lined with doors, three on each side, all with a four-inch gap at the top. Above her head an open skylight let in light, fresh air and the sounds of activity on deck as the ship made ready to sail. An oblong table with bench seats either side took up the middle of the floor. At the forward end of the mess, just in front of the bulkhead, a black stove radiated warmth. Standing on a large metal hearth it was flanked by a bucket of coal on one side and a basket of small logs on the other.

'I put you in here, miss.' Mossop indicated the cabin next to the armoury. 'You being the only lady aboard.'

He thought she should sleep next to muskets, pistols, cutlasses and boarding pikes? Her bewilderment must have shown because he jerked his head sideways.

'The jakes, miss,' he hissed. 'You'll be closest.'

'The–' Heat flooded her face as she realized what he meant. 'Th-thank you, Mossop. That was thoughtful.'

''S all right, miss. All part of the service.' He turned the handle and to Phoebe's surprise *pulled* the door open. That it should open outward into the mess seemed an odd inconvenient arrangement, for there was little space between the open door and the bench seat. But when he stepped back so she could enter she understood.

The cabin that for the next three months would be her only retreat, her only source of privacy, was no bigger than a cupboard. A single bunk filled most of it. The remaining narrow strip of floor between the edge of the bunk and the doorway was occupied at the forward end by a small nightstand crammed between bunk and partition wall. A short, railed shelf was attached to the ship's side and a small oil lamp hung from a hook in the deckhead.

The steward edged past to place the wooden case containing her herbal remedies on the bare mattress. 'Your trunk's in there, all right?' he pointed to the space beneath the bunk. 'You might have to pull'n forward to lift the lid. The boy will bring you hot water at seven-thirty each morning. Breakfast is at eight, dinner at noon, tea at five. Weather allowing, I usually make a hot drink about nine. Anything you need, you just ask. All right, miss?'

Weather allowing. Desperate to steer her imagination away from vivid images of wild seas lashed by gales, Phoebe said the first thing she could think of. 'H-how many other passengers are there?'

'Travelling light we are this time. There's only three more besides yourself.' He cocked his head, listening. 'I think that's the last two now arriving, miss. So I'd better go. We'll be leaving soon as Mr

70

Burley do come back with the mail. Why don't you go topside? Get a lovely view of the harbour, you will.'

Leaving. Swallowing the lump in her throat that made her feel as if she might choke, Phoebe stretched her quivering mouth into a smile. 'Maybe later. I just – I – thank you.' As he nodded and turned away she pulled the door closed and in semi-darkness sank onto the mattress. It was thin and hard.

She heard muffled grunts and curses as seamen brought down trunks and bags. Then came the clang of footsteps on the companionway stairs and male voices talking and laughing. Doors opened and closed. Then there were more foot-steps on the brass stairs receding as they reached the deck.

Above her head, the sounds of activity in-creased. There were thumps, creaks, shouts and the thud of running feet. The ship began to move, gathering way. Then it tilted as it picked up speed. Tipped gently backward she clutched the wooden edge of the bunk, rigid with fear, her heart threatening to burst from her chest. She could hear the slap and hiss of water. Turning her head and listening intently she realized it came from the other side of the planking: the only barrier between her and the sea beyond.

Panic began to bubble. She wanted to cover her ears to shut out the sound but dared not let go of the bunk edge. She could feel a scream forming in her throat. To stop it escaping she bit hard on the soft flesh inside her bottom lip. Feeling the packet's motion change to a slow rise and dip she

71

guessed they had left the shelter of the inner harbour. They were out in the Carrick Roads. She couldn't bear to look ahead to the prospect of three months aboard this ship. Yet it was too painful to look back. She could not remember her father. And her mother's face had faded from her memory. Only Aunt Sarah's image remained clear. But though sometimes it was strong and vivid at other times it seemed to blur.

Phoebe hunched her shoulders. Hot tears spilled down her cheeks to drip off her chin. What was the point of loving people? Losing them hurt so much. *Too much.* Suddenly she heard her aunt's voice as clearly as if she were sitting alongside.

'For shame, Phoebe,' Sarah scolded, clicking her tongue in reproach. 'I didn't raise you to waste time feeling sorry for yourself. You are alive and should be grateful for it. Make yourself useful. Then you'll have no time for this foolishness.'

Letting go of the mattress with one hand Phoebe wiped her wet face with shaking fingers then dragged in a deep breath. She couldn't get off the ship. Nor could she remain in this cramped hutch for the entire voyage. Meeting the other passengers would be an ordeal. But at least there were only three of them. She touched the wooden case drawing comfort from its familiar shape.

Scarred and scratched, the once sharp edges were rounded now with age and use. Yet what it contained – knowledge handed down through generations – was priceless. Both William Quintrell and Uncle George had assured her that when she reached Jamaica there would opportunities for her to use what she had learned. *But the ocean was so vast, the ship so small. And she was so horribly afraid.*

Drawing another deep breath she reached for the handkerchief tucked inside her cuff. She heard footsteps on the stairs and realized it was one of many sounds she would have to get used to. Wiping her eyes and nose she took off her hat and lay it on the nightstand. The best thing was to keep busy. Being occupied would leave her less time to brood, to miss all–

A knock on her door made her jump violently.

'Miss Dymond?'

'Yes?' Shock had tightened her throat so that the word emerged as a strangled hiss.

'Is everything all right?'

No. Phoebe swallowed hard. Rising from the bunk to her feet she steadied herself with one hand, used the other to make sure her face was free from tearstains, and spoke through the wood. 'Yes, thank you.'

'Miss Dymond, I have no wish to intrude on your privacy but nor do I have unlimited time.' His obvious impatience made Phoebe flinch. 'I have just learned that I am to act as your guardian for the duration of the voyage. That being the case would our conversation not be more easily conducted – and more private – without a door between us?'

Phoebe grasped the handle. The door remained shut. *She was trapped.* Terror seared her nerves. But as she opened her mouth to scream she was

73

pulled forward, the handle wrenched from her hand as the door flew open *outwards*.

Letting out a cry, she stumbled against a tall figure, gasping as she felt warm breath on her face. Gripped by her upper arms she was set down on the bench seat with the table at her back and immediately released.

Dizzy with relief and shock, deafened by her drumming heartbeat, Phoebe pressed both hands to her temples feeling utterly foolish. 'How stupid of me. I'm sorry. I forgot about the door opening out...' As she glanced up the words dried on her tongue. This wasn't the man she had seen on deck. 'Wh-who are you?'

His thick hair was the colour of clover honey and sprang back from his forehead in tousled waves. Beneath it his brows were drawn together in a frown. Without taking his eyes from hers he lowered himself onto the bench, deliberately putting distance between them.

'Crossley. Jowan Crossley.'

Phoebe's thoughts tumbled in confusion. *This* was the man her uncle had asked? No, he hadn't. Her uncle had asked the packet agent to inform the captain. Only the captain wasn't aboard. And either the agent had been too busy to mention it or had simply forgotten. 'You're the surgeon?' At his brief frowning nod, she moistened her lips. Clearly he was as unwilling a party to the agreement as she was.

'I'm sorry you have been put to such un-necessary inconvenience, Mr Crossley. My uncle made the arrangement with my best interests at heart. However, as you see I am not a child. I

74

have been used to going about the town quite independently. With only three other passengers aboard I cannot think I shall require protection. As you pointed out, you have too little time already. I do not need, nor do I want, anyone feeling responsible for me.'

As the silence stretched and she waited for his reply she could feel her cheeks burning. 'I intend no offence, Mr Crossley.'

'None is taken, Miss Dymond.' He stood up, his head almost touching the great crossbeams that supported the deck. 'May I escort you up on deck? It is a fine sunny day and—'

'No!' Phoebe blurted. Then collecting herself she forced a smile. 'No, thank you. I will stay here.'

But instead of taking his leave as she had expected, he sat down again resting one elbow on the table and briefly inspecting his fingers.

'You have not made a sea voyage before?' He made it a question but Phoebe guessed he was just being polite.

She shook her head. Then darted him a glance. 'Is it so obvious?'

He smiled and raised one shoulder in a shrug. 'I wouldn't know. This is my first trip too.'

Phoebe searched his face warily. Would he say such a thing if it were not true? What would he gain? 'Are you humouring me, Mr Crossley?'

'No, Miss Dymond. I am stating a fact. I did not mean to be impertinent. I asked only because I wondered if perhaps the ship's motion is affecting you. I understand it can sometimes take a day or two to get used to it.'

For the first time she was able to smile naturally. 'No, the motion has not disturbed me at all, at least not so far. But should it do so I have several remedies in my case.'

'Then why,' he quizzed gently, 'on such a beautiful sunny day do you choose to remain down here? Heaven knows there will be rain enough before–' He stopped, rising to his feet as Phoebe jumped up grabbing the table edge to steady herself.

'Because – because I have things to do. Excuse me.' Wrenching open the door to her cabin she whirled inside and pulled it shut. Leaning against the partition she pressed her palms to her fiery cheeks. He had no right to question her. She held her breath, waiting, counting the seconds as she willed him to go. She had reached six before she heard him move away, then the sound of his boots on the brass stairs.

Trembling, she took off her long cloak and hung it on the hook on the back of the door. Having claimed she had things to do she had better find something. Keeping occupied would pass the time. *And there was so much time to pass.* Kneeling she pulled her trunk forward, opened the lid and lifted out two sheets, two blankets and a pillowcase. As she shook out the folds and began to make up the bed she breathed in the sweet fragrance of lavender. A flood of memories made her eyes burn. Blinking away tears before they could fall she concentrated on tucking the sheet neatly over the grubby mattress.

Chapter Five

The smell of cooking made Phoebe's insides cramp and she pressed a hand against her stomach. Breakfast – the little she had been able to eat of it – had been a lifetime ago in a different world. Normally she enjoyed meeting and talking to people. But circumstances were far from normal. Though she would have preferred to remain in her cabin she knew that to do so would provoke curiosity, even censure, among the other passengers. It certainly would not help her prove to the surgeon that she was competent to look after herself and had no need of a guardian.

With difficulty – for her fingers were shaking – she poured out another small measure of valerian tincture, shuddering at its bitterness. *Please let it work quickly*. Smoothing her hair, shaking out her gown and fastening the top button of her short jacket, she opened her door.

Mossop entered the mess from the other end carrying a fistful of cutlery. 'Ready for your dinner, miss? Be ready in five minutes.' He began setting out knives and forks.

With a hand out to steady herself as the ship gently rose and plunged, Phoebe lurched into the short passage, past the armoury, and into the WC. It was much colder in here and she shivered. Warily approaching the wooden seat all she could see was an encrusted lead-lined chute.

But then she glimpsed white foam, became aware of how much louder the hiss and slap of the waves were, and realized the chute led directly into the sea. She flinched back, her heart giving a convulsive lurch. But, as she leaned against the unyielding wood, Sarah's words echoed inside her head: *Be grateful.* Phoebe swallowed hard. Yes, it was draughty. But what if the ship had not possessed this convenience? Had she been travelling in winter it would have been far colder than this, and the sea much rougher.

Back in the mess she slid onto the bench seat close to her door. Footsteps on the stairs grew louder.

'Are neither of the officers eating with us?' a man's voice enquired.

'It doesn't appear so, at least not today,' another replied. 'I overheard the master telling Mossop that he and the mate would take their meal later in the saloon.'

'You know why, don't you?' a third voice, edged with irritation, intervened. 'Several of the crew have never sailed before. The mate and the bosun have placed each new man with an experienced able seaman, and divided them so half are on each watch.'

'Well,' the second speaker placated, 'that makes sense. They do need to learn their way around the rigging as soon as possible.'

'No doubt they do. But everything is taking twice as long and the old hands are none too happy. What was the master thinking of, taking on crew who don't know one end of a rope from the other?'

'I don't suppose he had any choice. What with the war and everything, the best will already be on some ship's list. And the press gang will have snapped up any able-bodied man who doesn't have an exemption. He'd have to take what he could get.'

The thought of her life being in the hands of men with no more experience of the sea than she had herself dried Phoebe's throat. But though she could hear the fast throb of her own heartbeat, her fear no longer stabbed like steel blades. The valerian had begun to take effect. She felt an inner tremble of relief. As three men trooped in from the companionway passage, at the other end of the mess a door opened to admit the surgeon. Seeing her, the newcomers hesitated in surprise then bowed.

'Gentlemen.' Jowan came to her side. 'Miss Dymond, permit me to present your fellow passengers. This is—'

'Romulus Downey.' The older, cheery-looking man Phoebe had seen on deck earlier and assumed was the doctor immediately came forward and took her proffered hand. Holding it between both of his, he beamed. 'It is an honour and a pleasure to make your acquaintance, Miss Dymond. We are fortunate indeed that our small company should include a member of the fair sex. Though I travel a great deal it is all too rarely that I have the pleasure of sharing a journey with such beauty.'

Phoebe stiffened, darting a glance at Jowan Crossley. She heard the echo of her own voice telling him she had no need of his protection and felt her cheeks grow warm. She would deal with this. *She must. Or risk looking foolish a second time.* Withdrawing her hand she nodded coolly. 'You are too kind, sir.'

However, instead of taking the hint and backing off, Downey leaned towards her, subdued and anxious. 'Oh dear. Pray forgive me, Miss Dymond. You have my word as a gentleman and scholar that I am harmless. But I do so *enjoy* feminine company. The trouble is I lack practice. I never married, you see. I was always too busy, first with my studies then my expeditions. I fear my pleasure at a delightful prospect has offended you. Though I swear nothing could be further from my intention.'

It was so unusual an apology, and so obviously sincere, that in spite of the anxiety and exhaustion hovering over her like a dark cloud, a smile trembled at the corners of Phoebe's mouth. 'I am not offended, sir. Startled perhaps, and maybe a little sceptical, for I am not used to receiving such extravagant compliments.'

As the old man's gaze met hers his perturbation faded, replaced by warmth, intelligence and humour. Clicking his tongue he shook his head.

'Then you are not appreciated as you deserve.'

'I would like to think my value lies deeper than my appearance, sir.'

Phoebe glimpsed satisfaction in the twinkling eyes and received the impression that she had passed some kind of test.

'You must never doubt it, Miss Dymond.'

'That is brave of you, sir. For you do not know me.'

'Ah, but with your kind permission I hope to.'

He indicated the space alongside her. 'May I?' At her nod of assent he eased between the bench and the table and settled himself comfortably.

During the exchange Phoebe saw Jowan Crossley's features set into an expression that appeared to be almost a frown. Yet Mr Downey's apology must surely have removed any cause for concern.

'Mr Clewes, Mr Matcham,' Phoebe repeated the names as they were introduced. As everyone sat down she noticed that though the surgeon had been standing near Mr Downey, instead of sliding in beside the older man he moved to the opposite side of the table. *The better to observe her?*

She had told him she did not want or need his protection. Though after panicking because she couldn't open the door, then refusing to go on deck with him, it would hardly be surprising if he doubted her self-sufficiency. Her first task must be to reassure him. But pretending command of her body and her emotions would require strength she wasn't sure she possessed.

With her hands clasped in her lap out of sight she smiled politely at the man directly opposite. The same height as her he was plump and pink-faced. And though she would not have put him much above forty he looked quite old-fashioned in his long frock coat, breeches, buckled shoes and roll-curl wig with its short pigtail. 'Have you been to Jamaica before, Mr Clewes?'

He nodded quickly and the way his face twitched made her wonder if he suffered from some nervous affliction. Perhaps he was simply shy. 'Oh yes. Mr M-Matcham and I m-make this v-voyage almost every year.'

Glitter-eyed and thin-lipped, his colleague leaned forward. 'As agents for London merchant houses we negotiate with plantation owners to buy their sugar, rum, coffee and tobacco.' His mouth widened as his gaze flickered over the bodice of her close-fitting jacket before returning to her face.

'Indeed?' Phoebe responded coolly before looking away, startled and uncomfortable. The two men could not have been more different. Taller, leaner and – judging by his fawn pantaloons, Hussar buskins, and the wide lapels on his forest green cutaway coat – a keen follower of fashion, Horace Matcham had discarded his wig in favour of a Brutus crop. He had an unnaturally high colour that reminded her of William Quintrell.

'And you, Mr Downey?' she enquired, as Mossop carried in a large tray containing a steaming dish of boiled potatoes, another of boiled cabbage, a small bowl of mustard, one of butter, and a plate heaped with thick slices of cold ham. 'Have you visited Jamaica before?'

She had feared the sight of food would revolt her. Discovering that she actually felt hungry was both a surprise and a huge relief.

'I have, Miss Dymond. And not only Jamaica. I have visited most of the islands comprising the West Indies. However, my interest lies not in commerce but in matters of the soul.'

'Are you then a m-missionary, sir?' Clewes enquired, as Phoebe served herself from each of the dishes. 'If so, I f-fear you will have a hard time of it. Priests are not welcome on the p-plantations.'

Phoebe wanted to ask why, but did not like to interrupt.

Downey shook his head. 'Though I studied theology I did not enter the church. It is my good fortune to possess means that allow me to pursue my passion free from the necessity of earning my daily bread.'

'What is this passion of yours, sir?' Matcham helped himself to potatoes. 'I swear you have us all agog.'

'I am studying the development and practice of certain cult religions from the Dahomey region of Africa.'

'Africa? Then why–' Phoebe began but he forestalled her.

'Why am I going to Jamaica? Because the Africans transported from Dahomey and sold as slaves in Jamaica and Saint Domingue carried their religion with them, adapting the ancient traditions and keeping them alive.'

'Very interesting.' Matcham's comment was belied by his tone, and his rudeness turned Phoebe's unease to dislike.

'Indeed it is fascinating,' Downey blithely agreed. 'Though of course since the rites came to be known as *obeah* and myalism–'

'Obeah?' Both merchants blurted simultaneously, their food forgotten.

'And myalism,' Downey repeated.

'There's a difference?' Phoebe ventured, intrigued by the merchants' reaction. She saw from the surgeon's expression that he shared her curiosity.

'Black magic and murder,' Matcham muttered.

Glancing briefly at the merchant with a look that reflected disappointment, Downey turned his genial face to Phoebe. '*Obeah* is, as Mr Matcham says, a form of witchcraft. It is often employed as revenge by causing harm to the person suspected of causing injury or offence. Whereas myalism–'

'Tell her,' Matcham interrupted, 'how the *obeah*-man tries to scare his victims to death with fetishes made from bunches of feathers dipped in blood, or alligator's teeth and broken eggshells and snake's heads, or dead birds mounted on a pole.' He spread mustard on a forkful of ham. 'Should those not have the desired effect he resorts to poison.'

'Or s-shadow-catching,' Clewes added. As Phoebe and Jowan turned to him he shrugged, his cheeks twitching in an awkward smile. 'It's just a lot of mumbo-jumbo. Certainly nothing you need be concerned about.'

Dead birds mounted on poles. That was what Uncle George had seen.

'What is shadow-catching?'

She looked up quickly at the surgeon's question and saw Downey's delight at his interest.

'Ah. Well. First you must understand what it is not. When we refer to a shadow we mean an image cast by the sun. But in this context a person's shadow refers to the essence of his personality: his or her – soul. An *obeah*-man – on payment of a fee naturally – gazes into a gourd filled with water and calls upon his victim's shadow to appear to him. When it does he stabs it through the heart.'

Phoebe wasn't sure how to respond. On one hand it sounded ridiculous. Yet was it really any stranger than the superstition that breaking a mirror would bring seven years' bad luck, or that possession of a rabbit's foot conferred good fortune?

'You s-see?' Clewes's laugh had a ragged edge. 'M-mumbo-jumbo.'

'You are of course entitled to your opinion,' Romulus Downey said with gentle courtesy. 'However, many thousands of people do believe in these powers. And whether or not we share their beliefs I think it only courteous to respect their right to hold them.'

'People?' Matcham scowled. 'For God's sake, these are *slaves*. They don't have any rights.'

'Actually, that's not true–'

'Excuse me, Mr Downey,' the surgeon broke in, skilfully heading off a confrontation. 'But if what you have just described is *obeah*, then what is myalism?'

This was the question Phoebe would have asked had he not done so first.

Downey beamed across the table. 'In effect it's the opposite. Myalmen know just as much about the techniques and practices of *obeah*, but they use them for good rather than evil. Myalmen are able to *release* captured shadows. They are also gifted herbalists.'

Phoebe's interest increased.

'In fact,' Downey continued, 'the oldest and most experienced of them are often called *doctor*.'

The furrow between Jowan Crossley's brows deepened for a moment but he remained silent.

'Another difference,' Downey continued, 'is that *obeah* is usually an individual contract between

85

professional and client, agreed in secret. By contrast, myalism involves special dance rituals that are accompanied by drums. So it is more a cult or social practice.'

Instantly Phoebe remembered what Aunt Sarah had told her about the rhythmic drumming Uncle George had heard carried on the night wind. Beneath her jacket her skin seemed to shrink and her knife clattered briefly against her plate.

'Thank you, Mr Downey. It's most interesting.'

'So, Miss Dymond,' Matcham demanded, pushing his empty plate aside. 'What takes you to Jamaica? These are dangerous times. And if you'll forgive me for saying so, I'm astonished to see a young lady making such a hazardous journey alone.'

Though his mouth smiled, something in his speculative gaze brought Phoebe's chin up. But before she could reply Jowan Crossley leaned forward.

'Your concern does you credit, sir.' The irony in his tone sent a dart of surprise though her. 'Fortunately it is groundless. Miss Dymond's family recognized the potential risks and appointed a guardian to take care of her. I have the honour of being responsible for Miss Dymond's welfare until our arrival in Jamaica, and you may be sure I shall take that obligation very seriously.'

A flush darkened Matcham's complexion to crimson but he held the surgeon's gaze. 'I am grateful to you for the information, Doctor, but does not treatment of the sick and wounded command the majority of your time?'

86

Though the surgeon's mouth tilted upward at the corners Phoebe had never seen a smile so lacking in humour or goodwill. She sensed antagonism between the two men but had no idea of its cause. 'You may rest easy, Mr Matcham. I am happy to report that so far everyone aboard is in good health.'

'D-do you have f-family in Jamaica, Miss Dymond?' Clewes's blurted enquiry was clearly an effort to dispel tension that was almost palpable.

'No, not exactly. Well, not yet.' Blushing, Phoebe shook her head. 'Forgive me, Mr Clewes. I must sound very confused. It–' *It still feels unreal.* 'The fact is I am travelling to Jamaica to be married. M-Mr Quintrell's father owns a plantation north-east of Spanish Town.' She saw the two agents exchange a glance.

'I – er – know the area,' Clewes nodded.

'Perhaps you know the family?' Phoebe was hopeful. To learn more might make the future less daunting.

'Er, no. I don't, not p-personally.' He busied himself with his plate. 'Though n-naturally we have heard–'

'Indeed, who has not?' Matcham murmured, earning himself an anguished glare from his companion.

'W-what my c-colleague means,' Clewes said quickly, 'is th-that though we don't have any d-dealings with them, everyone t-tends to know everyone else.'

'If only by reputation,' Matcham added bitterly. He leaned forward. 'You are to marry Mr *Rupert* Quintrell?'

Phoebe nodded, struggling to keep her smile in place. Hadn't she just said so? What lay behind their questions and speaking looks? Did they know something she didn't? Of *course they did*. They were acquainted with many of the plant-ation owners and familiar with Jamaican society They knew all kinds of things that she had yet to discover. They probably thought her ill-equipped for plantation life. No doubt there was a great deal for her to learn. But William Quintrell believed her capable.

'Unfortunately, Mr Quintrell senior has been obliged to return to Cornwall due to ill health. My–' *Betrothed, husband-to-be, intended, fiancé?* Perhaps if she said the words aloud the situation would seem more real. 'I understand m–' But how could she speak in such intimate terms of a man she had never met? 'Mr Rupert Quintrell runs the plantation now.'

'Not an easy task at the best of times,' Romulus Downey sighed, putting his knife and fork together on his empty plate.

Not understanding why he should say so, and about to tell him that the Quintrells had recently enlarged their productive acreage, Phoebe didn't get the chance.

'And without wishing to alarm you, my dear,' Downey continued, 'I fear things are unlikely to improve.'

'How so?' Jowan asked from across the table.

'Surely it's obvious?' Downey spoke softly, sadly. 'An economy dependent upon the enslave-ment of one race by another has sown the seeds of its own collapse and will reap a bitter harvest.

The slaves exist in hopeless misery while their wealthy owners live in constant fear.'

'Oh, surely not.' Phoebe felt her face grow warm as they all looked at her. 'Certainly Mr Quintrell gave no such impression. Indeed, he seemed very contented. He spoke with great pride and pleasure of all that he and his son have achieved.'

Downey turned to her, his expression kind. 'Is that so? Then he is most fortunate. However, such peace of mind is rare.' He addressed the table at large. 'Much that occurred during the revolution in France cannot be condoned. Yet who can blame the many with so little for resenting the few who had too much? What no one expected, yet surely should have seen as inevitable, was that when news of the revolution reached Saint Domingue, the slaves would rise in similar fashion against their French owners and masters.'

'Yes, but S-Saint Domingue is a F-French colony,' Clewes reminded. 'J-Jamaica belongs to G-Great B-Britain.'

'Do you think the slaves care about the nationality of those who own them?' Downey said. 'It is only because of fear that this revolution might spread to Jamaica that the cruel treatment of slaves is at last being addressed with new laws–'

'Oh yes. And I'm sure protecting the rights of slaves has made the British courts feel very virtuous,' Matcham interrupted impatiently. 'But they don't have to apply them, or live with the results. Any owner will tell you that without the whip, controlling the blacks would be impossible. You've got to have punishment. How else can you stop the sabotage and malingering?'

'Or p-produce the c-crops?' Clewes shrugged. 'The d-demand for s-sugar, rum, t-tobacco, c-coffee and m-molasses increases every year. And though the *intention* might have been g-good, those l-laws have actually m-made m-matters worse.'

'It's true,' his colleague nodded. 'While costs are continuing to climb, production is falling.'

Phoebe's head began to ache as she struggled to reconcile two very different pictures. The lavish – if mercifully brief – flatteries at the beginning of the meal had been swept aside by topics both startling and brutal. She told herself that this was a compliment as it assumed both her interest and her understanding. And she *was* interested. After all, this was where she would be spending the rest of her life. But she hadn't realized the situation on the island was so volatile. Yet how could she have been expected to know such a thing? Mr Quintrell had said there wasn't any trouble. Surely he would never have encouraged her uncle to send her – nor Uncle George agreed – if there was real danger?

'Miss Dymond?'

The surgeon's voice made Phoebe start, especially as it came, not from where he had been sitting across the table, but above her right shoulder. She looked up, bewildered, and felt his hand cup her elbow. Almost without realizing it she was rising to her feet, politely excusing herself as he propelled her out of the mess and through to the bottom of the companionway stairs.

Phoebe blinked in the bright light from the open hatch. The air was cool on her hot face and smelled fresh after the heat and food aromas in the mess. His palm, warm through the sleeve of her jacket, gently urged her towards the half spiral of brass stairs. She stiffened, wrenching her arm free as she pressed back against the bulkhead, swamped by visions of mounded heaving water, dark and threatening.

'No!' Inside her ribs her heart clenched in a painful spasm, then fluttered so she could hardly catch her breath. 'No! I can't. I want to go back to my cabin.' She tried to turn, to run, escape. But the surgeon was in front of her, gripping her upper arms.

'What's wrong, Miss Dymond?' His voice was quiet, concerned. 'There's nothing to be afraid of.'

How dare he say that? What did he know? Beneath her anger she yearned to believe him. But the longing was crushed as all her childhood nightmares rushed back, filling her head like webs and flapping black wings. She attempted to pull free, expecting him to release her. But he didn't.

'Tell me,' he coaxed in a gentle tone that reminded her of something. As she realized what it was, a little of her rigidity seeped away. It was the same tone *she* used to fearful mothers in the throes of labour; the same tone she used to soothe a sick and fretful child to sleep.

When she used that tone it came from her heart. Did he really mean it? Or was he simply humouring her? A few weeks ago it would not have occurred to her to ask such a question: to doubt intentions or be wary of trusting. But much had happened since then.

She shook her bent head, suddenly over-

91

whelmed by the strain of the past two weeks and unease stirred by the mealtime conversation.

'Miss Dymond, I am a physician as well as a surgeon. I give you my word that whatever you tell me will remain private between us. I may have medicine that could –'

She shook her head again, feeling it throb. 'I thank you, sir. But should I require medicine I have my own.' The moment the words left her lips she wished them unsaid. She tensed, expecting from her past experience of physicians to be berated for her arrogance. But when he spoke his tone held more curiosity than condemnation.

'Indeed? Did you perhaps visit an apothecary in preparation for the voyage?'

'No. There was no need.' She raised her head. 'I–' But before she could mention her work or Aunt Sarah her gaze met his. The wooden walls enclosing the tiny space shimmered and blurred. *She was falling.* She tensed: the sensation startlingly real. His smile faltered as his features blanked with shock. But an instant later it was back in place. Phoebe assumed her tired mind had been playing tricks. Releasing her he took a step back, fiddling with his coat cuff.

'What–?' He cleared his throat. 'Is there something on deck that you wish to avoid?'

Having expected him to follow up her comment by asking the source of her medicine, Phoebe was taken unawares. 'No.' He didn't press, or argue. He simply waited. The burden of silence and the pressure of her fear were too great and her words spilled out in a whisper. 'The sea. I cannot – I'm afraid of the sea.'

'Why?'

She struggled to remain composed. It was so long ago. It shouldn't upset her now. 'My mother – she died on a ship. We were returning from America.' She fell silent, overwhelmed by renewed feelings of loss: grief for the mother she could barely remember, and for her beloved Aunt Sarah.

'Were you with her?' He was tentative, as if feeling his way. She nodded. 'And your father?'

'He had been killed several weeks earlier in the Battle of Yorktown.'

'He was with General Cornwallis?'

Phoebe nodded. 'He was a captain. His death was the reason we were returning to England.' She clasped her hands. 'I cannot picture my mother's face. But I still hear the sound of her weeping. It was a love-match, you see, and cost them both...' She pressed her lips together to stop the outpouring of things he had no right to know nor she to tell. 'There were dreadful storms and she suffered terribly from seasickness. Then she developed a fever. Because she was already so weak.' Phoebe swallowed and shook her head. There was another silence. She felt like glass, thin as a bubble and full to the brim with unshed tears. A wrong move and she would shatter. Or they would spill.

'How old were you?'

'Five.'

He nodded. He didn't say how sorry he was. He didn't say anything. She was deeply grateful. Yet it seemed wrong to thank him. How had he known she didn't want, couldn't have borne, the conventional expressions of sympathy? Then she remembered he was both physician and surgeon.

93

He would have considerable experience of death and of dealing with the bereaved. If only when Aunt Sarah died *he* had been–

'What happened to you when the ship reached Falmouth? Where did you go?' His quiet question brought her out of her scattered thoughts. She swallowed painfully.

'I was told that just before she – my mother spoke to the captain. When the ship arrived in Falmouth he carried me to relations who took me in. I was very happy there.' Her voice wobbled and she coughed to disguise it. 'My uncle and my two cousins are all packet men. They spend most of their lives at sea. My fear must have seemed very strange to them. But they were very kind.' She gestured helplessly. 'I know my dread is foolish. I am no longer a child. But–' Glancing up the companionway she shook her head, and shuddered.

'Miss Dymond, will you trust me?'

Phoebe gazed at her shoes, embarrassed by her own hesitation. 'I don't know you.' He was trying to be kind. But she was wary of trusting anyone now.

'That's true. But as a doctor I am bound by oath as well as by inclination to *preserve* life. You cannot spend the entire voyage down here. Your health would suffer. Look up. Do you see the blue sky? The sun is shining. It's a beautiful spring day. Come. No harm will befall you, I promise.'

As he held out his hand Phoebe could feel the familiar and dreaded stirring of panic. *She couldn't.* He had promised she would be safe. *She couldn't.* She shook her head.

'I-I can't.' She turned her face aside. He would

94

release her now and, his patience exhausted, walk away. But he didn't.

'All right, not today.' Cupping her elbow once more he steered her away from the stairs and turned towards the door leading into the captain's day cabin.

'Where are we going?'

'One moment.' Knocking, he waited an instant then turned the handle. Stepping inside he drew her gently after him.

Light streamed in from small-paned windows above a wide padded seat that almost filled the stern wall of the cabin. There was a cabinet to one side and a bookcase on the other. In the middle of the cabin stood a table covered with books and papers on which rested some kind of nautical instrument and an inkstand. A few feet from her along the bulkhead was a small black stove, and on the far side of that another door.

He released her arm and stepped away. 'Take a look.' He gestured toward the window.

She felt the blood drain from her face. Did he have any idea what he was asking? *Of course not. How could he?* Then anger as hot and bright as a flame scorched through her. 'You have no right to do this.'

After an instant's vivid shock, his face closed. 'I beg your pardon.'

Despite a shame so intense she could feel her chemise clinging to damp burning skin she would not apologize. Perhaps his intentions were good and honourable. But how could she be sure of that when people she had known for years – she closed her eyes. Then, raising her head, she half-turned towards the door.

'We should not be in here.'

'I thought,' he said quietly, meeting her fury with calm, 'if you could bring yourself to look at the water from in here, perhaps even allow me to open one of the windows, you might find the prospect of going up on deck a little less daunting.'

She wanted to run away and hide. And if he had responded with sarcasm or impatience or disdain she would have been able to justify doing so. But he hadn't so she couldn't. *Damn him.* Gripped by emotions terrifying in their strength and complexity she wrapped her arms tightly across her body as if this might keep it all inside and under control. Her mouth and throat were dust dry and it hurt when she swallowed.

She took a step forward, then another. *If he said a word* – but he didn't. *If she glimpsed the smallest hint of triumph* – but she didn't. He simply stood where he was, his eyes locked on hers. As she reached him he stepped aside so she could see the view he had blocked with his body.

'Oh,' Phoebe gasped. She gazed at the ship's wake spreading in a widening *vee* of sunlit foam that glittered like diamond-dusted lace on rolling swells of deep blue water.

Awestruck, she whispered, 'It's beautiful,' and felt the hard tangled knot of grief inside her soften.

Chapter Six

'We will go just as far as the top stair.'

'Then I can come down again?'

'If that is what you wish.'

Sliding a trembling hand through Jowan Crossley's proffered arm she followed him, one reluctant foot after the other.

He glanced back at her. 'The bosun tells me that *Providence* is a brigantine.'

Why was he telling her this, and why now? Did he not realize it was impossible for her to concentrate on what he was saying, let alone respond as good manners required? *Of course he did.* His conversation was a deliberate attempt to distract her. For though she could not give him her whole attention, nor could she focus exclusively on her terror.

She recognized the gambit as one she used herself to divert a sick or injured child. It felt strange to be on the receiving end. The very fact that he was even trying to win her confidence surprised her. Most of the doctors she knew were too busy or too impatient to bother with any except wealthy patients who kept a good table and a cellar to match.

But they were men in their middle years and older. Jowan Crossley was ... *tall, fair, with wide shoulders and...* Flushing to the roots of her hair Phoebe reined in her unruly thoughts. The surgeon appeared to be just short of thirty. His comparative youth was likely to make him less set in his ways, more open to new ways of thinking. That was the reason – *the only reason* – she had registered his appearance in such detail.

'Apparently that means she has square sails on her foremast and a fore-and-aft gaff sail on her main. She has a crew of twenty-two not counting the bosun, carpenter, sailmaker and gunner. Did you know those four are known as idlers?'

She strained to detect the smallest hint of impatience that would legitimize retreat, heard none, and was torn between gratitude for his tact and resentment of his gentle but relentless determination. *It's all for the best. I won't deny you might find things difficult to begin with. But you're not short of pluck, Phoebe. Once you're there you'll see it was the right move. Then you'll wonder why you ever had doubts.* That was what Uncle George had said. No doubt Jowan Crossley would use those very same words to justify his actions. Though she had to admit he had not said them yet.

'Personally,' he confided over his shoulder, 'I think calling them idlers is most unfair, and surely inaccurate. They are not part of a watch working four hours on and four hours off. Instead they are at their duties from seven in the morning until five-thirty in the afternoon. That cannot be called idleness. Would you not agree, Miss Dymond?'

To try and counter the clamour going on in her head, Phoebe had kept her gaze fixed on the pattern of holes and curls in each brass tread. But at her name she automatically looked up. He had hefted his bag out onto the deck, stepped after it, and was waiting for her. For a moment the temptation to turn and run back down the stairs to the sanctuary of her cabin was almost over-powering. Cramped, stuffy, and dark, it still represented safety. As if reading her thoughts he leaned down, extending his hand.

'Two more steps that's all.' His voice was low-pitched, for her ears only. Should anyone be close by they would not be able to hear. 'Already you've come this far.'

She shook her head, gripping the rail, frozen. Nausea churned in her stomach. 'I can't.'

'You can. You're safe, I promise. Come.'

She stared at his palm; at the long fingers slightly curled as he waited; *a hand that fought death*. She knew everything he had said was true. It *wouldn't* be good for her health to spend three months either in the mess or her cabin. Lack of sunlight and fresh air would make her ill. How could she be of use to anyone else if she was weak and unwell herself? He was trying to make it as easy as he could. And for that she owed him: not just gratitude but effort.

'Remember,' he murmured, 'you are not alone on this ship.'

Her head snapped up. Welling terror choked her as vivid images filled her head: a small child huddling, drenched and chilled in a corner of a storm-lashed deck. She struggled for control as he continued talking.

'You are in the company of men who know the sea, know their job, and want to reach Jamaica as quickly and safely as you do. All of us: the master,

99

the mate, the crew, the other passengers, and me, value our lives just as much as you value yours. If we are not fearful, why should you be?'

Everything he said made perfect sense; her brain knew it. But her body and her emotions – *help me.* She did not know to whom she was pleading. Then she pictured her aunt's face. Heard the brisk 'All right, my bird, steady now', with which Sarah had strengthened and encouraged her in everything from her first attempts at decanting tinctures to coping with the tragic aftermath of a stillbirth.

Her heart crashing against her ribs, every muscle taut, she reached for his hand. As his fingers closed over hers, a moment's blissful relief – *you're not alone* – was shattered by the jolt that tingled up her arm. She caught her breath. She was so anxious he should not see her confusion that she was hardly aware of stepping over the coaming and on to the deck.

Deeply disturbed by her physical response to his touch she swiftly pulled her hand free and used both to hold on to the edge of the hatch. He was a doctor, a professional man doing his professional duty, almost a stranger. And she was on her way to be married.

To avoid looking at him she turned her head and found her gaze climbing from the scrubbed deck to the vast expanse of water. Gilded with sunlight, the dancing surface rose and fell. It was the colour of sapphires under a cornflower sky dotted with puffs of cloud like cotton balls. Parted by the ship's bow, waves turned like earth beneath a plough blade and fell aside in a froth of foam to flatten and spread behind them. 'It's so ... *big*,' she whispered. 'And the ship...' She shuddered.

'Seems small?' He moved to her side. 'True. But *Providence* is in her element. This is what she was built for, where she is meant to be. She is not *fighting* the sea or the wind. She's using both to take her where she wants to go.'

Phoebe moistened her lips. 'But what if there's a storm?'

'Mossop tells me she's well found and will take anything thrown at her.' He grinned. 'And as Mossop has crossed this ocean at least a dozen times, who are we to doubt him?'

Relief brought a tremulous smile to her mouth. Suddenly self-conscious, Phoebe looked away. 'You have been very patient with me, Dr Crossley. But I have imposed long enough on both your time and your kindness.' Dipping her head she turned to start down the stairs.

'You will come topside again tomorrow?'

For an instant she wondered if he might be seeking her company. Then recognizing the vanity – and the impropriety – of such a thought, she blushed. What he sought was her assurance she would continue to get as much fresh air as possible. Despite being responsible for the welfare of twenty-eight men of the ship's company as well as the rest of the passengers, he had spent his valuable time helping her conquer a literally crippling fear. That alone meant to refuse would be unforgivable.

'Yes.' Head bent to hide her fiery colour she retreated down the stairs.

Watching her disappear, Jowan recalled his restless night and tried to make sense of turmoil that instead of diminishing was actually growing worse. He was her guardian, for God's sake. She was travelling to her wedding.

He had been furious when Burley, with a mumbled apology for it having slipped his mind, suddenly informed him of this additional responsibility. Tierney, the packet agent, must have known that chaperoning lone females was one of the surgeon's non-medical duties. Why hadn't *he* mentioned it? But even as the question formed Jowan guessed the answer. Tierney would waste neither time nor interest on anything that did not bring in money.

His irritation had grown during the hours that followed. As well as wanting to escape the demands of his grieving parents he had joined the Packet Service to get away from predatory females. His age, his professional standing, and the fact that he was not unpleasant to look at meant he had spent the past five years side-stepping increasing pressure to marry. After assuming he'd have a few months free of female company, the prospect of being required to spend a proportion of the voyage making conversation with a tongue-tied schoolgirl or a prune faced spinster had filled him with frustration.

Glimpsing Phoebe Dymond as she climbed aboard he had wondered briefly at her downcast eyes and hurried dash from gunwale to companionway. Assuming sadness at leave-taking, or possible seasickness, and relieved that she was neither child nor crone, he had shrugged thoughts of her aside and returned to his work.

But like a burr she had clung. And twenty-four hours on from that first glimpse he was beginning to realize that his imagined alternatives would have been far less disturbing to his peace of mind.

Though he now knew her anxiety to be rooted in her fear of the sea, he sensed this was not the only reason behind a nervous tension so strong that at times her slender body seemed almost to vibrate.

His first impression of reserve, almost shyness, had proved accurate – in some respects. The fact that she required a guardian, not merely an escort, indicated she was not yet twenty-one. Yet her cool response to the presumptuous Matcham and her banter with Romulus Downey indicated considerable social skill.

Guiding her into the saloon so she might look at the sea through the stern window he had acted on impulse. Her spirited response had been a revelation. Surprise had been shouldered aside by curiosity. Usually he could tell within minutes if a young woman possessed enough intelligence and breadth of interest for him to want to know her better. Few did.

Though his exchanges with Phoebe Dymond had of necessity centred on her debilitating fear, something about her intrigued him. He knew his interest was edging beyond the purely professional, and was not at all wise, yet he found himself reliving their conversations.

At dinner she had been willing enough to tell

them she was travelling to Jamaica to be married. But though her mouth had smiled, there had been more trepidation than pleasure in her tone. Looking back he was appalled at the pressure he had applied to get her up on deck. Medically he could justify it. But when she had spoken of losing both parents and being given to strangers he had found himself touched in a way he hadn't expected, especially as she had made it clear she was not seeking sympathy, nor would it be welcome.

Once more warning bells had jangled. Was he mad? Had he not left Cornwall to escape entanglement? In any case, if the fact of her being betrothed had not put her beyond his reach, his moral responsibility as her guardian certainly did. Yet in the hours since, he had not been able to get her out of his head.

Anger stirred as he recalled her hesitation when he had asked her to trust him. He'd been doing his best to help her, and she had looked at him with – not just uncertainty – but definite suspicion. Why should she not trust him? Then again, why should she? She didn't know him. Yet that fact alone should not automatically inspire doubt unless – had she trusted someone only to have her trust betrayed? Who had hurt her, and why? *It was none of his business.*

'Ready, sir?'

The bosun's voice jerking him back to the present reminded him of his duties. Angry with himself – for he should, and did, know better – he picked up his bag.

'Ready, Mr Hosking.' Shading his eyes, Jowan

peered forward along the deck to the group of men shuffling into a rough line. 'Where's Grigg?'

'Gone to fetch hot water and bandages, sir. There's a couple of gashes need stitching.'

Deliberately shutting Phoebe Dymond from his mind, Jowan strode briskly along the deck to take his first sick parade.

In the days that followed, Phoebe began to adjust to shipboard life. The varying trills of the bosun's whistle, the clang of the watch bell every half-hour, the thud and whoosh of water buckets and the rhythmic scrape of the bibles – prayerbook-sized blocks of sandstone used to clean the deck each morning – quickly became familiar. Already she had become so used to the rattle of blocks and the crack of canvas as sails were raised and lowered that she barely noticed them.

The tilting floor and the boom and hiss of the sea against the ship's side were taking longer to get used to. But they no longer filled her with dread. In fact during mealtimes, if the conversation was interesting, she could forget about them for minutes at a time.

Keeping her word she had gone topside every day, waiting until the other passengers were up there so no one might see how slowly she climbed the stairs. Or how often she needed to stop. From the second day she set herself targets. To start with they were very small: to take one more step up the companionway before stopping; to spend an additional minute on deck – counted in seconds under her breath – before returning to the mess.

She began keeping a diary, noting her achievements and setbacks. After a week, re-reading what she had written, momentary pride was eclipsed by shame. It was time to try harder. From this morning each time she went up on deck she would take note of what skills the old hands were teaching the new men.

'Ah, Miss Dymond,' Romulus Downey greeted her as she stepped over the coaming a few days later. 'Come to take the air? You have timed it well. Mr Burley tells me we shall have rain before nightfall. Already the wind is picking up. Still, it will speed us on our way, will it not?'

Phoebe tried to ignore the flutter of panic beneath her breastbone. 'Let us hope so, Mr Downey.' Keeping one hand on the hatch top she moved aside to allow him to go down. About to follow, she saw the familiar cluster of men waiting at the mainmast. It was past the usual time for sick call. As she wondered where the surgeon was she heard footsteps on the stairs. But they weren't his. Realization that she was able to distinguish Jowan Crossley's footsteps from anyone else's made her cheeks suddenly hot.

Grigg appeared, shaking his head and muttering to himself. Seeing her he raised his eyes skyward and clicked his tongue.

'Been one of they mornings, it have, miss. Two men down with fever, then Slush near chopped his finger off.'

'Slush?' Phoebe repeated blankly.

'The cook, miss.'

'I *am* sorry.'

'Not half so sorry as the men'll be if their

106

dinner's late,' Grigg retorted grimly. 'I'd best get on.'

As Grigg hurried towards the waiting men Phoebe heard Jowan's boots loud and fast on the stairs.

Bounding out of the companionway, he checked as he saw her. 'Miss Dymond.'

'Dr Crossley, Grigg says you have several men sick. I wondered if I might be of help? I have–'

'Thank you, no,' he cut her short. 'I don't doubt you mean well, Miss Dymond. But the injuries and ailments suffered by seamen are beyond the scope of a vinaigrette or hartshorn draught. Please excuse me.' With a curt nod he strode past her along the sloping deck.

Phoebe stared after the tall figure; her racing heartbeat loud in her ears as shock vied with fury at his snub.

Chapter Seven

Stung by the surgeon's rejection of her offer, Phoebe decided to return to the mess. Perhaps Romulus Downey would be willing to tell her more about life on the island that was to be her new home. No doubt the agents knew Jamaica at least as well as he did, perhaps even better. But she did not feel comfortable with either of them. Mr Matcham radiated bitterness and an anger that seemed on occasion to be directed at her, though she could not imagine why. Meanwhile Mr Clewes watched both his colleague and her with an anxiety she found unsettling. So as far as was possible she tried to avoid them.

She had almost reached the bottom of the stairs when Timmy Keast, the ship's boy, came through from the passage carrying a bucket. As he glanced up and saw her he tried to shield it from her gaze.

'Sorry, miss. If I'd known you was coming down I'd 'ave gone up through the fo'c'sle.'

'It's all right, Timmy. Don't concern yourself.' As she reached the bottom and he started past her she saw that the bucket was almost full of what looked like bits of greyish-brown fur. 'What on earth is that?'

'Dead rats, miss.'

A bucketful? Managing to mask her inward recoil, Phoebe tightened her grip on the rail. Two men were suffering from fever and Timmy was holding a bucketful of dead rats. Was there a connection? To betray horror or fear would achieve nothing. She must remain calm. *You are not alone on this ship.* 'Do you know what killed them?'

'Mr Grigg's oatcakes, miss.'

'I beg your pardon?' Phoebe was startled.

'He made 'em up special. Put poison in them, he did.'

'Oh, I see. Is this' – she indicated the bucket – 'all?'

'Shouldn't think so.' Timmy wiped his nose with the back of a grubby hand. 'Stuff do take a while to work, see? Then there's the job of finding them. Still, this is the third bucket this morning. So it look like it's working.'

The *third* bucket? 'How are you disposing of them?'

'Over the side, miss. Too many to put on the caboose stove. In any case, Slush do say they stink even worse than the salt pork.'

As her imagination supplied images that made her wish she hadn't asked, Phoebe tried desperately to divert her thoughts. 'Timmy, why is the cook called Slush?'

'On account of the fat, miss. From when the meat is boiled. He do skim it off, save it in a barrel, and when the ship get home he sell it to the soap makers. 'Course, some of it got to be set aside for greasing the foremast where the yards go up and down. But he don't like parting with it, miss. Not at all, he don't.' Grinning, the boy raised a finger to his forehead, sidled past, and hurried up the stairs leaning sideways to balance

109

the weight of the bucket. His feet were bare. The callused and filthy soles made little sound.

In the short passage to the mess Phoebe steadied herself against the bulkhead. The sideways tilt of the floor had increased. And the slow rise and plunge as the brigantine rode the deepening swell tipped her first forward then back making it hard to keep her balance. As she staggered into the mess Mossop was fitting fiddle rails round the edge of the table.

He looked up. 'Bit of a blow coming.'

Phoebe swallowed. *Coming?* It was going to get worse?

'Don't you worry, miss. You'll soon get your sea legs. Good sailor, are you?'

Phoebe shrugged helplessly. 'I don't know.' She couldn't remember.

'Well, it looks to me like you're doing all right. Mind you,' – he lowered his voice – 'there's others I aren't so sure about.' With a speaking look the significance of which she didn't have time to grasp, he turned back to his task.

As Phoebe hung up her cloak, oddly reassured by the steward's conviction that she would be fine, dawning realization made her pause. The fear that had clung to her like a dark shadow seemed to have diminished. It was still there, but fainter and less sapping. So much had happened – was still happening – she simply didn't have the strength to sustain intense fear and deal with the challenges that each new day at sea brought.

She was in a situation she had no power to change and over which she had no control. All she could do was accept each day as it came and try to make the best of it.

Returning to the mess, she sat in her usual place at the table. 'Mossop, have you seen Mr Downey?'

'I b'lieve he's just gone along the passage, miss. Looked to me like he was feeling a bit queasy. I reckon a chat with you would cheer'n up proper. Take his mind off things.'

'If Mr Downey is indeed suffering as you describe, then a peppermint infusion will do far more than conversation to improve his comfort.'

Sucking air through his teeth the steward shook his head. 'I haven't got nothing like that, miss.'

'Of course not. Why should you? But I have,' Phoebe said. 'Would you be so kind as to bring me a cup of boiling water and a teaspoon?'

'Dare say I can manage that, miss.' He headed for his pantry.

Phoebe returned to her cabin and opened the case containing her remedies. As she inhaled the scent of dried herbs her head was filled with vivid images of summer, of days spent gathering leaves and blossoms. She recalled the balm of the sun's heat and the lazy drone of bees around the hives in the garden. The painful sense of loss, of yearning for what had gone and would never be repeated, was acutely painful. Her hand went to the valerian bottle. About to grasp it she hesitated. There was still a long way to go. Fear raised gooseflesh on her skin. Better not to think of that. But once the bottle was empty there would be no more until she reached Jamaica. She must be strong and hold out until she really needed it.

Taking out a jar of honey and two linen bags, one containing crushed dried peppermint leaves and flowers, the other dried camomile, she closed the case and left it on her bunk. As she emerged and shut her door Mossop returned with a steaming jug.

'I brung two cups, miss.' He lowered his voice again. 'Seemed more sociable like. The gentleman might be a bit uncomfortable drinking alone, specially if need was seen as weakness.'

Phoebe was surprised by the steward's sensitivity. 'Thank you, Mossop. That was very thoughtful.'

Downey lurched into the mess from the passage, a handkerchief to his mouth, his round face wan and miserable.

'Oh, Miss Dymond. I must ask you to excuse me. I am feeling woefully ill.'

'I'm so sorry, Mr Downey. I am just making myself an infusion. I'd be delighted to share it with you.' Placing a heaped teaspoonful of dried herb in each cup Phoebe poured on hot water and added a small amount of honey.

Downey mopped his glistening forehead. 'You are kind. But I fear that if I stay I might embarrass us both. I think I should go and–' He sniffed, his brows puckering. 'Is that peppermint?'

Phoebe nodded. 'A wonderful settler and very soothing to the digestion. Please, do sit, Mr Downey. You *will* feel better, I promise.' Picking up her camomile tea, she took a sip.

He slid carefully onto the bench. Then wiping his forehead and upper lip once more he drew the cup towards him and lifted it with shaking

112

fingers. After several sips he turned to her, his expression softening as the strain melted away.

'That is remarkable. Astonishing, in fact. Miss Dymond, you are an angel.'

Phoebe laughed. 'I am nothing of the sort, sir. However I do have some knowledge of herbs and their properties. I take it you are beginning to feel a little better?'

'Much better.' He leaned forward a little, confiding. 'In truth, Miss Dymond, I had begun to wish I had never set foot on this ship. Usually when I travel by sea I bring a bottle of laudanum. When the weather turns bad I sleep for days and so escape the worst of the discomfort.'

Phoebe quickly raised her cup to mask her shock at such improvident behaviour with a powerful drug. Downey took another sip of his own infusion and sighed.

'I bought one from an apothecary in Falmouth. But I fear the servant I entrusted with my packing either forgot to put it in my trunk or else decided his need of it was greater than mine.' He sipped some more. 'This is indeed a miracle potion, Miss Dymond. I am more indebted to you that I can say.'

Phoebe smiled, pleased to see colour returning to his cheeks. He was visibly more cheerful.

'May I ask how you know about such things?'

'I was taught by my aunt. She was an expert in the use of herbs as medicine. I wonder if you are sufficiently recovered might I ask you about your studies?'

'Might you ask–? My dear Miss Dymond, I am honoured by your interest. I imagine that being a herbalist yourself you are interested in the myal cult?'

Phoebe nodded. 'How did it come to Jamaica?'

'With the Aradas Negroes from Dahomey who were captured and sold into slavery. Despite threats of dire punishment if they are caught performing any of the rites and rituals they refuse to abandon them, for this is all they have left of the life they were forced to leave.'

'They must be very brave.'

'There are those who think them very foolish,' Downey said. 'But courage is not all they require. The ritual dances demand a great deal of energy. This from men and women already worked to the limit of human endurance. Their willingness to deny themselves desperately needed rest and sleep is a testament to how much their religion means to them. One wonders,' he remarked wryly, 'how many plantation owners would do as much for their Christian faith.'

Cradling her cup in both hands, Phoebe frowned. 'I don't understand. Why are the owners so opposed to it?'

'Fear,' he said simply. 'The slaves' skin colour, way of life, beliefs, even the food they prefer, is different from ours. They are thought of as animals and treated as such. But the truth is that no matter how white men might wish it otherwise, blacks are human beings too. And no man can act with deliberate cruelty towards his fellows yet remain untainted. A slave trader will justify his actions by claiming that Negroes are savages. And because they are not Christians they and their dances and drumming must therefore be instruments of the Devil. But that is fear talking. Myalists believe as strongly in the soul as Christians do: perhaps even more so. For what man can call himself a Christian then commit acts of brutality so appalling–' He broke off, shaking his head. 'Forgive me, Miss Dymond. Sometimes I forget myself. I would not wish to upset you.'

Phoebe swallowed. 'It is an upsetting subject, Mr Downey. I had not realized...' There was so much she had been unaware of, or had shut her mind to, overwhelmed by its enormity and her own helplessness. But she was going to Jamaica to marry a plantation owner. Never again could she tell herself it was not her concern. 'But that doesn't mean we can simply shut our eyes and pretend horrors do not exist. And yet – didn't I read somewhere about slaves arriving from Africa being offered baptism? And those converting to Christianity being welcomed and well treated?'

His expression reflected sadness and cynicism. 'That was indeed the original intention. In fact it was cited as moral justification for the slave trade. But it's an ideal seldom observed. In practice most Negro slaves are denied any religious instruction.' He spread his hands. 'From whom would they receive it when, as Mr Clewes mentioned at dinner, planters refuse to allow clergy on their land?'

Now Phoebe understood much more clearly the reason for the planters' reluctance. They would not want any visiting priest seeing evidence of ill-treatment or brutal punishment. She recalled William Quintrell's jovial manner, the glimpses of a darker personality behind the heavy

115

charm, the tremor in his hand, and the amount he drank. But surely he could not be one of those men of cruelty? For if he were, Uncle George would never have welcomed him. Would he? Just how well acquainted were they?

Uncle George might know nothing at all about the way William Quintrell ran his plantation. Surely he would have wanted to find out? Why would he? Uncle George ran his ship as he saw fit. He would consider other men of business entitled to the same freedom. Yet he must have seen, as she had, numerous newspaper articles concerning the slave trade, and still others agitating for its abolition.

Yet whatever practices William Quintrell might or might not have employed in running the plantation he was no longer in charge. He had handed over control to his son *who had expanded the cane fields and doubled production.* Still, Uncle George must be convinced she would be in safe hands. Otherwise he would never have agreed to her betrothal. She had to believe that. Because to doubt would mean he had sent her away not caring what happened to her. She could not bear even to contemplate such an appalling possibility.

Phoebe moistened her lips. 'Surely not *all* plantations are run by barbaric methods?'

Downey gazed into his cup. 'I have visited only a few. But I would like to believe not.'

Though this did nothing to allay her deepening unease Phoebe forced a smile. 'Thank you, Mr Downey.'

He looked up. 'For what, Miss Dymond?'

'Being as honest as courtesy allows.'

116

'I have too great a regard for your intelligence to be anything else,' he said simply.

The compliment, clearly sincere, brought warmth to her cheeks. She set her own cup down. 'It is easy to understand that owners would not want their slaves hearing gospel teachings about the equality of all men before God.'

'Indeed not. Though given the inefficiency and corruption of a large portion of the clergy there is little likelihood of that happening. I understand they are currently charging three pounds to baptize a slave. As you might imagine few owners are willing to pay. Not only do they claim the blacks would be unable to understand the complexities of Christianity, they have even petitioned for a cut in the number of saints' days and religious processions.'

'Why?'

'To limit opportunities for slaves to meet each other. They fear further revolts,' he explained.

'But' – Phoebe met his gaze – 'these have erupted anyway. At least they have on Saint Domingue.'

'True,' Downey agreed. 'How could it be otherwise?' Resting an elbow on the table, he rubbed his forehead.

'Forgive me, Mr Downey. I fear I have wearied you.'

'Not at all,' he denied, straightening. 'I am tired, but it is from lack of sleep. In truth, Miss Dymond, I rarely have such an interested and attentive audience.' He beamed at her, his eyes twinkling. 'Especially–'

'I do hope,' she cut in, raising her brows at him,

'that you are not intending to qualify your remark with a reference to the fact that I am female.'

After a moment's surprise he grinned and slapped his thigh. 'I knew I was right about you.' He leaned towards her. 'Miss Dymond, you possess a mind more open and enquiring than many so-called men of learning I have encountered.'

'If that is so it may be because my own background is somewhat out of the ordinary.'

'I guessed as much. Were you perhaps a lonely child?'

Startled by the bluntness of his question, Phoebe studied him warily but saw only kindness in his gaze. She shrugged. 'I was happy with my own company and I've always loved to read. Besides, from the time I went to live with my aunt and uncle, quite literally an orphan of the storm, Aunt Sarah allowed me to assist her.'

'What did you do?'

'To begin with I was given simple jobs like stripping elderberries and flowers from their stems and into a bowl. I think she wanted to see how quickly I got bored. Only I never did. From those very first moments I knew I was doing something important and useful. I used to feel a glow of excitement when I came in and saw one end of the table covered with bundles of dried herbs and roots, or basins filled with steeping leaves and flowers. As soon as I was old enough to stand on a stool without fear of falling off she let me watch her make decoctions and ointments. And she promised that when I didn't need the stool any more I might help. Never has any child been so anxious to grow! I was far too enthralled with all I was learning to have time to feel lonely.' *That had come later.* 'But were we not talking about souls, Mr Downey?' she reminded, anxious to steer the conversation away from herself.

'Indeed, we were, Miss Dymond. And believers in *vaudou*, as it's known in Saint Domingue, take safety of the soul very seriously indeed. Many will go to a *mambo* or *hungan* – a priest or priestess – in order to have their soul protected from sorcerers, or indeed from anyone who might wish them harm.'

'How? I mean, what could the priest do?'

'First, with great ceremony he will take nail parings and a lock of hair from the supplicant and put them into a small bottle. Then the meat of a white cockerel that has been cooked without any salt or flavouring is shared with the supplicant's friends or family. While the meal is being eaten, a package of bread soaked in wine, rum, or cane juice, together with something sweet – maybe a small piece of sugar cane – is tied around the supplicant's head. Everyone must take great care not to break any of the cockerel's bones. After the meal the bones, the bottle and the package are placed in a little box. This represents the supplicant's soul and is hidden away in some secret place. Thus, though a slave's body might belong to his master, his soul is safely hidden elsewhere and remains free.'

'Why then do they dance?' Phoebe asked quietly. 'They have little enough to celebrate.'

'That is not the reason,' Downey said. 'They

dance to reach a state of trance. It is their only escape, other than death.'

The gusting wind ruffled Jowan's hair as he examined a rope burn that had left an able seaman with a ten-inch scar that curved across his inner arm from wrist to elbow. The pale pink streak was livid against the man's leathery sun-darkened skin.

'It's healing well. You were given olive oil to rub in?'

'Aye, sir,' the seaman nodded.

'Keep using it night and morning. It will protect the new skin and prevent it contracting.' Jowan nodded dismissal.

During the next hour he gave Blue Pills and mercuric oxide ointment to three men with syphilitic rashes, put a fresh dressing on a superficial leg ulcer, dosed an obvious malingerer with a strong cathartic and removed a large splinter from under the thumbnail of the carpenter's mate. By the time he had finished the wind was much fresher and the swell more pronounced.

Returning unsteadily via the fo'c'sle to the master's cabin, now rigged as a sick bay with two hanging beds, he saw that the James's powder he had given to both fever patients had taken effect. Their faces glistened, beaded with huge drops of sweat.

Leaving Grigg to wash them and attend to any other needs, Jowan crossed to his own cabin. Shutting the door he dropped his bag, crawled onto his cot, and lay with an arm over his eyes. He had tried telling himself the roiling discomfort in his stomach was due to something he had eaten. But he knew it wasn't.

He had believed himself prepared for whatever his new career might bring. He harboured no doubts about his professional expertise. But the possibility he might suffer from seasickness had never occurred to him. As well as feeling wretched he felt utterly foolish. For despite her desperate fear of the sea even Miss Dymond's stomach was proving stronger than his.

He couldn't give in to it. That would be too shaming. Besides, he had duties, responsibilities. There were records to be written up of patients seen and medicines dispensed. The men in the sick bay needed to be bled, and the cook's dressing changed. And according to Mossop this was just 'a bit of a blow'. He would get used to it. *He had to.*

Swallowing several times he carefully pushed himself up and swung his legs to the floor. Opening the medicine chest he took out a ribbed brown glass bottle. He was well aware of the risk he was taking. But he also knew his own strength and was clear about his reasons. He was not seeking escape or a permanent blurring of reality. All he wanted – needed – was a very brief respite to allow his body to adjust to the increasing motion of the ship. He poured a small dose into the measuring glass, tossed it down his throat, closed his eyes and waited.

Within seconds the horrible churning settled; soothed by a warmth that suffused his entire body. Replacing the bottle and glass Jowan closed the chest and returned to the sick bay and duties

121

that would keep him busy for the rest of the day.

'I have to allow,' Romulus Downey confided, 'that the dramatic descriptions of snake worship and magic cited by Mr Matcham and Mr Clewes do contain elements of truth. *Vaudou* gods may indeed be represented by stones, plants, birds, animals, by water or trees, or even by symbols drawn on the ground. And it is true that gifts in the form of food or a sacrifice are offered to them. But that is only one aspect of cult practice. You see though many priests were among those captured and sold into—'

'Priests were sold?' Phoebe blurted, shocked.

'Oh yes.'

'But—'

'You have read that slave ships carry only the dregs of Africa, criminals and so on. That is what supporters of the trade would have you believe. But in reality slave cargoes have always comprised a broad cross-section of African society. No doubt some were criminals. But far more were not.'

'So who were they?' Phoebe asked.

'Perhaps prisoners of war. Or simply people who had offended someone in a position of power. The only comfort the priests could offer these poor unfortunates was to keep their religion alive. They did this by teaching their fellow captives a simplified version of the names and characteristics of the gods, and the required rituals, dances and sacrifices. Though of necessity a very simplified version of a complex religion, this has been handed down through generations born in slavery on both Saint Domingue and Jamaica.'

'What kinds of gods and goddesses?' Phoebe asked, fascinated.

'Well, just as Christians believe in Christ the holy saviour as the epitome of goodness and the Devil as all that is wicked and evil, so it is in *vaudou*. There are different families of gods. The *rada loa* are gentle, helpful and good. But *petro loa* are associated with magic invoked by *obeah*-men for evil purposes.'

Shivering, Phoebe rubbed her arms.

'My dear, I do apologize. I shouldn't have–'

'No, no, please. The air seems suddenly cooler that's all. Mossop was saying it would rain before nightfall. Please go on.' Phoebe caught herself. 'Mr Downey, do forgive me. Perhaps you would prefer to be doing something else.'

'What could possibly be more rewarding that talking about my life's work to someone who shows such interest?' He beamed. 'I am astonished at how much better I feel thanks to your magic potion.'

'Then please tell me a little more?'

'Well, just as human beings have different facets to their characters, so do the gods. The goddess Ezili-Freda-Dahomey belongs to the family of sea spirits and is the personification of feminine beauty and grace.'

'Like Aphrodite?'

'Exactly so. But another Ezili is Ezili-of-the-black-heart. And one of the most dreaded *loa*, a servant of the devil, is Marinette-bwa-chech whose emblem animal is a screech owl.'

Phoebe shook her head in awe. 'How have you

123

been able to learn so much about something so secret?'

'You will be amazed to hear that I have been permitted to attend certain of the rites and dances.'

Phoebe gaped at him. 'Truly? But – but – what about the terrible punishment threatened for any slaves taking part in such ceremonies? How were you able to win their trust?'

But as Romulus Downey opened his mouth to tell her, the sound of footsteps on the companionway was lost beneath a hoarse cry of alarm followed by a clatter and several loud thuds.

Chapter Eight

'I fear that sounds as if–' Romulus Downey began.

'Someone has fallen down the companionway,' Phoebe finished, already on her feet. Thrown by the ship's movement she lurched towards the door. As she reached it, Bernard Clewes staggered in supporting his colleague who was limping badly. Blood trickled from beneath the hand Horace Matcham pressed to his temple. His face was pale with shock.

'He s-slipped,' Clewes panted, holding tight to the wrist slung across his shoulders. 'T-turned his f-foot when he went down.' His other arm was around Matcham's waist taking most of his weight. 'The deck's w-wet and s-so are the s-stairs.'

'Sit him down here, Mr Clewes.' Phoebe indicated the bench. 'Mr Downey, would you be so kind as to ask Mossop for a pint of cold water in a basin? I'll just–'

'B-beg p-pardon, M-miss Dymond.' Clewes eased the other man down. 'I m-mean n-no offence, b-but m-might it n-not be w-wiser to c-call for the s-surgeon?'

Reaching for the handle on her cabin door Phoebe stopped as a tide of heat climbed her throat to flood her face. She had acted instinctively, forgetting that the two merchants knew

125

nothing of her background or her skills.

'Of course. I'm sorry. I just–'

'Miss Dymond knows what she's doing,' Downey interrupted. 'She gave me a potion that cured my seasickness.' He turned to Phoebe. 'Can you do anything for Mr Matcham's ankle?'

Phoebe nodded, glancing uncertainly between the men. 'I have a herbal tincture that would reduce the pain and swelling.'

'B-but you d-don't even know – how c-can you be s-sure he hasn't b-broken a b-bone?' Clewes's face creased in anxiety.

'I think it unlikely,' Phoebe said. 'If it were broken Mr Matcham could not have borne to put weight on it. It's almost certain the injury is a severe sprain. But naturally you will wish to hear the surgeon's opinion.'

'You'd better be prepared for a long wait,' Downey warned. 'The surgeon's first responsibility is to the crew. Two men are laid up with a fever and there was quite a crowd waiting by the mainmast when the bosun blew his whistle for sick call. It could be a while before Dr Crossley is free.'

He addressed the man slumped over the table, his head buried in his hands. 'What do you say, Mr Matcham? Will you wait? Or will you place your injured ankle in Miss Dymond's very capable hands?'

Matcham looked up. Though his face was pale with shock his grimace of pain twisted into an expression that was almost a leer. 'Miss Dymond will satisfy me very well.'

Phoebe turned away. The man had all the

appeal of a toad. In fact if it came to a choice the toad would win.

'I'll find Mossop,' Downey said.

'Mr Clewes.' Phoebe glanced up. 'While I fetch the tincture would you be good enough to remove Mr Matcham's shoe and stocking?'

When she returned with her case and opened it Clewes's eyes widened as he gazed at the contents. 'G-good God! How d-did you c-come by all this? I've n-never s-seen – n-not outside an ap-pothecary's s-shop anyway. It m-must have c-cost a f-fortune.'

Smiling, Phoebe shook her head. 'Not at all. I do sometimes have to buy new bottles and jars. But most people are very good about returning empty ones when they have used up what's in them.' After applying a salve to the cleaned cut on Horace Matcham's temple she wiped her hands on a piece of muslin. 'As for the remedies, I prepared them myself.'

'*Y-you?*' Clewes's eyebrows shot up. 'B-but you're only–' He broke off, pink and flustered. 'T-that is to s-say–'

'It is unusual to find someone of my age and sex with such knowledge?' she suggested with only a hint of dryness.

'W-well, yes. I t-trust you will f-forgive my reaction, M-miss Dymond. It's j-just – I'm aston-ished.'

'It's true I am young.' Phoebe carefully poured out a teaspoonful of arnica tincture then tipped it into the cold water. 'But age is not the only mea-sure of experience.'

'Oh, well said, my dear.' Romulus Downey

clapped his palms together.

'So how long have you been doing this?' Matcham demanded.

'I have been watching and learning since I was a small child. But if you are referring to the actual making of medicines and ointments, my proper training began about ten years ago.' Phoebe squeezed excess liquid from the saturated compress and bent to lay it gently on the bruised swollen flesh that was already beginning to turn blue.

'Good G-god!' Clewes repeated, his amazement once again getting the better of him.

'What's in that?' Matcham pointed to the small pot of salve.

'Comfrey, elder and marigold flowers in a base of sweet oil and beeswax. It's an excellent wound cleanser and quickly stops any bleeding.' Phoebe finished bandaging the compress in place and looked up. 'How does that feel?' It was not simply the intensity of his gaze that disconcerted her, but the faint smile twisting one corner of his mouth.

'You have the touch of an angel, Miss Dymond. It is to be hoped Mr Rupert Quintrell truly appreciates the value of the jewel he has been so fortunate to win. Though I think it unlikely.'

As Clewes glared at his colleague, Phoebe simply inclined her head. Straightening up she turned from the bench to put the unused bandages back in her case. This allowed her to keep her gaze averted as she spoke.

'I will leave the bottle of arnica tincture with you for now, Mr Matcham. Though I would appreciate its return when you no longer have need of it. The compress should be soaked and reapplied every four hours until the swelling has gone down.'

'I don't think I can manage by myself.'

Phoebe could feel his gaze on her like grubby fingers. She continued replacing items in the case. 'I'm sure Mossop would be willing to assist you.' The look she darted at the steward combined apology with pleading.

His hands full of cutlery, Mossop glanced swiftly between Phoebe and the man whose bandaged foot rested on the bench.

'No trouble at all, miss. All part of the service.' He turned. 'You want to be a bit more wary on those stairs in future, Mr Matcham.'

'Yes, thank you, Steward. Much obliged I'm sure,' Matcham snapped. 'If you have finished dispensing unwanted and unnecessary advice, perhaps you'd be so good as to inform us when we might expect our dinner?'

'Just about to, sir.' Mossop's tone was as bland as his expression. 'Came in for just that purpose, I did. I'll be bringing it very shortly. If this wind gets much stronger I'll have to douse the fire.'

'I suppose that will mean cold fare tonight?' Romulus Downey ventured.

''Fraid so, sir.'

'Ah well.' Downey turned to Phoebe and beamed. 'In that case, Miss Dymond, I have even more reason to be grateful to you for that magic potion.'

Phoebe had returned her case to her cabin and was about to take her place beside Downey when the door to the fo'c'sle opened. As the surgeon entered she knew immediately something was wrong. Even allowing for dimness of the mess and shadows cast by the skylight his face seemed drawn. And there were dark rings under his eyes she was sure hadn't been there yesterday. It was a professional observation she told herself, looking away quickly. But the sudden small clutch at her heart betrayed a concern she had no right to feel. Aware of heat in her cheeks she edged along the seat.

'Well, Doctor.' Matcham's eyes glittered as he turned from the surgeon sliding onto the bench beside him to look across at her. 'Were you aware we have an angel of mercy among us?' His smile reminded Phoebe of a shark. 'We are extremely fortunate. And it appears you have a rival.'

Phoebe's blush owed as much to confusion as to embarrassment at being the focus of attention. There was nothing in Matcham's words to which she could take exception. Yet his manner made her acutely uncomfortable.

'Come now, Miss Dymond,' Matcham continued. 'There is no call for blushes, or false modesty. You do indeed have a magic touch. It certainly relieved *my* suffering.'

There it was again, that note of suggestiveness. But she had dealt with worse when out on professional calls. So she kept her face expressionless as she raised her head.

'You are kind to say so, sir. But I fear you exaggerate. An arnica compress on a sprained ankle is a simple but effective remedy. It owes nothing to magic.'

'Mr Downey would not agree with you. I distinctly remember him using that very word while singing your praises. Is that not so, Mr Downey?'

'Indeed it is,' Downey agreed, glancing at Phoebe with a smile. 'In fact, I would happily call her a worker of miracles.' He turned to the surgeon. 'And what of your morning, Doctor? How is the cook's hand? I hope he was able to prepare the crew's dinner. Mossop says that if the weather worsens the fires will be doused. So we must make the most of our hot meal for who knows when we may enjoy another?'

Jowan Crossley's expression hardened into a frown and a muscle began to jump in his jaw.

Interpreting this as anger at her encroachment onto his territory Phoebe dropped her gaze. With the benefit of hindsight she wondered if it might have been wiser not to offer assistance. But doing so had been instinctive.

On the opposite side of the table the two merchants murmured together, their heads close. Stifled voices and repressed gestures suggested an argument.

Phoebe glanced across at the surgeon who had served himself a small – very small – portion of the meat and vegetables. Something about his fixed stare as he chewed with slow deliberation stirred a memory. But before she could grasp it Downey addressed her softly.

'Is it my imagination? Or is everyone a trifle tense? I suppose it's the threat of bad weather. Were it not for you, my dear, I would be dreading it.' His forehead furrowed suddenly. 'You do still have plenty of that peppermint potion, I hope?'

Phoebe smiled. 'I do, Mr Downey.'

He blew a sigh. 'That's a relief. The thought of – well, best not to dwell on that.' He shot her a shame-faced grin.

The meal finished, Phoebe excused herself and stood up intending to fetch a book. The four men also rose: Downey and the merchants announced their intention of retiring to their cabins for a nap. She assumed the surgeon would return to the sick bay.

'Miss Dymond?' Jowan Crossley's manner was as unyielding as seasoned oak.

Reaching her cabin door Phoebe glanced back. 'Yes?'

'A moment of your time if you'd be so kind.' He had come round the table and with his back to the mess indicated the passage. 'In the saloon?' Politely phrased, it was nonetheless an order.

Silently she led the way. Acutely aware of his proximity she kept her face averted as he reached past her to open the door. As she entered she blinked at the brightness flooding in through the stern windows. After the gloom of the mess the daylight was a pleasure. It was also a relief to enjoy it without having to brave the spray-filled wind roaring across a deck whose lee rail seemed terrifyingly close to the heaving mounds of pewter-grey, foam-streaked water.

Looking away from the stern windows and what lay beyond them she saw the saloon was empty. Presumably both master and mate were topside because of the deteriorating weather. Had he known that? Intuition told her the surgeon had brought her here for a scolding. Would he have continued had they not been alone? Bracing herself Phoebe turned to face him just as he spoke.

'May I ask why you didn't call me to attend Mr Matcham?'

'I would have done so, had you not still been busy with the crew. But the matter was not serious and well within my capability.'

'With respect, Miss Dymond, I am the best judge of the seriousness or otherwise of any injuries sustained on board this vessel.'

'Indeed you are. But Mr Matcham seems in no way unhappy with–'

'Oh come now, Miss Dymond,' he interrupted sharply. 'With you fussing over him is it likely he would complain?'

Phoebe stared at him, stunned by the strength of his anger.

Compressing his lips and tightening his jaw as if to physically prevent any more words escaping, he glowered back then abruptly turned away. 'As to your capability–'

'You know nothing,' Phoebe stated, her chin high. They glared at each other. Realizing that her response – an amalgam of anger, hurt, and other deeper more complex emotions – was open to misinterpretation she took refuge behind a facade of cool reason. 'Perhaps, Dr Crossley' – she clasped her hands together – 'the best thing would be for you to examine Mr Matcham yourself. Then should you find my treatment lacking in any way you will enlighten me and I shall be suitably grateful.'

His narrowed glittering gaze and the rigidity of his expression distracted her from his pallor and the grape-coloured shadows beneath his eyes. 'Miss Dymond, what made you think yourself competent to offer treatment in the first place?'

'Mr Clewes asked me the same question, though his manner was less aggressive and he apologized lest I should be offended by his enquiry.' She saw him open his mouth to reply but raising her voice gave him no opportunity. 'I can only repeat what I told him and the other gentlemen. I am a trained herbalist.' Her experience and skills in midwifery were not relevant, nor were they likely to interest him.

His eyes widened and astonishment slackened the tense muscles in his face. He looked suddenly much younger. 'When you say trained, does that mean you served a proper apprenticeship?'

'It does, and I did. My teacher was the best in the county.' Pride in Aunt Sarah enabled her to bear the still-sharp stab of loss without flinching.

'Why didn't you tell me?'

'I would, had you given me the chance.'

'Given you– What are you talking about?'

'I offered my help earlier,' she reminded. 'I would have told you then had you allowed me time to finish what I was saying.'

Once more he took a breath as if to speak. But conditioned by experience of Falmouth's medical practitioners she knew an apology was unlikely. Nor was she willing to listen to excuses justifying his behaviour.

'Dr Crossley, you are the ship's surgeon. My skills, such as they are, pose no threat to your position or professional standing. The accident occurred when I was available to offer assistance and you were not. That is the sum of it. However, though I stand by the efficacy of my treatments, you would oblige me greatly by examining Mr Matcham's ankle so you may reassure yourself, and me, that I have done no harm.'

Jowan fought a maelstrom of emotions as he gazed at her. His first thought was that she looked magnificent. Despite her courteous tone there was no doubting the indignation betrayed by her rigid posture, the blaze in her eyes, a defiantly tilted chin, and cheeks flushed deep rose.

That she dared even suggest he might feel threatened had triggered a welling fury. But it had ebbed as swiftly as it had risen as he recognized the truth of her claim. He did feel threatened. But not for the reason she assumed. Her treatment of Matcham's injury was just an excuse. So she had bound up a twisted ankle. Any sensible woman could have done as much. Though few would have had arnica tincture available for a healing compress. What really unsettled him was his attraction to her. Perhaps if they had met under different circumstances... But they hadn't. He was a gentleman and must behave like one.

Yet the more he learned about her the harder that became. He bitterly resented the position into which he had been forced. Blaming her wasn't fair. He knew that. But she was the focus, the cause of a turmoil he had not expected and didn't know how to combat.

When he heard he had been appointed Miss Phoebe Dymond's escort and guardian he had wished her in hell. But now having met her, beginning to know her, he knew himself there.

She intrigued and attracted him as no other woman ever had. Being officially responsible for her safety offered him legitimate and unlimited opportunity to spend time in her company. But the inescapable fact of her being betrothed to another man meant this was a poisoned chalice. She was under his protection. How ironic that the person from whom she most needed protection was him.

'Doctor Crossley?' Phoebe's voice broke into his raging thoughts.

'Thank you, Miss Dymond.' The strain of his inner battle lent harshness to his voice. 'I do not think I need your permission to examine an injured passenger.' Listening to her and Downey talk with such ease at the table had been both revelation and torment. There was so much more to her than he had imagined, or her demure dress and reserved manner suggested. He had wanted to join in the conversation. But he was jealous of the rapport she and Downey shared. Besides, he had felt physically wretched. He still did. Forcing down even that small amount of food had drenched him with the cold sweat of nausea. Afraid of betraying weakness he had stayed silent.

'I will, of course, check Mr Matcham's ankle tomorrow,' he said. Seeing the colour deepen in her cheeks he cursed himself for a pompous idiot. Perspiration trickled down his sides and stuck his shirt to his back.

'I'm sure he'll appreciate the attention.' Her face was carefully expressionless. She had withdrawn like a snail into the protection of its shell. 'If there's nothing else you wish to say to me, Doctor?'

There was so much. Biting his tongue to stop a flood of dangerous words reaching his lips he jerked his head in abrupt denial.

'Then you will excuse me.' She nodded coolly and walked out, her head high, her back radiating – what? He didn't know her well enough and she was too skilled at masking her emotions for him to guess. But whatever negative feelings she harboured towards him – he deserved them all.

As the door closed behind her he turned away cursing violently under his breath. As it reopened he swung round, hope surging. It wasn't her. Why would it be? *What a fool.*

The master strode in, pausing as he saw the saloon's occupant. His bushy brows lifted. 'You looking for me, Doctor?'

'No, Mr Burley, thank you. I was just–' Jowan stopped. How could he explain his actions to the master?

'Miss Dymond all right, is she?'

Either Burley had seen her as he descended the stairs or he had passed her in the passage.

'Yes, she's–' Jowan's voice rasped and he cleared his throat. 'She's fine. Apparently Mr Matcham took a fall and sprained his ankle. She went to his aid.'

'She did?' Burley's bushy brows climbed higher.

'She informs me she is experienced in the use of herbs to treat illness and injury. I will, of course, take a look at Matcham myself, just to reassure myself, and him.'

'Now I think of it Tierney did say something about her being useful should we run into any trouble. But to tell you the truth I wasn't taking

137

much notice at the time. I had too much else to think about.'

'How would he have known?' Jowan strove to make his tone off-hand, as if he had little interest in the answer.

'Through her uncle,' Burley replied. 'George Oakes is a senior captain. He's on the Lisbon run now. His wife was a healer and midwife. Well known and well liked by all accounts. Sad business.' Burley shook his head.

'Sad?' Jowan prompted.

'Killed, she was. Must be, oh, a couple of years ago now.' Burley pulled a face. 'A horse pulling a timber wagon took fright in the main street and bolted. The wagon tipped over and Mrs Oakes was crushed under the load.' Jowan swallowed as Burley continued, 'Died before they could get her out.' He sighed and shook his head. 'I dunno, it always seem to be the best that's taken before their time.' He straightened. 'You needn't worry. If Miss Dymond was taught by her aunt then she knows what she's doing.'

Jowan nodded without comment. A little more of the tantalizing puzzle that was Phoebe Dymond had been revealed. Though it appeared her claim to some experience of diagnosis and treatment was proved, how could she compare her study of herbs to his intensive training in medicine and surgery? She couldn't. But nor had she. It was he who was contrasting the quality and worth of their knowledge. *Why?* Why should this girl's ability challenge his vastly superior erudition and expertise? It didn't, couldn't. So why did he feel the need to guard his professional territory so jealously? What was wrong with him? He was tired to his soul. His brother's death, his parents' grief and the weight of their desires and expectations had left him exhausted. At least his work aboard had posed no problems so far. Which was just as well considering his dreadful queasiness.

Burley moved behind his desk. 'Can't be easy for her. Being the only female aboard,' he added, as Jowan gazed at him blankly.

'Oh, no, indeed.'

'Look, you're more likely to see her than I am. Next time you do, tell her she's welcome to come in here if she'd like a bit of privacy. I'm topside most of the time.'

'I'm sure she'll appreciate the offer.'

'Right.' Sitting down in his chair, Burley waved the surgeon to the banquette. 'So, what we got? How many genuine sick and how many trying it on?'

Jowan sat. Thankful for an opportunity to steer his thoughts away from Phoebe Dymond he told the master his findings.

Chapter Nine

Phoebe sat alone in the mess, her journal open in front of her, one hand supporting her head while the other toyed with her pen. She had begun the journal to help pass the time by recording details of life on board a packet ship. But while she included information about the daily routine and all she had learned from her talks with Mr Downey, now she wrote to try and make sense of the chaos inside her.

It should have been easy. In theory all she had to do was focus on her destination: the end of a journey taking her from her old life to the new. But hard though she tried she could not maintain the necessary concentration. The thoughts and feelings invading her dreams as well as her waking hours were outside her previous experience. Willpower should have banished them. To discover hers wasn't strong enough suffused her with shame.

Instead of drawing comfort and security from the prospect of marriage and all its attendant benefits, she was growing more nervous as each day passed.

She had heard Jamaica described as a land of beautiful scenery. Its mild climate and fertile earth made it a major producer of wealth. The Quintrell plantation was one of many responsible for providing English homes with commodities once considered luxuries, now taken for granted and enjoyed without thought as to their origin.

She had never given much thought to how sugar was produced. She had read about slavery in editorials that quoted demands from one or two politicians for the trade in slaves to be abolished, and the roar of counter-arguments ridiculing such foolishness and warning of financial catastrophe – even economic collapse – should such demands be heeded. The facts, thundered the broadsheets, were self-evident. Slaves were merchandise just like the sugar, coffee, rum and cacao their labour produced. They were property to be bought and sold: the business governed by a system of laws designed to protect all concerned.

She had never been entirely comfortable with the concept of one man *owning* another. But her unease seemed totally out of step with general belief that the way things were was the way they should be: that white races – especially the English – were superior to all others, and that blacks were savages with strong backs but no souls.

Among her friends and acquaintances and even among her clients she occasionally heard a murmur of doubt that echoed her own. But this was drowned by louder voices declaring 'they aren't like us', and 'there's nothing we can do, so best leave it to those who understand these things'.

As a woman and one who had not even attained her majority her opinion was of no interest. With no voice and no power she had, for peace of mind, diverted her attention from matters outside her control to those within it. But since listening

141

to Romulus Downey all her doubts and all the unease so long repressed had resurfaced. Now, though deeply ashamed of her willingness to turn her back on such terrible injustice, she still did not see what she could do to change anything.

Regardless of what the merchants said it would be truly a miracle if the slave revolt on Saint Domingue did not spread to Jamaica. And if all that were not enough she had other far more personal reasons for feeling apprehensive.

She was making a lifetime commitment to a man of whom she knew nothing other than an image on a miniature and a proud father's praise. Surely these were sufficient reasons for the upheaval she was experiencing?

Of course they were. But the real source of her disquiet ran deeper and was far more unsettling. What she felt was wrong. Nor did it make sense. She wasn't even sure she liked Jowan Crossley. Certainly she found his superior manner – so typical of physicians – infuriating. That it should affect her at all only increased the anger which courtesy required her to keep hidden. To let it show might lead him to think his opinions mattered. She would not allow him the satisfaction.

If she could accept that the deriding of herbal remedies by Falmouth doctors was due to ignorance, and that the only response to such a shortsighted attitude was to ignore it, why could she not treat him the same way? For the simple reason that he wasn't the same.

How did she know that? Because most of the Falmouth doctors – had she confessed to them her fear of the sea – would have mocked her foolishness. They would have – metaphorically if not physically – patted her on the head while declaring there was nothing to be afraid of. They had not lived her experiences, but being men they naturally knew best.

He hadn't done that. Instead he had made her face her terror and helped her overcome it. It was thanks to him that she could climb the companionway by herself and stand alone at the rail to marvel at the ocean's colour and movement changing with the strength and direction of the wind.

When she boarded the ship her fear had reduced her to the status of a patient. As a doctor dealing with her *condition* he had shown great kindness. He had also been sufficiently confident of his ability to resolve the situation to overcome her refusals.

Gently but implacably he had forced her to face what she was most afraid of. What if she had collapsed, or thrown a fit of hysterics? He must have known either was possible. That he had been prepared to take the risk and deal with the consequences suggested considerable strength of character in a man not yet of middle years whose decision to join the Packet Service surely indicated greater familiarity with treating men.

Her disappointment with him was her own fault. She had been so sure he was different. But his reaction to her treatment of Mr Matcham's ankle had shown he wasn't. Discovering that he shared the bunkered opinions and attitudes of his colleagues should have made it easy for her to rid her mind of him and think of other things. *So why couldn't she?*

The door from the passage opened. She glanced up and immediately looked down again pretending to be intent on her journal as a wave of heat climbed her throat and burned her face. From the corner of her eye she saw him close the door behind him and stand with his back against it.

'Forgive me for interrupting you.'

Courtesy demanded she acknowledge him. Glad of the skylight's limitations she raised her head, hoping the dimness and shadows would disguise her heightened colour. 'It's of no consequence.' *His interruption, or her forgiveness?* Let him make of it what he would. Setting down her pen she closed the journal, conscious of the ship's increasingly pronounced rise and dip.

'Mr Burley asked me to tell you that he is aware of the difficulties attendant upon a lady travelling alone, particularly the lack of privacy. As he spends much of his time topside the saloon is often empty. He says you are most welcome to use it whenever you wish for solitude.'

Touched by the master's thoughtfulness Phoebe felt an easing of the tension in her neck and shoulders as relief rippled through her. 'How very kind of him.' That offer meant she would no longer have to retire early to her cabin in the evening. Or remain on deck in order to avoid Horace Matcham's scrutiny and remarks tainted with a suggestiveness or spite she found offensive yet to which she was reluctant to draw attention. 'Thank you, Dr Crossley.'

Leaning back against the door, he swallowed. 'I – er–'

144

She waited. Returning tension quickened her breathing and her heartbeat. Was he going to apologize? If he did, how should she respond? Telling him it didn't matter would be the polite thing to do. Then he would feel better, the incident would be behind them, and she would have lied. The fact was his criticism of her actions had mattered. It still did.

'Nothing. It's nothing. Excuse me.' With a curt nod, he headed towards the fo'c'sle.

Phoebe gazed after him, fighting an urge to hammer on the table with her fists out of sheer frustration: partly with him, but mostly with herself for her stupid hope that he might have made an effort and in doing so redeemed himself. She was a fool. Why should he care for her opinion?

The weather worsened during the afternoon. The merchants remained in their cabins. Mr Downey emerged briefly, wan and woeful.

'Miss Dymond, would you be so kind? Another of your peppermint infusions?' He sighed. 'I confess I am not feeling at all the thing.'

Phoebe closed the book in which she had sought escape from the clamour of her thoughts. 'I'm so sorry to hear it, Mr Downey. But don't worry, you will soon be more comfortable. Sit down while I fetch the herb and some hot water.'

'I'll just–' He indicated the door to the passage and the WC.

'Of course. It will be ready when you return.'

'All I got is what I boiled up in the kettle, miss,' the steward warned as he handed her a cup and spoon. 'There won't be no more for a bit. Not

145

now the fire's out.' He tipped the kettle.

'This will be more than enough.' Taking both the cup and steaming jug Phoebe smiled her thanks. 'Poor Mr Downey. The ship's motion is very unpleasant for him.'

Mossop shot her a knowing look. 'He isn't the only one.'

Phoebe's brows rose. 'Really? I thought Mr Clewes and Mr Matcham–'

'Not they,' Mossop interrupted. 'Used to it, they are.'

'Then?'

'Maybe I should keep my trap shut. 'Tidn really my place to say. But he've been looking sick as a shag for days.' As Phoebe gazed at him blankly he hissed, 'The surgeon, miss. I'm surprised you haven't noticed. But I daresay you've had enough to think about. Still, it don't make no sense to me. You'd think with him being a doctor and all he'd have stuff he could take. But if he have, why do he still look so bad? Comes to something when the doctor do look worse than his patients.' He shrugged then grinned. 'P'rhaps you should offer'n some of that there pepper-mint. Works a treat for Mr Downey, poor bug – poor soul,' he corrected hastily.

Phoebe smiled mechanically while her thoughts raced. She had noticed Jowan Crossley's pallor and the bruising shadows under his eyes, but she had assumed he was simply tired; assumed his absences at mealtimes were due to sick-bay demands or that he was eating at his desk. Now as she recalled how he had picked at his food it was obvious he'd had no appetite. Her lingering anger softened briefly to sympathy.

But as she berated herself for not recognizing what had been staring her in the face, her mind flew back over the sudden change in him to blank-eyed detachment shattered by flashes of irascibility. One might be tempted to think – *surely not*. She caught her breath as she understood how Jowan Crossley, miserably nauseous, had kept himself on his feet and carrying out his duties.

She wanted to be mistaken but knew she wasn't. She recognized the signs now. Though depressingly familiar she saw them mostly in older people: usually women.

That *he* would resort to – even now she found it hard to believe. As a physician he must have known the risk he was taking. Laudanum was highly addictive. Yet perhaps, responsible for the health and welfare of everyone on board, he had used it – not for escape – but simply to keep going.

'Thank you, Mossop.' Pouring hot water on to the dried herb she stirred in a spoonful of honey, her actions practised and without conscious thought. The idea of facing Jowan Crossley with what she now knew sent a wave of heat through her. Her skin prickled with perspiration that dampened the fine lawn of her chemise. It clung uncomfortably.

As Downey shuffled in, white to the lips, clutching at the doors and bulkheads for support, she forced an encouraging smile. 'Ah, Mr Downey. Would you be more comfortable back in your cabin? Then as soon as you have drunk the infusion you could try to sleep again.'

'My dear,' he murmured unhappily, 'you have read my mind. I am poor company.'

Holding the cup carefully she followed him as he lurched past the table. The battle inside her raged on. She shouldn't interfere. She had no right. She was taking too much upon herself. Yet how could she simply ignore it? Knowledge conferred responsibility. If she were wrong she would apologize. *If she were wrong his reaction did not bear thinking about.* But no matter how much she might wish it otherwise, she knew she wasn't.

Taking the empty cup from Mr Downey as he sighed and reached for his wig to remove it before lying down, she tactfully withdrew. Closing the door quietly she returned to the pantry.

'Mossop, would you be kind enough to take a message to the doctor? He's probably busy, so please make it clear that there's no urgency. But I would appreciate a few moments of his time sometime during the afternoon.'

'Mr Downey not too good?'

'I think he's going to try and sleep some more.' Phoebe evaded the question with a brief smile. While the steward was away she collected several small bottles from her case and stowed them in a drawstring purse of fawn kid. Carrying it into the mess with her she opened her book once more.

The clatter of pans from the steward's cubbyhole added their din to the wind noise and the dull thuds vibrating through the hull as *Providence* crashed through short steep seas. When she realized she had read the same sentence three times without taking in a single word Phoebe gave up and closed her book.

Wishing she had not sent the message, wondering what she should say, which phrases would be least offensive, she heard the fo'c'sle door open. His face was the colour of cold ashes. A frown creased his forehead and twin grooves bracketed his mouth.

'You asked to see me, Miss Dymond? Are you unwell?' His manner made it plain no other reason would justify such a summons.

Phoebe rose to her feet bracing herself as the ship swooped down into a trough then slowly climbed the face of the next wave. 'No, Dr Crossley. I am perfectly well, thank you. I apologize for calling you away from your patients,' she added quickly. 'But I need to speak to you.'

'Could it not wait?' Jowan snapped, gripping the edge of the table as he was thrown forward. 'This is not a convenient time–'

'Indeed, and I'm very sorry.' Phoebe could see the faint sheen of moisture on his face. 'But as you are here... Please.' She moved to the door leading to the passage and the companionway. 'May we go to the saloon?' As he approached, she explained quietly, 'The gentlemen are all in their cabins. But they may not be asleep. And I would prefer that we are not overheard.'

He gestured for her to precede him. 'You are being very mysterious, Miss Dymond. I must assume you have good reason.' He pulled the door closed behind him shutting off the only source of light. The sudden darkness and his proximity in the narrow passage made Phoebe's heart skip a beat. She took a quick breath but before she could speak the saloon door opened and she swung round as Burley appeared.

'Ah, Miss Dymond, Doctor. Good timing that is. I shall be topside for an hour or two so you'll have the saloon to yourselves. Having so much in common you won't be short of things to talk about.'

So much in common? Bewildered, Phoebe glanced from the master to Jowan who cleared his throat.

'I believe Mr Burley is referring to Mr Matcham's accident.'

Burley continued to address Phoebe. 'I know your uncle. He's a fine seaman. I wouldn't be so bold as to claim friendship, but we've enjoyed a chat and a glass or two. And your aunt: now, she was a remarkable woman. There's many in Falmouth would be long gone but for her.'

Phoebe nodded. 'She was very special.'

'Well, looks to me like you're making your own mark.' With a smile Burley turned to the companionway and hauled himself up the stairs.

Phoebe hurried forward into the saloon, desperate to put physical distance between herself and the surgeon.

'Am I to close this door as well?' he enquired acidly.

'If you please.'

He shut it. 'Considering the noise of wind and sea, not to mention the creaks and groans of the boat, an eavesdropper would be hard-pressed to catch anything less than a shout. Now, Miss Dymond, what is this secret you are so anxious to protect?'

Phoebe staggered across to the banquette. The

150

violent pitching made it safer and more comfortable to sit rather than stand. Folding her hands in her lap she gripped her left thumb tightly and out of sight in her right fist.

'It is not my secret, Dr Crossley, but yours.' The packet plummeted then rose. There was a brief, telling silence.

'I beg your pardon?' Soft, edged with warning, his voice stroked her taut nerves like a honed blade. But she heard the undertone of shock and that gave her the courage to continue.

Because of the weather noise and to be sure he heard her – for she knew she would not have the courage to repeat the claim – she kept her burning face tilted up so he could read her lips. But she could not look at him. Instead she fixed her gaze on the chimney pipe rising from the squat black stove to one side of where he stood.

'It is my belief that you are seasick and have been treating yourself with camphorated tincture of opium.' She moistened her lips and plunged on. 'I truly admire your determination to remain at your post. And no doubt that is what led you to take such a risk. But I can offer you a remedy that will swiftly banish the headache and queasiness so you need no longer rely on a drug best reserved for life-threatening situations.'

The blood drummed in her ears. She could feel her heart beating fast and hard against her ribs. As the silence dragged so her apprehension grew. She shouldn't have spoken. She'd had no choice. But that she, with no medical qualifications, should make such an accusation against a physician and surgeon was shocking in the extreme.

151

He would never forgive her. *She'd had no choice.*

Unable any longer to bear the silence she parted dry lips with her tongue and looked directly at him. 'I think you are angry and deeply offended. I beg you to believe that I wished only to help.'

He turned his head away, his features a taut unreadable mask.

Swallowing, Phoebe rose shakily to her feet flexing her hand to ease the ache from the pressure of her grip on her thumb. 'Please...' *forgive*. No, she would not ask the impossible. 'Please excuse me,' she whispered and started towards the door.

As she drew level his right hand lifted a few inches from his side. She stopped, poised to walk on if she had misread his intent. Side by side, a foot apart and facing opposite directions, they swayed with the pitching of the ship.

He cleared his throat but his voice remained low, the words emerging reluctantly. 'I never expected – I was not prepared – I have never in my life felt so appallingly ill.'

Phoebe kept her gaze fixed on the scrubbed planks of the cabin sole. 'I daresay it is small comfort but apparently Captain Nelson is also a sufferer. If such a brave man can be so afflicted then it cannot be taken as a sign of weakness.'

His brief gesture was dismissive. 'That's as may be. But pride demanded I save face by denying the truth: that the ship's surgeon possesses the stomach of a baby.' His bitter self-mockery tugged at her heart. 'The laudanum was a risk: I was fully aware of it. But without–' He shook his head. 'Believe me, Miss Dymond, when you feel as I did – still do – risk counts for nothing against the promise – the faintest hope – of respite.' He cleared his throat again. 'I was unforgivably rude to you earlier. But you are having your revenge.' His bark of laughter was harsh.

Phoebe looked up. 'Do you really think me so mean-spirited?'

Thrown against the table he braced himself with one hand and raised the other to rub his face. 'No. Of course I don't. It is myself I am angry with, not you. It's just – as physicians we are trained in theories whose practical application by way of various drugs or procedures is supposed to rebalance the body and free it of disease. And though I have never truly believed we have all the answers, that I should find myself so helpless... The shock was profound and deeply unpleasant. Then to learn that you – and I intend no disrespect – possess knowledge that succeeds where mine has failed deals one's pride a severe blow.'

Phoebe risked another sidelong glance. Though his face was greenish-white and haggard the set of his shoulders was less rigid. 'A rare experience,' she murmured, 'but one I have no doubt you'll survive.'

He winced briefly then nodded, flicking her a weary grin. 'Of course I will. And as a scientist I would be foolish indeed to reject an opportunity to widen my knowledge, or–'

'Or refuse to try a remedy that might work?'

'Except – is there an alternative to peppermint? I loathe the stuff.' He shuddered, his throat working. 'I don't think I could–'

'Yes, there is. If you will wait here I'll fetch

153

some hot water.'

Returning a few moments later she found him sitting on the banquette, elbows on his knees, his head in his hands. In the moment before he looked up she saw how his honey-gold hair curled thickly over his collar and how the brown superfine of his coat lay taut across unexpectedly broad shoulders. Tearing her gaze away she moved quickly to the table. Loosening the drawstring she removed the bottles from the kid purse and measured half a spoonful from each into the inch of hot water.

Handing him the cup she sat down at a discreet distance.

'What is it? Not that it matters,' he added, 'as long as it works. I'm just interested.'

'Black horehound, meadowsweet and camomile steeped in brandy.'

While he took a mouthful of the draught, Phoebe remarked once more on the master's kindness in offering her use of the saloon.

'For there is so much more light in here. Reading and writing will be far easier.'

Draining the cup he held it between his hands.

'Were you in practice in Falmouth, Dr Crossley?' she enquired.

He shook his head. 'No, in Plymouth. At the naval hospital.'

'I imagine it must be a very large establishment.'

'It is.'

'Have you ever had the opportunity to visit Flushing?' she enquired. 'It is such a pretty village, and enjoys a particularly mild climate. No

154

doubt that is why most of the packet captains and crews choose to live there.'

'I'm sure you're right.' His forehead puckered in a faint frown. 'Miss Dymond, you are clearly adept, but why have you chosen this *particular* moment to demonstrate your gift for polite conversation?'

Recalling her own half-bemused half-irritated reaction when he had insisted on telling her that the packet was rigged as a brigantine and the injustice of four of the crew being called *idlers*, she suppressed a smile. 'How are you feeling now, Dr Crossley?' She watched his expression change from uncertainty to wonder then amazed relief.

'Good God!' He looked up, tired eyes narrowing as he smiled. 'I can't believe – for the first time in days...'

Phoebe rose and busied herself returning the bottles to her purse. Her mission accomplished she had no reason – *no right* – to remain any longer. 'I mustn't take any more of your time. I know how busy–'

'*You* mustn't take.' Jowan Crossley lurched to his feet. 'Miss Dymond, I owe you more than thanks. I owe you not one but several apologies.'

'Then consider them made and accepted.' She continued edging towards the door. She had resented his short temper and taciturnity. But Jowan Crossley's smile posed a far greater danger to her peace of mind. 'Even if you were aboard as a passenger – which you aren't – being pleasant and cheerful to other people is impossible when one is feeling ill.'

'You are more forgiving than I deserve.'

'Not at all,' she said politely and reached for the handle.

'Miss Dymond?'

It was the strain in his voice that made her look over her shoulder. 'Dr Crossley?'

'I – I am reluctant to trespass further on your good nature, however' – a fleeting grimace twisted his feature – 'I have had little sleep for several days. No doubt you have a remedy that will help without risk of harm.' There was bitterness in his tone but she sensed his anger was aimed, not at her, but at the limitations of the medicines at his disposal.

'I do,' she said calmly. 'I will prepare it when everyone has retired.'

'I'm very much obliged.'

Phoebe turned again to the door.

'Just one more – I think it would be best if the – everyone remained ignorant of – of my indisposition.'

For an instant she could not believe what she had heard. Incensed, she whirled round. 'I am astonished you should think such a request necessary. No less than you do I respect a patient's confidence. Nor is it my habit to gossip. Did you know me better you would certainly know that. It is to protect your privacy that I said I would prepare your sleeping draught *after* everyone had retired. However, if you imagine the crew unaware, I'm afraid you are mistaken. Though, of course, it may not be generally known. But it was Mossop who alerted me. He has been aware – yes, and concerned – these past four days.'

156

Breathing fast, her face on fire, she turned to leave. But in a couple of strides he was beside her, his palm against the door holding it closed.

'Once more I must crave your pardon, Miss Dymond.' Twin patches of colour burned high on his cheekbones in vivid contrast to the haggard pallor of the rest of his face. 'I beg you will stay and take advantage of Mr Burley's offer. You will be undisturbed here. I shall return to the sick bay.' He made a jerky formal bow. 'Your servant, ma'am.'

Chapter Ten

After he'd gone, Phoebe leaned her forehead against the wood, listening to his footsteps and the slam of the mess door. *Undisturbed.* How little he knew. And would never know. In fact she must put an end to this foolishness at once. Instead she could take pride in knowing that because she had found the courage to challenge Jowan Crossley, *he* would never again be able to deny the effectiveness of herbal remedies.

Daylight faded to dusk. Phoebe heard the bosun's shrill whistle, running feet and rattling blocks as sails were shortened. The wind howled and shrieked like a soul in torment. The mess lamps were lit. Mossop brought in bread, cold meat and slices of cheese. Downey's cabin door remained firmly shut.

As the evening wore on, the merchants played cards and drank brandy at the mess table. Horace Matcham tried to engage Phoebe in conversation. But sensing that to respond at all would make it more difficult to extricate herself should his manners dip with the level of the spirit in his glass, she excused herself and retreated into her cabin. Wedging herself against the bulkhead she opened her journal.

Instead of writing, she found herself reliving those minutes in the saloon with Jowan Crossley. Swiftly, deliberately, she turned her thoughts instead to Matcham's behaviour. Though his ankle was almost healed he had not yet made any effort to go up on deck. He clearly harboured a grudge against the Quintrells. But whether this sprang from a business matter or something more personal he had not said and she could not ask. To do so would invite gossip about men not here to defend themselves: men to whom she owed a duty of loyalty.

After trips down the passage and much slamming of doors the merchants eventually retired to bed. Within twenty minutes she could hear both of them snoring.

Creeping out into the mess Phoebe set her case carefully on the table. Hearing a groan she knocked softly on the door next to hers.

'Mr Downey? Would you like some more peppermint?'

'Would you be so kind, my dear?'

'I will bring it very shortly.'

Returning from the pantry where Mossop was slinging his hammock, she swiftly prepared the dose.

'Mr Downey?'

'Come in, my dear. Forgive me for not getting up, but–'

'You had much better stay where you are.'

He heaved himself up on one elbow, wincing as light from the mess lamp spilled over his bleary, unshaven features. Without his wig he looked strangely defenceless. What little hair he possessed was thin and white. Odd strands stuck out untidily from his skull.

Phoebe pretended not to notice. 'As the fire is

out there's no hot water,' she explained. 'So I've mixed you a tincture instead of an infusion. But I promise you will find it just as effective.'

Whispering his thanks he drained the cup, gave it back, and with a soft moan subsided once more on to his pillow.

Bidding him a good night she backed out and closed the door just as Jowan came in from the fo'c'sle and glanced quickly round the mess.

'Is this a convenient time?'

Phoebe nodded, aware of her racing pulse. Horribly afraid her face was glowing like a beacon she turned to the table and swiftly mixed valerian and skullcap. 'I should warn you it is not pleasant. I would recommend–'

'As long as it works' – he reached for the cup – 'I don't care what it tastes like.'

As he took it his fingers brushed hers. The shock tingled up her arm and sent a flash of heat through her. But his attention was on the cup and its promise of sleep. Relieved at his preoccupation, Phoebe caught her lower lip between her teeth. She watched as he swallowed a mouthful, knowing what was to come.

Immediately his face contorted and he gave a violent shudder. 'God Almighty!' He glared at the cup, then at her.

Without a word, compressing her lips on a shaky breathless laugh that was as much a release of unbearable tension as genuine amusement, she held up a jar of honey. He thrust the cup forward for her to add a spoonful. But as the water was cool it took a few moments to mix. Burning under his gaze she jumped when he spoke.

160

'Such forbearance.'

Glancing up she saw that despite the ravages of exhaustion a wry smile lifted one corner of his mouth. She glimpsed the boy he had once been.

'I would not have been able to resist saying "I warned you".'

With a shrug and a quick smile she hoped concealed her thrill of pleasure she removed the spoon. 'Ah, but you have not had my training – in forbearance.' While he drank she turned away to replace the bottles and honey jar in her case. Removing one of the small brown bottles she offered it to him without looking up.

'It's the same mixture I gave you earlier. I've made up a blend of the three herbs. If you keep it with you no one need be aware. I would recommend one to two teaspoonfuls mixed with a little water taken three times a day. In a few days you might find you no longer need it, in which case–'

'In which case I will return it.' She felt him take the bottle and saw it tucked into the pocket of his waistcoat. 'You are very generous, Miss Dymond. And very kind.'

'As you were to me when I first came aboard,' Phoebe said quietly, checking that everything in her case was secure before she closed the lid and snapped the catches. She wanted so much to look up and knew she mustn't. He sounded so different. But that was because she had done him a kindness. Now they were even. And that was the end of it. 'I'll just take the cups–'

'Allow me. It's the least I can do.'

'Goodnight, then,' she murmured. Quickly lifting her case over the fiddle rails that edged the table, she opened her cabin door, stepped inside, and pulled it closed behind her.

Later, lying in her bunk, she tried to rationalize her attraction to him. It was their profession, just as Mr Burley had said. That was what they had in common. Though their methods, training, and treatments were very different, their aim – to ease suffering – was identical.

Two days later, Phoebe woke early and was immediately aware of the change. The wind had stopped howling and the ship's motion had eased. For the first time in days the deck angle was barely noticeable as the packet surged forward on a long rolling swell.

Craving escape from the confinement of the shared mess and her cramped quarters, she dressed and swiftly pinned up her hair. Wrapping herself in her cloak against the early-morning chill, she closed her door carefully despite the steady snores reverberating from three of the cabins, then slipped along the passage and climbed the brass stairs.

Stepping out on to the deck she inhaled deeply. The air was sweet and clean. She drew in as much as her lungs would hold. The cool freshness on her face was blissful: a stark contrast to the close, stale atmosphere below.

With a nod to the wheelman who knuckled his forehead and murmured a greeting, she crossed to the weather rail. Gripping it with both hands she looked towards the bow. The morning's work was well under way. Several seamen on hands and knees were holystoning the deck. Seawater hauled over the gunwale in canvas buckets sluiced loosened grime into the scuppers and out over the ship's side. Other crewmen worked the bilge pump, polished the brasswork and coiled down ropes before hanging them neatly on wooden pins. Up in the ratlines two men were greasing the areas of the foremast down which the yards were raised and lowered.

Resting her arms on the rail, Phoebe breathed in the nutty fragrance of linseed oil rubbed into the wood to stop the salt water turning it black. Gazing out over the sea towards the east she watched the sky change colour from pearl through primrose to pale pink and gold. A fiery crescent appeared on the horizon. It climbed slowly, growing in size and splendour until the entire shimmering disc had risen out of a gilded ocean.

The sun rose every morning whether or not anyone was there to see it. It was all too easy to be distracted by the upsets and pressures of life and forget to look. But how much was missed. There was such beauty in the world. There was ugliness too. Yet even that was part of the cycle: darkness and light, good and evil, birth and death, joy and grief. Nothing lasted forever. Change was inevitable. But it was so hard to let go of a familiar past and trust in an unknown future.

'You're up early, Miss Dymond. Everything all right?'

Phoebe looked round to see the master emerging from the companionway. 'Fine, thank you, Mr Burley,' she lied.

'Lovely morning, isn't it?'

163

'Truly beautiful.'

'With the north-east trades behind us we should have a good fast run down to Madeira.' Touching the brim of his hat in salute he went to check the compass.

Phoebe looked from the drying deck to the sails, smiling as she recalled Mr Downey identifying each one for her. When she had marvelled that he should know, he had laughed and shrugged.

'I am a scholar, Miss Dymond. You might compare me to a sponge. Only instead of water I soak up knowledge. I am fascinated by facts.'

Phoebe tested her memory. The three triangular sails whose leading lower corners were attached to the bowsprit were the staysail, jib and jib headsail. On the foremast an additional square topsail, a royal, had been added above the course, topsail and topgallant. Each was smaller than the one below it but all were taut and full-bellied as they drove the ship forward. The boom of the huge gaff mainsail was swung out, scooping the breeze and directing it on to the square sails in front of it. Behind the packet, sparkling white foam left an arrow-straight trail marking the vessel's speed and passage.

The subtle hues of sunrise had melted into a sky of light clear blue. Mossop opened the mess skylight releasing the smells of coffee and frying bacon. Phoebe's stomach growled. If a few weeks ago she had been told she would be aboard a ship, not paralysed by fear but looking forward to her breakfast, she would not have believed it. But so it was.

By the time she had hung up her cloak, tidied her hair and returned to the mess, Downey had emerged and was closing his cabin door. Thinner and pale but freshly shaved, wearing his bushy grey wig and a clean shirt and neckcloth beneath his black coat and breeches, he beamed at her.

'Good morning, Miss Dymond.'

'Good morning, Mr Downey. You look in much better heart. I trust you are recovered?'

'I'm relieved and delighted to say I am. After some food and fresh air I will be quite myself again.' He shuddered. 'Though I have to confess it was a most distressing experience. After fearing I might die so awful did I feel, I began to wish death would come and relieve me of my suffering. But thanks to you, my dear, I am so much restored that after breakfast I plan to take a turn about the deck.'

'You will enjoy it. The sun is shining and the air is delicious.'

'Capital! Then I shall find a quiet spot and do some work on my new book.'

Phoebe faced tasks of her own that could no longer be put off. Carrying a bundle of washing, a cake of soap and bag of pegs in the large enamelled bowl Mossop had loaned her she followed him up the companionway to an area in the stern behind the wheelman.

'If you want more water take it from that one.' Mossop pointed to the cask lashed to the side of the companionway hatch. He poured the bucketful he had boiled for her into the bowl. 'There'll be plenty more rain to fill'n up again.' He looked around. 'Good bit of breeze. Dry nice and quick, it will.'

The thought of her underwear and nightdresses blowing like flags for all to see was not a comfortable one. But even had her trunk been big enough to accommodate them, she didn't possess sufficient clothes to make a three month voyage without the need to launder essentials. And after the gales and rain, today's warmth and sunshine offered ideal conditions.

Mossop leaned towards her. 'If you peg it inside the hammock nettings' – he jerked his head – 'no one will even know 'tis there.'

They would, of course. But it might be less obvious. And with Horace Matcham still reluctant to risk his tender ankle by climbing the stairs she would be spared the discomfiting remarks he was almost certain to make.

As she soaked, rubbed, rinsed and wrung until her forearms ached, Phoebe thought back to Mondays at home when Sally Endean came to do the laundry. Mary always had the fire under the copper lit by six. By nine the scullery was usually full of steam and the first load flapped on the line.

Phoebe realized suddenly how much she had taken for granted. After Aunt Sarah died she had taken over the housekeeping. She had discussed each week's menus with Mrs Lynas, regularly checked kitchen stores and the condition of the household linen, and ensured Uncle George always left sufficient money for her to settle the tradesmen's accounts each month. She had ordered salting, pickling and bottling according to the season. But it had been Mrs Lynas and

166

Mary who carried out those orders* and did the actual work.

Not that she had been idle. With patients to visit and herbs to be planted, tended, picked, dried, and transformed into a wide range of remedies there had always been more jobs to be done than time in which to do them.

Emptying the bowl she refilled it from the cask. Had she been wealthy a personal maid would have accompanied her to take care of her laundry. But had she been wealthy she would not be making this voyage at all. And that meant she would not have–

Recognizing danger she tried to stop the thought before it completed. She wasn't quick enough. *She would not have met Jowan Crossley.* Would that have been better? Easier perhaps. Wiser and less stressful, certainly. But better? She couldn't answer that. Hauling her mind from a quicksand that might swallow her, she directed her attention to the wet linen.

At least by sundown she would be able to remake her bunk with sheets that smelled of fresh air and sunshine. Her trunk would contain clean – if creased – chemises, nightgowns, and camisoles neatly folded around gauze sachets of dried lavender. And if right now her hands were red and the ends of her fingers resembled pale prunes, she had a nourishing hand-cream made of almond oil and beeswax infused with comfrey and essential oils of lavender and geranium with which to treat them once the job was finished.

Rupert Quintrell would not expect his bride-to-be to arrive with work-roughened hands. What, in fact, was he expecting? Back in Falmouth, lying in her bed after another day of preparation and packing, she had tried to imagine what her new life on the estate would entail. Given the circumstances of her marriage she did not anticipate love. Nor did she seek it. Everyone she had loved had been taken from her. She could not bear to relive that pain.

She hoped they would deal comfortably together in liking and respect. If they were fortunate, affection would grow through shared experience as they came to know one another. She wondered how tall he was. What his interests were. How his voice sounded.

Such had been her imaginings as she tried to envisage talking to the man portrayed on the exquisite miniature. But lately as she drifted into sleep, lulled by the sounds of the ship and the sea, it was the surgeon's eyes and smile that filled her restless dreams: his voice that echoed in her ears.

Jowan Crossley dipped his pen in the standish. Sitting at the small writing-desk in his cabin, the ledger open in front of him, he was supposed to be writing notes detailing the condition and treatment of patients he had seen that morning. But though his eyes were on the page his mind was in another part of the ship.

While stitching a gash, re-dressing a persistent ulcer, or bleeding a man with fever while Grigg administered doses of calomel or medicinal rhubarb, he had been able to shut out everything but the job in hand. But now his attention was no longer focused on practical matters he found concentration impossible.

Though he hoped never ever to experience the misery of seasickness again, being fully recovered meant – paradoxically – that life had become not easier but far more difficult. Then he had been absorbed by wretched discomfort. Now he had too much time to think.

His recovery had not even come about through his own efforts. Despite everything he had learned during years of study, training and practice he had been helpless. Relief and restoration had been granted by a simple blend of herbs. A mixture so swift acting he was almost inclined to agree with Downey's claim of miracle potions.

To have been cured by someone outside his profession was embarrassing enough; that he should owe his deliverance to a young woman made it worse. That his saviour should be Phoebe Dymond–

Throwing down the pen he raked his hair with both hands. He was supposed to be responsible for *her*. If, when he had first been told, he had known what he knew now – what would he have done? Refused the obligation? The terms of his employment meant that was not within his power. And as her guardian he could not entirely avoid her even if such a thing were possible on a vessel this size. Besides, God help him, he wanted to see more of her, not less.

Her air of reserve was misleading. She wore it like a cloak, a protective shell. But beneath it she was fire and passion. There was no doubting her kindness and generosity, or her temper. Yet

169

though swiftly roused her anger soon passed. She bore no grudge and possessed a dry wit that delighted as much as it had surprised him.

Based on the little he had been told he had made assumptions about her that seemed perfectly reasonable at the time. At ease in society and always a welcome guest, he knew well how to conduct himself. So why in her company did he so often find himself wrong-footed: feeling clumsy, foolish or ashamed? This was a new experience, unpleasant and bitterly resented.

Shoving back his chair he thrust his arms into his coat and left the cabin to make his weekly inspection of the galley. The cook had better have heeded his warning about cleaning the pease-soup cauldron.

'According to the master,' Downey told Phoebe, as they stood at the larboard stern quarter enjoying the afternoon sunshine, 'we are roughly five hundred miles south-west of Lisbon. The coast of Morocco is about three hundred and fifty miles in that direction.' He gestured with his left arm.

Phoebe shivered, masking it with a quick smile. 'That sounds as though we are a very long way from land.' *From rescue, from safety, from people and houses and–*

'Not at all,' he beamed. 'We will reach Madeira tomorrow. And though we stay only long enough to pick up mail it will be–'

'Oh my goodness.' Phoebe's hand flew to her mouth as a seaman hurtled out of the fo'c'sle and flung himself at another near the foremast.

Accusations erupted into violence. As fists flew, others joined the fray. Phoebe winced as the shrill note of the bosun's call pierced the grunts and roars. He plunged into the scrum, laying about him with the short length of rope that was as much a badge of office as his whistle.

'I think it better we go below,' Downey announced quickly. And cupping Phoebe's elbow he steered her towards the companionway.

They were all sitting down to tea when Jowan came in from the fo'c'sle.

'Was anyone badly hurt?' Phoebe asked.

He shook his head. 'Just cuts and bruises. One man will have a black eye by the morning and another's nose is broken.'

'What was it all about?' Downey enquired.

'Theft.' Jowan was grim. 'It's a tradition in the fo'c'sle that sea chests are never locked. Most of the men are carrying ventures to trade in Jamaica. Apparently some shoe buckles have gone missing. The master is questioning the crew now.'

Matcham clicked his tongue. 'And to think I missed all the excitement.'

'W-what will happen t-to the thief?' Clewes put Phoebe's thought into words. 'Assuming they f-find out who d-did it, of course.'

'Will he be flogged?' Matcham's eyes gleamed.

'No,' Jowan said. 'Though the thief might prefer a flogging to the alternative.'

'Why not?'

'Why?' The two merchants demanded simultaneously.

Phoebe watched the surgeon as he answered.

'Why won't he be flogged? Because flogging is

171

a naval punishment and a tradition the Packet Service does not follow. Why might he prefer it? Because instead he'll be put ashore at the first landfall.'

'Madeira,' Downey reminded Phoebe.

'Well, what's so bad about that?' Matcham snorted. 'Unless he's thrown in jail, of course. Which no doubt he's used to.'

'He'll lose his protection from the press gang,' Jowan said. 'And Madeira is a regular port of call for naval vessels, many desperate to replace men lost to battle wounds or fever.'

The following morning Phoebe stood in her usual place in the stern. With Downey beside her she gazed at the islands that were growing larger. She had watched the master issue orders, heard the bosun's whistle, seen the huge boom swing across the ship from one side to the other, and felt the deck change its angle beneath her feet as the packet altered course to make her approach.

'That's Porto Santo.' Downey pointed. 'There's not a single tree on the island. Over there are the Ilhas Desertas, literally the deserted islands. And ahead' – he gestured towards the island – 'is Madeira.'

Three hazy peaks clothed in swathes of dense forest rose out of the blue sea. Patches of paler green showed where the lower slopes had been cleared of trees.

'Some of the land is used to grow sugar cane,' Downey said. 'But most is devoted to vines. No doubt you are familiar with Madeira wine? I confess I find it a touch heavy and sweet for my

172

palate. But apparently it is very popular in America as well as in England.'

By mid-afternoon *Providence* lay at anchor off Funchal and the deck seethed with activity. A small leather portmanteau containing mail was lowered into the larger of the packet's two boats now bobbing gently on the turquoise water.

Closely guarded by two of his erstwhile shipmates the thief, his hands manacled in front of him, stood near the side ready to follow. Phoebe recognized him as the man she had glimpsed involved in a snarling argument the day she boarded.

The bosun jerked his head and the two seamen pushed their prisoner to the opening where a section of the gunwale had been removed and a ladder hung over the side. Instead of removing the manacles to allow the thief to climb down by himself the crewmen passed a length of rope through his pinioned arms. Yelling and cursing, he was lowered with swift efficiency into the boat.

Wearing his best uniform, the master emerged from the companionway followed by the surgeon.

'Limes, was it?' Burley said over his shoulder, as he strode to the opening.

'If possible,' Jowan said. 'But lemons will suffice.'

'I'll see what I can do.' Burley disappeared down the ladder.

Phoebe felt her colour rise as Jowan turned and his gaze caught hers. After an instant's hesitation he nodded briefly and went back down the stairs.

Phoebe remained on deck enjoying the mild air as the sun sank slowly down the western sky. It cast soft golden light over whitewashed houses dotted across the hillside amid vine terraces and small patches of cultivated land.

It was almost five and halfway through the first dogwatch when she heard sounds on deck that signalled the master's return. Closing her book she left the saloon and returned to the mess.

Matcham looked up. 'Come and join us, Miss Dymond,' he demanded. After a brief turn about the deck the two merchants had returned to the mess and had passed the remainder of the afternoon playing cards.

'Thank you, but no,' Phoebe demurred.

'We are starved of good company,' he pressed.

'I think not,' she replied politely, without breaking her stride, 'for you have each other.'

'We want you, Miss Dymond,' he insisted with a glittering smile.

'I do not play cards, Mr Matcham.'

'Then we will devise some other amusement–'

The door opened and Burley looked in. 'Surgeon here, is he?'

'I b'lieve he's in the sick bay, sir.' The steward's entrance from his pantry allowed Phoebe to escape into her cabin. She sat on her bunk, her heart racing, furious that she had fallen into Matcham's trap. She wished she need not speak to him at all, but that would make her appear ill-mannered.

She remained in her cabin until Downey tapped on her door and called her to tea. She enquired about progress on his book. Then listening to the surgeon's reply when asked the purpose of the lemons – apparently useful in preventing a debilitating disease common among seamen on long voyages – she was able to eat without taking any further part in the conversation.

The sounds of urgent activity filtered down from the deck. The boat had been hoisted inboard and secured on its cradle. Men swarmed up the ratlines and out along the yards to ready the sails while others heaved on the capstan bars to raise the anchor.

Having rid *Providence* of a thief and picked up the mail Burley did not intend to linger.

A few days later the passengers were at breakfast when Andy Gilbert clattered down the companionway and poked his head around the mess door.

''Morning all. Master says not to worry when you hear the guns. 'Tis only a practice, all right?' With that he disappeared again.

Phoebe decided to take advantage of both master and mate being on deck. The empty saloon would allow her privacy to wash her hair.

After unpinning and thoroughly brushing the dark rippling curtain that fell almost to her waist, she put a towel around her shoulders and sat down on the banquette. Uncorking a bottle of lotion made from rose-water, pearl ash and spirits of wine she had just tipped it against a piece of flannel when the first gun boomed. Despite the mate's warning the noise made her gasp and her heart gave a painful thud. Chiding herself for an excess of sensibility she moved across and closed the side window.

Holding the bottle between her knees she gently worked the flannel over her scalp from forehead to neckline. Even down here with doors and windows closed the noise was deafening. Bellowed orders, thumping feet, the rumble of the heavy trucks as the guns were run out, the crump and roar of ragged cannon blasts were followed by more shouted orders. The whole process was repeated several times.

Taking a section of hair at a time she ran the re-wetted cloth from root to tip until it had all had been thoroughly washed. After towelling it thoroughly she combed out the tangles. Then lifting the damp mass back over her shoulders she left it loose to dry.

The smell of burnt gunpowder and hot metal pervaded the saloon and stung the back of her nose. Wrapping the bottle of lotion in the folded towel with her brush and comb Phoebe lay them beside her on the red plush seat and opened her journal.

A tremendous explosion made her start violently. Above the fading echoes she could hear heavy thuds, yells, the throat-tearing scream of a man in mortal agony and someone shouting for the surgeon.

Should she stay here? *Whatever had happened sounded bad.* Should she offer help? *This was outside her experience.* How many were hurt? *She would offer. She must. She had no choice.* But she could not be seen like this.

Swiftly twisting her hair into a coil she anchored it with pins at the nape of her neck.

Then snatching up her belongings she hurried along the passage and through the mess to her cabin. Tossing the bundle on to her bunk she grabbed her case. She had just slammed her cabin door when Jowan burst in from the fo'c'sle.

'What happened?' she began.

'One of the carronades exploded and snapped the restraining ropes. It's like a butcher's shamble up there.'

Chapter Eleven

As Jowan strode toward the steward's pantry Mossop hurried out into the mess wiping his hands on a grubby cloth.

'Bad is it?'

Jowan nodded grimly. 'One man dead, half-a-dozen injured. Mr Downey was knocked out but I doubt it's more than just simple concussion. Those with burns and splinter wounds are being carried down to the sick bay through the fo'c'sle. Grigg should be able to deal with them. He's taken young Timmy with him to fetch and carry. But Jenkins–' He shook his head. 'His foot was crushed.'

'Any chance–'

'I wish there were. But it's beyond saving. Andy Gilbert is pouring rum into him to deaden the pain. I'll need the table.'

Heaving a sigh the steward clicked his tongue. 'Poor bug – soul. Got a wife and a couple of kiddies he have. Youngest is no more'n a babby.' He shook his head. 'Someone bringing sand buckets are they?'

'What for?'

'The floor,' Phoebe supplied, seeing Jowan's momentary confusion. 'So you won't slip on spilled blood.'

Both men turned startled faces towards her. *How did she know?* She answered their unspoken question: 'Uncle George's ship has been chased by privateers on several occasions.' She lifted one shoulder. 'Though the packet escaped capture it was inevitable there would be damage and injuries. He always talked over such events with my aunt.'

'Why, for heaven's sake?' The surgeon was visibly shocked.

'Because my aunt was often asked to treat injured men who could not afford a doctor's fee.' Phoebe replied, carefully expressionless. His hard frowning gaze bored into hers but she met it steadily. 'As Grigg is already busy you'll need someone to assist you.'

Glancing from one to the other Mossop announced, 'I'll go and fetch the buckets,' and hurried out.

Never had Phoebe been so glad of her ability to mask her emotions. The façade of calm confidence was as familiar as her favourite winter cloak and as easy to slip into. Jowan Crossley couldn't see her heart thumping or the tension in her muscles as she tried to prepare herself. This was after all just one more new experience in a whole procession that had begun the moment she set foot on this ship and met the man charged with her safety and well-being.

A wild giggle suddenly bubbled up. She cleared her throat to disguise it. He would not understand. How could he when there was so much about her reactions she didn't understand?

Since meeting Jowan Crossley she had never felt more protected or less secure. She had always considered herself level headed, *sensible*. But the

179

turmoil inside her, as conscience warred with overwhelming attraction, mocked any claims to sense or decency.

Sounds from the deck broke into her troubled thoughts and she forced herself to concentrate on the task ahead. She wasn't exactly afraid. But she couldn't deny being apprehensive about her ability to detach herself from the horror. Yet she must if she was to provide the surgeon – and the injured man – with the help they both needed. She sensed the battle raging inside him.

His frown deepened. 'I appreciate your offer, but Grigg can–'

'Grigg cannot be in two places at once,' she reminded.

He dragged a breath. 'It will be a bloody business.'

'So are scythe wounds and so is childbirth.'

He looked startled. 'What would you know–'

'I told you I was Aunt Sarah's apprentice.'

'You mean *you* have delivered–' He raked his hair. 'You continually amaze me, Miss Dymond.'

'Then you must have lived a very sheltered life.' The curt words were out before she could stop them. For an instant she wished she had held her tongue. But his astonishment each time he learned she was capable of doing something useful fanned flames of resentment whose source she didn't dare examine. Should she apologize? It was too late. In any case more important things demanded their attention.

She turned as the steward came in with two sand buckets. 'Mossop, will you bring boiled water and two – no – three basins?' She turned

180

back to Jowan projecting calm efficiency. 'The point is I am no stranger to bloodshed.' *But an exploding gun? What damage would that inflict on flesh and bone?*

'Very well. If you're sure...'

'Perfectly,' she lied, not waiting for him to finish.

While Jowan went to fetch the instruments he would need, she helped Mossop push the benches out of the way. Then she sprinkled sand over the cabin floor. Grunting with effort the two merchants staggered in carrying Downey's slumped form between them.

'Would you lay him on his bunk?' Phoebe hurried to open the door for them.

'What's going on?' Matcham demanded. 'Why have the benches been moved? Why is there sand–'

'Dr Crossley has to perform an amputation.'

'W-what? In h-here?' Clewes glanced over his shoulder at the mess table as his eyes widened in horror.

'I'm afraid there's nowhere else,' Phoebe said.

Having deposited Downey on his bunk, Matcham straightened his coat. The smile that oozed across his mouth was slick with triumph and satisfaction. 'Miss Dymond, you must allow me to escort you to the saloon.'

'B-but w-what about the m-master–?' Clewes began.

'What about him? Given the damage on deck he'll be up there for hours,' Matcham cut in impatiently. 'He certainly wouldn't want us under his feet. Nor, I imagine, would he expect us to

181

stay in here and watch.'

'N-no, indeed! I c-can't s-stand the s-sight of – never c-could. Hopeless w-with–' As he backed away shaking his head, Clewes darted Phoebe a look that reflected shame at his anxiety to escape. 'I'd b be useless.'

'Miss Dymond?' Matcham repeated, crooking his elbow and offering his arm. 'This is no place for a young lady.'

'Thank you, but I am staying to assist.'

'Y-you're what?' Clewes said, horrified.

Shock blanked Matcham's features. 'You cannot possibly.' Disbelief, resentment and anger chased each other like storm clouds across his face. 'Has the surgeon taken leave of his senses that he would expose you to–'

'Gentlemen, I appreciate your concern but truly it is unnecessary.'

'My dear Miss Dymond,' Matcham began, 'no doubt your intentions are of the best, but you cannot know–'

'Indeed I can,' she interrupted, polite but firm. 'And I do. Now if you will excuse me I must see to Mr Downey.'

'I fear I shall have to inform the master–' Matcham warned, the threat cut off as Clewes pushed him out, slamming the door in his haste to be gone.

Clenching her fists, Phoebe closed her eyes. Of all the odious, interfering, patronizing – taking a deep breath she deliberately flexed her fingers, squared her shoulders and thrust the merchant from her mind.

'The explosion,' Downey mumbled, wincing as

182

Phoebe gently examined the swelling above his temple. 'It made me jump and I tripped over. Damn silly thing to do. I feel such a fool.'

'Indeed you should not. For though I was below deck in the saloon the noise gave me a dreadful fright,' Phoebe confided. 'When you fell did you hurt yourself anywhere else?'

'No. Well, I jarred my shoulder. I'm a bit shaky. Feel a little queasy too.'

'That's probably shock. It can have very unpleasant effects. Will you turn onto your side, Mr Downey?' She covered him with the blanket, opened the cupboard in his nightstand and took out the pewter chamber pot. 'I'll leave this within reach. And I'll bring a draught for your headache as soon as–'

'Don't you worry about me,' Downey waved her away. 'I'm just an old man making too much fuss. Go and do what you can for those poor sailors. But once you've finished, perhaps–'

'I'll be back, I promise.'

Returning to the mess, Phoebe saw that another bucket half-full of sand had been set beneath the table. Mossop had put the water and basins she'd requested on one of the benches standing against the merchants' cabin doors.

'Here, miss.' He took a torn length of grubby lightweight sailcloth from under his arm. 'It'll save your dress from – well, you know.'

She looked up, her throat suddenly and painfully dry as Jowan came in. He had removed his coat and rolled up his shirtsleeves. A wooden tray was balanced on his bare forearm. It held a loosely wrapped gauze bundle on top of which was a folded piece of canvas-like fabric. Once off-white it was now dirty grey and smeared with stains that had dried dark brown and stiff. As he closed the door the tray tipped slightly and she heard the clink of metal against metal. She saw him register the makeshift apron she was tying around her waist. A muscle jumped in his jaw as he leaned forward and spoke with soft urgency.

'Are you absolutely sure?' He stopped, glancing up as approaching voices and footsteps in the passage grew louder.

Phoebe turned as the door was flung open and two seamen staggered in carrying the injured man between them. Her gaze was drawn to the unrecognizable mess of mangled flesh and splintered bone at the end of his leg. A bitter taste flooded her mouth.

Jenkins' whole body trembled. His head lolled sideways on one shoulder as if too heavy for his neck. His face was grey-white, glistening, and contorted with pain and fear as his eyes rolled beneath fluttering lids. The acrid stench of his sweat reached her in waves, battling with the pungent burnt-sugar smell of rum.

Phoebe looked again at the dreadful injury and swallowed hard.

'Miss Dymond?' The surgeon's murmur was harsh and urgent.

'Poor *poor* man,' she whispered. Then resolve tilted her chin. Turning her head to meet his gaze she gestured toward the bundle on the tray. 'Dressings?'

She saw him release a breath as he nodded. 'I had to leave half with Grigg so I hope there may

184

be enough. Be careful when you lift the bundle. Of your fingers, I mean. The instruments are underneath and the knives are exceptionally sharp.'

As she took the tray he whisked the dirty cloth off the top and shook it out to reveal a blood-stiffened apron. She cleared her throat. 'I have linen and gauze here should you need them.'

Looping the apron over his head, he quickly fastened the strings then beckoned the two seamen forward. Helping them place the injured man on the table he looked at each in turn. 'I'll need you to hold him down.'

They nodded: their faces as white as that of their shipmate who moaned and babbled incoherently, turning his head one way then the other on the scarred wooden tabletop.

Jowan flipped back the cloth to uncover three steel knives with handles that appeared to Phoebe to be covered by some kind of braided material – presumably to prevent blood-wet hands from slipping. One had a short straight blade. The other two had longer blades with a curved edge. There were two saws: one large and broad, the other thin and D-shaped, and suture needles. Beside him Phoebe laid out dressings and bandages. Reaching into her case she took out a bottle and set it on the bench.

He paused in his preparations. 'What's that?'

'An antiseptic lotion made from marigold and golden seal.'

'I've never heard of it.'

She looked up. 'Why would you?' Turning her back on the seamen she dropped her voice to

185

avoid being overheard. 'But I can vouch for its usefulness. As well as being antiseptic it also has an astringent action that shrinks the cut edges of flesh and reduces bleeding.'

His brows rose. 'You have personal experience of this?'

She nodded quickly. 'I've used it on scythe wounds. There are always some during hay-making and harvest.'

He shook his head. 'This is different.'

'Only in degree.' She moistened her lips. 'Do you have an alternative? Something of your own you prefer to use?'

The fact that he didn't annoyed him. 'No.'

'Then I don't understand your reluctance. You have seen my other remedies work.'

'You cannot compare this to seasickness.'

'The principle is the same. And I promise you it is effective. None of the mothers I delivered died from childbed fever. Can you claim as much?'

He stiffened. 'I don't deliver babies.'

'But you must know doctors who do. And you must know how many women die. Women who were healthy before—' She fastened her teeth on her lower lip to stop herself saying any more.

But he silently completed the sentence: *before they were attended by doctors who arrived on the delivery ward with bloody hands having come directly from performing dissections in the mortuary.* He caught himself. She could not possibly know anything about that. Nor could he be certain that any connection existed between this practice and the high death rate among women delivered in

186

hospital. He saw her draw a ragged breath before completing the sentence.

'Before they went into labour.'

But he could not deny it. He had heard the talk, read the articles, shaken his head over the mortality figures. And she must have seen that in his face.

'Why are you refusing something that will–'

'Because I can't take on trust something of which I have no knowledge and no experience.'

'You were glad enough to do so when you were suffering,' she shot back in a fierce whisper.

'Yes, I was,' he hissed. 'But I was making that decision for *me*. And had anything gone wrong it would have been *me* who faced the consequences, not someone else.' He watched angry colour bloom in her cheeks at the implication her remedies might harm. But it faded as she recognized and conceded his point. She bent her head and smoothed her palms down the sailcloth.

'I'm sorry. I shouldn't have spoken so. But please, I beg you to reconsider. Jenkins must lose his foot. Will you risk his life as well?'

Denial sprang to Jowan's lips. How dare she assume the man would die? And how was it possible that she, a mere girl, should possess the means to defeat infection: a curse that had puzzled and worried medical men for centuries? But, as he hesitated, his own words returned to haunt him. *As a man of science how could he turn down an opportunity to try something that might work? What right had he to do so?*

'You must realize it's very difficult for … someone in my position to … to–'

187

'Take a gypsy remedy on trust?' she offered with deceptive mildness.

'All right, yes.'

'So how many more people must suffer and die? Not because of what ails them, but because men of science' – her tone mirrored her derision – 'are too arrogant to accept that someone not of their elite, someone not even of their sex, might know what they do not. Such men place a high value on their pride if they think it worth another man's life.'

Her words stung like a whiplash. Anger burned, firing his skin, curling his nails into his palms. Everything in him rebelled against her accusation. How dare she challenge him? She had no training. She claimed success but could not explain the science. Though it did not occur to him to doubt her, there might be any number of reasons entirely unconnected with use of her lotion why infection had not developed. *But was he prepared to risk Jenkins' life to prove his point?*

He had performed scores of amputations at Plymouth. Yet despite his speed and technique winning praise from senior surgeons he had still lost over half his patients to post-operative infection. The mortality rates for some of his colleagues were even higher. He had even begun to question the point of putting a man through the agony of having a limb cut off in order to save his life, only for him to die anyway from putrefaction.

As his rage cooled it lost power. 'And if I use it and he dies?' He was not seeking a scapegoat. It would be his decision and therefore his responsibility. But he needed to know how she would react should the worst happen.

Phoebe's stormy gaze held his without flinching. 'If he dies it will be from shock or loss of blood or some other cause. Not from infection.' Her conviction was absolute.

'All right.' He gave a brief nod. He hoped she understood that had he possessed an alternative he would have used it. Then he wondered why he should care what she thought. The question of why hospitals either did not know about these anti-infection measures or – if they did know, still refused to adopt them – was one to be explored some other time.

While Phoebe poured lotion into one of the bowls Jowan nodded to the two men and they stationed themselves on either side of the table. Slicing off the remnants of Jenkins' trousers, he buckled a canvas tourniquet around the man's thigh, turning the brass screw to tighten the strap and cut off the blood flow. Phoebe moved one of the buckets so it stood beneath Jenkins' foot. Then with a hand whose steadiness inspired in him both relief and admiration, she carefully poured the diluted lotion over the terrible wound.

Selecting a knife and bone saw Jowan nodded to the two men who stepped close and took hold of their shipmate, glancing at each other then at the terrified face of the man on the table.

'Now,' Jowan said quietly.

He heard the soft hiss of Phoebe's in-drawn breath an instant before Jenkins' first shriek of agony. Knowing what to expect he was able to block out screams that pierced his eardrums and made his teeth and the bones of his skull vibrate. They seemed to go on forever. But he knew from experience they rarely lasted longer than the twenty or so seconds it took for most men to pass out from pain and shock.

Working fast, his movements practised and sure, Jowan cut and sawed. The mangled foot dropped into the bucket with a soft thud. Phoebe passed him the suture needle. By the time he had secured the skin flap she had prepared a cool compress.

While he bandaged the compress around the stump of Jenkins' lower leg Phoebe heard Jowan murmur to one of the seamen who picked up the bucket containing the severed foot and, with his face averted, carried it out.

'Mossop,' Jowan called over his shoulder. 'Will you go and make sure Grigg has left a bunk free? Tell him we'll be bringing Jenkins through in just a minute.'

'Dear life,' the steward grunted. 'That there sick bay'll be as packed as a pilchard barrel.'

He returned with Timmy loping along behind him. Jenkins was carried out. Timmy fetched a broom and had just begun to sweep up the blood-soaked sand when the bosun stuck his head round the fo'c'sle door.

'What you doing in here, boy? Dinner's all behind and Slush wants you in the galley.'

'Hang on a minute,' Mossop charged in from his pantry. 'What about all this?' He waved at the wet, grit-strewn planks. 'I can't be–'

'I'll see to it.' Phoebe put down a bowl of

190

blood-soaked dressings on the bench and held out her hand. 'Give me the broom, Timmy, and do as Mr Hosking says.'

Looking from Phoebe to the bosun Timmy shifted uncomfortably, shuffling his bare feet as he passed it over reluctantly. 'Sorry, miss.'

'It's all right. Off you go.' As the boy vanished in the bosun's wake, Phoebe resumed sweeping. 'Mossop, could I have a jug of boiling water? I promised Mr Downey an infusion for his headache.'

'Make something for yourself while you're at it, miss,' he advised. 'Done wonders you have. But – no offence – you're looking fagged. You won't have been expecting nothing like this.'

Phoebe's smile cost her huge effort. He would never know how truly he spoke. 'No,' she agreed. 'But my life lately has been full of surprises. I'll need another bucketful of hot water as well, to scrub the table.'

'I'll do that, miss.'

'Yes? And who will prepare dinner?' she enquired gently.

'Bleddy 'ell,' he muttered. 'Beg pardon, miss. But 'tis never right you doing–'

'I promise I won't make a habit of it,' Phoebe assured him.

She had swept up the sand and was swabbing the table when Jowan returned. The furrow between his brows deepened as his gaze flicked from her face to the cloth she was wringing out. 'Are the other men all right?' she asked, to forestall him.

'Grigg coped well. Why are you doing the boy's job?'

191

'Because he's needed in the galley. And because...' She looked away for a moment. 'Because I – it was–' *a horrible, wrenching experience and I can't bear to think about it, or about the things I said to you.* Inspiration struck. 'I'm just waiting for Mossop to boil the kettle again. I've given Mr Downey an infusion for his headache. I thought – with your permission – I would prepare one for Jenkins. A combination of nettle and raspberry leaves to minimize any bleeding, and camomile with valerian and a little honey to relieve his anxiety and help him sleep.'

'Object? How could I?' Wearily, he rubbed his forehead. 'The truth is–' His mouth quirked in a smile laced with irony. 'Miss Dymond, I find the need to offer you yet another apology most unsettling.'

Bewildered, Phoebe twisted the cloth in her hands. 'Apology? For what?'

'For more reasons than I care to think of, but in particular for doubting your fortitude. Yet this was a situation for which none of your previous experience – no matter how extensive – could have prepared you. And though you demonstrated remarkable pluck, I'm ashamed to have asked it of you. The strange thing is that once I had begun the operation I-I actually forgot you were...' He shook his head.

The silence stretched. Eventually Phoebe could wait no longer. 'You forgot I was – what? There?'

He looked up, startled. 'God, no. Your efficiency – you were certainly more useful an assistant than some of my previous–' He stopped himself. 'No, the truth is I forgot you were a woman.'

'Ah.' Biting the inside of her cheek Phoebe nodded slowly.

'I hope you're not offended.' He sounded concerned. 'I meant it as a compliment.'

She forced her lips into a smile and dipped her head in acknowledgement. But she could not meet his eyes. It did not feel like a tribute. It felt as if he saw her professional skills as something separate and distinct from her personality and her gender: as if her ability made her an honorary man. *Yet wasn't it wiser for both their sakes that he should see her so?*

Of course it was. But that didn't stop it hurting.

In her cabin, Phoebe inhaled the fragrance of the nourishing cream she had smoothed into her hands. Her hair was freshly brushed and she had braided it high on her crown. She was wearing a short jacket of rose-pink velvet over her dotted white muslin in an effort to reflect colour into her pale cheeks. Her looking-glass confirmed a neat and tidy reflection. Considering the events of the morning, the tension lines around her eyes and mouth were unlikely to warrant remark.

Downey did not appear for dinner, remaining in his cabin. With the two merchants sitting opposite in their usual places, Jowan shared the bench with Phoebe. Despite the space between them she was acutely aware of him and kept her head bent and her eyes focused on her plate.

'Are you quite well, Miss Dymond?' Matcham's solicitous enquiry forced Phoebe to look up.

'Yes, thank you.'

His gaze snaked to Jowan and back as he shook

his head. 'I think your family must surely be appalled if they knew what had been asked of you.'

From the corner of her eye, Phoebe saw Jowan stiffen. As he shifted on the seat she spoke quickly. 'You are under a misapprehension, Mr Matcham. Nothing was asked of me. I offered my help. As for my family, given the circumstances they would have been ashamed of me had I not done so.' She watched a dull flush climb Matcham's face and though she knew it was unworthy she could not deny the tiny glow of satisfaction. 'I was glad to be of use. Fortunately the need is past, and–'

'Er, not quite, Miss Dymond.' Jowan Crossley cleared his throat as he pushed his plate aside. 'I must ask a little more of your good nature.' As she turned to him he continued, 'Grigg would be grateful for your advice regarding the compresses. Would you mind?'

Pleasure and self-consciousness flooded her face with warmth. She knew Matcham was watching and must have seen the response over which she had no control.

'Not at all. Shall I–' She set down her cutlery, about to rise.

'No, no.' He gestured for her to remain where she was. 'There is no urgency. Please finish your dinner. After such a morning you need to rebuild your strength.'

'Miss D-Dymond, it is a m-marvel to m-me that you c-can eat at all after w-what you m-must have endured,' Clewes shuddered.

'I fear I lack sensibility.' Phoebe pulled a wry face.

'I c-cannot b-believe—' Clewes began but was cut short.

'If indeed that is so,' Jowan said glancing at her, 'then Jenkins and I must both be grateful for it.' Rising, he nodded across the table. 'Gentlemen. Your servant, Miss Dymond. Perhaps you will come to the sick bay when you are ready?'

As the door closed behind him, Phoebe returned her attention to her plate. The surgeon was right. The experience had drained her. But now he'd gone she had no desire to stay for Horace Matcham had been steadily drinking throughout the meal.

'Miss Dymond? Have I offended you?'

It was as if he had divined her thoughts. Honesty battled with good manners. He was one of the most offensive men she had ever had the misfortune to meet. But to tell him so would fly in the face of every courtesy she had been taught. Yet if she denied his claim she was as good as giving him permission to continue. Her only hope lay in prevarication. But before she could ask him why he should think so he was speaking again.

'Because it seems to me that you go to great lengths to avoid my company. Are you avoiding me, Miss Dymond?'

'M-Matcham, n-no,' Bernard Clewes murmured.

Phoebe's throat tightened and she knew she would eat no more. Assuming an expression of cool politeness that masked seething anger she deliberately put her knife and fork together on her plate.

195

'I am astonished that you should ask such a question.'

'You haven't answered it,' he pointed out.

'I am under no obligation to do so.' Phoebe stood up.

'M-Matcham, p-please,' Clewes's tone sharpened with a mixture of warning and anxiety.

'You're happy enough to spend time with Mr Downey.' Though Matcham's words rang with accusation the undertone of jealousy took her by surprise. The truth in his statement forced her to respond.

'Indeed I am. Mr Downey is a gentleman of wide interests who has been kind enough to share with me some of his knowledge of Jamaica's religious customs. If you'll excuse me.' She moved along the bench seat.

'So what has the surgeon been teaching you? Is that equally interesting?' He slapped the heel of his hand against his forehead in exaggerated realization. 'How foolish of me. Indeed it must be. For you spend an astonishing amount of time together. What would Rupert Quintrell think about that, I wonder?'

Phoebe could feel her face burning. Only a determination to deny him the satisfaction of seeing her upset enabled her to keep her expression under control. 'As a *gentleman*,' she gave the word deliberate emphasis intending Horace Matcham to infer that he had forfeited all claim to such description, 'I imagine that–' But before she could say more the merchant gave a bellow of coarse and bitter laughter.

'Rupert Quintrell a gentleman? Oh my poor

196

innocent, you're fair and far out there.'

'T-that's *enough*,' Bernard Clewes broke in, seizing his colleague's arm and shaking it hard. 'You g-go t-too f-far.' Crimson with embarrassment he turned to Phoebe. 'I am m-most d-dreadfully s-sorry, Miss D-Dymond.'

'You have no reason to apologize, Mr Clewes.' She completely ignored the man mumbling next to him.

As Clewes began a strangled and convoluted explanation of which she heard only, '...history b-between them ... b-bad b-blood...' Phoebe walked out.

Chapter Twelve

Showing Grigg how to prepare the compresses and leaving him sufficient lotion to make fresh ones during the night, she left the sick bay. Alone in the saloon, she tried to write up her journal but the events of the morning were still too painfully vivid. She attempted to read but found it impossible to concentrate.

Though she loathed Matcham she could not deny there was a kernel of truth in his accusations. Despite the fact that most of her conversations with the surgeon sprang from strongly opposing views, when he was busy with his duties and out of her sight and hearing she felt both restless and oddly flat.

This was deeply unsettling. It wasn't as if she lacked alternative company. Romulus Downey was interesting and informative. She enjoyed his companionship and learned something new each time they met. And unlike the surgeon he was easy and comfortable to be with.

Jowan Crossley stirred emotions she had been unaware of. Intellect and conscience told her what she felt was wrong, but her heart refused to listen.

After tea, Phoebe climbed the companionway seeking escape from her confused thoughts and an atmosphere in the mess so tense and claustrophobic she could not bear it a moment longer.

She wanted peace and space and clean fresh air. She knew it was only her imagination playing tricks but the hot metallic stench of blood still lingered in her nostrils.

Burley was by the binnacle and came forward as she emerged.

'Miss Dymond,' he bowed. 'I want to thank you for what you did this morning. There aren't many–'

'Please, Mr Burley,' Phoebe interrupted. 'Think no more of it. I was glad to be of use.' With a nod and a smile she moved past him to the weather rail and a moment later heard him clatter down the brass stairs.

She watched the sun sink towards the ocean turning the streaks and puffs of cloud from gold to salmon pink then deep rose. The sky paled from a clear azure to the soft lilac grey of a pigeon's breast. Above her head, beyond the range of the sun's last rays, the clouds darkened to plum and purple.

The watch changed. Men moved about the ship. Side lamps were lit and sails trimmed. The sea had turned from rich burgundy through slate to black, except for the frills and streaks of white foam curling back from *Providence*'s cut-water as she drove on into the deepening darkness.

Through the skylight Phoebe saw the glow of the mess lamps. Announcing his presence with a polite cough, the mate offered to escort her down.

'That's kind of you, Mr Gilbert. But I prefer to remain up here a little longer. I'm not ready to sleep yet and have no interest in cards.'

'If you're sure, miss.'

'I am, thank you.'

Phoebe rested her forearms on the rail, soothed by the rhythmic *shush* of water against the hull. Then footsteps on the stairs made her stiffen.

'Ah, Miss D-Dymond,' Bernard Clewes said. 'I th-thought I m-might s-smoke b-before retiring. I've n-never been one for s-snuff, you know. However, if you w-would find the s-smell offensive...' He left the sentence unfinished, forcing her to reply.

She didn't want to be drawn into conversation with him. Yet good manners demanded she respond. 'Not at all, Mr Clewes. My uncle used to enjoy the occasional cigarillo.' She heard the scratch of a match then inhaled the fragrance of burning tobacco. He came to the rail, careful to remain an arm's length from her.

'Miss D-Dymond, I d-don't wish to c-cause you further d-distress.' His worsening stutter betrayed obvious discomfort.' B-but I f-feel I m-must apol–'

'Please, Mr Clewes.' Phoebe had no desire to revisit the subject. It would resurrect too much she wasn't capable of dealing with right now. 'I meant what I said at the time. You were not at fault, therefore no apology is necessary.'

'Indeed it is, though p-perhaps n-not from m-me. B-but if you will p-permit me, I'm s-sure I c-can–'

'Mr Clewes.' Phoebe was firm. 'I would really much rather you didn't.' His intention might be worthy. But what if it was not his idea at all? What if Matcham had sent him to offer apologies and explanations intending to question him later about her response? To what purpose? What would he gain from such an exercise? Perhaps she was doing him an injustice. But though her experience of him was limited, the little she knew suggested it was exactly the kind of manipulation he would enjoy. Well, he must look elsewhere for his amusement.

'I beg you will not concern himself with what is, after all, a matter for your colleague's conscience, not yours. I really do not wish to discuss it further. Please excuse me.' Turning to go below she caught her breath on a soft gasp. Jowan Crossley was standing at the companionway hatch. Usually able to distinguish his footsteps among all the others she hadn't even heard his boots on the stairs.

'Forgive me, I have no wish to interrupt.' His voice was icy.

'You're not,' Phoebe said. 'Mr Clewes has just come up to smoke, and I am on my way down.'

'Before you go I would appreciate a quick word.'

Glad the darkness hid the sudden rush of heat to her cheeks Phoebe took a quick breath as anxiety shivered down her spine. 'It's not Jenkins?'

'No, he's as comfortable as can be expected.'

Her profound relief made her aware how much it mattered that her antiseptic lotion should not fail. 'And the other patients?'

'It is on their account that I came looking for you.'

Not on his own account, not because he

wanted her company, or to discuss the morning's events or indeed anything else. He was here on behalf of his patients. He could not have made himself plainer.

'For the healing process to begin they need sleep. But crowded conditions in the sick bay, coupled with the constant noise from the deck and fo'c'sle–' His brief shrug made further explanation unnecessary. 'I am reluctant to give laudanum because of its depressing effect on respiration.'

'You require a sleeping draught?'

'If you would be so kind.'

'Of course. For how many?'

'G-goodnight, Miss D-Dymond, D-Doctor C-Crossley.' Clewes bowed himself past them. No sooner had his head disappeared down the companionway than Phoebe felt her elbow grasped and she was hustled out of the wheel-man's hearing.

'What were you thinking of?' Jowan grated. 'Up here alone in the dark with–'

'Sir, you forget yourself.' Phoebe jerked her arm free, unnerved by the warmth of his hand through her sleeve and the treacherous shocking desire to lean, just for an instant, against his tall frame. 'I neither sought nor welcomed his company. But after what happened in the mess–'

'What are you talking about?' His voice was sharp. '*What* happened?'

She realized she could not tell him about Matcham's snide allusions. Her face burned and she swallowed, trying to lubricate her dry throat. 'The – the operation. It is not an experience one can easily banish. I wanted some fresh air before retiring. When we left Falmouth you were most insistent concerning its importance to my health. But perhaps you have forgotten.'

'I have an excellent memory.' His voice was grim. 'Indeed, I could wish it was less – never mind.' He stood aside, gesturing for her to precede him down the stairs.

But Phoebe wasn't ready to go. There were things that needed to be said and this was too good an opportunity to waste. She turned to the rail.

'Doctor Crossley–'

'I am not deaf, Miss Dymond.'

'I wasn't shouting.'

'No, you were not. But have you noticed how sound seems to travel much further at night?'

It was a warning that whatever she was about to say might be heard by people other than himself. His interruption reminded her once again of the need to be constantly on her guard. As if she didn't already spend every waking minute mindful of what she said and to whom she said it. Frustration flared into anger and her lowered voice vibrated with the strength of it.

'You praise my skills and show respect for my remedies yet still you act as if I were just out of the schoolroom and required your advice on how to behave. I-I find your manner suffocating.'

She had not known silence could be so *loud*.

'My concern for your welfare is offensive to you?'

Phoebe clasped her hands tightly. 'I would not have phrased it in exactly those – but as you have

– yes,' she blurted finally.

'Then I must remind you that your safety and protection are my responsibility.'

His tone ignited a rage in Phoebe that caught her unawares. 'And I can only repeat what I told you when I first came aboard. The arrangement was made without my knowledge or consent. Have I not demonstrated capabilities that are defined not by age but by learning and experience?'

'I agree that in some respects – very important respects – this is indeed the case. But the fact remains that your uncle made the arrangement with the best of intentions. And having accepted the responsibility I must honour it. Only when I hand you into the care–' His voice roughened and he cleared his throat. 'Only when we reach Jamaica will my duty be discharged.'

Phoebe could feel herself trembling. Her throat ached from the strain of keeping her voice low. 'Is that how you see it? A duty?' These were questions she should not be asking. What was she seeking? Confirmation? Denial? And if she received either: what then? What would it achieve? She hated the injustice of a society whose rules permitted a man like Matcham to speak and act as he pleased yet denied her the right to express her contempt: rules that permitted her uncle to give this man, this stranger, the right to dictate her actions and behaviour. 'A burden unsought and unwanted?'

She could not see his features in the darkness but his voice was harsh.

'You have left me in no doubt that you see it so, Miss Dymond.'

'And how do you see it?' Shaken by turbulent emotions she sensed were not what they seemed she clung to defiance. 'The truth, Doctor. Surely I deserve that at least.' She heard him swallow.

'I see it exactly as you do, Miss Dymond, a burden unsought and unwanted. You want honesty? You shall have it. I was not consulted: I was informed. Though not until I was already on board. It was as much of a shock to me as it was to you. And you should know that it is not a situation I would have chosen.'

He looked away, his profile a hard-edged silhouette. 'But we must live with what is, even if it is not how we might wish it to be.'

After a moment her anger drained away. His flat statement made too much sense to permit argument. Yet something in his tone jarred. Shivering from cold and reaction she tried to work out what it was.

'The sleeping draught, if you would be so kind?'

Guilt suffused her in a scalding flush. 'Of course.' His quiet reminder was the least of many reasons that made her grateful for the darkness. 'I'll fetch my case.'

Romulus Downey beamed. 'Well done indeed, Miss Dymond. Mr Matcham's ankle is fully mended. Mr Jenkins is still with us and without any sign of infection. The men who suffered burns, or were wounded by shrapnel and splinters, are back on light duties. The two with fever are recovered and the cook's hand is healing. I am sure the surgeon must give thanks a dozen times

205

a day for your presence on board.'

Leaning on the rail beside him, Phoebe smiled but said nothing. It was her impression during recent weeks that Jowan Crossley wished her a million miles away. Yet the morning after their encounter on the night-shrouded deck he had declared his interest in the methods of preparing herbal remedies as well as in their applications. Wary at first, her suspicion had quickly dissolved in the face of questions that indicated a genuine interest also shared by Romulus Downey.

'Can we not change the subject?' Matcham had complained last evening. 'Which month this leaf should be picked, how long that root takes to dry, it's all so boring.'

Biting her tongue, Phoebe had dropped her gaze to the table. She knew what he was doing. If she reminded him how the arnica tincture had helped his ankle he would draw her into a conversation the direction of which he would dictate.

He wanted to cause trouble and he had made her his target. She had no idea why this should be so. And instinct warned her not to ask. For that would play right into his hands, offering him an opportunity to repeat his insinuations linking her with the surgeon.

Yet the facts could not be simpler. She was travelling to Jamaica to be married. Because she was not yet of age, in accordance with custom and tradition the ship's surgeon had been appointed her guardian for the duration of the voyage. That was the extent of her relationship with Jowan Crossley. So why didn't she say so? *Because facts were not the same as truth. She would be lying. And Matcham would know she was lying. The truth, whatever that might be, was far more complicated.*

'So what would you have us talk about?' Jowan had enquired with deceptive mildness.

Phoebe had glanced at him then across the table at the merchants. Clewes continued eating with no sign of his habitual anxiety. Matcham's mouth pursed in a satisfied smirk. Had neither of them recognized the implied warning? Anticipation flared in Matcham's eyes. Instantly Phoebe had tensed, mentally bracing herself.

'Surely Miss Dymond must be longing to know something of Jamaican society? We can enlighten her, can't we, Clewes?' Without waiting for his colleague's response he had switched his gaze to Phoebe.

'Kingston is a most lively place. For gentlemen's enjoyment there is racing and gambling. Meanwhile the ladies occupy themselves planning elaborate balls. Because there are three times as many men as women, even the least attractive female finds herself in great demand. You, Miss Dymond, will be danced off your feet. And when wine has been flowing and spirits are high, as they invariably are on such occasions, the evening turns into something of a scrimmage which is tremendous fun.' His eyes glittered.

Clewes shifted uneasily. 'M-Matcham, p-please.' He laid a hand on his colleague's arm. It was shaken off.

'Then there are the visits.' Matcham's tone had been boisterously enthusiastic, but his narrowed gaze was as cold and sharp as splintered ice. 'Not morning calls. Oh no, in Jamaica things are not so brief or so formal. It's the distance, you see. Estates are often many miles apart. And even those considered close neighbours may find themselves cut off by a river in flood, or find the road is washed out after a heavy storm. So the usual short call of an hour or less isn't feasible. Instead families come to stay, sometimes for weeks, bringing their slaves and their pets: the entire household in fact. So of course they must be amused. Mr Rupert Quintrell is exceptionally generous in this respect. The entertainment provided for his male guests has made him famous throughout the island.' His sly mocking smile made Phoebe's skin crawl. 'Nor does work on the plantation stop, despite so many of the ripe young slaves being taken out of the gangs–'

'Enough, f-for G-God's s-sake.' Creased like a withered apple from anxiety, Clewes's face was deeply flushed. 'Miss D-Dymond, take n-no notice I b-beg you.'

'Take no notice? My dear Clewes, I'm doing her a favour. She must surely want to know what will be expected of her.'

'Miss Dymond.' Touching her elbow Jowan had risen from the bench. His face might have been chiselled from stone. 'Perhaps you will allow me to escort you to the saloon?'

'Thank you.' Her own face felt hot and her head throbbed. She wanted to get as far away from the merchant as possible. What did he mean *entertainment*? What had the slaves to do with it? Glancing down at Romulus Downey to bid him goodnight she saw he was gazing at the merchant with a thoughtful frown.

'I b-beg you w-will excuse m-my c-colleague,' Clewes pleaded, his face shiny with perspiration. 'He's n-not hims-self.'

Matcham drained his glass. 'A lamb to the slaughter,' he muttered, seizing the bottle. His hand shook and the wine spilled onto the table forming a small crimson pool that instantly reminded Phoebe of blood.

'Miss Dymond?' Downey's voice shattered the spell.

As memories of the previous evening receded she looked up, grateful to be freed from their grip.

'I'm so sorry, Mr Downey. I didn't quite catch that.'

'I was saying that I hope Dr Crossley has told you what a valuable contribution you are making to the welfare of everyone on board.'

Not everyone. Certainly not Mr Matcham. Why had he taken against her? It was almost as if he wanted to punish her. But that made no sense. They were strangers. Then it must be something to do with the Quintrells. He appeared to know a great deal about Rupert. Yet he denied any personal acquaintance. Was that where the problem lay? Had something happened to make him feel slighted? In a small community, especially where business was concerned, a snub — real or imagined — could assume an importance out of all proportion to the event.

'Miss Dymond?' Downey's voice held a note of concern. 'Are you unwell?'

'No, no, I'm fine. I was just thinking about all that's happened since we left Falmouth.' Phoebe

209

rested her arms on the rail. 'It is so strange to realize that only because of Dr Crossley's cruelty am I able to stand here and look out at the sea.'

Downey's brows climbed as his face mirrored shock. 'Cruelty?'

Phoebe nodded. 'That was how it felt at the time. Though of course I see it very differently now.'

'I beg you, Miss Dymond, explain.'

'When I first came aboard I was absolutely terrified of the sea. But Dr Crossley encouraged me to face my fear and by doing so to overcome it. He was very kind and very patient.' *So why is he now so cold and withdrawn?* Suddenly aware of the risks she was courting by talking of him, the danger of betraying thoughts and feelings to which she had no right and of which she should be – and was – deeply ashamed, she straightened up and forced a smile. 'I understand you have visited several plantations, Mr Downey. Were your experiences anything like those described by Mr Matcham?'

'My interest was in the slaves, Miss Dymond, not social activities at the big house.' He began to tell her how the Revolution in France had created profound unrest on Jamaica's neighbouring island. By the time she realized he had not answered her question it no longer seemed so important.

'When the uprising on Saint Domingue began four years ago,' he said, 'everyone believed it would soon be crushed. But the slaves were better organized than was realized. They had formed themselves into armed groups bound by a blood oath and their sworn aim was to kill every white man and free every slave. You can imagine how terrified the plantation owners must have been, especially at night when the drums began.'

Shivering at the thought of the fear and bloodshed, Phoebe wrapped her arms across her body. 'It must have been terrible for them. And yet I'm amazed the slaves had not rebelled before.'

'Oh, they had. There have been several revolts in the past hundred years. One was led by an African slave called Macandal whose ambition was to drive out all the whites and turn Saint Domingue into an independent black kingdom.'

'What happened to him?'

'Like so many men who acquire great power he began to believe he was immortal. He was sufficiently bold, or foolhardy, to attend a *calenda* – a night-dance – on one of the plantations. Of course he was recognized and arrested. His sentence – intended as a warning to others – was to be burned alive. As he was tied to a stake on top of a pile of wood he was still shouting that his captors would not hold him, that he would escape.'

Phoebe shook her head, awed by such mad courage.

'Do you know, for one brief moment it looked as if he had.'

'How?' Phoebe was both appalled and fascinated.

'As the flames leapt up around the stake his desperate throes wrenched it free and he plunged off the pyre. There was uproar as word spread

211

through the huge crowd that he had disappeared. Of course he hadn't. He was tied to another plank and – well, suffice to say that the sentence was carried out.'

Phoebe swallowed hard as she nodded.

'Others tried to imitate him. One leader used *vaudou* ceremonies to inspire his followers, promising that the soldiers' bullets would not harm them.' The new harshness in Downey's voice was reflected in his expression. 'The only weapons these desperate slaves had were knives, hoes and sticks. Believing they were protected, the bravest thrust their fists into the cannon barrels to stop them firing and urged their comrades forward, promising to stand fast.' He shook his head. 'They were blown to bits.'

'Where–' Phoebe cleared her throat. 'When was this?' *Please, please let it have been in the distant past.*

'Two years ago. I was on Saint Domingue when it happened.'

Her skin tightened and her mouth grew dry. Would the unrest in Jamaica explode into something similar?

Chapter Thirteen

Jowan dropped suture needle and scissors into the bowl and passed them to Grigg.

'That's some 'andsome job, Doctor,' the seaman perched on the stool gazed at the neat row of stitches on his brawny forearm.

Jowan bit back a smile. 'Thank you, Sykes.'

'He's the last of 'em, Doctor,' Grigg announced. 'Want me to bandage him up?'

Flexing his shoulders, Jowan nodded. He needed fresh air. As the sick bay opened directly off the fo'c'sle he had swiftly grown used to the thick fug of stale stew, damp wool and unwashed bodies. But several days of wet weather meant he'd had to take sick call below deck. This morning alone he'd drained an abscess and stitched two bad cuts by lantern-light. Though this was not the cause of the tension encircling his skull like an iron band, he needed to get out of the cramped and foetid space. Perhaps looking out at the vast expanse of ocean would help him find fresh perspective on a situation that was causing him too many sleepless nights.

'Here, you got any of that there stuff Miss Dymond put on Jenkins' stump?' Sykes asked. 'Healed him up a treat, it did. And he never had none of that green muck coming out. Not like poor Janner. Poor bugger stank like a midden. Afore your time that was, doctor.'

As Grigg glanced at his superior, his brows rising, Jowan shrugged and nodded. Though sailors were reputedly the most superstitious bunch of men regarding anything to do with women and the sea, *Providence*'s crew had taken Phoebe Dymond and her remedies to their hearts. He didn't blame them. How could he resent something that made his job so much easier? Yet sometimes – when he recalled the long years of work and study – it was hard not to.

She could not match his knowledge of anatomy or the required balance of humours, tones and acidity. Yet her success in preventing putrefaction of wounds put his efforts to shame. A man would have boasted, demanding acknowledgement and praise before sharing. She had willingly given him whatever he needed. He had never met anyone like her. Nor would he, for she was unique. *And it was his duty to deliver her to a man she had not met, did not know, and who might not value her as she deserved.*

'I'm going topside, Grigg.' Opening the door into the mess he almost collided with Romulus Downey who was hovering on the threshold apparently waiting for him.

'Might I have a word, Doctor?'

Resisting the temptation to put him off, Jowan forced a brief smile. 'Certainly. Are you not well?'

'I'm fine, thank you. I wish to speak with you concerning...' Glancing round the empty mess he pointed at the closed door of Matcham's cabin from behind which issued loud rhythmic snores, and lowered his voice to a whisper. 'Do you think we might find somewhere more private? It's

214

important we are not overheard.'

'If the master is not in the saloon we could–'

'He is on deck. I saw him myself a few minutes ago.'

Jowan gestured. 'After you then, Mr Downey.'

Once inside the saloon, Jowan closed the door and indicated the padded stern seat. Both men sat. Downey hunched forward, rubbing his hands together.

Jowan recognized deep unease in the gesture. 'What's the matter, Mr Downey?'

'This is very difficult. Unfortunately I see no alternative.' He paused, chewing his lip.

Resisting the urge to hurry him Jowan held onto his patience and his temper, and waited, experience telling him that silence would prove more encouraging than questions.

Downey drew a deep breath. 'As you are Miss Dymond's guardian it is only right that you be informed of anything that affects her well-being.' He paused again and it took all Jowan's strength to maintain an outward calm that masked the fact that every nerve was taut, every fibre of his body willing the man to get a move on.

'Mr Clewes is upset and deeply uncomfortable about the way his colleague is behaving towards Miss Dymond. Unfortunately his remonstrations have been ignored.' Downey moistened his lips. 'I intend no criticism when I describe Mr Clewes as a man – shall we say – less robust in personality than Mr Matcham. And having tried and failed in his efforts at dissuasion he was in a quandary. To come and tell you the reasons behind his colleague's behaviour would have meant betraying a confidence.'

'Yet he's told you?' Jowan enquired, having great difficulty holding on to his temper. *He* was Phoebe's guardian; Clewes should have come directly to *him*.

Downey shook his head. 'Not willingly. That's the point. I came upon him alone last evening. No, I must be honest. I followed him up on deck with the express intention of questioning him. Had you been aware just how unpleasant things have become I'm sure you would have acted. But when it happens you are usually elsewhere busy with your duties. I think – no, I'm sure – the timing is deliberate. And of course Matcham is often drunk. Though I–'

'When what happens?' Jowan interrupted brusquely.

'Well, not to put too fine a point on it, Matcham's manner towards Miss Dymond has always been ... difficult. But just lately it has bordered on persecution.' Jowan opened his mouth, but Downey forestalled him. 'Clewes has tried, but seems unable to stop him. Yet someone must.'

Jowan's surprise and his gratitude for Downey's intervention were thrust aside by urgency. 'So you questioned Clewes. What did you learn?'

Downey's deep sigh told Jowan the information had been hard won. 'Mr Clewes's speech impediment does not respond well to stress. Also, every reply was hedged about with explanations. But as I understand it the facts of the matter are these. As the only child of an overbearing widow, Horace Matcham was raised with an exaggerated idea of his own importance. He is able to turn on charm

216

when it suits him, but turns arrogant and spiteful if thwarted. However, his self-esteem was severely dented when, one after another, the families into which his mother hoped to marry him declined any match. Apparently she was absolutely furious. Eventually, using contacts of her late husband, she found him his current position which requires him to make regular voyages to Jamaica.'

Jowan's impatience gave way to admiration for Downey's detailed but succinct presentation.

'There he received many invitations to social gatherings. But none of the young women he met was acceptable to his mother. Then for the first time in his life he fell in love. Annette Kendall was the daughter of a wealthy merchant, a widower. She had recently returned to Kingston from England where her education and social debut had been supervised by her aunt.' He cleared his throat darting Jowan an apologetic glance. 'I assure you this is all relevant, Doctor.'

Jowan nodded. 'Please go on.'

'According to Clewes, Matcham tried desperately hard to impress Miss Kendall's father. The young lady appeared to encourage him. They danced together as often as decorum permitted, and she frequently allowed him to escort her to supper at balls and parties. Naturally, Matcham took these as signs of her particular interest in him and spoke in confidence to Clewes about his hopes of a future with Miss Kendall.' Downey paused, running his tongue across his lips, and Jowan realized the recital was nearing its climax.

'Another regular guest at these events – despite his reputation – was Rupert Quintrell.'

'Reputation?' Jowan queried.

Downey cleared his throat again. 'At best a flirt, at worst a rake and a libertine. But apparently Miss Kendall found him very agreeable.'

'I'm astonished her father did not warn him off.'

'You have to understand that Jamaican society is much less rigid than English. The owners of the biggest estates rarely set foot in Jamaica. They leave their plantations in the hands of attorneys, agents and overseers, most of them single men. The smaller estates are owned or run by men who were either born on the island or came to it as bachelors and started out as merchants. Because they greatly outnumber white women, their domestic lives are less – formal – than would be acceptable in England. Also, despite Miss Kendall's apparent advantages of education and a London season, she was in fact far more naïve than Jamaican-born girls her age.' Downey paused again.

Guessing what was coming, hoping he was wrong, Jowan remained silent.

'Can you imagine how Matcham felt when Miss Kendall told him she was in love with Rupert Quintrell and wanted his help with an elopement?'

A pang of sympathy caught Jowan by surprise. But it dissolved instantly as he recalled the merchant's smirking attempts to unsettle and embarrass Phoebe. 'What did Matcham do?'

'Told Miss Kendall's father. Despite everything he was still willing to marry the girl. Though whether it could ever have been a happy union...' He shook his head. 'In any case, she would have

218

nothing to do with him. To Miss Kendall's shock and her father's chagrin Rupert Quintrell publicly disclaimed all responsibility, acknowledging he had dallied and flirted as he had with a dozen other young women, but denying hc had ever intended, let alone promised, marriage.'

'And Miss Kendall?' Jowan ground out. 'What became of her?'

'She tried to take her life. She had believed all Quintrell's pretty speeches; believed he loved her. So the shock and pain of such a brutal rejection coupled with guilt at the shame she had brought on her father, and the knowledge that everyone thought her a fool were all too much to bear. She was found in time. But it was a near thing. As soon as she was fit to travel she returned to her aunt in England. Matcham had already left.'

'What about Quintrell?' Disgust roughened Jowan's voice. 'Was he still everyone's welcome guest?'

Downey shook his head. 'A few took his side, blaming Miss Kendall's father and her chaperon for not being sufficiently vigilant, and citing her attempted suicide as evidence that she was emotionally unstable. But many agreed that this time he had gone too far. As invitations dwindled he responded by throwing riotous parties that lasted for days with dancing and other entertainment involving certain of the slaves.'

'Indeed?' Jowan's distaste coloured his tone. 'And while he was occupied hosting this *entertainment*, who was running his estate?'

'He was. No matter how wild the revelry – and rumour has it he often went without sleep for days – he was out in the plantation every morning organizing the gangs for the day's work and checking to see it was carried out.'

'His slaves never took advantage?'

Downey stared at his hands. 'A few of the men tried. He had their hands tied to a rope and made them walk behind his horse to the edge of a deep ravine where their feet were tied as well. Then he instructed the gang they worked with to throw them over. He warned that any man refusing to obey his orders would be shot, and for each refusal two children under the age of five would be turned off the estate to fend for themselves.'

Jowan felt the blood drain from his face. *'What?'* This was the man Phoebe was to marry?

'It sounds barbaric,' Downey said. 'It *is* barbaric. But it must be remembered that slaves vastly outnumber whites. The threat of revolt is ever present. An owner who wants to keep his plantation operating must maintain control. He cannot afford to display the smallest sign of fear or leniency. Slaves who have been brutalized and treated as less than human mistrust compassion. They see it as a weakness to be instantly exploited.'

Jowan nodded. But his concern for the slaves was forced aside by his anguish over Phoebe. He looked up, met Downey's gaze, and saw his own uncertainty reflected back at him as he wondered what in God's name he should do.

Downey's shoulders were hunched in distress. 'Will you tell her?'

'About Matcham's history? If I do she'll want to know how I learned of it.'

'I'm more than willing–'

'I'm sure you are, and I appreciate the offer, but that's not my point. Can you imagine how she'll feel knowing everyone in the mess is aware of her fiancé's part in Matcham's misery? In any case, the fact that she knows the reason behind Matcham's behaviour won't stop it happening.'

'Not even if you tell Matcham you're aware of the bad turn Rupert Quintrell served him?'

Jowan realized he dare not take that chance. The voyage still had several weeks to run. Given the restricted space and lack of privacy, to inflame an already tense situation would be not just foolish but dangerous.

'I cannot imagine Matcham reacting well to sympathy: least of all from me. The blow to his pride and loss of face would be too great.'

'I fear you're right.' Downey sighed. 'It would only make matters worse.'

Unable to remain still, Jowan jumped up from the seat, raking his hair. 'There's no doubt Matcham was ill-served by Rupert Quintrell. But why take it out on Ph– on Miss Dymond? What sort of a man makes an innocent young woman the target of his malice? What can he hope to gain?'

'This is only a guess,' Downey said. 'But I wonder if Matcham's plan, once he discovered Miss Dymond's reason for making the voyage, was to pay Rupert Quintrell back in his own coin by trying to win Miss Dymond's affection?'

'Even to contemplate such an action shows the man is devoid of all decency,' Jowan snapped.

'Or reacting to the pain of a grievous wound,' Downey murmured.

Jowan swung round, glowering at the older man. 'Surely you are not condoning–?'

'Of course not. I merely seek to understand. In its twisted logic and hunger for revenge Matcham's response resembles that of a spiteful child rather than a mature man. However it is my belief that his efforts were doomed to failure from the start.'

'So I should hope,' Jowan spat. Then he glanced up. 'What makes you say so?'

Downey lifted one shoulder: his gesture implying the answer was as obvious as the question was unnecessary. 'Miss Dymond loathes him.'

Jowan blinked, taken aback.

Downey smiled. 'Come now, Doctor. Surely you must have noticed?'

Noticed *what?* And how could he have missed it? Whenever he was in her company he was torn between wanting to study her every movement, and constant anxiety lest he betrayed an interest far beyond that suitable for a temporary guardian.

Like him she had learned to conceal her emotions. Her distant half-smile and lowered lashes gave little away. But he had learned to read her reactions in the tilt of her chin, the manner in which she clasped her hands, the shade of rose in her cheeks. *At least he thought he had.*

He frowned at Downey. 'She is always perfectly polite.'

'But of course she is. Would you expect otherwise? Courtesy is as natural to her as kindness. But with you and me she jokes and teases, and has even been known to lose her temper.'

Instantly Jowan saw what Downey meant. 'She only speaks to Matcham when he addresses her directly or asks her a question,' he said slowly. Though he had noticed her reticence he had not understood its significance.

'And except for mealtimes, when she has no choice,' Downey said, 'if Mr Matcham is in the mess she avoids it.'

'Still, thanks to Mr Burley she has use of the saloon. And,' Jowan added, as jealousy pricked like an embedded thorn, 'considering the hours you and she spend talking together on deck she cannot have much time left to fill.'

Downey beamed, blushing like a schoolboy. 'I confess her interest in my work gives me enormous pleasure. The demands of my chosen life have limited my opportunities to enjoy female company. Meeting a young lady as intelligent and open-minded as Miss Dymond has been an unexpected delight.' His smile faded and he heaved a sigh. 'However, the frequency and duration of our conversations has been remarked upon by Mr Matcham in a manner that appears jocular but which inevitably contains a sting in the tail.' He hesitated. 'As has the interest in medical matters you and she share. But no doubt you were already aware of that.'

At Jowan's expression he pulled a wry face. 'Oh. I see you were not.'

'Do you know if he has made any such comments to Miss Dymond?' Fury tightened Jowan's throat, as he strove to keep his voice level.

Downey clasped his hands together. 'I have not heard him do so but I think it more than likely.

Quite apart from the fact of Miss Dymond being your ward, the professional relationship that has developed between you is bound to have increased Mr Matcham's sense of exclusion.'

Jowan turned away, unable to hide his rage at Matcham's behaviour towards Phoebe and guilt that he had been unaware of the unpleasantness to which the merchant had subjected her. *Why had she not told him?*

'I make no excuses for him,' Downey said. 'Even allowing for the man's obvious unhappiness I find it hard to comprehend his actions.'

Jowan paced the saloon, his brows drawn down. 'Surely Miss Dymond's uncle must have made enquiries before agreeing to this marriage?'

Downey examined his nails then raised his eyes. 'I understand Captain Oakes is preparing for his own remarriage.'

'And was too distracted by his own concerns to give proper attention to his niece's future safety and happiness?' Jowan's fingers curled. He wanted to hit something.

Downey spread his hands. 'Of whom could he enquire except the young man's father? And what father would want to speak badly of his son? Perhaps both Captain Oakes and Mr Quintrell were persuaded that once married the young man would put aside his rackety bachelor ways and adopt a more sober and responsible way of life.'

'Do you think it likely?'

Downey shook his head. 'I am not the man to ask, Doctor, having no experience in such matters. Though it is often said that dissolute young men fortunate enough to find strong sensible wives do abandon their wild ways and embrace respectability.'

'And that is to be Miss Dymond's role?' Jowan flared, tortured by the images conjured by Downey's explanation. 'Not a loved and respected bride, but an animal tamer?' The instant the words were out he regretted them. They betrayed a depth of emotion he had no right to feel. 'I beg your pardon, Mr Downey. I should not have spoken so.'

Downey waved the apology aside. 'I understand your concern, Doctor.' *Did he? Jowan hoped not.* 'And I would like to believe such transformations possible. Perhaps in England they are. But given the lack of moral leadership from the church and the majority of the plantocracy, plus the pervading atmosphere in the island of time running out, I would say Jamaica is as stable as a barrel of gunpowder. And the fuse is already burning.'

'What shall I do?' Jowan burst out, unable to contain his anger, anxiety, and frustration.

'There is nothing you *can* do.' Downey's plump features puckered in sympathy and concern. 'Not about Matcham. But when duty demands your presence elsewhere, I shall offer my company to Miss Dymond. Between us we will shield her from any further unpleasantness.'

'I'm most grateful.' Jowan offered his hand, touched by the elderly scholar's offer.

Downey rose and clasped it. 'You need not thank me.' He smiled. 'It will be my pleasure and privilege.'

After Downey had gone Jowan threw himself down on the padded seat, stretched his arm along the back and gazed blindly out of the stern window. He was damned if he told her, and damned if he didn't.

If her uncle considered the arrangement suitable, then for an outsider to interfere was indefensible. But what if her uncle did not know the whole story?

Yet if *he* told her what he had learned about her betrothed what would he achieve? Would she believe him? If she did, she would have to face the terrible realization that her uncle was either guilty of appalling naïvety in accepting Rupert Quintrell as a suitable husband for her without making any enquiries, or that, anxious to secure his own future happiness, he had deliberately sacrificed hers.

And once you've done that to her, Jowan demanded of himself, *what then?* Having shattered her dreams and destroyed her future you would be responsible for her. Do you want that? *Yes, by God, he did.* The immediacy and certainty of his response stunned him.

But would *she* want it? Was it likely? When he had just turned her world upside down? She had made no secret of her rage at his being appointed her guardian without her knowledge or permission. To present her with such information about her fiancé now: to expect her to make a decision about her future now, was out of the question.

She had to meet Rupert Quintrell. She had to see for herself what manner of man he was. Until then Jowan knew he had no choice: he must remain silent.

Chapter Fourteen

Following days of damp humid weather a morning of blue sky, hot sunshine and a stiff breeze promised ideal drying conditions. Phoebe noticed clouds massing low on the western horizon. But they were much too far away to be of concern.

After an hour's hard work she pegged her washing inside the hammock netting, rubbed a nourishing calendula and arnica cream into wrinkled reddened hands, and retired to a corner of the stern.

Sitting on the warm deck, dry now after its early scrubbing, she drew her legs up, tucked her feet beneath her skirts and opened her book. If Romulus Downey came topside she would enjoy his company. Meanwhile she was content to be alone.

Glancing forward she was surprised not to see the surgeon taking sick call at the mast. After the recent poor weather she would have expected him to take advantage of the sunshine. But perhaps none of the crew had reported ill or injured. Or maybe he was seeing them below deck. That would obviously be more convenient as he had his drugs, dressings and instruments to hand.

She caught herself. *The pattern of Jowan Crossley's working day was none of her business – unless and until he made it so.* She stared hard at the printed page, trying with an effort that bordered on desperation to turn her mind from areas too fraught with danger to explore.

A warning shout coupled with the shrill of the bosun's call jerked her back to full awareness. Starting up from a half-waking dream that had filled her with sweet warmth, shocked to feel the gentle half-smile curving her mouth, she looked round swiftly, hotly ashamed of this betrayal by both her mind and body.

'Best get below, miss,' the helmsman shouted. 'Quick as you can. You'll get caught else.'

A low-pitched rumble was growing louder by the second. Scrambling to her feet and shaking the creases from her gown Phoebe glanced westward. She caught her breath. A thick purple-grey curtain was hurtling towards the ship. Falling from dense roiling clouds it met the sea in a line of churning white froth. The wind suddenly dropped away. Against the increasing roar and hiss of the approaching squall, Andy Gilbert bellowed a stream of orders and the bosun's whistle shrilled.

Half the watch was already racing up the ratlines to reef the square fore and topsails on the foremast. The rest pounded along the deck reaching for halyards to drop the huge gaff on the main. They were halfway through their task when the wind suddenly returned in a violent gust. Had the men been a few seconds slower it would have split the canvas or forced the packet over on her beam-ends.

Tearing her gaze from men clinging on as best they could while tying the reef-points, Phoebe tucked her book under her arm, turned to the hammock netting and snatched up the garments hanging inside. Bundling them together as a brilliant flash coincided with a deafening crack of thunder she hurried towards the companionway. In an instant daylight turned to menacing gloom.

The wind shrieked through the rigging. Ropes thrummed under the strain. Thick cloud the colour of slate and gunmetal swallowed the topmasts and released a torrent of rain that drummed on the deck with a sound like rolling cannonballs. Phoebe flinched as another thunderclap cracked. It was so close and so loud, that she felt it through the soles of her feet. The sheer volume of water sheeting down made it impossible to see or breathe. The drops stung and bruised like pellets of lead shot.

She reached blindly for the hatch, drenched to the skin before she could step over the coaming. At the bottom of the stairs she stood breathless and gasping as water trickled down her face and soaked into her sodden gown. Her heart raced, banging against her ribs from shock at the suddenness and ferocity of the storm.

So much for her lovely drying day. Sagging against the bulkhead she began to giggle. Part astonishment and part relief to be out of the downpour, it released some of the tension that of late had become a constant and draining companion.

Hearing the door open behind her she straightened up and turned, expecting to see the master. Instead Jowan Crossley emerged from the saloon, a frown darkening his features. He hesitated for an instant, his expression so swiftly controlled she could not read the fleeting changes. As the master appeared behind him, Jowan moved aside to allow him to pass.

Burley's gaze flicked over Phoebe. 'Got caught, did you?' He grinned. 'Oh well, you aren't the first and you won't be the last. A squall do make its own rules.'

Shy under the surgeon's gaze Phoebe glanced down at her dress, pulled a wry face, and wiped the back of one hand across her wet forehead. 'It was like standing under an upturned bucket.' She winced then shrugged at the long roll of thunder, raising her voice above the din. 'Only louder.'

Burley nodded. Phoebe saw him dart a sideways glance at the surgeon who hadn't said a word but was still staring at her, a fact of which she was embarrassingly conscious. ''Tis violent all right. But it don't last long.' He cocked his head. 'See? 'Tis passing over already.'

As he had to shout Phoebe assumed he was humouring her. But before she could accuse him of doing so, the unrelenting barrage began to diminish. She glanced at the deckhead, astonished. And moments later, as if a spigot had been turned off, it ceased altogether.

With a smile and a nod to them both, Burley climbed the brass stairs.

'You should–' Jowan began.

'I must–' Phoebe said simultaneously. Clutching the bundle of washing she felt the book's cover hard against her breast. 'Excuse me.'

'Of course.' He gestured for her to go first.

Acutely aware of him, of her own dishevelled state, and of the blush that fired her skin from her scalp to her toes, she turned to the doorway. As she hurried through the mess, Clewes exclaimed in concern. Though she didn't want to stop, courtesy demanded she make some response.

But even as she hesitated Jowan placed himself between her and Clewes, his body a shield as he opened her door.

'Go on in,' he murmured. 'I'll make your excuses.'

Clutching bottle and glass, Matcham was slumped over the table mumbling incoherently. Phoebe was inside her cabin, the door shut, before he had raised his head.

As she dropped her bundle on the bunk she heard Jowan's brief explanation, his voice fading as he continued through the mess towards the sick bay.

By mid-afternoon the sun had dried the deck and her washing, including her saturated dress. Having changed into a clean if slightly creased gown of lavender muslin with elbow-length sleeves, she stood at the stern quarter rail with Romulus Downey.

'According to Mr Burley,' he was saying, 'we're approaching Antigua–' He broke off. 'Did you hear that? It sounded like thunder.'

'Oh surely not another storm.' Phoebe scanned the sky warily. But it was a crisp clear blue. The only clouds were small puffs and streaks of pristine white. A warm breeze filled the packet's sails, tilting the deck as she cut through sparkling indigo water. The morning's tempest might never have happened. 'Well if it is, at least it's a long way away. I'm sorry, what were you saying?'

Downey was watching the lookout at the top of the main mast and didn't answer. Phoebe wondered if he'd even heard her. She looked up to see what was holding his attention. Cupping hand to mouth the lookout yelled down to the mate. Before he had finished footsteps rang on the stairs and the master emerged, his bushy brows drawn together in concern.

'But how did he know?' she began.

'A seaman's sixth sense, my dear,' Downey murmured, as they watched the lookout point over the starboard beam.

Snatching up a glass, the master scanned a small area of the western horizon. Moments later orders were being rapped out and repeated. A new urgency imbued the piercing tones of the bosun's call, swiftly drowned by the thud of running feet as men poured out of the fo'c'sle and swarmed over the deck.

The helmsman spun the huge wheel. Within moments topgallants and skysails filled. The jib topsail was hauled up the stay and sheeted in. As *Providence* altered course and leapt forward with new urgency Phoebe and her companion exchanged a glance.

'It's not a thunderstorm,' she said, a statement not a question.

Downey shook his head. 'I fear not.'

'What?'

'A ship of the French navy? A privateer?' He shrugged. 'I hope we remain too distant to find out.'

As Burley turned to speak to the helmsman, he caught sight of them. This time he didn't smile.

'You'd best go below.'

Nodding, Downey cupped Phoebe's elbow. She went reluctantly. At lunchtime Matcham had been drunk and belligerent. Hoping he might have retired to his cabin to sleep it off, her stomach tightened at the sound of his voice raised in slurred argument with his colleague.

Reaching the door into the mess she spoke over her shoulder, 'I think I should warn Dr Crossley.'

'Please don't upset yourself, my dear,' Downey soothed. '*Providence* is a fast ship. And I'm sure Mr Burley will do everything in his power to avoid any ... unpleasantness.'

'I'm not upset, Mr Downey,' Phoebe broke in gently. 'And I have complete faith in Mr Burley's seamanship, but I think the doctor would appreciate being informed so he can make preparations, even if, as we both hope, the warning proves unnecessary.'

'Yes, well, perhaps you're right.'

Phoebe had already opened the door. Matcham and Clewes both turned to see who had come in. Ignoring Matcham's loud greeting she felt a leap of relief as Mossop emerged from his pantry.

'Doctor's in there, miss.' He pointed to the cabin next to Downey's that was being used as an additional sick bay.

She had quickly realized that Mossop too possessed a sixth sense for trouble. Whether he had felt the ship change course, recognized the urgency in the shouts and running feet, or whether he was simply trying to protect her from Matcham's drunken overtures, she was grateful.

'Thank you.' She smiled at him and tapped

233

lightly on the door. At Jowan's 'Come in' her heart gave a brief flutter. She entered, pulling the door closed behind her.

Sitting at the head end of the single bunk, his bag open in front of him, Jowan looked up from the ledger in which he'd been writing. In the flickering yellow light from the two lanterns his features appeared drawn, the skin tight across his cheekbones.

Phoebe moistened her lips. 'I thought you'd want to know that there's a possibility—' On deck shouts and more running feet were followed by a grinding rumble. Instinctively she looked up, her skin tightening as she recognized the sound. The guns were being run out.

'A certainty I'd say.' His grim tone matched his expression as their eyes met. Shutting the ledger he slotted it behind the rail on the shelf above the bunk. 'Will you tell Mossop to boil some water? I'll get Grigg to start preparing dressings and bandages.'

'Could you ask him to help move Mr Matcham into the saloon?' Phoebe blurted. 'I don't think Mr Clewes will be able to manage alone.'

His face tightened and a muscle jumped in his jaw. On the verge of saying something, he thought better of it. 'Yes, of course.'

'I expect Mossop will already have sent Timmy for sand buckets.' She swallowed. 'I'd like to help.'

'Thank you.' His nod was brief but immediate.

Her heart leapt with relief and a delight that was instantly swamped by guilt. Of course she didn't want anyone to be hurt. But if they were then her skills would be useful. And an opportunity to work alongside a qualified physician and surgeon, to be treated as an equal, how could she help but be thrilled at the prospect? It was something Aunt Sarah would not have imagined possible.

The fact that a trust had developed between herself and Jowan Crossley was undeniable. But was this sense of affinity purely professional? It ought to be, had to be. She had no right to anything else. Yet it was becoming increasingly difficult to separate her admiration for him as a doctor from her awareness of him as a man. How could she divide the two when each aspect was so much a part of the other? But she must. *She must.*

'Perhaps some antiseptic lotion? And the poultices and compresses you used on Jenkins?' Jowan reached for his tray of instruments.

'I'll prepare them at once.' She left the cabin and returned to her own, glad to have something on which to concentrate, something that would keep her busy and leave no time for thoughts that were wrong and wicked and hopeless.

The next hour flew as preparations continued. Mossop came in from his pantry, glared at the sloping deck and clicked his tongue.

'Good job we got dinner over afore all this started. 'Tis some job to keep pans and kettles on the stove. I daren't fill 'em more'n halfway. That's how 'tis taking so long to fill the jugs you asked for.'

Seated on one of the benches Phoebe looked up from the bowl in which she was steeping squares of gauze in a hot infusion of marigold and goldenseal to make wound-healing compresses. 'Don't worry, Mossop. We're doing very well. And if all these preparations turn out to be unnecessary' – she shrugged – 'the rest of the water can be used for tea and the bandages put away for another time.'

Once everything was ready they could only wait. Their pursuer had been identified as a French privateer. Though the master had bent on every sail he could find and was coaxing the last ounce of speed from the packet, slowly but surely the Frenchman was gaining on them.

Phoebe went to her cabin and changed her lavender muslin for an older gown. As she emerged, she noticed the mess door had been fastened back. She glanced along the passage and her skin erupted in goose pimples as she saw Andy Gilbert unlocking the armoury. Men formed a human chain passing cannonballs and bags of grapeshot to be stacked beside the guns. Then pikes, axes and muskets were handed up the companionway to be distributed among the crew.

She guessed that as the youngest and smallest of the crew Timmy would be acting as powder monkey: bringing up gunpowder cartridges from the magazine. Soon the slow matches would be lit and laid for safety in a sand bucket beside each gun.

Phoebe tied the sailcloth apron around her waist. The knowledge that it was only a matter of time, that a fight was now inevitable, made the tension almost unbearable.

She knew from her uncle that Packet Service

rules decreed that if a packet ship was attacked she must run. Only when escape was impossible was it permitted to turn and fight. To ensure this rule was obeyed, packets were armed only for defence. Smaller than most enemy vessels, and outgunned, packets relied on the courage of the crew and the skill and ingenuity of their masters to keep out of trouble.

But if trouble was inevitable the crew was supposed to keep the enemy at bay for as long as it took either to escape or to sink the mails. Then the packet was supposed to strike her colours and surrender. These rules were bitterly resented by packet men.

A booming explosion made Phoebe start violently. Her hand flew to her throat.

'All right?' Jowan murmured.

She nodded, drawing a steadying breath. 'Yes, it's just – I wasn't expecting...' She could feel her heart galloping. Yet in a strange way that first shot was a relief. At last the waiting was over.

'Was that a warning?' Downey enquired, busily rolling another bandage with hands that had developed a slight tremor.

'The Frenchie testing for distance more like,' Grigg announced.

There was another rolling boom, swiftly followed by a much louder explosion as *Providence*'s stern-chaser roared defiance.

For a while Phoebe sat with every muscle tense, hardly daring to breathe as shots were exchanged. Then came the crunch of splintering wood. *Providence* had been hit.

The screams of the wounded were lost in a

shuddering crash as something fell to the deck. Within moments, injured men began arriving in the mess. Phoebe lost all track of time as she and Jowan and Grigg worked amid deafening noise. Removing a six-inch splinter from one man's calf she washed the wound with a lotion of marigold, yarrow and comfrey and bandaged on a compress. As he tugged his forelock, muttered his thanks, then limped out to return topside, another man slumped on to the bench holding a rag to his head, his face a crimson mask.

While she washed off the blood then stitched the scalp flap back in place, Jowan set a broken leg. Falling from the yard when the topmast was shot away, the man had got tangled in the rigging. It had saved his life but snapped his femur.

Trying to shut out everything else but the injury in front of her, Phoebe swabbed cuts, applied soothing ointment to shrapnel grazes and burns, bound healing compresses to wounds. The guns thundered. The mess grew stuffy and rank with the stench of blood and sweat. Her dress clung uncomfortably and she could feel beads of perspiration trickling between her breasts and down her temples. Wiping a forearm across her forehead and upper lip it came away wet.

'Phoebe!'

Jowan's voice. She whirled round, startled by his use of her name, and saw a brawny figure being laid on the table. She recognized him. It was one of the helmsmen. His face was a rictus of agony as he cradled his right arm against his chest. But as

Grigg gently eased away the blood-soaked shirt someone had wrapped around his hand Phoebe caught the inside of her lower lip between her teeth. What remained of the helmsman's hand wasn't recognizable. It was just mangled flesh and jagged white bone. Her throat tightened and her stomach heaved. She closed her eyes and swallowed hard again and again.

Forcing her head up she met Jowan's gaze, nodded, then turned aside. 'Grigg?' Her voice sounded hoarse. She cleared her throat and tapped him on the shoulder. 'As soon as you've finished, can you bandage Thomas's arm? I've already applied burn salve.'

'I'm right there, miss.' As they passed each other both nearly slipped. Despite the earlier covering of sand the floor was slick with blood and water. Phoebe scooped another handful from one of the buckets. It felt cold and gritty, and stuck to her damp fingers. Quickly scattering it beside the table she moved the bucket so it stood close to the surgeon.

As Mossop lifted the man's shoulders so Jowan could pour laudanum into his mouth, she rinsed her hands, Drawing deep breaths and willing herself to be calm and steady she reached for the bowl of antiseptic solution.

The horrendous noise made conversation impossible. But having assisted with the amputation of Jenkins' foot Phoebe knew what to do and when to do it.

While she helped Jowan, Downey continued giving drinks, emptying bowls, collecting blood-soaked dressings in a bucket and fetching more

239

bandages from the saloon where Clewes was rolling them after tearing another sheet into strips.

The operation completed, Grigg and Mossop carried the unconscious helmsman through to the sick bay. As she and Jowan turned to their next patients, Phoebe felt someone tap her on the back. She turned, flexing painfully stiff shoulders. Downey pointed at the deckhead. At first she didn't understand. Then she realized that though she could still hear gunfire, *Providence*'s cannons had fallen silent.

Immediately she looked across at Jowan. His face was drawn and pale except for brownish purple shadows beneath his eyes and a streak of dried blood across one cheek. As his gaze met hers there was a roar from the men on deck and a thump as someone jumped down the last few stairs. Then a crewman burst into the mess, his smoke-blackened, sweat-streaked face split by a huge grin.

'The navy's come! 'Tis the *Vanguard*. Look like she been in a fight herself but she's seeing the Frenchie off.' Instantly the atmosphere lightened. Some of the injured men gave a ragged cheer. Others nodded, their shoulders slumping in relief.

As she exchanged a smile with Jowan, Phoebe felt her eyes prickle. Instantly she bent her head, blinking away tears of relief as she squeezed excess solution from a gauze pad and bound the hot compress onto the seaman's shoulder. Swallowing the stiffness in her throat she helped the seaman to his feet. She had never been so tired in her life. Every muscle ached and her head was throbbing from the strain of working under such intense pressure amid indescribable noise.

She staggered slightly, finding it suddenly harder to keep her balance. Was it exhaustion? Or had the packet's motion changed?

'*Vanguard* has signalled us to heave-to,' Grigg announced, as he came in from the sick bay. 'They're sending a boarding party across.'

As Phoebe opened her mouth to ask why, the packet wallowed, rolling heavily. She saw Jowan grab at the table to steady himself. But he missed. Losing his footing on the wet floor he fell. Phoebe gasped, wincing at the sickening crack as his head hit the edge of one of the benches.

Mossop burst in. 'That boarding party want to take some of our crew to replace their dead and injured.'

Phoebe flew to Jowan and knelt beside him, heedless of the filth or her dress. 'They can't do that.' Her voice reflected her fear for Jowan and shock at Mossop's announcement.

The steward nodded grimly. 'They can. 'Tis wartime. They can do what they bleddy like. They want the surgeon as well.'

'Bugger that,' Grigg snapped. 'Beg pardon, miss.' Crouching, he whipped off Jowan's blood-streaked apron. 'But they aren't having him. He's ours.' Clutching the surgeon under the arms, Grigg started hauling him towards a bench. 'Someone give us a hand.' He glanced over his shoulder. 'And you lot budge up.'

While Phoebe watched, frozen with fear and exhaustion, Grigg propped Jowan in a corner and, tucking the ties out of sight, draped the bloody canvas across shirt and breeches that might otherwise betray him. Grabbing a sopping crimson rag from the swab bucket he wound it around Jowan's head. The injured crew huddled around until he was virtually invisible.

'C'mon now, miss.' Mossop gently lifted Phoebe to her feet. 'Just a bit longer. Once they've gone I'll make a nice cup of tea.'

Phoebe stared at him, felt her insides shake like jelly, and pressed her fingers to her mouth. If she started laughing she wouldn't be able to stop.

The bosun's call shrilled. Booted feet strode across the deck and clanged noisily on the companionway.

Phoebe drew a deep breath and straightened her shoulders, wiping wet hands down her bloodstained sailcloth apron. As she turned, a tall figure in white breeches and a navy coat with lots of gold braid strode in.

'Where's the surgeon?'

Phoebe's chin rose. She stepped forward. 'My name is Phoebe Dymond.' She paused. 'Whom do I have the honour of addressing?'

He stopped abruptly. As colour rushed into his face Phoebe realized he was younger than she had first thought.

He bowed briefly. 'Lieutenant Waddington, at your service, Miss Dymond. Forgive the intrusion, but I need the surgeon.'

'Can I be of assistance, Lieutenant?'

'You?' His expression echoed his astonishment.

'Looked after us 'andsome, she 'ave, sir,' one of the injured men announced.

'Aye, good as any doctor she is,' another agreed.

'Miss Dymond is a trained herbalist and healer, Lieutenant.' Downey clutched the table to steady himself as the ship wallowed and rolled. 'I don't know what we would have done without her.'

As the lieutenant glanced swiftly around the mess, Phoebe tried to see it through his eyes: the injured men slumped on one of the benches and on the wet floor propped against the merchants' cabin doors; the swab bucket, the blood, the smell.

'*You* have been treating the injured men?' he demanded, clearly finding it hard to believe.

'Indeed she has, Lieutenant,' Mossop confirmed. 'Watched her myself. As neat a bit of stitching as I've ever seen. We'd 'ave been in some bad way without her and that's a fact.'

'You're bound for Jamaica, Miss Dymond?'

Phoebe nodded. 'I am.'

'May I ask for what purpose?'

'With respect, Lieutenant, I fail to see why the circumstances of my journey should be of any interest to you.' His colour rose again. 'However,' she added, before he could respond, 'it is no secret. I am travelling to Jamaica to join–' She took a breath, clasping her hands in front of her and forced the words out. 'To join my f-fiancé. He owns a sugar plantation there.'

'I see.' He made a stiff bow. 'My question was prompted not by idle curiosity, Miss Dymond, but by concern for your safety. Recent news from the island is not good. Refugees are flooding in from St Domingue and the militia have been deployed in the north-west of the island to deal with an uprising among the Maroons.'

'I appreciate your consideration in warning me, Lieutenant. Now if there is nothing else, I must beg you to excuse me. Some of the injured men have not yet been treated.' A low-pitched groan tensed Phoebe's stomach. *Jowan*. As the lieutenant glanced round the sound of swift footsteps in the passage preceded Clewes who rushed in.

'Miss D-Dymond, I'm s-so s-sorry t-to interrupt, b-but c-could you spare G-Grigg or M-Mossop? M-my c-colleague – oh.' Seeing the newcomer he stopped short.

'Obviously you are busy, Miss Dymond. I'll delay you no longer.' With a brief bow the lieutenant strode out, nodding to Clewes as he passed.

Phoebe swayed, suddenly light-headed.

'Everything's all right, miss,' Mossop soothed. 'You jest sit down here. Grigg, will you see to–'

'I'm gone. Now, Mr Clewes, do I need a bucket?'

'I'm fine,' Phoebe said, wondering why her voice sounded so far away. 'Oh, that's marvellous,' she murmured, as a cool wet cloth was placed on the back of her neck. She raised her head. 'Doctor Crossley...'

'Thomas and Mr Downey are carrying him to his cabin.'

She straightened up. 'I ought to...'

Mossop pressed her down gently. 'You stay right there. He won't come to no harm while you have a cup of tea.'

Chapter Fifteen

Dimly aware of movement, of pressure under his arms and knees, not knowing where he was or what was happening, Jowan began to struggle. He felt sick and dizzy and a sword-thrust of pain lanced through his temple.

'Easy now, Doctor.' Grigg's voice came from above and behind him. 'We're just taking you to your cabin.'

'Put me down.' Jowan felt his lips move. But hearing the words emerge in a hoarse mumble shook him. He cleared his throat, flinching as pain shot through his skull again. 'I can walk, dammit.'

'Are you sure that's wise?' Downey fretted.

'Yes,' Jowan hissed. Everyone else had managed to keep their footing. He was the only one to have made a fool of himself.

'Well, if you say so.' Downey released his legs, grunting as he straightened up.

Unable to suppress a groan as nausea churned his stomach Jowan reached blindly for his cabin door murmuring, 'Phoebe–'

'Just fetching lotion and bandages she is,' Grigg said, shifting his grip so Jowan was leaning on him. 'Come on, better get you laid down before you fall down.'

Grigg was becoming far too familiar. But right now Jowan hadn't the strength to reprove him.

Lying flat on his bunk, eyes closed and feeling marginally better, he heard the scrape of a match and smelled oil as the lantern was lit. Then he heard the soft swish and rustle of skirts.

'Ah, Miss Dymond.' There was pleasure in Downey's voice. 'You must allow me to congratulate you on the way you dealt with Lt Waddington.'

'Oh, I didn't intend – it was just that he–'

'Indeed, you were superb.' Downey was not to be stopped. 'I would go so far as to say that the lieutenant's understanding of the world and women's contribution to it has been considerably broadened.'

'There, miss.' The lantern glass clattered onto its base. 'Should be able to see what you're doing now. Need anything else, do you?' Mossop enquired.

'Not for the moment, thank you.'

'Well, if you do, just give us a shout. All right?'

As the steward opened the door, Jowan eased himself up. Gingerly touching his tender scalp he winced. And glimpsed fresh blood on his fingers.

'I'll leave you to Miss Dymond's care then, Doctor,' Downey announced, moving towards the door Mossop still held. 'As I can be of little help I'll only be in the way.'

'Indeed, Mr Downey,' Phoebe said quickly, 'your assistance this past hour was invaluable and much appreciated.'

'You are too kind, my dear. I'll close this, shall I? Then it won't slam.'

Jowan swallowed. He was alone with her. Never had his cabin felt more claustrophobic. Swinging his feet over the edge of the bunk he gazed blindly at the door, shoulders tensed, his hands gripping his thighs while she bathed the cut on his head. The herbal lotion was acrid in his nostrils. Yet beneath its sharpness he detected the floral soap and dried lavender that were unique to her. Lack of space and the task she was performing required her to stand close. There were still inches between them yet he could *feel* the fragrant warmth of her body. A groan escaped and he closed his eyes.

'I'm so sorry,' she murmured. 'I'm being as careful as I can. At least the cut has stopped bleeding.'

'It's not that.' His tone was rough. He could not tell her the truth. 'Your touch is exquisitely gentle.' Hearing the soft catch of her breath and aware of the sudden tremor in her hand as she wiped the wound with a clean wad of gauze, he hurried on, 'No, it's this awful queasiness.' Though it wasn't the whole truth, nor was it a lie.

As she turned, dropping the gauze in the bowl and picking up a small jar of salve, he inhaled the air stirred by her movement. He bit hard on his lower lip as he fought an overpowering urge to rest his forehead against the softness of her bosom.

'It could be the result of the blow as you fell,' she suggested. Jowan's eyelids fluttered down as he abandoned himself to the sensation of her fingers applying the salve. 'Or it might be due to the ship's motion. Is your sight clear? You have no blurred or double vision?'

Carefully tilting his head he looked into her

face. 'No.' He bent his head again, swallowing the hoarseness in his voice as he pressed one hand to his stomach. 'Just nausea and a very sore head.'

'That's not to be wondered at. You took a hard fall.'

'I must have a thick skull.'

'Well, on this occasion you should be thankful for it.'

This time his wince held wry humour. 'What happened?'

'The ship rolled and because the floor was wet...' She swallowed and he guessed she was seeing again the crimson wash of blood and spilled water on the cabin floor. 'You slipped and hit your head as you fell.'

'No, I meant what happened about our crew? The last thing I remember was Mossop saying the boarding party had come for men to replace *Vanguard*'s dead and injured.'

Phoebe wiped her hands on a linen rag. 'I don't know. I'm sure someone will tell us as soon as there is further news. I think Lieutenant Waddington must still be with Mr Burley. I know we are still lying hove-to, which is why *Providence* is rolling so badly.' She hesitated. 'Apparently their own surgeon was killed and they wanted you as his replacement. But–'

Startled, Jowan looked up. 'Then how is it that I'm still here?'

'Well,' she hesitated, 'for a start you were unconscious. And – and the crew didn't want to lose you. They hid you among the injured and–' Her hands were surely dry, yet she continued to wipe each finger with great care. 'You must understand,' she blurted, 'no one actually lied.'

'But?' Jowan prompted, as the silence lengthened.

'But they – we – allowed the lieutenant to assume we didn't have a surgeon on board.'

Jowan studied her. Even in the lantern light he could see a flush had suffused her face and throat. Avoiding his gaze, she replaced the top on the salve jar. Her fingers, usually so deft, were clumsy and awkward. 'So who did he imagine had been treating the wounded?' He heard Phoebe swallow.

'Without actually saying so, Grigg and Mossop implied that I...' Her voice trailed off.

'And the lieutenant believed them?' Uncertain whether he felt relieved or angry he gave her no chance to reply. 'Indeed, why would he not? Evidence of your industry was all about him.' Guilt added to the crushing weight on his heart. He dared not tell her of his admiration for her courage, her strength of character, or even the breadth of her knowledge. To say anything would be to say too much. He would not be able to disguise the depth of his regard, his longing. And that would place an intolerable burden on her. But for how long could he continue to hide what he felt? Perhaps the lieutenant's arrival was fortuitous. He could leave now, honour intact, and spare them both. And if his heart were as battered as his skull no one but he would know.

He straightened, fighting increasing queasiness as he started to rise from the bunk. 'I must see the lieutenant. My – my duty is to the frigate's crew, the fighting men.'

She reached out to stop him but withdrew her hand immediately, as if the move had been instinctive and only after it was made had she realized what she'd done. She clasped her hands together, fingers entwined, the knuckles gleaming like bare bone in the soft light.

'And, if you go, what will happen to *Providence*'s crew? They are not trained for battle like naval men. Their job is the safe delivery of mail and passengers. Yet because the enemy considers them fair game they are forced to fight. Had you wanted to be a naval surgeon surely you would have joined a naval ship? In any case, surely a frigate the size of *Vanguard* must have at least one surgeon's mate and – and perhaps several sick bay assistants?'

Though she kept her voice low she was talking faster and faster, clearly driven by powerful emotions. But what were they? Disgust that he could so easily abandon men who relied on him for their well-being? Dismay that he might leave her to face Matcham without protection? And she was right. He could not leave. He took a breath, but she had not finished.

'You made it very clear you resented having responsibility for me foisted on you. But I have tried hard to be more help than nuisance. And – and when I told you I did not require your guardianship you said I had no choice in the matter. If that is so, surely you owe a duty to my uncle? After all it will not be very long before you can hand me over to – to Mr Quintrell. Then your obligation will be discharged.' Pitched higher than usual her voice cracked. 'You will be free.'

Free to recall her courage, her compassion, her spirit, and every moment spent in her company. Free to miss her, to ache. Free to worry about her being ill-used or unhappy.

'As you say. Then I will be free.' He could not contain his bitterness and saw her flinch.

'I–' She cleared her throat. 'I'll fetch something to ease your nausea. Excuse me.' Snatching up the bowl and salve she whirled out oblivious of the bloodstained water slopping on to her dress.

The door slammed and he was alone with his thoughts. Lying back he gazed at the deck head, his wretchedness unconnected with nausea or injury.

Believing him angry, and that he held her responsible for being forced to remain aboard the packet, that he would rather have left with Lieutenant Waddington, Phoebe withdrew into herself.

Losing eight men to the *Vanguard* left *Providence* dangerously shorthanded. And though every man who could hold a hammer or sew canvas was put to work on basic repairs, the packet would need a lot more done at the shipyards in Jamaica.

Phoebe was torn between wishing the voyage over so she would no longer have to face Jowan every day and dreading arrival at Kingston. *Providence* was a tiny world unto itself, cramped, smelly and uncomfortable. It lacked the conveniences she had always taken for granted at home. But she had found a friend in Mr Downey and won the respect and affection of the crew. She had survived a battle, greatly expanded her

251

medical knowledge, assisted at two amputations, *and fallen in love*. And the thought of leaving surroundings that initially had appalled and terrified her yet were now so familiar was unbearable.

She coped with her dread as she had coped with losing her aunt and the prospect of the voyage: by keeping so busy she didn't have time to think. Working wherever she was most needed she changed dressings, removed stitches, applied salves, prepared draughts and tinctures. She rose early and retired late. Most of the hours in between she devoted to helping get the wounded fit enough to return to their duties.

It was inevitable that on occasions she found herself alone with Jowan. But as soon as the patients had been treated she quickly excused herself, citing medicines to be prepared or notes and records to be written up. Sometimes she yearned to linger. Then she would recall his bitter expression the day she had reminded him of his duty to the crew and to her uncle. That was all it took to make her flee.

The fact that she was aboard the packet and sailing to Jamaica proclaimed to the world her acceptance of the proposal made by William Quintrell on behalf of his son. By marrying Rupert Quintrell she would acquire status, responsibility, and the opportunity to continue her work. She had never expected the arrangement to include love.

Everyone she had ever loved had been taken from her. But her vow never again to risk such terrible pain had crumbled to dust scattered on the wind. How could she have been so weak, so stupid? She hadn't chosen this. It had just ... happened. But no one knew. Nor would they ever. The guilt, the dreadful shame, of loving a man who did not love her, a man who was not her betrothed, was a secret she would carry to her grave.

As the crewmen recovered there was less for her to do. Grigg and Mossop both told her she was looking pale and it was time she took things a bit easier. Deeply preoccupied, Jowan did not seem to have noticed. But it could only be a matter of time before he did. Then he would question her. What would she – could she – say?

Dreading the prospect of empty hours with nothing to keep her mind busy Phoebe sought out Downey. He was delighted to see her.

'I have greatly missed our conversations,' he confided with a broad smile. 'Do you know I even considered pretending some minor indisposition?'

'For shame, Mr Downey,' Phoebe scolded, warm with pleasure that this learned man enjoyed her company.

'I know,' he sighed. 'It is a terrible admission. I had not thought myself so selfish. Anyway, I am much relieved not to have such underhand behaviour on my conscience. Now, what shall we talk of today?'

'Who are the Maroons?' she asked, resting her arms on the rail, suddenly aware of how long it was since she had felt the warm breeze and tasted sweet fresh air. 'Lieutenant Waddington said something about them being involved in an uprising.'

'Ah, the Maroons. Well, originally they were a gang of slaves who ran away from a plantation and made a home for themselves in the mountains and ravines of north-west Jamaica. As their numbers gradually increased, bands of white men set out with guns to try and wipe them out. But after one such band found itself surrounded by the very men it had come to kill and completely at their mercy, the Maroon leader, a man called Cudjoe, showed himself to be very shrewd.'

'How so?'

'He negotiated a treaty. In return for some land and freedom to hunt game he would set up a court to punish crimes that did not deserve death. In addition the Maroons would police the forests and capture runaway slaves.'

'Why are they called Maroons? It seems an odd name.'

'It comes from the Spanish word *cimaron*, meaning wild or unruly. And no doubt they were at the beginning. But over the past sixty years, and without help of any kind, they have resisted the lure of rum and entirely by their own efforts set up businesses selling tobacco and cured meats.'

'Really?' Phoebe was astonished.

'That's not all. Because the mountain passes are so difficult and precarious it can take days to get from one village to another. So they developed a system of communication using a cow horn, rather as we would use a bugle. Every man in every village has his own particular call. This allows important information to be passed along

254

far more quickly than would be possible on foot.'

'That's amazing.' Phoebe shook her head, gazing for a moment across the restless inky water. 'Lieutenant Waddington said there has been an uprising and the militia have been sent in.'

Downey sighed, his expression grim. 'No doubt the cause is something that could easily have been settled with a little tact and goodwill. Instead it will have been blown out of all proportion by some clumsy and overzealous government official.'

Phoebe was startled. 'Why should you think that?'

Downey grimaced. 'Because I have experience of such men. There are two thousand regular troops stationed in Jamaica and seven thousand men enrolled in the militia. The total number of Maroons is perhaps thirteen hundred. And I doubt even half of them will be involved in whatever's going on. The decision to send in soldiers is the government using a hammer to crack an egg.' He caught himself, drew a breath, and smiled at her. 'I daresay it will all be over by the time we get there.'

Once she would have welcomed his reassurance, accepting it without question. But her experiences aboard *Providence* had taught her that life was rarely that simple.

Wearing a dress of white cambric and a wide-brimmed hat to shade her eyes, Phoebe watched the island of Barbados grow larger. The dark swells of the Atlantic gave way to sapphire and jade that paled to turquoise as the ship skirted expanses of coral reef on the approach to Bridgetown. After so long at sea she found the intense greens of the luxuriant vegetation startling. Golden sand fringed the shore. Behind it were fine colonial buildings flanked by smaller brightly coloured wooden shacks that tumbled over the hillside like a child's bricks.

Providence anchored in Carlisle Bay. While Mr Burley took the mail ashore to Government House and collected the bags for Jamaica and the return trip to England, other boats ferried fresh water, chickens and fruit out to the ship. After a few hours during which Phoebe remained by the rail absorbing the sights, sounds and smells, and talking to Downey, *Providence* weighed anchor and headed into the Caribbean.

The July days were hot, the nights warm and humid. Already difficult, sleep became almost impossible for Phoebe. Most of the men were back at work. Grigg looked after the few who still needed care.

She tried to restart her journal. But the need to censor her thoughts and guard her pen took all pleasure from it. She spent some time on deck with Downey each day. Then, when the master went topside, she retired alone to the saloon. Solitude meant she could put aside the mask, drop the pretence of looking forward to arrival in Jamaica. She could sit on the padded bench seat, gaze out through the stern window at the ship's wake and try desperately to empty her mind and not think at all.

She sometimes saw Jowan taking sick call at the mainmast. Often she wouldn't see him for the rest of the day. Except for meals. She found that strange. Because often he ate very little yet he still came to the table, and always sat beside her. Though his silent presence was torture it protected her from Matcham's attentions.

Obviously some kind of exchange had taken place between them. She had no idea when it had occurred or what had been said. But though she often sensed the merchant's eyes on her, he no longer attempted to draw her into conversation. Nor did he make any further insinuating remarks about Rupert Quintrell. Most nights he remained at the table after the meal was over and drank himself into insensibility, relying on his colleague and Mossop to put him to bed.

One morning, stepping out of the companionway onto the deck, she sensed a change. There was more banter among the crew who tackled their tasks with new enthusiasm. Before she could ask, one of them knuckled his forehead, his face split in a wide grin.

'We'll reach Jamaica tomorrow, miss. Best look to your packing if you want to be ready.'

Chapter Sixteen

'That is Fort Charles.' Downey pointed to the squat building of weathered red brick on the end of the long narrow spit of land they were passing. 'It was the only one to survive the earthquake.'

Phoebe gazed out over the stern quarter as *Providence* sailed into a vast and crowded harbour. 'The only one? How many forts were there?'

'Six.'

'Why so many?'

'Because a hundred years ago Port Royal was the wealthiest town in the Caribbean. Houses here cost more to rent than in the most expensive parts of London.'

'And all that wealth came from trade?' Phoebe was impressed.

Downey hesitated. 'Not exactly. There was trade, of course. But most of the town's prosperity sprang from piracy and its attendant evils; drink and – and so on.' He faltered and Phoebe nodded, pretending she hadn't noticed. But her profession, coupled with growing up in a port, meant that despite her youth she was well aware of prostitution and its tragic consequences.

'So when the earthquake struck and the sea swallowed up two thirds of the town the clergy declared it to be God's revenge.'

'Did many die?'

'Over two thousand. Yet some escaped. And in

ways that were little short of miraculous.'

Fascinated, Phoebe turned to him. 'How? What happened?'

'During the first shock huge crevices opened up and hundreds of people tumbled into them. One was a man named Louis Galdye. When the next tremor forced all these gaping fissures closed, crushing everyone inside them, he should have been killed. Yet somehow he wasn't. Instead he was catapulted out into the sea. Fortunately he could swim. And he managed to stay afloat until a boat picked him up.'

Phoebe stared at the scholar. What he had told her seemed utterly incredible. Yet he must believe it for he would never deliberately tell her a falsehood. 'Are you– I mean–'

'Am I sure? And how do I know?' he smiled. 'No, no, it's all right.' He patted her arm, stopping her apology before she could speak. 'I scarcely believed it myself until I visited St Peter's churchyard and read that very same story etched on his gravestone. And his wasn't the only astonishing escape. The quake was followed by a massive tidal wave that hurled a ship called *The Swan* on to rooftops in the centre of the town. Not only did it land on its keel, it remained upright, providing shelter for those who were able to climb aboard.'

Awed, Phoebe shook her head and looked once more towards the spit of land. Now *Providence* was through the gap she could see the town. 'But it all looks so – established. It's hard to believe it was ever...'

'A heap of rubble? Port Royal was far too

important to the British Government to be left in such a state.'

'Why? I thought you said it was an evil wicked place.'

'And so it was. But don't forget it was also the centre of Caribbean trade. Not only that, the huge sheltered harbour made it an ideal base in the West Indies for the Royal Navy to store supplies and make repairs. So rebuilding began immediately.'

'But if so many had died and so much was destroyed how could those who were left *afford* to start again?'

Downey raised one shoulder. 'By returning to what had built the town in the first place.'

Phoebe caught her breath. 'Piracy? Surely the British Government would never–'

'Oh they would,' Downey said drily. 'And they did, claiming necessity as justification. And I have to accept that they had a point.' He pointed east beyond the town to a busy area of wharves and docks that rivalled Falmouth. 'That's the naval dockyard. Though we have come direct from Cornwall, our voyage has lasted almost seven weeks. Naval vessels are at sea for months, sometimes years. What would become of our ships and men if there were nowhere for them to make repairs in safety? No source from which to obtain fresh food and water or materials with which to make repairs.' He pointed again. 'You see that long low wooden building on this side of the town? That's the naval hospital. It's the only place in this part of the world where sick and wounded English sailors can be put ashore to receive treatment.'

Phoebe bit her lip as, amid the chaos in her head, she heard once more her uncle's damning condemnation of the calibre of doctors sent out to Jamaica.

The sky was brassy with heat, the breeze thick with humidity. Beneath her wide-brimmed straw hat perspiration prickled Phoebe's forehead and the nape of her neck.

Ships of every size, shape and nationality crowded the harbour. Some rode at anchor, others were dropping canvas to slow their approach, or setting sails as they headed seaward. The packet's route across the busy waterway took her past two dilapidated hulks moored side by side, their topmasts missing.

'Have they been in a battle?' Phoebe asked. Before her companion could reply she heard the muffled sound of men shouting and caught her breath at a foetid stench carried on the breeze. 'Ugh. What on earth—'

'They are prison ships,' Downey said.

Phoebe looked up quickly. Opening her mouth to ask why men were confined in rotting ships when there must be gaols in Port Royal and Kingston, she closed it again. The answer was obvious. The prisons ashore must already be full. Lieutenant Waddington had spoken of refugees flooding in from Saint Domingue. Clearly it was not only the wealthy and well-to-do who had escaped the uprising. Like rats fleeing a sinking ship, the thieves and murderers had followed those on whom they preyed.

Downey patted her arm. She wasn't sure if he was attempting to offer comfort or distraction.

Glad of either she looked to where he was pointing. 'There is Kingston.'

Shaped like an open fan the town spread over a plain that rose gently from the waterfront to the foothills of the Blue Mountains. Behind the forest of masts crowding the busy waterfront, elegant buildings of stone and brick dazzled in the blinding sun. The distant mountains were purple-hazed, the lower hills intensely green.

This was the end of her voyage. It was time to abandon any foolish dreams and half-formed hopes. Arrival at Kingston meant leaving the ship and its familiar routines, saying goodbye to people she had come to think of as friends *and so much more.*

'I must confess there were times when I wondered if we would arrive safely.' Beside her Downey sighed, resting his arms on the rail. 'But here we are.'

Phoebe said nothing. She didn't dare open her mouth, afraid that instead of making a polite response some other sound might emerge: a desperate cry, a wordless plea. She had not looked for – had not intended – had fought so hard, and lost. And now she would lose again. She caught the soft inner flesh of her lower lip between her teeth and bit down hard, finding in the sharp pain a brief respite from agony she wasn't sure she could bear.

'My dear, are you all right?'

Darting a helpless sidelong glance, Phoebe saw the concern furrowing his round pink face soften to sympathy.

He clicked his tongue. 'A foolish question,

undeserving of an answer. You have come halfway around the world to begin a new life among strangers. Of course you are feeling nervous. It would be odd indeed if you were not.'

The shrill tones of the bosun's whistle followed by thudding feet made him look round. Phoebe drew a deep shaky breath. Her heart thumped against her ribs. Relieved and grateful for his assumption and his understanding, she pulled herself together. She must not fail now.

'They are making ready the jollyboat to take Mr Burley ashore with the mail,' he observed, raising his voice so she might hear him above the increased activity.

Phoebe looked forward along the deck and saw the huge gaff mainsail being lowered. Up aloft men were bent over the foremast yards gathering up canvas and lashing it in place.

'Time to go below,' he smiled, offering his arm. 'It will soon be our turn to leave the ship. As soon as he can spare them the bosun will send men down to carry up our trunks.'

Phoebe nodded, still not trusting her voice, and let him guide her to the companionway.

In her cabin she removed her hat, wiped her damp forehead with a crumpled square of lace-edged lawn, and sank onto the edge of her bunk alongside her wooden medicine chest.

For the past two months *Providence* had been her home, the link between a past she could never return to and a future she had begun to dread. She had learned so much aboard this ship. But the most unnerving discoveries were those she had made about herself. She was not the person she had believed herself to be. Nor could she simply *unlearn* what she now knew. Yet if such a thing were possible, would she choose it?

If her uncle had placed her in the care of Romulus Downey for the duration of this voyage she would have arrived in Jamaica with her mind broadened and her heart intact, reconciled to the future arranged for her by her uncle and William Quintrell.

Instead, fate had made Jowan Crossley her guardian. When for the first time at the bottom of the companionway stairs she had met his gaze directly the shock had been profound. Everything she had known and trusted and believed in had shifted, and the world – apparently unmoved – was no longer the same. In that instant she had recognized that what had happened was irrevocable.

Why had life played such a cruel trick? Throwing them together just long enough for her to recognize the qualities that set him apart from other men. Just long enough to realize that what she had tried to convince herself was merely admiration and respect was in fact something far deeper, and far more damaging to her future peace of mind.

The conflict between desire and duty was tearing her apart. And yet there was no choice. Jowan Crossley had befriended her, treated her kindly, and shown genuine respect for her skills. He had fulfilled the obligation thrust upon him as her guardian. But his recent coolness as the end of the voyage approached made very clear the limit of his interest.

Had she, in spite of all her efforts, inadvertently betrayed herself? Was his reserve a warning? Had he deliberately created this distance to spare her humiliation and himself embarrassment?

Heat blossomed beneath her ribs, climbed her throat and flooded her face. She pressed cold palms to her burning cheeks. Her anguish was punishment for breaking her vow. Had she not sworn never to risk her heart again? She had adored Aunt Sarah. Yet that love paled beside her feelings for Jowan Crossley. And the pain was all the more acute for being self-inflicted.

Once Jowan had handed her over to Rupert Quintrell he would return to the ship and she would travel to the plantation. She would never see him again. There would be no more arguments, no more discussions, no more teasing. Never again would she watch his frowning concern soften to surprise and relief as one of her remedies took effect. Never again would she experience the privilege and terror of assisting him, awed by his deftness and skill as he set shattered limbs and repaired torn flesh and muscle.

But she would remember. And she would not taint their parting with embarrassing tears. Pride was all she had left: pride and memories. But these were so vivid, so powerful, they must be put away until the wounds had begun to heal and the scars would not break open again. Her pride was strong, but not strong enough. To get through the coming days with any semblance of serenity she would need help.

Her fingers were shaking as she opened the wooden case and surveyed its depleted contents.

She took out a small brown bottle. Thank God she had waited. Removing the stopper she gulped down a mouthful, shuddering violently at the bitter taste. Breathing deeply to combat nausea she sat perfectly still, waiting.

Beyond the tiny cabin doors opened and slammed. She heard voices, thuds, grunts and scraping sounds as trunks were hauled out into the mess.

The powerful tincture began to work its miracle, warming away the painful tension in her stomach, soothing and loosening over-stretched nerves, blunting the jagged edges of grief and apprehension. She replaced both stopper and bottle. As she closed the case there was a rap on her door. Releasing a slow deliberate breath, she rose and opened it.

A crewman she had treated for splinter wounds raised scarred knuckles to his forehead. 'Come for your trunk, miss.'

'Thank you.' Phoebe stepped out into the mess to leave room for him.

'M-Miss D-Dymond, I w-was hoping to s-see you.'

'Mr Clewes.' Phoebe nodded politely as he came round the table.

'I j-just w-wanted to s-say th-that I c-count it a p-privilege to h-have known you. And – and I w-wish you very h-happy.'

'Thank you, Mr Clewes.' Wrapped in the sedative's effects, calm and untouchable, Phoebe inclined her head.

'Want me to take yer wooden case as well, miss?' The crewman enquired behind her.

Phoebe turned. 'No, thank you. I'll bring that.' As Clewes stuttered his farewells to Downey, both were ushered towards the companionway by the burdened crew. Phoebe crossed to the pantry and tapped on the open door. 'Goodbye, Mossop. Thank you for everything.'

Abandoning his ledger, the steward rose from his stool. 'Off, are you, miss? Dear life, 'tisn't you should be thanking me. I don't know where we'd 'ave been without you and that's God's own truth. You'll be missed something awful. And not just by me and Grigg neither.'

For an instant hope flared, bright as a spark from a beacon on a dark night. It faded and died as the steward continued.

'I tell you straight, miss, there isn't a man in the fo'c'sle won't be sad to see you go. Half of 'em wouldn't be alive now if it wasn't for you. Nothing against the surgeon, God bless'n. But he didn't have nothing like your herby stuff. Worked bleddy miracles that did, miss, begging your pardon.'

'Thank you, Mossop.' Phoebe was aware of her mouth smiling. Her vision was clear, her eyes perfectly dry. Like an ebbing tide the anguish of imminent separation and anxiety about what was to come had receded to lap softly at the further-most edges of her mind.

Leaving the steward to his lists she returned to the mess and picked up her medicine chest by the handle on the lid. As she headed for the passage and the companionway Matcham's door opened. Automatically she quickened her steps.

'Miss Dymond?' His voice was low-pitched, urgent.

267

Part of her wanted to keep moving, pretend she hadn't heard. But the voyage was over. Their paths would not cross again. It was possible he wished to apologize. She turned. 'Mr Matcham?'

He leaned towards her, his expression intense. 'You don't like me, Miss Dymond. Perhaps I have given you little cause. But I bear you no ill will. And others won't tell you so I must. Don't do it. Escape while you can. You don't know–' His gaze flickered sideways. Straightening, he took a quick step away from her. After momentary shock his features hardened into a cynical mask. 'Ah. I should have guessed.' He swept an exaggerated bow. 'Your pardon, Miss Dymond.'

Bewildered, she watched him retreat into his cabin and pull the door shut.

'Are you ready?'

She whirled round, clutching at the table as the world rocked. 'You startled– I didn't hear–'

'I'm sorry.' Jowan was brusque. 'It was not intentional. Are you ready?'

Moistening dry lips she nodded and started towards the companionway. The sedative had muffled her confusion and unhappiness, but the merchant's warning pricked like a thorn. *Escape.* From what? Matcham had spent much of the voyage drunk. And on the rare occasions he was coherent it had been obvious he was fighting demons of his own for which he blamed the Quintrells.

Yet just now he had sounded sober enough. But what had provoked his final remark, and the sudden change in his expression and manner? What had he meant? She slowed.

Jowan cupped her elbow, keeping her moving. The warm pressure of his palm made her melt inside. Acutely aware of him, of his physical proximity, she felt her face grow hot and dreaded its betrayal.

He cleared his throat. 'Take no notice.' He was curt. 'Matcham is not himself.'

Grateful for the dimness in the passage Phoebe kept walking. Not daring to look round she was unable to see his face.

'He's deeply unhappy,' she said, recognizing the fact for the first time. The sound torn from Jowan's throat was so quickly stifled Phoebe did not know if it was laugh or groan. Nor could she ask.

Heat and bright sunshine spilled down the brass stairs. She hesitated, but the pressure on her elbow increased and she was forced to climb.

Sitting straight-backed in the stern of the launch with Jowan Crossley beside her, Phoebe gazed past the crewmen bending to their oars, past Matcham, Clewes and Downey in the bow.

Her throat ached. She tried to swallow the hard lump that made breathing so difficult, moving hands clasped tightly in her lap so that the nails of one dug unseen into the palm of the other. Determined that no one, especially Jowan, should detect her brief loss of control she turned her head and gazed blindly at tear-blurred ships that shimmered in the brilliant sunlight.

Suddenly her mind was filled with a vivid image of Lizzie Gendall in the kitchen of her cottage in Flushing. Phoebe could hear Lizzie's voice as clearly as if she were sitting alongside. *It won't be like you think, girl. But you'll come to no harm.* Please God, let her be right.

Phoebe put her hand into the rough calloused paw. As she stepped onto the wooden jetty she swayed and would have fallen had the crewman's fingers not instantly tightened.

'All right, miss? I 'spect it feel a bit strange being on dry land again. But you'll soon get used to it.'

With a nod and a brave attempt at a smile she withdrew her hand and took a few steps forward. It wasn't just the sensation of having solid ground under her feet again. After weeks during which the ship had been so much a part of the boundless vistas of sea and sky, a small self-contained world within an infinitely larger one, the impact of so many people, such bright colours, the noise and squalor was overwhelming.

People shouted in a variety of languages and dialects, trying to make themselves heard above creaking wheels, jingling harness, clopping hoofs and squealing dolly winches hauling cargo out of holds.

Catching her arm, Jowan drew her out of the way as a file of black sweating men with satin-shiny skin grunted past. Some were pushing loaded barrows. Others, bowed under the weight of sacks, breathed in gasps, their faces contorted with strain. Their torn shirts and ragged knee-length trousers revealed limbs criss-crossed with scars. None wore shoes and Phoebe was surprised how pale the soles of their dusty feet were. All headed towards the warehouses at the rear of the wharves.

The humid air was already thick with the smell of sewage, rotting fruit, fried fish and burnt sugar. The hot feral stink of the sweating men caught the back of her throat. Despite the comforting blanket of the sedative she felt a flutter of fear. Instinctively she gripped Jowan's sleeve.

'Don't—' *leave me.* She caught herself just in time, and coughed to disguise the tremor in her voice. 'Don't worry,' she amended quickly. 'I'm – it's all just a bit new and strange.' She attempted a wry shrug.

'Come. This is not a place to linger.' Brusque and unsmiling, carrying her medicine chest in one hand, Jowan crooked his elbow. 'Please take my arm, Miss Dymond.'

Longing to, she resisted. 'It was only a moment's unsteadiness.' She was no weak wilting female and she would not have him remember her so. 'Really, I'm fine now.'

'I'm glad of it. But among such a jostling crowd we might easily become separated. This is not Falmouth, Miss Dymond,' he warned before she could speak. 'You are a stranger here and at greater risk of harm.'

Colouring, for he was right, she bit her lip and linked her arm through his. *Miss Dymond. So formal. Yet on the ship he had called her Phoebe.* But this had usually occurred during an emergency when convention bowed to speed and efficiency. He probably hadn't even been aware of doing it.

But all that was over. He would take her to the address given her by William Quintrell. Then he would leave. And she would never see him again.

Chapter Seventeen

Jowan guided Phoebe across the large open space that separated the upper town with its more opulent buildings from the lower part where houses and shops close to the waterfront were smaller and shabbier.

Open carriages drawn by pairs of gleaming horses criss-crossed the square. Smartly dressed and obviously wealthy, the occupants were attended by black servants wearing liveries of green, blue, purple or crimson decorated with gold.

Jowan glanced round to ensure that the boy he'd hired to bring Phoebe's trunk aboard his barrow was following close behind then steered Phoebe into a busy street lined with town houses. Built of brick and timber each had a pillared porch and steps leading up to the front door.

There was as much bustle and noise here as there had been down on the waterfront. And though this was clearly a well-to-do part of town many of the people were travel-stained and visibly weary. Several carried travel bags or small bundles. Some moved purposefully and appeared to know where they were going. Others seemed bewildered. More than a few men were drunk.

The prevailing atmosphere was tense. Jowan had experienced something similar while training in London when the wounded returning from battle had poured into already crowded wards.

Impossible demands on limited facilities had created conditions that were dangerously volatile. It looked as if the same thing was happening here.

At the next house, a group of people were being turned away from the front door. Retreating with obvious reluctance they almost collided with the two servants who stood at the edge of the steps guarding bundles made from knotted blankets, apparently the only luggage. The middle-aged man and his son gesticulated as they pleaded in a mixture of French and broken English with someone inside. The man's wife, her face ugly with grief and exhaustion clung to her two weeping daughters.

Feeling Phoebe hesitate, Jowan gently pushed her forward. 'No, don't stop.'

'But surely–'

Forcing her on up the steps he brought his head close to hers. 'What comfort can you offer? Do you think they will welcome or appreciate sympathy when what they obviously need is somewhere to stay?' He felt a pang of guilt as her cheeks flamed. But surely she saw he was right?

He tugged the bell pull, conscious of the father's bitter gaze. Perhaps the family had tried here earlier. He rapped hard with the knocker.

The door opened to reveal a short, grizzle-haired Negro wearing a black coat and breeches, white stockings and black shoes.

'You wastin yo' time. Mizz Stirling ain't got no room.' He started to close the door again but Jowan's arm shot out.

'This is Miss Dymond. Mrs Stirling is expecting her.'

The butler frowned. 'She never said nothin' to me.'

'Perhaps you will fetch her?' Jowan hung onto his temper. 'Miss Dymond has just arrived on the packet from England. She has a letter directing her to this address. She is to meet her–' *He couldn't make himself say the word. God, what a fool he was. As if not articulating it would change anything.* 'To meet Mr Rupert Quintrell.'

The butler stepped back smartly. 'Here, you c'mon in quick.'

As Phoebe entered, Jowan turned to drop some coins into the barrow-boy's grubby hand. The beaming grin told him he had over-tipped. But the lad willingly helped him carry the trunk and Phoebe's medicine chest up the steps and over the threshold.

Jowan straightened. Glancing across at Phoebe he saw she had removed her hat and was holding it in front of her like a shield. It was trembling. *How could he leave her here?*

'People banging on the door day and night,' the butler grumbled as he closed the door. 'Mizz Stirling got a kind heart. But this old house is just 'bout ready to burst. What Mastuh would say if he was alive–' He shook his head. 'You wait while I go and – ah, she coming.'

Emerging from the back of the house a woman hurried towards them. In her forties she was still handsome, and her elaborate hairstyle and high-waisted gown were modish if not quite the height of London fashion. As she bore down on them it occurred to Jowan that the only visible difference

274

between her and many prominent Falmouth matrons was her complexion, for her skin was the colour of toffee.

'Julius, I thought I made it clear–'

'You did. And I ain't forgot. But these folks is from England. Mr William sent young missy with a letter. She come here for Mr Rupert.'

Jowan detected an odd inflection in the butler's announcement but dismissed it as simply the old man's way of speaking. The omission of any surname signalled that the Quintrells were well known in this house.

'Ah.' The woman's mouth widened in a bright smile as her gaze darted between them. 'You're very welcome. I'm Rose Stirling.'

'My name is Crossley,' Jowan made a brief bow. 'I'm physician and surgeon aboard the packet ship *Providence*. May I present my ward, Miss Phoebe Dymond?' Sensing Phoebe's quick glance before she shook Rose Stirling's proffered hand, Jowan kept his gaze on their hostess. No doubt Phoebe was incensed by his mode of introduction and would take him to task as soon as an opportunity arose. But right now, though he couldn't have said why and suspected he was being ridiculous, he was acutely conscious of her vulnerability. It would do no harm to make the point that she was not without friends or protection.

But for how long? And who would watch out for her after the ship sailed? He steeled himself. That was not his concern. Delivering her into Rupert Quintrell's care would bring his duty to an end. But that hadn't yet happened. And until it did, even should this occur within the hour, her

275

welfare was his responsibility.

Rose brought her palms together over a voluptuous bosom. 'Well, you're here at last. William – Mr Quintrell, that is – did write and tell me to expect someone. But that was before Christmas. You must forgive me. What with all that's happening I've been so busy I'm afraid it slipped my mind.'

Tension tightened Jowan's forehead as his mind raced. Phoebe had been introduced to William Quintrell when her uncle invited him to dinner. That dinner had taken place two months ago in April. So how could he have written before Christmas to book a room for her when they hadn't even met? The answer – shocking, yet obvious – appalled him. It hadn't been specifically for Phoebe. Quintrell had determined to find a wife for his son. It was sheer chance that had thrown Phoebe into his path. Did she know this? *What difference did it make?* He wrenched his thoughts away before horror and dismay could betray him.

'Invasion,' Rose was saying. 'There's no other word for it.' She sighed, shaking her head. 'The town is full to overflowing. There's not a room to be had anywhere. Yet they still keep coming.' She shrugged, half-apologetic, half-defiant. 'It's terrible. The stories I've heard. People forced off their land and out of their homes. Fleeing for their lives with little more than the clothes they were wearing. And they're the lucky ones. At least they got away. The others–' She shuddered.

'Mrs Stirling–' Jowan began, but Rose simply carried on, anxious to explain. 'Anyway, you do see my problem, don't you?' She spread her

276

hands, the bright smile flashing once more. 'I didn't know when you'd be coming. You might not have come at all. And there was one of my best rooms standing empty. Well, it wasn't right. Not with so many in need. I've even given up my drawing room to a family of four. Mind you, that's only temporary. They're just waiting for a ship–'

'Mrs Stirling,' Jowan interrupted, his tone edged. 'Presumably Mr Quintrell had good reasons for arranging that Miss Dymond should stay here?'

'Well, of course, he did. He knows–'

'Are you now saying you don't have a room for her?'

'Good heavens, no.' Her high-pitched laugh sounded strained. 'Of course there's a room for her. It's just not the one–'

'Why don't you show us?'

Her brief shrug conveyed both resignation and defiance. 'This way,' she called over her shoulder, and started up the wide staircase.

As they climbed, Jowan could hear muffled voices from rooms below and above them. Catching Phoebe's eye he raised his brows. He hoped the silent exchange might reassure her and perhaps ease the quivering tension he could feel as he cupped her elbow. But she did not respond. Her blank-faced pallor as she stared ahead pierced him like a blade.

At the far end of the wide landing Rose opened a door. She stood back, indicating the short flight of steep wooden stairs. 'It's not exactly spacious. But you won't find anywhere else, not in Kingston. I could have let it a dozen times over.

And got far more than William Quintrell paid me.'

So why didn't you? Jowan wondered. As he followed Phoebe up the narrow stairs he guessed it was profit not altruism that had motivated Rose Stirling to open her house to refugees. Given the desperate shortage of accommodation, had she returned William Quintrell's deposit to his son she would have been absolved from the agreement and could have let the room. The fact that she had not done so, and that Phoebe had somewhere to stay, should have filled Jowan with relief. Instead it increased his unease.

At the top of the stairs he stepped into a circular space about eight feet across. The floor was dusty, the only item of furniture a narrow wooden bedstead. The rear half of the room was planked from floor to conical roof. At the front the planks reached hip height. But above that a semi-circle of windows allowed the afternoon sunshine to stream in.

'I'll send one of the maids up–' Rose began.

'This is impossible!' Jowan snapped. 'I've seen larger closets. This isn't a proper bedroom–'

'It's a watchtower,' Phoebe said quietly over her shoulder, then looked out of the windows once more. 'Several of the houses have them.'

These were the first words she had uttered since entering the house. Crushing a surge of tenderness, he moved to her side. 'What do you suppose they're for?'

Her brief sideways glance acknowledged both his kind intent and the patronizing tone of the question. 'I imagine the houses are owned by

278

merchants who like to know the moment their vessels enter the harbour.'

'Sorry,' he mouthed.

'Exactly so, Miss Dymond,' Rose said, only the top half of her visible as she shrewdly remained on the stairs so as not to overcrowd the cramped space. 'My late husband, God rest his dear soul, had it built. He was up here every morning and evening.'

'No doubt it was ideal for that purpose,' Jowan began, 'but–'

'I like it.' Phoebe turned from the window. Jowan tried to read her expression as she looked around. 'It reminds me of my cabin.' Her mouth quivered in a fleeting smile. 'Though that had the luxury of a nightstand and a shelf. But this is wonderfully light.' She turned again, gesturing. 'And I have a magnificent view.'

'It's never the same two days together,' Rose said. 'Ships are coming and going all the time. No doubt you'll still be here when the packet sails so you'll be able to watch it leave.'

'Still here?' Jowan said sharply. 'Why?'

'Well, I'll have to send word to Grove Hill to let Mr Rupert know she's arrived,' Rose said.

'He's not in Kingston?' Phoebe blurted.

Rose Stirling's brows arched in amusement. 'Good heavens, no. What would he be doing here? We don't see him much at all now. Mind you, he's not the only one who's become a stranger. None of the resident owners likes leaving his plantation. Not while there's this trouble–'

'The Maroons,' Jowan interrupted. 'We heard.'

'Yes, well, by the time he's arranged for some-

279

one to come and collect Miss Dymond–'

'Surely–' Jowan fought rising anger. Rupert Quintrell's absence was not Rose Stirling's fault. 'Surely, given the importance of the occasion, he'll come himself?'

Rose hesitated then flashed her bright smile again. 'Yes, you're right. Of course he will.'

Jowan could see she didn't believe it. He glanced at Phoebe who was looking out of the window and saw her shoulders drop slightly. Was she very disappointed? Of course she was. She would surely have expected the man she was to marry to be here to meet her. Why wasn't he?

Fragments of what Downey had told him about the planter's way of life and behaviour whirled through Jowan's mind. He didn't know what to feel. Brief fierce joy at the realization he had a few days longer with her was eclipsed by anxiety over how soon repairs to the ship would be completed. He must see Burley as soon as possible. He had to find out how long the work would take. He would also need to rearrange his shipboard duties to allow time ashore. While on the one hand the prospect of spending part of every day with her was an unexpected pleasure, on the other it would prolong and intensify the agony of their eventual parting. He only just had time to control his expression as Phoebe turned.

'Well, if I am to remain here for – for a while I think I should use the time to replenish my stock of herbs. Mrs Stirling, perhaps you can tell me where–?'

She was interrupted by a wild cry that faded to a moan. On the landing below a door slammed and a female voice called, 'Mizz Stirling? Where are you? We got to get a doctor. Mizz Stirling?'

'This really is–' Rose shook her head. 'If I'd known she was so close to her time I would never have–'

'Is there a doctor nearby?' Phoebe asked.

Rose nodded. 'But he won't come. None of them will.'

'Why ever not?'

As Rose's head withdrew, her voice floated back to them, 'The last one I could find to ask was English. He said he was already working eighteen hours a day and had neither the time nor the wish to treat people his country is at war with.'

Phoebe's expression reflected her shock. 'That's terrible.'

Shaking his head, Jowan followed her down.

A middle-aged creole woman in a grubby blue dress came panting up the main staircase, her eyes wide with anxiety.

'There you are. Mizz Stirling, she got to have a doctor. She's wore out and nearly mad with grievin'. She don't got no strength to bear this child.'

'That's enough, Jenny,' Rose scolded. 'Calm down.' As Jowan closed the door to the little tower room, Rose laid her hand on his arm and lowered her voice. 'You're a doctor. I know they'd be willing to pay whatever–'

'I'm sorry. I'd help if I could.' He moved so she was forced to release him. 'But I have no experience in such matters. However...' His gaze met Phoebe's.

'I have,' she said. 'Perhaps you would introduce me, Mrs Stirling?' Without waiting for an answer

281

she turned to the quivering Jenny and smiled. 'Would you bring me the wooden case standing beside my trunk?'

'Yes, miss.' Nodding feverishly, the slave bolted down the stairs once more.

'But you're so – are you sure?' Rose Stirling's expression reflected astonishment and doubt.

'I can vouch for Miss Dymond,' Jowan said. 'I've seen her work. She knows what she's doing.'

Still Rose hesitated. 'If anything was to go wrong...'

'I'd trust her with my life,' Jowan said briskly. 'Besides, unless you intend to leave Jenny to cope on her own, with all the risks that would entail, what choice do you have?' Walking past her he knocked on the door.

It was wrenched open. A dishevelled man in a crumpled shirt, mud-streaked pantaloons and scarred halfboots gazed at them wildly. A livid and swollen gash above one eye contrasted vividly with his pale haggard face, and exhaustion made him look much older than he probably was. His anxiety was evident as he seized Jowan's arm and pulled him inside.

'You are doctor? Please, you help. My wife, she has suffered too much. I fear for the child.' His English was fluent but heavily accented.

'My–' Jowan caught Phoebe's eye, 'my colleague is a midwife.' He returned his gaze to that of the distraught Frenchman. 'Madame will be in excellent hands.'

The man's eyes widened briefly then he frowned. 'She? She is only a girl.'

Recognizing his own initial reaction Jowan felt

a stab of shame, and wondered how many times Phoebe had faced similar doubts and prejudice before being permitted to get on with the job at which she excelled.

'Nevertheless, she possesses skills that I do not.' Taking the man's arm he steered him gently towards the door. 'Sir, this is women's work. Mrs Stirling, will you escort the gentleman downstairs?'

'There's only the kitchen–' Rose began.

'Splendid. I'm sure Mr–?'

'*Vicomte.*' The man drew himself up, inclining his head with bitter irony. 'I am the Vicomte de Saint-Michel-sur-Vienne.' A muscle jumped in his jaw, and his eyes as they met Jowan's were filled with burning anger and self-loathing. 'My family are nobility since 1565, but I-I could not protect my land or save my children.'

'Sir,' Jowan said quietly, 'you have my deepest sympathy. But if even half of what we have heard about the situation on Saint Domingue is true, to have brought your wife and unborn child to safety is a remarkable achievement. Hold fast to that.' He turned to Rose. 'Perhaps you'll take the *vicomte* downstairs and arrange for some tea or coffee? I will be down in a moment.'

As they left, Jenny arrived with Phoebe's case. 'I stays with madame,' she announced defiantly.

Jowan nodded. 'Of course.' He looked across to the *vicomtesse* lying curled on her side on the double bed one fist pressed to her mouth the other gripping Phoebe's. She tensed and started to groan as another contraction took hold.

'Miss Dymond?' Jowan said. 'I must return to

the ship.' She whirled, unable to hide her shock or the brief flash of fear. Steeling himself he continued, 'You do not need me here. And I should inform Mr Burley about ... developments.'

Phoebe nodded jerkily. 'Yes, of course. But–' She bit her lip.

'I'll come back tomorrow.'

Her relief was visible. She had been holding herself stiffly, braced against further trouble. Now he saw that brittle tension dissolve as she released a deep breath. 'Thank you.'

She turned to Jenny. 'Go down and ask Mrs Stirling for one jug of boiling water and one of cold, clean towels and an old clean sheet, also a small teapot, a cup and a spoon so I can make Madame an infusion that will help the contractions.'

As Jenny disappeared again Jowan hesitated. He didn't want to leave but knew he could not – must not – stay. 'May I – some antiseptic lotion? The *vicomte*'s head wound appears to be infected.'

'Of course.' Phoebe's smile softened the taut planes of her face. The transformation was startling, and brought home to him the true scale of her anxiety. He had expected her to be nervous. It would have been strange if she were not, considering she had come ashore expecting to meet for the first time the man to whom she was betrothed. But this was something far deeper. She had hidden it well, but at great cost. She looked desperately tired. Yet suddenly she appeared less apprehensive. Perhaps that was because she had a job to do, something that would keep her fully occupied for several hours at least.

'Please take whatever you need. The bottles are

labelled marigold and golden seal. I think there are two.'

'Found them,' Jowan said. 'I'll borrow a blade if I may.' She nodded, her gaze fixed on the *vicomtesse*. 'Jenny will return both to you as soon as I've finished.' He paused at the door. 'Good night.' There was so much more he yearned to say, and clamped his jaws together to hold it back.

She looked up, her mouth soft and vulnerable as the corners lifted briefly. 'Good night.'

Down in the kitchen, while Jenny shifted impatiently from foot to foot as one of Rose's maids gathered the items Phoebe had requested, Jowan swabbed, lanced, drained, then re-bathed the ugly wound on the *vicomte*'s forehead.

'This will combat the infection and quicken the healing. But you'll be scarred.'

The *vicomte* glanced up, his voice hoarse, tortured. 'You think I care?'

'What happened?' Jowan prompted quietly as he bandaged a soaked gauze pad in place. He recognized the signs. The *vicomte* needed to talk. Not because he wanted sympathy: any offered would be violently rejected. After all, only those who had lived through it could possibly comprehend the horror he and his wife had experienced. But relating something of what had happened would relieve the pressure. For like so many who survived when others – comrades or family – had perished, the *vicomte* was crucified with guilt.

'They burned the house. We got out just in time. They were armed with machetes. The ones they use to cut the cane. My daughter and her nurse were– I shot the one who– Then I found

285

my son.' He swallowed audibly. 'My wife knows they are dead, but that is all. I could not tell her – never will I forget–' He passed a shaking hand across his face. 'I had to leave them. There was no time to bury–' His voice cracked and he shook his head, fighting for control. 'All our house slaves ran away, except for Jenny. And him.' He indicated the stocky, dark-skinned figure with bloodstained rags wrapped round his upper arm who had limped in carrying an armful of wood.

Jowan beckoned to the slave. 'Let me see your arm.'

'It is not necessary.' The *vicomte* was dismissive. 'They are used to such things and take little account of them.'

Jowan caught the flash of hatred in the creole's dark eyes as he placed the wood in the hearth then silently left. Why then, when he could have joined the rebels, had the slave risked his own life helping the family to escape?

'Madam Stirling says you are from a ship?' the *vicomte* said.

Jowan nodded. 'The packet *Providence*. We arrived yesterday.'

'When will you return to England?'

'I'm not sure. The ship needs repairs and will remain here at least a week.'

The *vicomte* nodded. 'That is good, for madame will be stronger. She has family in England. We must go to them. Your captain carries passengers, yes?'

Jowan nodded. 'Yes, but I don't know if the cabins are already booked.'

'You will tell him of our need,' the *vicomte* commanded. 'We cannot return to Saint Domingue, nor can we stay here.'

'Four berths will cost–'

'Four?' The *vicomte* frowned. 'Why four?'

Though the *vicomte*'s imperious manner grated, Jowan remembered what the man had been through and swallowed his irritation. 'Surely you will take Jenny and – I don't know his name – will you not? Your wife will need continued care, and help with the child. And though the ship carries a steward, his duties do not allow him time to be anyone's personal valet.'

The *vicomte*'s mouth tightened as he thought. 'Jenny we will take,' he announced. 'But not the other. He is strong. Someone will buy him.'

Jowan saw that as far as the Frenchman was concerned the slave was simply a piece of property that had served its purpose and would be too costly and inconvenient to keep. Masking his shock at the *vicomte*'s attitude towards the man to whom he owed his freedom if not his life, Jowan turned and picked up a wad of gauze and the bowl of diluted lotion.

'More reason then for me to treat his wound. You would not wish to lose money on the deal.'

Clearly the *vicomte* had no ear for irony. He lifted one shoulder in a shrug both careless and dismissive. 'As you wish. But for him I do not pay.'

Clenching his teeth to hold back words he would only regret, Jowan made a brief bow and strode out into the sunny yard to find the wounded slave.

Chapter Eighteen

'It's coming too quick,' Jenny muttered, her brown shiny face creased with anxiety as she took the full cup from Phoebe.

Phoebe understood her concern. The contractions had been strong and frequent from the start. Yet when all was taken into account... 'It's for the best,' she reassured. 'Madame is already exhausted. The sooner she delivers the better.'

'What you say this is?' Jenny frowned at the steaming brown liquid.

'An infusion of raspberry leaves sweetened with honey.'

'What for you give it to her?' Jenny demanded.

'To strengthen and tone the womb and minimize the risk of bleeding,' Phoebe replied patiently. 'Would you rather I–?'

'No,' Jenny said quickly. 'She *my* lady.' Setting the cup carefully on the table beside the bed she slid an arm under her mistress's shoulders and gently propped her up, crooning and encouraging as she held the cup to pale lips. While the *vicomtesse* sipped, Phoebe continued her preparations.

After Jenny had bathed the perspiration from her mistress's face and neck with lavender water Phoebe asked her to help turn the *vicomtesse* on to her side.

'Oh,' she sighed, as Phoebe began to massage

her back. 'Yes.' She lay quietly for a few moments. Then suddenly she shuddered, her face contorted and she gave a great tearing cry that convulsed her body.

'What you done?' Jenny's hands flew to her face. She rounded on Phoebe. 'You hurt her.'

'The hurt was already there,' Phoebe said, steeling herself against the *vicomtesse*'s dreadful anguish. 'I am setting it free.' She had seen this same reaction among the pregnant wives of fishermen lost at sea; and women who, while carrying a child, had lost another through illness or accident. Aunt Sarah had warned her not to be deceived by the façade of stoic acceptance among such women. They carried on because they had no choice. With too much to do and too many responsibilities they had no time to mourn properly. But while grief remained trapped inside it wreaked havoc, sapping the strength and crippling the spirit.

'She must let the pain out or she may never recover. Nor will she be able to accept the new baby.'

Watching her mistress writhe as she sobbed her children's names over and over, Jenny's mouth trembled. She wrung her hands. 'I never seen – all the time we was on the boat she was so quiet. Oh, miss, she look like she could die from grievin'.'

Phoebe touched the slave's arm. 'She won't die, I promise you.'

After a while the sobs diminished and the contractions increased. Jenny gently wiped her mistress's tear-swollen eyes then helped Phoebe prepare the bed, removing the covers and making a large pad of newspapers wrapped in an old sheet. Then they eased the *vicomtesse* up on the pillows. Phoebe prepared a warm solution of golden seal and marigold.

'What that for?'

Phoebe noticed Jenny's tone had changed from suspicion to curiosity.

'It's an antiseptic. You've heard of childbed fever?' Phoebe asked over her shoulder as she gently pushed up the *vicomtesse*'s nightgown.

Horror rounded Jenny's eyes and her hands flew to her mouth. 'Oh, lord, she ain't–'

'No, no. And this will keep her well.' Phoebe cut in. 'You must bathe her night and morning while she's lying-in.'

'But we ain't got–'

'I'll leave you some.' She turned to the *vicomtesse* who was watching her with pain-dulled eyes. 'Not much longer now, ma'am. Your baby will soon be here.'

'It's a boy, madame! You have a fine healthy son!' There was so much relief in Jenny's voice that Phoebe glanced up as she placed the baby between the *vicomtesse*'s thighs. Totally drained by her final effort, the exhausted woman lay back against the pillows. Her closed eyes were sunk deep in purple sockets. Her face, ash pale, was beaded with perspiration. But the corners of her cracked lips lifted briefly.

'A son,' she murmured hoarsely. 'Thank God.'

'Master will be kinder to madame now he has a son to replace little Pierre,' Jenny whispered to Phoebe.

Tying and cutting the cord, Phoebe handed the baby to Jenny to wash while she delivered the afterbirth.

'Listen to him,' Jenny beamed, as the shivery cries grew stronger. 'Ain't that a fine set of lungs?'

After bathing the *vicomtesse*, helping her into a fresh nightgown and making her comfortable in the remade bed, Phoebe watched Jenny place the baby, now clean and wrapped in soft muslin in his mother's arms.

The *vicomtesse* looked up, holding Phoebe's gaze for a long moment. 'Thank you.' Her voice was a cracked whisper.

Phoebe understood all that could not be spoken. Smiling, she nodded and turned away, suddenly aware of her own tiredness.

There was a knock on the door.

'The *vicomte* sent me to see if there is any news,' Rose murmured when Jenny opened it. 'He's wearing holes in my carpet with his pacing.'

'He has a fine son,' Phoebe said.

'And madame?'

'She's well, but very tired.'

'He'll want to see them,' Rose said.

'Madame?' Phoebe enquired.

'Yes, let him come up.'

'Mrs Stirling,' Phoebe said, as Rose turned to go. 'May I have another cup of hot water?'

'More infusions?' Rose's brows lifted. 'I declare, Miss Dymond, you could set up as an apothecary. What is it this time?'

'Camomile and honey,' Phoebe responded calmly, used to reactions that combined uncertainty, curiosity and a hint of envy. 'It will help

291

the *vicomtesse* relax and sleep.'

While Jenny carried all the debris down to the kitchen, Phoebe received the *vicomte*'s thanks and an apology so stilted it was clearly a rare event.

'I was glad to be of use. Now I'm sure you would prefer to be alone.' Picking up her little wooden case she left the room, closing the door quietly.

Rose was waiting. 'Well, what an afternoon! Thank goodness everything went well. The *vicomte* has his new son. His lady's life will be the better for it. And while you were busy, so was Ellin. Go on.' She ushered Phoebe up the wooden stairs to the tower room, following close behind.

The floor had been swept and washed, and the bed made up with fresh sheets. A nightstand had been carried up and placed next to Phoebe's trunk opposite the bed. On the top stood a large porcelain jug inside a basin with a matching soap dish alongside. Fresh towels were folded over the rail. Phoebe guessed that the small cupboard underneath would contain a chamber pot.

'Thank you.' She forced a smile, feeling drained and flat in spite of her relief that all had gone well.

'You are exhausted,' Rose observed. 'Ellin unpacked your trunk and took your gowns and linen for the laundry slaves to wash. I told her to prepare a bath for you in my room. She's waiting there now.' As Phoebe hesitated, Rose beckoned her towards the stairs. 'Come, just think how refreshed you will feel.'

Phoebe was tempted. 'You are very kind.' Yet she hesitated. Why was Rose Stirling going to so much trouble?

'Not at all.' Rose was brisk. 'Mr Quintrell insisted you were to receive every care and attention. And had he been here to see for himself the care you gave the *vicomtesse*, I'm sure he would be proud and delighted.' She smiled warmly. 'Now, as soon as you have bathed you must eat.'

Hungry though she was, Phoebe recoiled from the prospect of sitting down to dine with strangers. It rekindled too many unpleasant memories of Horace Matcham. 'I don't think–'

'But after such a day,' Rose interjected smoothly, 'I think you would prefer to be quiet this evening. So, if you wish, Ellin can bring a tray to your room.'

Relief and gratitude flooded over Phoebe. 'Oh yes, please.'

Clean and cool, her hair washed and loose about her shoulders, wearing a clean nightgown, a loose wrap and slippers, Phoebe scuttled up to her tower. Ellin had insisted she leave her clothes, which would be returned washed and pressed along with the others.

Grateful to relinquish a task that had been such a struggle aboard the ship Phoebe promised herself never again to take having her laundry done for granted. And smiled wryly, acknowledging that as time passed she almost certainly would.

A few moments later, Ellin arrived with the promised food. After she had gone, Phoebe sat on the bed with the tray on her knees and lifted the cloth to reveal a plate containing spiced chicken, fried plantains, black-eyed peas and rice, and a glass of guava and peach juice.

She ate ravenously, and when she had finished,

took the tray down the steep stairs and put it outside the door to signal that she wanted no more visitors or conversation that evening.

Back in her tower she looked out of the window. It was impossible to pick out one ship among the many crowding the wharfs and jetties. *Jowan. Where was he? What was he doing?* Slamming a mental door on thoughts that shamed her, she watched the sky change colour as the sun went down and was astonished how swiftly darkness fell. Stars appeared, like diamonds scattered across blue-black velvet.

Two months after leaving Falmouth she was in Kingston, Jamaica. Having imagined Rupert would be here to meet her, the fact that he wasn't had been a huge relief. Such a reaction was something to be deeply ashamed of. And indeed she was. But it was not enough to vanquish the hopeless yearning she felt for Jowan Crossley.

Swaying with tiredness, she climbed into bed and curled on her side. Images whirled through her weary brain: the *vicomtesse*'s wrenching grief; Jenny's relief that the child was a boy; Rose Stirling's assertion that the *vicomtesse*'s life would be easier because of it.

What was she to do?

Phoebe woke with a start.

'Good morning, miss.' Ellin held a cup of chocolate in one hand. A freshly ironed dress hung over her other arm.

'Oh, thank you.' Sitting up, Phoebe pushed her hair back and took the cup. 'What time is it?'

'Nearly nine, miss. You were very tired. And no wonder.'

'How is the *vicomtesse?*'

'Jenny says madame and the baby had a peaceful night. The baby is suckling. Madame is quiet, still very tired of course, but calm. You did a fine job, miss. There's hot water in the jug.' Nodding, Ellin took the empty cup. 'You want me to come back and help you with–'

'No, no,' Phoebe said hastily. 'Thank you, I can manage.'

Twenty minutes later, washed, dressed, her hair brushed and twisted into a simple coil, Phoebe descended the two flights of stairs. Looking around, not sure which rooms were occupied or where she should go, she headed towards the back of the house.

Reaching a door, hearing voices, she hesitated, not wanting to interrupt. Then she heard Rose say Rupert's name.

Had he come? Was he here? Phoebe froze, uncertain whether to open the door or retreat to her tower.

'Oh, he's got a way with him, all right. He could charm snakes.'

Phoebe realized that Rose was talking not *to* him, but *about* him. She knew she ought not to stay. It was rude and ill-mannered to eavesdrop on other people's conversations. *But if the conversation concerned the man to whom she was betrothed, surely she had a right to know what was being said?*

'Especially,' Rose continued, 'when he wants something he can't simply take. But he'd better get the ring on her finger before she finds out what he's really like. God alone knows what she'll

295

make of him, or he of her for that matter. I wonder where William found her? She's not at all what I expected.'

'That man always did have the devil's own luck.' Shivering now despite the heat of the summer morning, Phoebe recognized Ellin's voice. 'Anyway, there's no reason she should find out what he gets up to in the fields. And as he ain't been in town these past few months there ain't been no new scandals. But she'd be wise not to keep any young girls in the house. You going to warn her?'

'Me?' Rose gave a harsh laugh. 'Do you think I'm a crazy woman? For ten years I ran William's house, warmed his bed, and double-checked his accounts. I watched Rupert go from bad to worse while his father refused to hear a word against him. Everyone said he was out of control. But William wouldn't have it. Just high spirits, he called it: a young man sowing his wild oats. Then that girl nearly died. Well, even he couldn't ignore that. But by then he was too afraid of Rupert to do anything. So he left the estate, his son, and me' – her tone was bitter – 'and went back to England for his health.'

'You didn't do so bad,' Ellin reminded her. 'He made over this house to you and gave you shares in two trading ships.'

'I earned them. But I wouldn't keep them long if Rupert found out I'd spoken against him. And someone would tell him. He knows too many secrets. No, she'll have to take her chances, same as the rest of us.'

'She's only young,' Ellin began.

'She'll grow up fast,' Rose said. 'Anyway, she's

no fool. She'll soon realize certain things are best ignored.' She paused. 'She's got a kind heart. Jenny's very taken with her and she guards madame like a tigress.'

'A kind heart?' Ellin mocked. 'You think that will tame him? Or stop him fouling his own doorstep?'

'No,' Rose sighed. 'He'll go on doing exactly what he wants, just like he always has. But at least Phoebe Dymond won't fasten a thumbscrew to the hand of any slave girl Rupert's had his way with, then make her do needlework. I hear that's Dora Ballantyne's favourite revenge whenever her husband can't keep his breeches fastened.'

Phoebe pressed one hand to her mouth as her head swam. Normally she was able to deal calmly with situations that caused many of her sex to swoon. But shock at what she had overheard made her stomach heave. Swallowing repeatedly and steadying herself against the wall she backed away.

Desperate to escape before Rose or Ellin came out, before anyone else staying in the house should see her, she stumbled up the main staircase, clinging to the banister, her slippers blessedly silent on the carpet. Reaching the door to her room she was gasping for breath as she fumbled the latch.

Up in her tower she sank onto the side of the bed, hugging herself, her heart hammering against her ribs as Rose and Ellin's conversation replayed in her head.

Rupert and the slaves: Rupert cruel and selfish: Rose Stirling not after all a respectable widow but William Quintrell's ex-mistress.

When she accepted this match she had also accepted, trusted, believed, the picture William Quintrell had drawn for her. Yet knowing what his son was he had looked her in the eye and lied.

Her uncle could not have known. *He couldn't.* William Quintrell must have lied to him as he had lied to her. Even to allow the possibility that – no, she could not afford such thoughts for they would destroy every good and happy memory of her uncle.

Suddenly she recalled Rose's reaction to the birth of a son to the *vicomtesse*, Jenny's claim that her master cared more about getting another son than he did about his wife, and Rose's statement that a man of wealth and position must have an heir. In that moment Phoebe recognized the stark truth.

Her sole reason for being here was to provide the Quintrells, father and son, with an heir for Grove Hill. It was clear to her now that despite his wealth Rupert's behaviour must be too well known throughout the island for him to be acceptable to any family who valued their good name.

She, on the other hand, had been perfect for William Quintrell's purpose. An orphan in the care of her widower uncle, who was very much preoccupied with his forthcoming marriage, she knew little about Jamaica, and nothing about his son except what he chose to tell her.

Unable to keep still, chilled and shaking despite the warm sunshine that filled the little tower, Phoebe leapt up. Arms clasped across her body as if to hold herself together she paced between the window and the short wooden rail that guarded the stairs: three steps one way, three steps the other.

Her first impulse was to tell Jowan. Instantly she knew she must not. *He had been made her guardian against his will.* Though he had been kind and they had developed a professional relationship that exceeded all her hopes, she could not burden him with this. His duty to her uncle would demand that she honour the engagement. If she persuaded him this was impossible, that same sense of honour and duty would compel him to take responsibility for her himself.

She recalled the bitter expression she had glimpsed when she caught him unawares. She shuddered. Such an imposition was impossible. He would resent and despise her. The thought was unbearable.

But what was she to do? How could she marry such a man as Rupert Quintrell? Yet what choice did she have? She was alone: a stranger in a strange country. Back and forward she paced, rubbing her arms.

Possibilities flared like sparks from a burning log. She could return to England on another ship. *Did she have enough money for a ticket?* And if she went back, where could she go? Not to her uncle and his new wife, nor to Cousin Amelia in London. No one would welcome her, and in all fairness why should they?

She could not return to England. But she would not marry Rupert Quintrell. So what was left? She could stay in Kingston.

That was impossible. *Why was it?* Because she had very little money and nowhere to live. *But she had skills.* Hope flowered. Given the desperate shortage of doctors, surely it wouldn't be difficult for her to find work as a midwife? And provided she could pay for her keep perhaps Rose would allow her to remain here? *And face Rupert Quintrell's wrath?* Rose's response to Ellin had made it clear she had no intention of putting her home and income at risk.

Phoebe would have to find somewhere else to stay. *In a town overrun by refugees, where there was not a room to be had?* Pressing icy palms to her cheeks Phoebe fought rising panic. *What was she to do?*

A sharp tap on her wooden door made her start. She heard the latch rattle then Julius shouted up, 'You there, Mizz Dymond? Doctor's come.'

Phoebe moistened dry lips. 'Please tell him I'll be down directly.' As the latch clicked shut at the bottom of the stairs she adjusted the muslin folds over her bosom, picked up her hat and drew a deep breath. She had made her decision. She could not, would not, marry Rupert Quintrell.

However, courtesy demanded she tell him in person. But to wait for news of her arrival to reach him, then for him to come to Kingston – she couldn't. Events aboard the ship coupled with the effort of concealing what she felt for Jowan Crossley had stretched her nerves almost to snapping point. To continue with the charade and at the same time cope with the stress of what she had learned this morning would demand strength she wasn't sure she possessed.

She had to settle the whole unfortunate business as swiftly as possible. There was only one way to do that. Instead of waiting for Rupert to come to her, she must ride out to Grove Hill.

She could not go alone. As her guardian Jowan would never permit it. Though he would be angry at the inconvenience he would nonetheless insist on accompanying her. And there was no one with whom she felt safer.

But because she could not tell him the real reason for her desire to leave at once for Grove Hill, naturally he would assume she was anxious to be with her betrothed. In truth she would have given what little she possessed to be spared a meeting she dreaded.

'Ah, here she is,' Rose looked up, beaming as Phoebe descended the carpeted staircase.

How can she smile at me as if she were my friend? Phoebe widened her mouth, desperately hoping it looked more natural than it felt. 'Good morning, Mrs Stirling.'

'I've just been telling Dr Crossley how delighted the *vicomte* is with his baby son. He has much to thank you for, Miss Dymond, as I'm sure he knows.'

Glancing towards Jowan Phoebe saw his eyes narrow and realized he had been watching her. As the crease between his brows deepened she knew it would be an uphill battle to convince him all was well. *Maybe she'd be wiser not to try.* 'Good morning, Dr Crossley.'

'Do I find you in good health, Miss Dymond?'

The fact that he asked indicated doubt. 'Yes, thank you. Though I think perhaps I'm still a

301

little tired.'

'You need make no excuses for that, Miss Dymond,' Rose said. 'Yesterday afternoon left me as limp as a rag.'

Ignoring her, Jowan turned to Phoebe and cleared his throat. 'I was going to suggest visiting an apothecary, but if you are not feeling up to–'

'No,' Phoebe blurted. 'I mean yes. Yes, I would – I do–' Feeling the flush climb from her throat to her hairline she stopped, then started again. 'Thank you, Dr Crossley. I would like that very much. I do need to replace quite a few of my herbs. But I think perhaps I'd better find out the prices before I–'

'Forgive me,' Jowan broke in. 'I should have mentioned this as soon as I arrived. I have a message from Mr Burley. He presents his compliments and apologies. He had intended you to be reimbursed before you left the ship.'

Bewildered, Phoebe stared at him. 'Reimbursed? For what?'

'Any and all remedies from your supply that were used to treat passengers and crew aboard the packet. Naturally such expenses are the responsibility of the ship's master.'

Relief poured through Phoebe like a warm tide. Though she had been only too happy to help, and to prove how useful herbal treatments were, she had feared she might have to use her own money to buy replacements. Even if William Quintrell's assertion that her skills would be welcome had been the truth – and she no longer knew what to believe where he was concerned – it might still have been weeks before she had time or the facilities to make fresh tinctures and decoctions.

'How very kind of Mr Burley.' Yet even as the words left her lips shadows of suspicion were forming. 'But when did he–?'

'Yesterday,' Jowan was abrupt. 'When I got back to the ship. I – I was able to – we had dinner together. I have the money with me.' Jowan patted his well-cut coat. 'You may buy whatever you need.'

Chapter Nineteen

'I should also tell you,' Jowan continued, 'that the ship will remain here for at least five days while repairs are made. Mr Burley has insisted that during this period I am to continue as your guardian and escort. So until your ... until Mr Quintrell arrives and my obligation is fulfilled I am at your service.'

'Oh, well said, Dr Crossley.' Rose clapped her palms together.

Phoebe was too wretched to care whether Rose's gesture was mocking or sincere. By making his announcement in front of Rose and Ellin, Jowan had indicated that responsibility for her was a duty he took seriously. Yet though he was bound by honour she could tell from his set expression and the timbre of his voice that he wished with all his heart he were not.

Stiffening her resolve and her spine she turned to him. 'Thank you.' She swallowed the sudden dryness in her throat. 'But I don't wish to cause any further inconvenience either to Mrs Stirling, or to you. So I think it would be best if, instead of waiting here, I travel to Grove Hill as soon as can be arranged.'

Shock blanked his expression and his face turned pale. Taking a breath he seemed about to speak but compressed his lips instead. Then he inclined his head, the movement jerky and abrupt.

'As you wish.'

'Why, Miss Dymond, that's an excellent idea.' Rose's smile softened her face and warmed her eyes. And Phoebe realized that this was the first genuine emotion Rose Stirling had shown since their arrival. Even her professed delight at the safe delivery of the *vicomtesse*'s baby had been tinged with irritation at the inconvenience. 'Of course you would rather be on your way, I am sure if I were in your position I would not be able to wait to see my new home.'

Knowing Rose would be glad to see her gone and cared nothing for her safety or happiness, it cost Phoebe a huge effort to smile in response. But it was vital she keep up the pretence that all was well and that her decision was based simply on the desire to be with her betrothed. 'I thought – hoped – you would understand.'

'Indeed I do. Now–'

'You are truly determined on such a course?' Jowan demanded, sounding both shaken and angry.

'I am.' Phoebe knew she must not betray even the smallest doubt.

'Then I must arrange mounts for us both–'

'There is no need.'

'Miss Dymond,' Jowan interrupted sharply. 'I hope you do not intend to tell me there is no need for me to accompany you. You are in my care. The matter is not for discussion. Now as I was saying, I must arrange mounts for us both and for your luggage.'

Phoebe remained silent, biting the inside of her lip as her cheeks burned.

305

'There is an excellent livery stable across the square,' Rose said. 'Mention my name and they will give you a good price. But if you are travelling on horseback, Miss Dymond, it will be impossible to carry a trunk with you. Might I suggest that you pack some essentials into a saddle-bag and leave your trunk to follow next week on the supply cart?'

Phoebe looked up, her relief intense. 'Of course. That's an excellent idea.' What to do about the trunk had been one of many anxieties that had kept her awake until the early hours. To take it would have meant she had to bring it back again. But to announce she was leaving it behind might have aroused curiosity or even suspicion. Now Rose had solved the problem for her.

Suddenly aware of Jowan's frowning scrutiny and Rose's puzzlement, Phoebe realized that because they didn't know the real reason for her relief her response to Rose's suggestion appeared exaggerated. *She must not arouse curiosity.* Swallowing, she spread her hands. 'You will think me very silly but I had been worrying about how to carry it on horseback. Obviously it is not possible. I should be very grateful if I could leave it here – just for a few days,' she added quickly.

Shifting his gaze from Phoebe who sensed his uncertainty, Jowan inclined his head to Rose. 'You are most helpful, madam.'

'It is no trouble. Now, you will need a guide and at least one guard. Ellin will know–'

'I shall take the *vicomte*'s slave,' Jowan announced.

'Matthieu?' Rose's expression betrayed her astonishment.

'That is the name the *vicomte* gave him. But his real name, I learned yesterday, is Quamin.'

'Why take him? He is as much a stranger here as you are,' Rose pointed out.

'That may be so. But I know him to be brave and loyal. Besides, the *vicomte* told me he has served his purpose and will be sold.'

Shocked, Phoebe turned to Jowan. But before she could speak the door opened and Ellin entered.

'Ellin,' Rose said, 'who would you recommend to escort Dr Crossley and Miss Dymond up to Grove Hill? They have decided not to wait for Mr Quintrell to come to town.'

Ellin's glance darted from her mistress to Phoebe and back again. Phoebe wondered if her hesitation was more than just a search for a name. But when Ellin spoke the certainty in her voice was matched by her nod. 'Oscar. He knows that area well.'

'Is he also a slave?' Jowan asked.

Ellin shook her turbaned head. 'No. He's a free man, so he'll expect to be paid. But he's more honest than most and he's reliable. He's got his own gun too.' She looked at Jowan. 'You carry a pistol?'

Jowan stiffened. 'I'm a doctor.'

'You're safe enough here in town. But doctor or no, in the hills you should be armed. You heard about the trouble?'

Jowan nodded, then turned to Phoebe. 'Miss Dymond, are you sure–?'

'Yes,' Phoebe said quietly, but with absolute determination. 'I want to go as soon as possible.'

Phoebe was up before dawn the following morning. Ellin brought hot water, then a breakfast of fruit, bread spread with guava jelly, and a cup of hot fragrant coffee. Though her stomach was tense with nerves Phoebe forced the food down. She would need every ounce of strength during the coming days. The prospect of leaving Kingston and riding into territory where armed guards were a necessity would have been daunting enough without the additional stress of concealing her real reason for the journey.

The sun was up, the air already hot and humid when Jowan arrived. Phoebe met him in the hall. His bow was punctilious, his greeting polite. But he avoided her eyes and her heart plunged at his set expression. Had her decision cost her his respect? *What did it matter? He would sail with the packet and she would never see him again.* She closed her eyes at a stab of pain so sharp it took her breath away.

Julius had carried her medicine chest downstairs. Setting it on the floor he grunted as he straightened up, pressing one hand to his back. 'You sick, miss?' he murmured.

Forcing a smile Phoebe shook her head. 'No, I'm fine. I was just – I'm fine.'

Ellin came to tell them Oscar had arrived. Phoebe followed Jowan through to the kitchen to meet the man they would be relying to lead them swiftly and safely to Grove Hill. Of medium height and heavy-set his dark skin was already beaded with sweat. He had a broad nose, thick lips, and hair as tight and curly as a black lamb cropped close to his skull. His check shirt and canvas trousers were faded but clean and in large scarred hands he held a frayed straw hat. Beneath the red cotton kerchief loosely knotted round his throat Phoebe glimpsed a thin leather cord and wondered at its purpose.

Dispatching him to find a couple of mules, Jowan suggested Phoebe visit the *vicomtesse* and her baby son and check that Jenny remembered her instructions. Meanwhile he would re-dress the wound on Quamin's arm. Fifteen minutes later they met again in the hall.

'All is well?' Jowan inquired.

'Yes,' Phoebe's voice was husky and she swallowed hard to try and shift the lump in her throat. Seeing the *vicomtesse*, still marked by exhaustion but clearly captivated by her new baby, had been a forcible reminder that this was something she would never experience. For she would not marry Rupert. And Jowan, her first love, the only man she wanted, was becoming ever more cold and formal. She clasped her arms across her waist to try and contain misery that was a physical ache.

With a nod Jowan picked up her medicine chest, freshly stocked after their visit to the apothecary, and carried it outside where a boy from the livery stable waited with two horses.

Ellin hurried from the kitchen with a canvas bag that she thrust into Phoebe's hands. 'There's cold chicken, fresh bread, fruit and two bottles of juice.'

'Thank you. Is there enough here for Oscar and Quamin?'

Ellin hesitated. As Phoebe realized that no food had been put aside for the guide and the slave, Ellin said, 'It's in the kitchen,' and bustled away. Returning with another napkin-wrapped package, Ellin thrust it into the bag then frowned at Phoebe. 'You all right?'

Phoebe forced a smile. 'Yes.' She sucked in a deep breath. 'Just a little nervous.'

'That's only to be expected. Listen–' But whatever she had been going to say remained unspoken as Jowan strode back in. 'Are you ready, Miss Dymond?'

Phoebe nodded.

Ellin turned to Jowan. 'You got a pistol?'

He shook his head. 'A Ferguson breech-loading rifle. From the packet's armoury,' he added, glancing at Phoebe. 'At Mr Burley's insistence.'

Ellin's brows shot up. 'You know how to use it?'

'I do now.' His tone was grim.

'Please God you won't need it. But make sure you can reach it fast.'

Phoebe felt her skin tighten. Jowan was a doctor, dedicated to saving life. Yet it was clear that since leaving the previous evening he had spent time learning to use a firearm. Guilt consumed her. This was her doing, her fault. But there was no going back.

She put on her straw hat and tied the ribbons under her chin with shaking fingers. On the doorstep she turned and thanked her hostess. Though Rose's kindness had been rooted in fear and lies, nonetheless Phoebe was grateful for fresh food, clean clothes, two nights' rest between crisp sheets, and the peace and privacy of the little watch-tower.

Jowan had strapped her medicine chest to a pack behind his own saddle. Cupping his hands for her foot, Quamin tossed her up onto her mount behind the leather bags resting on the horse's withers. Phoebe's murmured thanks earned her a startled look then several bows from the slave as he backed away. There was a brief hiatus as Oscar – who had a musket and a machete strapped to his pack, pointed to Quamin who was tying a musket to the roll slung over his mule's back and asked Jowan what he was thinking of allowing a *slave* to carry a weapon.

Phoebe's heart lurched. They hadn't even begun the journey and already there were problems. Jowan drew both men aside. Glaring at Oscar, Quamin spoke quietly but fervently. With a nod Jowan sent him to his mule. After a final word to Oscar, who shrugged, Jowan swung himself into the saddle.

Then with Rose Stirling's farewells following them down the street, they set off, Oscar leading, Quamin bringing up the rear.

The streets were already busy. Dust kicked up by feet and hoofs swirled in the hot humid air. The sky was a clear pale blue, the sun painfully bright. As perspiration broke out on her forehead and upper lip Phoebe pulled the brim of her hat down to shade her eyes from the glare.

Acutely aware of Jowan alongside her, aware also how important it was that she did not inadvertently betray her real feelings about the journey and the inevitable repercussions she pretended great interest in her surroundings. She

311

had been afraid he might try to make conversation. When he didn't she found his continued silence a relief yet unsettling.

Her mind bombarded her with memories: conversations they had shared aboard the packet: the range of subjects they had covered, the arguments, the different things she had learned from him, and her shock and delight at his admission of how much he had learned from her. Her eyes burned and filled and she turned her head away, mourning the loss of an unexpected friendship that had meant more to her than she could ever have dreamed: a friendship that had so swiftly and unexpectedly deepened into love.

Enough. She straightened her back. If these few weeks were all that was possible between them then she would be grateful. Jowan Crossley had treated her with kindness and respect. She knew from experience and observation that few women were as fortunate. And she had her memories. No matter what happened those were hers forever. Nothing could touch them, nor anyone take them away.

They left the town and followed the road northwest, through rough grassland and brackish swamps where clouds of insects hung over stagnant pools heavy with the sweet smell of decay. The sun rose higher turning the sky brassy and intensifying the heat. Phoebe was wearing her lightest long-sleeved gown. Though she was protected from sunburn and insect bites, the primrose muslin dragged uncomfortably against her damp skin.

She ran her tongue over dry lips. As this had

been her idea she could hardly complain of discomfort. But her throat was parched and she was not accustomed to riding for hours without a break.

The road began to climb through low wooded hills. Moving out of the blazing sun and into dappled green shade was a huge relief. Cornish woods always inspired feelings of tranquillity. But here she felt tense, uneasy. She tried to shrug it off. It was the trees. They were unfamiliar. Instead of oak, lime, sycamore and alder there were thick stands of bamboo, different kinds of palms, and huge ferns whose fronds erupted like a fountain from trunks that looked like matted hair.

In their own way the vivid greens were as intense as the sun's glare. She gasped as a sudden shriek brought her heart into her mouth. She jerked on the reins and her mount skittered sideways, colliding with Jowan's which flattened its ears and tossed its head.

'Steady.' Quickly controlling the fractious horse he turned to Phoebe. 'Are you all right?'

She nodded, though her heart was hammering painfully. 'I'm sorry. I didn't mean to – the scream – it startled me.' Even to her own ears she sounded breathless, her voice pitched higher than usual. 'What on earth was it?'

'Parrot,' Oscar pointed.

Looking up, Phoebe glimpsed flashes of scarlet and vivid blue. More screams were followed by a burst of chattering.

'We eat now,' Oscar announced, throwing one leg over his mule's shoulder and sliding to the ground.

313

As Jowan dismounted, Phoebe unhooked her leg from the pommel of her sidesaddle. She was a competent rider but she hadn't sat on a horse for over six months. Her bottom was sore, she ached in places she hadn't known existed and she had no idea how far they still had to travel. Reminding herself yet again that it had been her decision to make this journey, she smiled down at Jowan, determined not to betray her discomfort.

He did not smile back, but extended his hand. 'Allow me to help you.'

For an instant she debated declining, telling him she could manage. But dismissed the thought even as it occurred. How would it prove her self-sufficiency if she twisted an ankle or collapsed in a heap at his feet? *But to take his hand, to feel his touch, his fingers warm on hers – she had no choice.*

'Thank you.' Making sure her gown was clear of the saddle she leaned forward and slid off. But as her feet touched the ground and took her weight her knees buckled. She clutched Jowan's shoulders as his hands gripped her waist.

He made a soft sound deep in his throat. It sounded almost like a groan. She felt his breath warm against her forehead and a hot rush of longing swept through her body like a tide. Her legs were weak and trembling but she willed them to hold her as she snatched her hands away.

'Thank you. I-I haven't ridden for a while, so I'm a little out of practice.' Refusing to meet his gaze, painfully aware of her high colour, she turned away forcing him to let go. 'I'll – I must – will you excuse me? I'll just walk a little.' Now that she was on her feet another discomfort

314

demanded her attention, one she had been trying to ignore.

'Of course.' He stepped back. 'Take your time. But don't go out of earshot.'

She could hear Jowan's voice as he talked to Oscar and Quamin and guessed he was doing it deliberately so she would know where they were and feel safe while she snatched a few moments of privacy. The relief was tremendous.

Within an hour they had eaten and were on their way once more. The road followed the contours of the land, winding around thickly forested hillsides. Phoebe had quickly grown used to the smell of damp earth and rotting vegetation and the occasional sweet breath of jasmine. She stopped noticing tall nests swarming with white ants. Her anxiety increased. When should she tell Jowan she did not intend staying at Grove Hill?

Need she tell him at all? Once he had delivered her to the door he was free to return to Kingston. She could leave later. But what if Rupert refused to provide an escort for her? *What if he tried to keep her there against her will?* Surely he wouldn't? But if he did, who would know? Who would care? She could not believe in anyone any more. *Except Jowan.* But if she told him what she planned he would feel responsible. Though it was certainly not her intention, he might assume she was manipulating him into remaining her protector. She could not do it. The guilt would be unbearable.

It was late afternoon when they came to a wooden bridge on a span of cut stone foundations that indicated the river beneath had once been much wider. Phoebe's head was pounding as they rode into Spanish Town. Like Kingston it was busy. But here uniformed soldiers and militia moved among the throng. The atmosphere of tension was palpable.

Moistening dry lips she leaned towards Jowan. 'Who are all these people?'

'Some are probably refugees from Saint Domingue. Others may well be plantation owners and their staff. According to Mr Burley some estates have been attacked by slaves using the Maroon uprising as opportunity for revenge.'

Oscar led the way to a plaza bordered by elegant houses, some with pillared balconies. In the centre of the square, a lush garden and shrubbery was surrounded by wrought-iron railings. 'That is the governor's residence,' he said, as they passed an imposing red brick building with a two-storey portico.

Phoebe didn't care. Hot, tired, her nerves strained to breaking point, all she wanted was to reach wherever they were staying so she could get off her pony and lie down somewhere cool.

'Are you unwell? Miss Dymond?' The concern in Jowan's tone pierced her shroud of discomfort.

'Just tired.' She forced her mouth into a smile. But his answering frown told her he wasn't convinced.

'It shouldn't be long now.'

Within an hour it had become clear they had no chance of finding rooms for the night. They would have to ride on.

'You no worry,' Oscar told Jowan as Phoebe wondered how much longer she could remain in the saddle. 'I find a place. First I buy food. You

316

give money.'

Jowan handed over several coins and, leaving Quamin holding his mule, Oscar hurried away.

Phoebe wondered if they would ever see him again. Guilt-stricken she glanced at Jowan. 'I'm so sorry. This is all my fault.'

As he turned to her she saw that strain had etched deep grooves across his forehead, between his dark brows and either side of his mouth. 'You are claiming sole responsibility for this island's influx of refugees and civil unrest?'

'No, I didn't mean–'

'Of course you didn't. Forgive me. That was–' He shook his head. 'But apologies are pointless. We are here now and must deal with the situation as best we can.'

He was right. But it was her refusal to wait, her determination to tell Rupert as soon as possible that she could not – would not – marry him, that had put them in this position. And yet – Rose had known the journey would require an overnight stay. Surely she must also have known that Spanish Town would be overrun with refugees? So why hadn't she warned them? *Because she had wanted Phoebe out of her house as soon as possible.*

A short time later Oscar returned, a half-full sack slung over his shoulder. 'Now we go.'

'You've found us somewhere to stay?' Jowan said.

Oscar nodded. 'Not here. All full. But I know a place. We go?'

After the briefest hesitation Jowan gave an abrupt nod. Phoebe wanted to ask if it was far but caught her lip between her teeth instead.

317

They had to go. They had no choice.

Throwing himself onto his mule Oscar clattered off ahead. Jowan urged his mount forward and Phoebe's pony followed.

Soon they had left the town behind. The sun was low, casting beams of gold through the trees, when Oscar turned off the track and onto a narrow overgrown path. Jowan followed, leaving Phoebe no alternative but to do the same. Her doubts were expanding into fear when the trees thinned and opened into a small clearing.

A small wooden shack thatched with palm leaves sagged drunkenly. The doorway was a gaping hole. The door itself – ragged planks held together by a crosspiece – lay a few feet away. Part of the clearing had once been cultivated. But the abandoned vegetable patch had swiftly reverted to a tangle of grass, weeds and creeping vines. The sound of a stream bubbling along a meandering channel cut in the earth increased Phoebe's raging thirst.

Knowing she could not dismount without help she turned, and realized Jowan was watching her. No doubt he was wondering how she would react. Forcing a smile she shrugged. It would soon be dark and riding at night was far too dangerous. They would have to make the best of it.

Swiftly dismounting Jowan tossed his reins to Quamin and came to her side.

Phoebe slid to the ground. His hands steadied her as she flexed aching shoulders and trembling legs. But as soon as she was sure she wouldn't stagger or fall she smiled politely and stepped back. To lean on him now would only make it

318

harder to stand alone when he had gone.

As Quamin unsaddled the horses Phoebe removed her hat and took soap and a towel from her saddle-bag. 'I'll just – I won't go far,' she reassured Jowan, who nodded and turned away, but not before she had glimpsed a spasm of pain tighten his face. Her heart went out to him. He was probably as unused as she was to so many hours in the saddle.

She walked a little way downstream and knelt to cup water in her palms. She drank deeply. It was cold and clear and soothing. After washing her face she pressed wet hands to her throat and the back of her neck, then slipped off her shoes and stockings. The cold water trickled over her feet like silk. Drying herself quickly she tidied her hair as best she could then returned to the clearing. Though still physically weary and aching she was sufficiently refreshed to feel hungry.

Quamin was carrying a huge armful of freshly cut palm fronds into the shack while Oscar knelt on the edge of a grey blanket spread like a rug. From the sack open in front of him he lifted out two roasted chickens and a calabash of cooked mixed vegetables.

Emerging from the shack Quamin bobbed his head respectfully as he passed Phoebe. Untying the reins of the horses and mules, now relieved of their packs, he led them to the lower side of the clearing so they could drink.

Phoebe glanced round the clearing. 'Oscar? Where's my saddle-bag?'

The creole nodded towards the open doorway. 'Doctor put bags inside.'

Both bags? His and hers? Of course. Why not? It was sensible to put them out of the way. A shiver tightened her skin. The hut wasn't very big. Edging round the blanket Phoebe had to bend her head to enter. The first thing she saw was a mattress of leaves covering one half of the floor. Her heart tripped on an extra beat. Surely they weren't all going to sleep in here? But as her mind raced through the alternatives the reality of her situation hit hard.

Back in Kingston, alone in the little watch-tower, it had all seemed perfectly simple. Telling Rupert in person and as quickly as possible that she could not marry him had seemed the only honourable course. Potential risks to her safety or damage to her reputation had not occurred to her. Now she was facing the consequences of that naïvety. She tightened her grip on the towel. They were here at her insistence. Whatever the conditions she had no right to complain.

Hanging her towel on a twig stump sticking out of the wall, she opened her bag and took out a short bottle-green jacket, her teeth chattering as she buttoned it up. She took a deep breath, telling herself she would feel better after something to eat.

As she went outside again she saw Jowan re-appear on the far side of the clearing. Holding a towel in one hand he was straightening his coat with the other. His hair was wet and marked where he had raked it with his fingers.

'Shall we light a fire?' Phoebe suggested. The temperature was dropping with the fading light.

'No fire,' Oscar said, before Jowan could

answer. 'People smell smoke maybe they come. Maybe they want our food.' He continued emptying the sack, taking out mangos, bananas and guavas.

Biting her lip Phoebe shivered again. She jumped as Jowan spoke.

'Miss Dymond, I'd like to change Quamin's dressing before it gets too dark.'

'Yes. Of course.' Relieved to be distracted from anxieties she was finding hard to control Phoebe fetched her medicine chest and set it on the far edge of the blanket. While Jowan removed the old dressing from Quamin's arm she soaked a square of muslin with antiseptic lotion. After passing it to him she smeared healing salve on a fresh pad. Quamin sat quietly his head turned away while Jowan worked.

Oscar watched; frowning as he fingered the talisman suspended on the leather cord around his neck. It was almost an inch long, as pale and smooth as ivory and shaped like an arrowhead.

Phoebe realized it was a tooth that had once belonged to a large predator. Refusing to speculate about what kind of animal, or where it lived, she wrenched her gaze away and passed Jowan a clean bandage.

By the time they had eaten night had fallen and bats swooped silently across the clearing.

Quamin edged closer to Jowan. 'Please, massa, I take chicken bones?'

'Why?' Jowan asked.

Phoebe was curious too. The food had been shared equally between the four of them so it was unlikely the slave was still hungry. 'For Marinette,'

Quamin mumbled.

'Who is Marinette?' Jowan frowned.

'She a devil, live in the forest and hunt at night. We make gift to her, she not hunt us.'

'Tell him yes,' Phoebe whispered.

Jowan's eyes gleamed in the moonlight. 'Surely you don't believe–'

'No, but he does.' She saw him shrug. Then he turned to the slave.

'All right. But stay close to the clearing.'

Replacing the remaining fruit in the sack Oscar tied it to the branch of a tree and went to check the animals.

As Phoebe started to get up Jowan rose swiftly and offered his hand. She took it, her heart beating wildly, and forced herself to let go the instant she was upright. She heard him clear his throat.

'I'll just fetch my blanket if I may. Obviously Oscar and Quamin will sleep out here. And though I have no reason to suppose they would steal the horses I think it best that I do the same.'

Gratitude for his tact and consideration battled with a surge of fear. *If anything happened to him–* 'Wh-where? I mean, you won't go...?'

'I thought – across the doorway?'

'Yes. Yes, that's an excellent idea.' The tremor of relief in her voice echoed the weakness in her legs. 'Please, take some of the palm leaves. Quamin brought in a huge amount. Far more than I need.' *She was babbling.* Though they were not touching his breath feathered against her face and she could feel the warmth of his body. So close, too close. Too far. She felt herself sway, drawn to him like iron to a magnet, or *a moth to flame.*

'Thank you.' His voice was husky. 'If you are sure you can spare them?'

Such formality, such politeness. As she choked down giggles that were making her chest heave Phoebe knew she was on the brink of hysteria. It would not do. She swallowed hard and dug her nails into her palms. 'Yes. Of course I can spare them. Let me help—'

'No!' His abruptness startled her and she flinched back, catching her breath on a gasp. 'No,' he repeated. 'You may cut yourself or tear your gown. I will – it's best if you just...'

Clasping her upper arms she moved to the back of the hut as he scooped up his blanket with the gun still tied to it. Placing both outside he swiftly separated an armful of palm leaves. Phoebe listened to the scrape and rustle as he dragged them out.

Silhouetted against an indigo sky sequinned with stars he paused in the doorway. 'Good night, Miss Dymond. Try to sleep.'

'Good night.' Her throat was so stiff it emerged as a whisper. Fighting tears she told herself were due simply to exhaustion and nerves Phoebe wrapped her blanket around her and lay down facing the doorway. She looked at the darker shadow blocking the threshold and, comforted, allowed her heavy eyelids to close.

Gasping, she jerked bolt upright, the scream still ringing in her ears. Jowan was trying to calm Quamin and Oscar who were shouting. Scrambling to her feet she stumbled to the doorway, her heart thudding painfully against her ribs.

In the moonlight, Quamin, eyes rolling, skin

gleaming with sweat, trembled violently as Jowan reassured him. The slave's obvious terror sent a shaft of fear through Phoebe.

'Is Marinette, is Marinette,' he moaned.

'It's a screech owl,' Jowan told him. 'It can't hurt you.'

Muttering under his breath, Oscar was trying to calm the animals that tugged against their halters, jigging nervously and bumping each other.

As Phoebe hurried forward, Jowan saw her and shook his head. 'No, Phoebe—'

Ignoring him, she touched Quamin's forearm. He jumped as if he'd been stung. His chest was heaving as he panted and though the night air was chilly, sweat trickled in rivulets down his face and neck.

'Quamin, listen,' Phoebe looked into wildly rolling eyes. 'You made an offering to Marinette. You left her a gift. She will not harm you. Yes, you heard her. But she stayed in the forest. You are safe.' She held his gaze, telling him again that he was safe. After a moment his breathing slowed and the trembling eased. Wiping his hands down the sides of his trousers he bowed his head. After a moment he darted a resigned glance at Jowan.

'You whip me now?'

Phoebe pressed her fingers to her mouth.

'No!' Jowan rubbed the back of his neck. 'Everybody go back to sleep.'

As Phoebe turned towards the shack he followed.

'You shouldn't have—'

'It worked, didn't it?' *Why was he so angry?*

'It was dangerous.'

'Quamin wouldn't–'

Her arm was seized and he jerked her round. 'For God's sake, Phoebe. You don't know what he's capable of.'

'You saved his arm. Surely–'

'You think that's enough to secure his loyalty? His trust?'

'If you don't believe that then why did you bring him?'

'Who else was there?' In the moonlight his eyes gleamed as black and hard as obsidian.

Chapter Twenty

Phoebe shifted in the saddle trying to ease the strain in her back. They had set off soon after daybreak. Now the sun was high overhead, the humid heat stifling. Surely it couldn't be much further?

As if he had divined her thoughts Oscar glanced back. 'Grove Hill not far now.'

Though she wasn't looking forward to telling Rupert there would be no wedding, reaching the plantation couldn't come quickly enough. Even the roughest weather aboard *Providence* had not wearied her as much as this long ride.

Rounding a curve in the track Oscar reined in his mule and looked over his shoulder, his expression uneasy.

'What is it?' she asked Jowan, whose shrug indicated he didn't know. Following him forward she heard him enquire, 'What's wrong? Why have you stopped?'

Phoebe looked where Oscar was pointing. Lying on the track were chunks of feathers, some black, some white, surrounded by stones. Carefully placed amongst them were empty eggshells encircled by zig-zag lines scratched in the earth. Small patches of damp slime were all that remained of the raw eggs.

'Oh.' Phoebe gulped. She knew from her discussions with Romulus Downey that these were *obeah* signs. A shiver trickled down her spine like a drop of icy water. She turned to Jowan. 'It's a warning.'

Oscar's head jerked up. 'How you know that, miss?'

Frowning, Jowan waved the question aside. 'A warning? About what?'

'Telling us to go no further.'

Jowan nodded. 'Obviously it's intended for the rebel Maroons or the runaway slaves.'

'What makes you think so?' Phoebe asked, fervently hoping he was right.

'How likely is it that white people would know what such signs mean? In any case they couldn't be meant for us because no one knew we were coming.'

'No, of course not. You're right.' Phoebe nodded as relief coursed through her. What he said made perfect sense. The signs could not possibly apply to them. But just supposing there was an outside chance that they did – she had come too far – in every sense – to turn back now.

Shaking his head, Oscar hauled his restive mule round. 'I no cross that.' He jerked his head indicating the patterns on the track.

'We have an agreement,' Jowan reminded the guide while Quamin moaned softly, terror-filled eyes darting between them. 'You are being paid to take us to Grove Hill. If you refuse to go any further you won't get your money.'

'Money?' Oscar's voice climbed. 'Money no good if you is dead. This is bad place: bad magic. I don't go there. I go home.'

'You can't!' Phoebe cried.

'Yes, miss, I can. I is a free man. You want stop me? You shoot me.' Yanking on the rein he swung his mule round and kicked it into a gallop.

Helpless, Phoebe stared after the disappearing figure.

'Well?' Jowan barked at Quamin. 'Are you going to run away too?'

Trembling violently, sweat streaming in rivulets down his face and neck, the slave shook his head. 'N-no, massa. Me slave. Me run, me dead.'

In the brief silence, Jowan's gaze caught and held Phoebe's. 'Look, are you sure–?'

'Yes,' she didn't wait for him to finish. 'Oscar said it isn't far. We'll go on.' Having embarked on this journey, involving him against his will, she must see it through. But she was careful to guide her pony around the edge of the track so as not to disturb the feathers, shells and stones. Watching Jowan and Quamin do the same she felt relieved. She wasn't sure if she believed in the power of *obeah*. But the people who had made those patterns did. It cost nothing to show respect.

At last they reached the boundary fence with its tall solid wood gates. Quamin jumped down and opened one gate, holding it wide as Phoebe led the way through. Once inside she halted her pony, surveying the estate spread before her across a broad shallow valley. The way it was laid out – with the mill, workshops and other buildings forming a hub at the centre of the cane fields – meant that the slaves had the same distance to walk no matter which field they were working in.

The big house stood on a grassy knoll to her left. A cattle pen flanked the huddle of workshops and sheds. A short distance away two lines of huts with palm-leaf thatch reaching almost to the ground were shaded by coconut trees and thickets of bamboo. They were backed by vegetable plots, chicken runs and pig pens. A stream ran along the lower side.

A large area of cane had already been cut: the bare burned earth fuzzed green with fresh shoots. The rest still stood, dwarfing slaves whose machetes flashed in the sun felling cane stalks twice their height then cutting them into manageable lengths. Women followed, picking up the cut pieces and loading them onto carts drawn by pairs of oxen led by a small boy. These plodded continuously between field and mill yard where the carts were unloaded. More slaves fed the stalks into the vertical rollers geared to a long pole harnessed to a mule that trudged in an endless circle.

A white man in shirtsleeves, breeches and boots, a wide-brimmed hat shading his eyes, rode along the line of field slaves. He stopped his horse to speak to the one on the end. The man straightened. He nodded, gesturing towards the working gang. The rider sat for a moment, then leaning from the saddle he struck the slave across the face with his whip.

Phoebe gasped, her hand flying to her mouth. The other slaves didn't even look up.

'Come,' Jowan murmured, placing his horse between her and the field. Feeling queasy Phoebe urged her pony forward. Was that Rupert? Why had he hit the man? The other slaves had not faltered in their rhythmic slashing of the tall canes. Did that mean they were used to it? That violence was commonplace?

As they rode towards the house it was not only the heat that bore down on her like a weight. What manner of men were Rupert Quintrell and his father? *How much – or how little – had her uncle known about them?*

She had expected – and tried to prepare herself – for life here to be different from anything she had known in Cornwall. Aboard the packet she had made a real effort to understand when Mr Clewes and Mr Matcham talked about the difficulties plantation owners faced trying to control slaves who vastly outnumbered them.

Her own profession demanded strong nerves and a strong stomach. She had grown used to sights that caused others – men as well as women – to faint dead away. But the sudden unprovoked brutality of that blow – a whip against an unarmed man – had shocked and sickened her.

The forest smells of damp earth and decaying vegetation were lost beneath new sharper odours carried towards her on the breeze – wood smoke, burnt sugar, cattle dung, and the acrid stench of sweating bodies.

Viewed from a distance the sweeping roof, verandas and grand entrance of the large two-storey house were impressive. But as they drew closer Phoebe could see peeling paint and rotting woodwork.

Suddenly gooseflesh rose on her arms. Something was wrong here: something more than mere neglect. The house radiated an atmosphere so dark and malevolent that her heart began to

330

race and her nerves tightened. She looked up, expecting to see a flicker of movement or perhaps a face. But though the windows remained as blank as the eyes of a corpse, she couldn't shake off the conviction that they were being watched.

Stony faced, his manner withdrawn, Jowan dismounted at the bottom of wide steps that led up to the front door. As she watched him hand his horse's reins to Quamin then come towards her, Phoebe yearned for one of his brief smiles of encouragement. Though he had no idea of the real reason she was here surely he must realize how nervous she was?

Taking the hand he offered she slid to the ground. As he released her and stepped back she shook out her gown, trying to mask sudden inexplicable dread. Telling herself she was being ridiculous, that her reaction was due partly to the long ride and partly to the prospect of the task ahead, she tried hard to pull herself together. She had no desire to impress, but couldn't help wishing she didn't feel quite so disadvantaged.

Seeing Jowan's gaze flick towards the dilapidated building Phoebe knew he would soon begin to wonder at her reluctance. She must move now, at once. If she didn't her courage would fail. There was something wrong with this house. She didn't want to go inside. But the whole point of the journey had been to do the honourable thing and tell Rupert to his face that she could not accept his proposal. Drawing a deep breath she started forward.

Jowan tugged the rusting bell-pull. After several seconds the huge front door creaked open to reveal an elderly man in grubby livery. His brown face was lined and weary, his eyes red-rimmed.

'Massa's sick,' he said, before Jowan had time to speak. From the darkness behind him came the sound of women arguing, a rising scream quickly muffled, then a slammed door. 'Can't see no visitors.' He started to close the door. Jowan's hand shot out, pushing it wide again.

'What's happening here?'

'That ain't yo' business.'

'On the contrary,' Jowan snapped. 'It's very much my business. If your master is unwell then who is the white man on horseback in the cane field?'

'Mistah Edward, the overseer. He come for crop. Massa send for him when he took sick. Now you–'

'I'm a doctor.' Jowan's announcement clearly startled the old man.

'Abba never sent for no–'

'Hush your mouth, Isaac.'

The old man turned as a figure pushed through the whispering group loitering in the shadows at the back of the hall.

Tall, imposing despite a simple apple-green gown covered by a white apron, her skin was the colour of creamed coffee. A length of matching green muslin was wrapped around her head hiding her hair. She was, Phoebe guessed, no more than twenty-five yet had the manner and presence of a woman twice that age. Like the manservant's her face was ravaged by exhaustion.

'We don't need no doctor. I look after massa.'

'Is that so? And who are you?' Jowan enquired.

His cool tone brought quick colour to the woman's face. But she stood her ground, her chin lifting.

'Me name is Abba. I keep house for massa. You a real doctor?' she demanded.

'I am.'

'What for you come? Nobody send for you.' Her gaze flicked to Phoebe. 'What for you bring her?'

Phoebe stepped forward. 'My name is Dymond. I've come to–'

'Miss Dymond is my ward and therefore under my protection,' Jowan broke in, startling her. What was he doing? But his interruption and the swift glance that accompanied it contained a warning. Instinctively trusting him she quickly changed what she had been going to say.

'Mr William Quintrell was my uncle's guest in Cornwall. It was arranged that I visit Grove Hill,' she said carefully. 'Surely you were told I was coming?'

'Mr *William?* But–' Abba was interrupted by another rising scream. As the sound faded to a moan she turned to Phoebe, her features devoid of expression. 'Go back where you come from, miss. This ain't no place for you.'

'On the contrary, I have a particular reason–'

'You hear what I say? You don't belong here.'

'Right now I do,' Phoebe said quietly. 'I'm a midwife.'

'Phoebe.' Jowan was terse. 'What are you–?'

'Midwife?' Abba repeated above a rustle of whispers from the women watching at the back of the hall.

Phoebe nodded. 'Quamin,' she called to the slave, who was waiting on the steps. 'Will you bring my medicine chest?'

One of the women called out something Phoebe didn't understand. Without looking round, the housekeeper raised a hand and the woman fell silent.

'You got white medicine?' Abba's eyes narrowed.

Phoebe shook her head. 'I use herbs.' This evoked another rustle from the watching women. 'How long has she been in labour?'

'Too long.' Abba said flatly. Her voice dropped. 'Look, it ain't safe here.'

'Isaac said Mr Quintrell is ill. If that is so then Dr Crossley should be taken to him at once.' She wanted to get the whole wretched business over with as quickly as possible. She turned to Jowan. 'Shall I?'

'No,' Abba interrupted sharply, shooting Jowan a look Phoebe didn't understand. 'Miss don't go up there. No good for a lady.'

'But–'

'Try to contain your impatience,' Jowan murmured, making Phoebe wince. *If he only knew.* 'It is unlikely Mr Quintrell will be prepared for visitors. Nor would it be wise for you to be exposed to any risk of infection.'

'What about you?' Phoebe could have bitten off her tongue as she felt hot colour climb her throat. She had not intended nor did she wish to accompany him. When she spoke to Rupert Quintrell it would be in private.

'You may be sure I will take all the necessary

precautions.' The note of reprimand increased the warmth in her cheeks.

'That was what I was trying to suggest,' Phoebe said. 'Shall I leave you some antiseptic lotion?'

'Thank you, but should I need it I'll send for it.' He turned. 'Isaac, take me to your master's room.' He paused beside the housekeeper. 'I'd be obliged if you will provide Quamin with hot water and clean towels. He can bring them to me. Obviously you have other matters to attend.' As the old manservant led Jowan up the curving staircase another scream rang out.

Phoebe turned to the housekeeper. 'If you will allow me I may be able to help.'

'A slave?' Abba's expression reflected incredulity and suspicion.

Phoebe nodded. 'I will help any woman in labour.'

Abba shrugged. 'You the lady. I can't stop you.'

As they crossed the dark and dusty wood floor Phoebe's gaze was drawn to a small table. On it stood a lamp made from a black-painted calabash filled with oil. As they passed Phoebe saw that the burning wick floated above two splinters of bone arranged in a cross.

'Why is it lit at this time of day?'

'Is a charm lamp. To make a wish come true.' Abba's tongue snaked over her lips. But when she spoke her words were cold and clear. 'I burn it for massa.'

Jowan walked past the four-poster and threw open the window to release the foetid stench. Any physician working in a sailor's hospital quickly learned to recognize that smell. Inhaling deeply to cleanse his lungs he turned. It was hard to reconcile the man shifting restlessly beneath a single soiled sheet with the handsome smiling image in the miniature Phoebe had shown them at the beginning of the voyage.

Observing hair that had once gleamed like gold and now lay lank, matted and dark with sweat; closed eyes sunk in deeply shadowed sockets, cheekbones stained with the hectic flush of fever above an untidy beard, he fought down fierce exultation. *Phoebe could not possibly marry him now.*

Treatments involving arsenic, bismuth and mercury sprang to mind. He instantly dismissed them. It was far too late. The swollen arthritic knuckles and the small coppery spots peppering Rupert Quintrell's arms and visible at the open neck of a filthy nightshirt were confirmation that years of wild excess had not only caught up with him but were exacting a terrible price.

Rubbing his face, the stubble rough against his palms, Jowan turned toward the window once more. What in God's name was he going to tell her? That the uncle she loved and respected had agreed to marry her off to a syphilitic libertine? What would that do to her treasured memories?

But he would have to tell her something, and she was too intelligent to be fobbed off with lies. Nor would she thank him for trying to spare her feelings. He had made that mistake once and knew better than to repeat it. In any event, considering her profession and the fact that she had grown up in a port where on certain streets every building was either an inn or a brothel, it was surely inevitable that she would have some knowledge of the results of licentious behaviour. *But this wasn't some anonymous sailor or wharf-rat. This was the man to whom she was betrothed.*

'Who the hell are you?' The rasping whisper held an arrogance that instantly banished any thoughts of pity.

Concealing his warring emotions, Jowan turned. 'My name is Crossley. I'm a physician and surgeon, and the guardian of Miss Phoebe Dymond.'

'Is that so? How nice for you.' Rupert coughed weakly. 'But it still doesn't tell me what you're doing in my house or in my room.'

Reminding himself that this man was no longer a threat Jowan clung grimly to courtesy. 'I'm here because your father made Miss Dymond a proposal of marriage on your behalf which she accepted.'

Rupert's gaze widened. 'Good God.'

'As ship's doctor aboard the packet that brought her to Kingston I was made responsible for her safety and well-being.'

'Against your will?'

Startled by the shrewd question Jowan thought quickly. Had he somehow betrayed the conflict that had been tearing him apart since he first laid eyes on Phoebe Dymond? Rupert Quintrell might be mortally ill but it would be very foolish to underestimate him.

'Yes.'

'Is she such an antidote, then?'

Images of Phoebe: white-faced with fear at the

337

bottom of the companionway, wind-blown and laughing at something Romulus Downey had said, frowning in concentration as she dressed a wound raced through Jowan's mind.

'No.'

Rupert stared at him for a moment. Then his mouth twisted and his shoulders began to shake.

The sick man's expression was so akin to anguish it was a moment before Jowan realized he was laughing. 'Have I said something amusing?'

'It all depends,' Rupert rasped. 'One thing's as clear as the pain in my bones. You've fallen for her. Have you told her?'

'Certainly not.' Jowan couldn't entirely hide his anger and instantly regretted it, instinct telling him that emotion of any kind would be used against him.

'Oh dear. An honourable man,' Rupert mocked, then caught his breath. For an instant the agony that racked his body was vivid on his face. As it loosened its grip he sagged against the stained pillows cursing under his breath as fresh beads of sweat trickled down his temples. He moistened fever-cracked lips with the tip of his tongue.

'Where is she? In Kingston?' His eyes glittered as he frowned. 'No, you wouldn't have left her there by herself. So she must – she's here, isn't she?'

Jowan gave a curt nod.

'Go and fetch her,' Rupert ordered. 'I want to see what my father chose for me.'

Clenching his jaw so hard his teeth ached Jowan shook his head. 'Later perhaps.'

'For Christ's sake–' A paroxysm of coughing seized Rupert and shook him like a terrier shaking a rat.

Pouring water from the carafe on the bedside table into a smeary glass, Jowan masked his revulsion for both the man and the disease that was destroying him and slid his arm beneath Rupert Quintrell's shoulders, startled at the sharpness of the bones. *How long was it since this man had eaten?*

Rupert only managed a couple of sips, then choked. 'Throat – sore – can't...' Weakly shaking his head, he sank down on to the pillows as Jowan removed his arm and opened the door to Quamin's knock.

'Put the water down over there. Take those away,' he pointed to the carafe and glass, 'and tell Abba to give you clean ones.' As Quamin retreated, closing the door quietly, Jowan allowed his gaze to roam as he washed his hands. The room stank. The sheets and pillows were stained and damp. The man in the bed had not been washed, shaved, or fed for several days. Why, when there might be a dozen slaves in the house, had he been left in such desperate straits?

'They're afraid,' Rupert rasped, once again startling Jowan with his perception. 'So they should be. Damnable cowards the lot of them. They want me dead. But none of them has the courage to do anything about it. Not even Abba. And God knows she has reason enough–' He broke off, stiffening as his face twisted. As the agonizing spasm passed, his grimace softened into exhaustion and he gave a harsh croaking laugh. 'I know what they are doing down there. I see them in the shadows, waiting. But I'm still here.' His gaze was far away, his face haunted. 'Can't live, can't die, cursed...'

Jowan cleared his throat. 'Mr Quintrell, under the circumstances '

Rupert turned his head, studying Jowan through half-closed eyelids. 'Circumstances?' he mocked.

'Your condition,' Jowan kept his face expressionless. 'And the uncertainty of–'

'Doctors,' Rupert sneered. 'Always so mealy-mouthed. We both know what's wrong with me. And that I'm too far gone for cure or recovery. What neither of us can be sure of is how long it will take me to die.'

'Exactly,' Jowan said quietly. Predisposed by everything he had heard and by his own impressions to loathe this man, he was astonished to feel a brief flash of admiration. There was something almost heroic about Rupert Quintrell's disdain for slaves who lacked the courage to take advantage of his physical weakness and kill him.

Yet by leaving him lying helpless in his own filth, without food or clean water, they were exacting a slower and far crueller revenge. Doubtless he fully deserved to experience the same degree of suffering he had inflicted on so many others. But if they hoped to break him, or make him beg for mercy, Jowan knew they were doomed to disappointment. Rupert Quintrell would defy them to his last breath.

'So.' Jowan was relieved that his voice emerged in exactly the tone he had aimed for: off-hand, bordering on irritation that the long journey had been such a waste of time and effort. 'Presumably you will release Miss Dymond from the engagement and send her back to Cornwall?'

Rupert's eyes opened wide. Though his gaze was as merciless as a bird of prey his cracked lips curved in a cynical smile. 'Do you really imagine she would go? Oh, Doctor. How little you know of women. The instant she is informed of my condition she will insist that we are married at once.'

His words hit Jowan with the shock of a musket ball or sabre thrust. 'Don't be ridiculous!'

'You doubt me? Then you are even more of a fool than I thought,' Rupert retorted. 'From bride to wealthy widow in what may be a matter of weeks, perhaps days? Few women would turn down such an opportunity.'

Jowan didn't even try to hide his disgust. 'Among your circle perhaps.'

'In any circle. You don't believe me? Then we must have a wager on it.'

'Certainly not!'

'You know you'd lose,' Rupert crowed, eyes bright with malice. 'That's why you won't bet.'

'To hold such a cynical view of women,' Jowan said, 'is in my opinion as sad as it is distasteful.'

Rupert gave a bitter laugh. 'Obviously you've had very little experience of the so-called fair sex if you still hold such foolish notions. Women's affections are bought and sold as easily as sugar or rum. And as cheaply,' he added.

'That would depend on one's choice of company,' Jowan retorted, turning away as the door opened to reveal Quamin.

341

'You think so?' Rupert mocked. 'Wait and see. Now go and fetch her. She is, after all, my affianced bride. I have a right to meet her.'

'Not in that state you don't.' Jowan's stomach knotted with rage and a fear he didn't dare acknowledge as he beckoned Quamin forward.

'Ah. So will you leave me like this?' There wasn't a trace of anxiety in the question. It was both a challenge and a simple request for information. Jowan knew that whatever his reply, Rupert would simply shrug. He didn't care. And that gave him an unbeatable advantage.

'No.' Jowan forced the word through gritted teeth. While he and Phoebe remained in the house he was required by the oath he had sworn as a physician to do everything possible for this man.

Rupert grinned, enjoying his victory. 'Clean me up if it appeals to your sense of propriety. I will not deny I shall feel more comfortable. But I tell you this, had you left me in my squalor it would make no difference to her.'

Every instinct urged Jowan to find Phoebe and take her away right now. But he couldn't. He didn't have the right. Nor would she listen if he tried. She had insisted on coming here. Though she had not known and still did not know the state of Rupert Quintrell's health.

But in a very short time she would have to be told not merely the fact that his illness was terminal, but the nature of it. And being the woman she was she would insist on seeing the man to whom she was betrothed. Her integrity – and her courage – would demand it.

Then what? Undermined by Rupert's cynicism, overwhelmed by anxiety for Phoebe, and fear that Rupert Quintrell would be proved right, though not for the twisted reasons he stated, Jowan remained silent, clinging with grim desperation to his façade of professional detachment.

'Get on with it then,' Rupert taunted. 'Sweeten me up for my bride.'

Chapter Twenty-One

As Phoebe followed Abba through a door that separated the domestic quarters from the rest of the house, the savoury aroma of frying meat and onions made her mouth water. Her growling stomach and hunger pangs reminded her it was hours since she had eaten. She pushed the thought from her mind. She had work to do.

The sounds of heated argument grew louder: the source of the altercation becoming evident as Phoebe paused to glance through the open kitchen door. Several women were busy. One stood at the iron stove stirring and shaking a large skillet, two more were seated at one end of a big wooden table chopping vegetables. Opposite them with floury hands resembling white gloves against her dark skin another slapped and shaped corn bread dough. Two more lingered by the back door, one with an old basket full of vegetable peelings on her hip, the other leaning back to balance the weight of a large pot of water.

Though their complexions varied in colour from ebony to bronze, all wore dresses of the same coarse blue linen. Glimpsing her they fell instantly silent. Phoebe's tentative smile wilted beneath their sullen suspicion and quickly turned backs.

As she moved on, Phoebe heard whispers grow into a hum of murmuring. She couldn't understand their dialect but it was probable they were speculating on who she was and why she had come.

Abba opened a door. As warm foetid air wafted against her face Phoebe heard a moment of breathy low-pitched crooning before it was cut short by a hiss of indrawn breath then a shrill voice began to scold. She was definitely not welcome.

In the gloom from a grimy, cobwebbed window, Phoebe saw a slight figure sprawled between the gnarled knees of an elderly black woman hunched in the corner.

Startled to see the girl's face was even lighter than Abba's, Phoebe's gaze swept past slender limbs to the swollen belly beneath a chemise of fine white lawn the quality of which contrasted with the old woman's garment. Her heart lurched in shock and alarm. 'She's just a child.'

The girl moaned, her legs twitching as another contraction began. The old woman continued berating Abba, waving them both away with a scraggy arm.

'She twelve,' Abba stated, adding with caustic irony, 'old enough.'

Putting her medicine chest on the floor Phoebe crouched to open it. 'What's her name?' She could smell the girl's fear, hear the terror as her breathing quickened with the increasing pain. The moan rose to a hoarse yelping scream.

As she rocked the girl, the old woman screeched in fury, her lined face contorted. She jerked her chin at Phoebe, ignoring all Abba's attempts to explain. Losing patience, the housekeeper began shouting back.

345

The noise was deafening in the small stuffy room. Phoebe's head began to pound. 'Abba, please don't. It's not helping.'

Grabbing the old woman's arm the housekeeper pulled her roughly to her feet, heedless of the girl who tumbled sideways and curled over, drawing up her knees as she keened, sobbing for air.

The wizened old crone struggled and fought but was no match for Abba who spat a warning as she thrust her out through the door.

'Is she a relative?' Phoebe asked.

Abba's face was stony. 'One time she have power. Now is gone. What you do with this girl?'

'I'll do my best.' Phoebe's glance swept over broken furniture piled against one wall. The shelves lining another held old boots, shoes, baskets and other indefinable bundles. A low cupboard stood beneath the window. The girl lay on a makeshift bed of palm fronds covered with old straw mats between the cupboard and the wall. Conditions were far from ideal, but no worse than some of the rural cottages she had attended back in Cornwall.

'I need more light. Oil lamps rather than candles. Two buckets or iron pots, clean rags, soap, towels, scissors or a sharp knife, thread, a jug of hot water, several cups and a small spoon.'

Abba gave a brief nod and started for the door.

'What's her name?' Phoebe repeated.

The housekeeper looked down at the girl. The light was too poor for Phoebe to read her expression. 'She called Chalice.'

Abba brought the items Phoebe had asked for

then left again. Talking softly, hoping that even if Chalice did not understand the words she would be reassured by a soothing voice, Phoebe washed and examined the labouring girl, telling herself that the knots in her stomach were due to hunger rather than anxiety. In the distance she could hear Abba's voice overriding protests from the women in the kitchen.

Minutes ticked by. Each time the door opened as Abba came and went the volume of on-going argument accompanied by the clatter of pots and pans increased then subsided again. Unwilling to help she still kept returning, watching in silence, snapping fiercely at any slaves who dared open the door.

An hour passed, then another.

While she drew on everything she had learned, Phoebe's was a jumble of conflicting thoughts and emotions. Though she hadn't been sure what to expect, she had been shaken by the silent animosity of the kitchen slaves. They did not want her here. Yet had things gone as planned; had she intended to stay; had meeting Jowan Crossley not turned her life upside down, they would have been her responsibility.

Romulus Downey had told her they viewed kindness or compassion as a weakness to be exploited. But surely there had to be a way to obtain their obedience that did not depend on violence or cruelty? It was a task of such enormity she felt both guilt and relief that she didn't have to face it.

She tried different herbal infusions to ease Chalice's pains and speed the process. The half-empty cups had long since grown cold. None had worked. But there were no more screams. Chalice was too exhausted even to moan as the contractions racked her slim body.

Her back and knees aching, Phoebe knew she dared wait no longer. Lathering her hand with soap she felt for the baby's head. Trying to shut out the echo of Abba's voice, *too long, too long*, she reached in, fingers probing, trying to discern features. Another contraction began. Using it, Phoebe hooked the baby's chin. Oh *no*. She must not panic. She might be mistaken. Concentrate. *Gently, gently*. Her shoulder muscles burned and trembled in protest. Her gown clung, hot and clammy. Beads of perspiration slid into her eyes making them sting. She blinked hard.

Then at last: 'It's coming. There, that's the head. Now...' Her voice dried in her throat. She had so hoped she was wrong. But that brief touch had warned her. The tiny face was dusky grape-purple above the silver-blue coils of the umbilical cord wrapped tightly around the baby's neck.

Chalice grunted and the rest of the little body slid out into Phoebe's hands, inert, lifeless. 'A little girl,' she said over her shoulder.

Abba did not move from her position near the door. 'Dead?'

Phoebe nodded. 'I'm sorry.' Though Aunt Sarah had warned her and she had quickly discovered for herself that for every five healthy babies she delivered there would be one stillbirth she still felt a wrenching pang of sadness when it happened.

'Better this way,' Abba said.

Phoebe opened her mouth and closed it again without speaking. Who was she to argue? What did she know of their lives? As she lay the child between Chalice's slim legs she was struck by the contrast between the congested face and the colour of the tiny body. 'How pale the baby's skin is. She could almost be...' She stopped in confusion.

'Chalice got white blood,' Abba said. 'She Massa William's child.'

Because she was bent over the exhausted girl Phoebe was able to hide her shock. *Chalice was William Quintrell's daughter?* But as she sat back on her heels her head swam. She sucked in a deep breath, her hair prickling where it clung to her temples and neck. *Chalice was William Quintrell's child?* She reminded herself she was in Jamaica not Cornwall. Everything from climate and countryside to people's behaviour was totally different. She needed to remember that the conventions governing respectable society back home did not apply here. *Home. Where was that? Where did she belong now?*

Plunging her blood-smeared hands into the bucket of water she washed them thoroughly before drying them on a fresh towel, Aunt Sarah's insistence on cleanliness instinctive to her now.

In this country white people 'owned' black and were allowed by both law and church to treat them cruelly. All she had heard and the little she had seen disturbed her deeply. But to say so would invite derision.

Maybe she was foolish and naïve. As an outsider she could not possibly understand the problems

349

facing the ruling class of plantation owners responsible for producing the sugar, rum and coffee demanded by the rest of the world. Yet even allowing for all that, she knew in her heart that no matter how many people explained, excused or justified, certain things were just plain wrong.

But such thoughts were for another time. Right now, Chalice needed her. Bending over the comatose girl she pressed down on the flaccid belly to stimulate contractions that would deliver the afterbirth. *Twelve years old. An almost-white baby.* Phoebe recalled Mr Matcham describing Rupert Quintrell's house parties and the entertainment arranged for his guests ... young slaves brought in from the fields. But as a mulatto Chalice would have worked in the house, not the fields. *She'd be wise not to keep any young girls in the house.* Ellin's words echoed. Despite the heat and stuffiness, despite the perspiration beading her face and trickling between her breasts Phoebe's mouth was dust dry.

'Abba, the baby's father...'

'You don't ask 'bout him.' Scooping up the little corpse Abba moved away to wrap it in a rag.

'But Chalice is still a child. Whoever is responsible?'

''Course she a child. That why he wanted her.'

Phoebe was appalled. *'What?'*

'You a midwife. You not *know* men think if they go with virgin girl it make them clean again?' Abba's incredulity stung.

Yet Phoebe hadn't known. For who would have told her such a thing? *Sick men? A dead baby so light-skinned she could have passed for white?* A rush

350

of heat flooded through Phoebe followed by icy chills that goose-pimpled her skin. Her stomach clenched with foreboding. *If only she hadn't asked.* But she had. And though she suspected – and dreaded – the answer, it was too late now. She had to know. She moistened her lips.

'Who, Abba? Who is the baby's father?'

Abba looked up. 'Who you think, miss?' She sounded impatient.

'I won't guess. Tell me his name.'

'Massa Rupert.'

'You are sure? Because such an accusation–'

'Ain't no doubt.' Abba stated flatly. 'Massa Rupert father this dead child.'

Phoebe swallowed. 'But – but if Chalice is William's daughter, that makes her Rupert's half-sister. Surely he didn't – I mean, he couldn't have known?'

'He knew,' Abba said. 'I try to keep her away. But one day he see her. He tell me...' Her expression was as cold and flat as her tone. 'He tell me he will have her.'

'I don't understand. Why tell you?'

Abba's chin rose. 'He say I too proud. He want break me like he break his horses.'

'No, I meant why tell *you*? Where was Chalice's mother?'

Abba's brown gaze held Phoebe's. 'You looking at her. Chalice is my child. Born on me by Massa William when I was thirteen.'

'Oh dear God,' Phoebe whispered. Her head whirled and dark spots danced in front of her eyes. She shut them tightly, wishing she could as easily shut out what she had heard and all its

351

dreadful implications. Queasy and faint she swallowed hard.

'I beg him, not Chalice.' Abba continued. 'What for he want her? I still pretty. But he just smile,' she said softly, 'Give her beads and ribbons and lies. She laugh at me. Say she his woman now.'

Trying to shut out the horrific tormenting images that filled her head Phoebe had gradually increased the rhythmic pressure of her massage. But it was having no effect. She glanced up. 'Help me, Abba.'

The housekeeper looked down at her daughter. 'No hope for her.'

'Don't say that–' Phoebe began.

'No, you listen.' Abba grasped her arm, hauling her upright with surprising strength. 'You tried for her. But better she die.'

Chalice's smooth young features contorted in a grimace as her body tensed. Blood gushed, thick and dark, from between her thighs.

Phoebe tried to break free: to reach for rags to staunch the flow, but Abba held her fast.

'Let her be.'

Chalice's breath fluttered out on a soft sigh. Her head sagged, her limbs relaxed and she looked suddenly boneless, like a discarded rag doll. In the silence Phoebe barely registered the sounds beyond the little room.

'Why, Abba?'

The housekeeper drew herself up, dry-eyed and formidable. 'Chalice done got away. She free. And that baby girl be no man's slave.' She gripped Phoebe's shoulder. 'Now you go. Lamp is burning.'

Before Phoebe could ask what she meant, brisk footsteps approached. Phoebe heard Jowan's voice. As Abba released her and turned away he rapped on the door and opened it. Ignoring Abba who was crouching to cover her daughter's body with an old blanket, he frowned at Phoebe. 'How much longer–?'

'It's over,' Phoebe said softly. 'The baby was stillborn and the mother did not survive.' A short simple explanation for a situation infinitely more complex and tragic.

'Ah. A pity. I know you will have done your best. But now you must leave.'

'Doctor is right, miss,' Abba said.

Giving her a brief quelling look Jowan turned back to Phoebe. 'Mr Quintrell has a virulent fever. Quamin is presently upstairs making him comfortable.' His glance flicked to Abba. Phoebe had sensed anger boiling beneath his controlled façade. Now it spilled over. 'Call yourself a housekeeper? You should be ashamed.'

'Dr Crossley–' Phoebe began.

Abba's chin rose. 'You a stranger here, Doctor. Better you take miss and go.'

'Stop it, both of you,' Phoebe blurted, folding her arms across her aching stomach. She longed to leave. But she couldn't. Not until she had done what she came here to do. 'I'm tired, I'm hungry, and as for getting on a horse again...' She shook her head.

Jowan grasped her shoulders. 'Phoebe–'

'Doctor.' Abba moved out of Phoebe's line of vision. 'You take miss down hall. Nice room, plenty chair. She rest awhile. I bring food for her.'

353

Phoebe closed her eyes, bracing herself for an icy response to the housekeeper's impertinence. *He wanted to break me like he break his horses*. Abba had been Rupert's mistress. Rupert had seduced her daughter, his own half-sister, and fathered her child.

Jowan's grip loosened. 'Er, yes. Perhaps that would be for the best.' He sounded almost conciliatory.

Phoebe was so relieved she dismissed the fleeting suspicion as a reflection of her own anxieties. Lord knew she had plenty. But they were not for sharing. And to ask what had prompted his sudden reversal would be like throwing a gift back in his face.

He stood aside. 'After you, Miss Dymond.'

Taking a step forward, Phoebe stopped. 'Oh.' She indicated her medicine chest standing open on the cupboard beneath the window.

'I bring,' Abba said. 'You go.'

'As soon as possible if you please,' Jowan instructed the housekeeper. His palm warm beneath her elbow as he guided her along the hall, a sensation that was both comfort and torture. She had expected life here to be different from Cornwall. But the reality was far beyond anything she could have imagined. She felt naïve and foolish and terribly alone.

'I think this must be–' He leaned past her to open the door. He was so close. She longed to rest her head against his shoulder, to draw on his strength. Terrified he might notice the surge of hot colour in her cheeks she immediately lowered her eyes.

'Ah yes.' He ushered her inside.

A veranda shaded the windows from the sun, and gauze curtains filtered the late afternoon light. Elegant chairs, sofas and side tables were grouped around the spacious high-ceilinged room. Gilt-framed portraits hung on the walls and a Turkey rug covered half the dark-wood floor. But the musty smell hinted at damp and lack of use.

'This house is filthy,' Jowan grated. 'It's obvious that Quintrell's – illness – has been seized on as an excuse for idleness. And the housekeeper must bear responsibility for–'

'No doubt you're right.' Phoebe moved away rubbing her upper arms. 'But there are circumstances – perhaps a little compassion.'

'Compassion?' Jowan's brows lifted.

'The girl who just died.'

'What about her?'

Phoebe's throat closed. *So young to die, and in such a way.* Was Abba right? Was Chalice better off dead than living as a slave breeding more slaves? 'She was Abba's daughter and only twelve years old.'

'*Abba's* daughter? But she looked–' The shock on Jowan's face was followed by another emotion so swiftly masked it was gone before Phoebe could identify it. 'This godforsaken place–' he broke off. 'Forgive me, I...' He stopped again and took a deliberate breath. 'The situation here makes it imperative that you return immediately to Kingston until' – he hesitated – 'until the danger is past.'

Phoebe's thoughts raced. She had never intended, nor did she want to stay. But nor could

355

she leave without fulfilling her obligation. 'I can't just go. Not until... I-I haven't even seen him.'

'It really would not be wise. Mr Quintrell's condition.'

'Yes, so you have said. I understand the risks.'

'No, you don't.' Jowan was grim. 'Or you would not be arguing.'

'It's not that simple,' Phoebe cried. Despite the humid heat she felt shivery. 'While you were upstairs–' She broke off. She would not add to his burdens by confiding what she had learned. Rupert Quintrell's morals – or lack of them – were not Jowan Crossley's concern. She had virtually blackmailed him into escorting her here. He had complied with more grace and kindness than she deserved. And the prospect of a future without him in it...

Swallowing the painful stiffness in her throat she forced a smile. 'It was very good of you to accompany me. I appreciate your kindness more than I can say. Naturally you must return to Kingston as soon as possible. Mr Burley will want you aboard the ship. But I cannot go.'

Not immediately. Unable to keep still she moved about the room, touching an ornament, straightening a china bowl. 'By your own admission Mr Quintrell is desperately ill. Both he and the house have been dreadfully neglected. If I were to go now what is to prevent the slaves once again leaving him alone and untended? I cannot simply abandon him.' *Even if he deserves no better.*

Striding forward Jowan spun her round to face him. His features were taut and she winced as his fingers dug into her flesh. 'You don't understand.'

His expression frightened her but she stood firm. 'No, it's you who don't understand. I have an obligation.'

He shook his head violently. 'You don't. Believe me. In fact, you–' About to say something else he clenched his teeth as if to physically stop the words spilling out. 'Phoebe, listen. You cannot stay here.'

She spun round, the strain beyond bearing. 'Why not?'

His eyes bored into hers. 'Because – because...'

Her heart skipped a beat.

Terrified of betraying herself, terrified she might be wrong, she looked down so her lashes veiled her eyes. She could not breathe, hardly dared to hope. But if he acknowledged what she had glimpsed, if he said what was in his heart, then she could do the same. And that would change everything. For though she must still see Rupert to tell him she could not marry him, and ensure he would be properly cared for, after that she would be free.

Abruptly releasing her he turned away, raking his hair with both hands. 'Because' – his voice was harsh – 'you are not of age, nor yet married.'

The disappointment was crushing. *She had been so sure.* How could she have got it so utterly wrong? Swaying, she reached blindly for the carved back of the sofa. Pride alone kept her upright. She spoke wildly, no longer caring. 'If that is your only objection then it is easily remedied. Send for a clergyman.'

'My only?' A raw laugh ripped from his throat as he paced up and down. 'If you but knew.'

357

'Then tell me,' she hurled the words at his back. 'Is it your duty to my uncle? Is that what is preying on you? If so, be reassured. By bringing me here your obligation is discharged. My actions are no longer your concern, nor my welfare your responsibility. You are free to leave at once.'

'*Free?*' He turned, and the anguish on his face shocked her. 'I wish–' He inhaled deeply. 'Believe me, if there was any way to spare you, but there is not. Phoebe, Rupert Quintrell has syphilis.'

Phoebe felt her legs give way. *Syphilis?* The man to whom she was betrothed had *syphilis?* Her mind flashed back to what Abba had said. *Men think if they go with virgin girl it make them clean again.* She had seen what the disease could do. The uncle of one of Aunt Sarah's clients had turned from neat, cheery shipping clerk into a foul-mouthed man whose sudden inexplicable rages had terrified his family. He had hoarded old newspapers, prowling the town at night to find more, forgetting who or where he was. Grossly fat from morbid eating he had lost control of his bladder and bowels and began having convulsions. During one of these he had fallen and cracked his skull on a brass fender. His death shortly after had been a blessed release, both for him and for his shattered family.

Had William Quintrell been aware of his son's condition? No, she would not believe – surely he could not have known yet still sought a wife for Rupert? *And what of Uncle George?* The possibility that he too might have– Her vision went dark and the room spun. She was vaguely aware of a strong

358

supporting arm, her shoulder pressed against a broad chest, and a great wave of relief as she sank down onto a sofa. She drew deep shaky breaths and the blackness receded.

'Is he...?' She tried again. 'Has he lost his senses?'

Jowan turned from the window. 'No. His mind is still sound – or as sound as it ever was. But I believe him to be in the final stages of the disease.'

'How–' Her voice emerged as a cracked whisper. She cleared her throat and tried again. 'How long?' she couldn't finish the question.

'Will he live?' Jowan shook his head. 'A few weeks at most. But who knows how many others in this house have been infected? You must see you are in danger. And every hour you spend here increases the risk. Look at this place,' he gestured angrily. 'Look at the state of it.'

Phoebe rose and moved away. Only by putting physical distance between them would she be able to do what was necessary. She prayed silently for strength. 'It's filthy,' she agreed. 'Without super-vision it will get worse. So will everything else.'

'That is not–'

'My concern?' Phoebe interrupted. 'I cannot agree. All I know of Rupert Quintrell's character is what I have heard from his father who spoke nothing but praise, Mr Matcham who bore him great ill-will, and Abba whom he taunted with her twelve-year-old daughter. He may indeed be everything that is unpleasant. But my own situ-ation – an orphan with no dowry – hardly recom-mended me. This marriage offered me status, a

359

home, and–'

His face was rigid. 'And that will make you happy?'

Though she had used the past tense to describe her reasons for accepting Rupert's proposal, Jowan's question implied she still intended to accept it. She dared not correct him. If she did he would feel constrained to continue as her guardian, a situation intolerable to them both.

'Happiness cannot be bought,' she said. 'Nor did I expect it.' She tilted her chin, drawing on every ounce of courage. 'I do not tell you this in a bid for sympathy, Doctor Crossley. Indeed I'm sure there are others who find themselves in far worse situations. But as far as my uncle was concerned I had become something of a problem. Mr Quintrell's proposal offered a satisfactory solution. I would not have chosen to marry a stranger. But someone in my position does not have the luxury of choice. Mr Quintrell's offer included a promise that not only would I be permitted to continue my work, I would be encouraged to do so. You cannot understand what–'

Jowan's features were bleak. 'On the contrary, I understand perfectly. You are declining my offer of escort to safety. You prefer instead to marry a man of notorious reputation who is dying from the effects of a lifetime's debauchery.'

'No!' Phoebe tried to stop him. 'That is not it at all – if you will let me explain.'

'Do not trouble.' He was icy. 'You have made yourself abundantly clear. And you will be a widow soon enough. No doubt inheriting the plantation will soften that blow and compensate for all the unpleasant tasks you must face in the meantime. Forgive my impertinence. Clearly my concern was neither necessary nor welcome.'

Phoebe stared at him, stunned by both his bitter hostility and his refusal to let her explain that though she intended breaking her engagement to Rupert Quintrell, she could not walk away and abandon him to slaves who had little reason to be merciful. Grief was a solid leaden lump in her chest. She swallowed painfully.

'If that is how you view my actions then we have nothing more to say to one another – ever.'

Turning her back so he would not see her desperate battle to retain control, she heard the door open. Isaac shuffled in with a tray containing a bowl of savoury stew, two slices of corn bread on a small plate and a glass of mango juice.

'Dis here is calalou, miss. Abba say you eat, then sit a while and rest. Doctor, please you come long a-me.'

Responding to Jowan's formal bow with an equally formal curtsy Phoebe watched him leave, her back straight and her head high. But after the door closed behind Isaac, she sank down onto the nearest chair. She was beyond pain, too shocked even to be angry. No doubt both would come later. She looked at the food then turned away. How could she eat? *But she must, for how else would she remain strong? And if she were to fall ill what use would she be to Rupert or Abba or anyone else?*

The first mouthful rekindled her hunger. Refusing to think she concentrated fiercely on the flavours of beef, chicken, shrimp, tomatoes, onions and greens in their spicy broth. Spooning up the last of the stew she slowly chewed the corn bread crust. Rinsing her mouth with the remaining mango juice she set down the glass. She felt soothed and replete, but suddenly irresistibly sleepy. The intense demands of the past two days had finally caught up.

She stumbled over to the sofa and lay down. She shouldn't really – there was so much to do. And that was good because she wouldn't have time to think. Or to remember the suffering in Jowan's eyes or the bleakness of his expression, or those terrible wounding words he had hurled like daggers. Why had he been so angry? Why had he refused to listen?

She felt herself falling and fought to keep her eyes open. She was so dreadfully tired. Just a few minutes' rest... Then she would... Darkness enveloped her and she sank into oblivion.

Chapter Twenty-Two

She knew she was dreaming yet the sensations were frighteningly real. She was lying down so she must be in bed. But it was jolting and swaying. She could hear creaking and rumbles and complicated drum rhythms that rose and fell in waves. They were faint but insistent and reached inside her touching something in her soul. No, this was wrong. It was Uncle George who had heard them. And he had refused to talk about it. Now she understood why, for they stirred feelings that were strange and unnerving. How was it possible that in the multi-layered sound she could recognize rage against injustice, aching homesickness, and grief for everything lost? *She was dreaming.*

The stifling darkness was thick with the smell of straw, earth, old vegetables, raw sugar, rum, and soap. *Soap?* As it dawned on her that the warmth against her side was another body, the deep boom of an explosion made her heart leap violently and stopped her breath.

She didn't only hear it she felt the vibration through her body. Panic choked her and she struggled desperately to sit up. But something was holding her down. She tried to fight but her arms and legs wouldn't respond. Trapped, helpless, she became aware of a quiet voice – *Jowan's voice* – saying over and over again that she was

363

safe. But she wasn't. If he was here she was in terrible danger because she might betray herself, and he didn't want her. She was screaming but no sound emerged. No one could hear her. No one was listening.

The drumming faded and in its place she heard the simple reassuring rhythm of a heartbeat. Too exhausted to struggle she gave up and drifted away from sounds she didn't understand: and from the discomfort, the fear, and sadness as cold and deep as the Atlantic swell.

No longer an enemy, the darkness absorbed her and she became part of it. She felt warm breath against her face as the quiet voice murmured. She couldn't hear the words but it didn't matter. Nothing mattered any more.

A deafening crack followed by a low rumble jerked her back to consciousness. With a gasp she jerked up, wincing and covering her eyes against the brilliant lightning flash. Thunder cracked and rolled once more. She sagged as relief loosened muscles rigid with terror. It was just a storm. *That other blast had been part of her dream.* She rubbed her forehead. It felt stuffed with cotton and her bones ached.

'Good morning.'

Her eyes flew open and she gasped, bewilderment growing as she looked round. She was in a four-wheeled wagon surrounded by pots, baskets and canvas-wrapped bundles. Isaac was driving. He had exchanged his livery for a ragged shirt but she recognized his grey woolly head. Quamin was beside him with a musket across his knees.

Jowan sat with his back against the tailboard, his booted legs crossed at the ankle inches from her hip. His face was tired and drawn, his expression sombre.

'I thought–' *She hadn't been dreaming. But how much of the nightmare was real.* Her throat was dry, her voice husky. 'Where are we?'

'Approaching Kingston.'

Withdrawing as far as the confined space would allow, Phoebe hugged her knees. *Kingston?* She opened her mouth to ask, but closed it again. Her head hurt. Lightning flashed, instantly followed by deafening thunder so close she felt the vibration. Overhead the treetops disappeared into frayed purple cloud. She flinched as a large raindrop hit her cheek. Another splashed onto her hand and slid between her clenched fingers.

Seizing some roughly folded canvas Jowan shook it out and swung it over his shoulders, holding it forward. 'Come, it's not much, but it may keep off the worst.' Confused by his reserve – so different from yesterday's contempt *and his gentle reassurance in her dream* – Phoebe didn't move. Still groggy, not sure what was real or what was happening, she gazed dully at the straw mats and rumpled grey blanket spread out beneath her.

Realization pierced her like a blade. *This was last night's bed. Here she had slept in Jowan Crossley's arms.* Vivid impressions tumbled through her mind: of terrors soothed, of peace and safety. But these were pushed aside by contrasting images of his bleak bitter expression and devastating accusations before he had walked out, leaving her annihilated.

Embarrassed, mortified and furiously angry, she felt a rush of heat surge from her toes to her scalp. Turning away from him her gaze fell on the baskets, iron pots and calabashes crammed against the sides of the cart.

The calabash lamp: alight when Abba had taken her to Chalice. Later, when Jowan had led her away she had noticed, but her mind had been on other things. She remembered now. The table had been dark, the flame extinguished. Abba had called it a charm lamp. She'd said she was burning it to make a wish come true: a wish for Rupert. Phoebe had assumed she meant for his recovery. But that was before she learned the truth about Chalice's baby.

On the driving seat Isaac and Quamin hunched their shoulders against the downpour.

'Phoebe – Miss Dymond,' he corrected himself, his voice low. 'Please, there is no need for you to get wet.'

He had kidnapped her and now he was offering shelter? *She hadn't wanted to stay.* But he hadn't known that nor had he allowed her to explain. *If he could believe her capable of such reasoning, such actions, as those he'd accused her of, why should he care if she got wet or caught cold?* That was obvious. He still felt responsible for her. *A burden neither of them wanted.* She longed to jump out of the cart, run away from the scene of her humiliation, away from him. But she had no idea which way to go. And she felt horribly weak.

She shook her head. 'The rain isn't cold.' She looked down at primrose muslin now wet as well as creased and grubby, and the green jacket that someone – Abba? *Him?* – had buttoned her into

366

after she had fallen asleep.

Startled, she saw him toss the canvas aside and raise his face to the teeming rain. Within moments his hair was plastered to his scalp.

'You're right,' he said.

The deluge stopped as suddenly as it had started. Rays of sunlight slanted through the trees and a soft pattering filled the steamy air as water dripped from foliage. Darting from the under-growth a huge iridescent dragonfly hovered above a puddle on the rutted track then zig-zagged away through a spiralling cloud of midges.

Pressing fingertips to her temples, Phoebe tried to concentrate. She remembered eating the calalou Isaac had brought into the drawing-room. Afterwards she had felt overwhelmingly tired, and must have fallen asleep. But to have slept for so long, and not woken even when someone – *Jowan?* – had lifted her off the sofa and carried her to this cart.

She stiffened, her head jerking up. 'You drugged me.'

'Actually, it was Abba. While you and I were talking in the drawing-room she added some sedatives from your medicine chest to the food.'

'*Abba?*' Phoebe struggled to accept that the housekeeper would do such a thing entirely on her own initiative. Then realized she hadn't. 'But you knew.' It was a statement not a question. She remembered how Abba had moved round behind her, the sudden alteration in Jowan's voice. Abba must have signalled her intention, *and he had agreed.* But if he had known what was planned, known he intended to take her away from the

367

plantation, then why *why* had he said such terrible things?

'Yes, I knew. And had she not done it, I would have.' His gaze flickered before returning to meet hers directly. 'There was no alternative. You had refused to leave. I could not risk you being harmed.'

Phoebe hugged her knees. She didn't understand. 'Why would anyone want to harm me?'

'Don't be naïve, Phoebe. You're white. As far as the slaves are concerned that alone is sufficient reason.'

'But I've never—'

'I know. You have never ill-treated anyone. And you did your best to help Abba's daughter. That's why she had the cart made ready and sent Isaac with us. She wanted us away from Grove Hill before dark.'

Phoebe recalled her nightmare: so vivid it had seemed real.

She moistened her lips. 'Last night – I dreamed...' She hesitated, not wanting to ask him, needing to know, yet not wanting to hear. 'An explosion.' She knew at once from his expression. 'It was real?' At his brief nod shock tingled down her arms in pins and needles.

What had happened last night? 'Was it – did it come from Grove Hill?'

'Yes.' He was terse.

'The house?'

'I don't know,' he admitted. 'It might have started in the processing works or the distilling shed.'

'Started? You mean–?'

368

'In wooden buildings where rum is made and stored, an explosion would inevitably lead to fire. And with so much fuel available any fire is likely to have spread.'

She bit her lip. They both knew that the house was some distance from the processing plant. So if the house had burned it would not have been an accident.

'Who?' Her throat dried and she had to swallow before she could continue. 'The Maroons?'

He shrugged. 'It's possible.' But she could see he didn't believe it. 'I think it more likely to have been the Grove Hill slaves.'

'But why?' Before he could reply she added quickly, 'I'm not totally ignorant. I'm well aware most slaves endure a wretched existence. But they have put up with it for many years. And Mr Downey told me that though plantation owners live in constant fear of rebellion, the risks are actually quite low, only because Creole slaves born in Jamaica would never join any uprising led by an African-born slave.'

Jowan nodded.

'So something must have happened to–'

'It did. The new overseer was promised a bonus if he could bring the crop in by August. So he's been making the slaves work eighteen to twenty hours a day. That means they haven't had time to tend their vegetable grounds. And those are their main source of food.'

'Were they starving?'

'They were certainly hungry.'

But not actually starving. Phoebe forced herself to think. Blowing up the boiling and cooling

369

houses, the workshops and the still would leave the slaves without work, without a place to live, and facing the death penalty. 'Something else must have happened.' She saw the flash in his eyes and instantly dropped her gaze. *Admiration?* It was more likely to be impatience.

'Several slaves were caught pilfering cane syrup. They distil it to make a rough spirit. Apparently such theft is universal during crop time. Most owners and overseers ignore it because if the slaves are happier they are less likely to cause trouble over the heavier workload. But in this instance the slaves were punished in a way intended to act as a deterrent.'

'What?'

'I think it's better that you don't–'

'Oh please,' Phoebe didn't hide her impatience. She was in turmoil. She felt raw and exposed: angry and betrayed by his connivance with Abba in removing her from Grove Hill, and ashamed of her relief that the decision had been taken out of her hands. But uppermost in her mind was the agonizing realization that she had spent the night in his arms, that she had sought *and found* comfort from the man whose withering contempt and terrible accusations had wounded her beyond bearing.

She could hear her racing heartbeat and relived the shock and excruciating hurt. Her eyes burned but she swallowed the tears. She would die rather than let him see her weep.

'When we were aboard the *Providence* and you needed my assistance you managed to forget my gender. Try to forget it again now and tell me what was done to them.'

His jaw tightened and she saw a tiny muscle jumping at the corner of his mouth. 'As you will. Their right hands were cut off and the stumps sealed with hot pitch to prevent them bleeding to death thus evading the full effect of the punishment.'

Phoebe fought nausea. She had wanted to know. Now she did. 'But surely the overseer would have neither the right nor the authority.'

'You're correct, he didn't. It was the owner's decision.'

Oh dear God. Rupert had sent such an order from his sick-bed? 'When did – when was the punishment carried out?'

'Two days ago. Yesterday afternoon when I left you, Isaac took me to Abba. She warned me that a *calenda* was planned. Do you know what that is?'

'Yes, it's *vaudou* night-dance.'

'I understand from Mr Downey' – his gaze caught hers. 'I too was fortunate enough to enjoy several stimulating and informative conversations with him. I learned things that–' He stopped. 'Well, no matter.' Drawing a breath he continued in a more detached tone. 'He told me that these dances provoke powerful emotions. Coming so soon after being forced to watch the mutilation of their work-mates and taking into account the effect of any cane spirit that had not been confiscated, one slave calling for revenge would have been all that was needed to set off a conflagration.'

Phoebe's imagination conjured the scene in horrifying detail.

371

'We had to leave while it was still possible to do so,' Jowan said. 'Had we remained...' He fell silent. 'Abba reasoned that with most of the slaves taking part in the dance that any rebel slaves or Maroons lurking in the area would also be drawn to it. Those few hours offered the best – the only – chance for us to get away without anyone noticing.'

Phoebe remembered the women working in the kitchen. 'What about the household slaves? If the others – if the house was...' She swallowed.

Jowan shrugged. 'No doubt having stolen what-ever they could carry they would flee to safety in the north-west of the island where there are steep forested hills and ravines. Few whites are brave or foolhardy enough to go there.'

Phoebe moistened her lips. 'And Rupert?'

Jowan's face grew still and cold. 'Dead. And if his end was swift it was more than he deserved. At least he has been spared slow starvation or insanity.'

Shock widened Phoebe's eyes. She would never have expected such words from a man she knew to be a dedicated physician and surgeon. *But nor would she have expected the accusations he'd hurled at her yesterday afternoon.*

Though Rupert's death released her from a commitment she had dreaded, it did not alter the situation between her and Jowan. She would never have his love. He must return to the ship and to Cornwall. For her there was no going back.

As her gaze fell once more on the straw mats and crumpled blanket, she wondered what

Cousin Amelia would say. She could hear her now, complaining to Uncle George. *Phoebe always was difficult and headstrong. I cannot profess surprise that she has ended in such straits. She was never fit for proper society. Such wilful independence was bound to be her downfall. Well, she made her bed, now she must lie in it.*

Burying her head in her arms Phoebe tried to block out her cousin's *I-told-you-so* voice and critical expression.

She had come to Jamaica to start a new life. So that's what she would do. She caught her breath, raising her head with a jerk. 'My medicine chest.'

'It's here.' Jowan pushed aside the crumpled canvas to reveal the wooden box.

'Thank you,' Phoebe murmured. The violent lurch from fear to relief left her weak. Her wooden case embodied far more than the remedies it contained: it signified who she was and her value to the community. The realization that despite the threat of imminent danger, despite his low opinion of her and of her motives, Jowan had remembered to pick it up and put it in the cart deepened her confusion and her pain. She turned away, compressing her lips to stop their betraying quiver.

Isaac glanced back. 'Soon time you get out, massa. Better you and miss not seen in this old cart.'

'Where are we?' Jowan looked around.

'Down there is big square. Slaves coming from all over for Sunday market. I go sell calabash sugar.'

Looking forward Phoebe saw men and women

of every shade heading in the same direction. They came on foot, on mules, in carts and leading heavily laden donkeys. Some walked alone, others in chattering groups. Barefoot men clad in rags plodded wearily, bent beneath the basket of produce on their backs. Giggling girls wearing gaudy dresses hobbled in heeled shoes they weren't used to and waved their arms so that the trinkets they wore glittered in the sunlight.

There were none of the wealthy residents' carriages drawn by gleaming horses that Phoebe had seen on her arrival. The hour was too early.

'What will you do then?' Jowan asked.

'Go back to Grove Hill.'

'But if it's been destroyed,' Jowan began.

Isaac shrugged. 'I live there fifty year. Maybe others stay too.'

Quickly wiping her face with her fingers, from the corner of her eye Phoebe saw Jowan lean forward.

'Miss Dymond?' His voice was quiet, concerned.

'The rain,' she said briefly. 'I'm perfectly well.' She wasn't but that was not his concern. She straightened her jacket and made a vain attempt to brush the creases from her damp gown, acutely conscious of her dishevelment. Occasional drops of water still trickled down her neck. Finding her straw hat she shook off the water and put it on, tucking her wet hair up into the crown.

'Don't worry about Mrs Stirling,' he said grimly, startling her. It was as if he had somehow divined what she was thinking. 'I'll deal with her. Quamin?'

'Massa?' The slave looked over his shoulder.

'You have earned your freedom. I'll have a paper drawn up.'

Quamin's eyes widened in horror. 'What I do?'

'Nothing.' Jowan reassured. 'I'm not angry with you. On the contrary, but for your loyalty and courage.'

'No, massa,' Quamin babbled. 'What I do? This town got too many people, no work for all of them.'

'Well, perhaps you could go back with Isaac?'

Quamin shook his head. 'I stay with you.'

'I appreciate the offer, but you can't. I'll be returning to Cornwall in a few days.'

'I go on ship,' Quamin nodded feverishly. 'I work hard.'

'Perhaps,' Phoebe ventured, 'Mrs Stirling would be able to find Quamin a position? She must know a great many people in Kingston. In the meantime he can earn his keep doing jobs for her and some errands for me.'

'Quamin?' Jowan said.

'No go with you?'

Jowan shook his head.

Quamin nodded. 'Go with miss.'

While Isaac held the mule team Quamin lowered the tailboard. Jumping down Jowan lifted out Phoebe's medicine box and her bag then held out his arms. Avoiding his gaze, Phoebe put her hands in his, pulling free and moving away the instant she was on the ground.

With Jowan at her side carrying the two guns and her bag, and Quamin behind with her wooden chest, Phoebe kept her eyes lowered as

375

they walked along the quiet streets. Each step was an effort. Despite her drugged sleep she was still tired and the night's jolting had made her aching muscles painfully stiff.

Ellin opened the door to Jowan's brisk knock. Her expression didn't alter, but Phoebe saw her eyes widen briefly. 'What you? Mizz Stirling ain't–'

Using the guns to push the door wider, Jowan stood back to allow Phoebe to pass. 'Tell Mrs Stirling I wish to speak to her. Then prepare some breakfast for Miss Dymond. Her room is not let?'

Ellin shook her head. 'No, her trunk still up there.' She frowned as Phoebe removed her hat and her hair tumbled down. 'God sakes, what happened to you, miss?'

Phoebe gestured vaguely. It would take too much effort to explain. She didn't feel well. Beneath the wet clothes that were making her shiver her skin was burning.

On the upstairs landing, a door slammed and Rose Stirling skimmed down the staircase in a full-skirted dress of pink silk, her hair covered by a white mobcap. 'Doctor Crossley, Miss Dymond, this is a surprise. I didn't expect–'

'Why didn't you tell us how things were at Grove Hill?' Jowan demanded.

'I don't know what you mean,' Rose blustered.

'Mr Quintrell's illness? It was not sudden. So you cannot have been unaware.'

'Good heavens, if I believed all the rumours I hear – anyway' – her chin rose – 'it was Miss Dymond's decision to go. In fact she insisted on it. It wasn't my place to try and stop her. If Mr Quintrell is ill, well, you are a doctor. And Miss Dymond is skilled with herbs. So why have you come back?'

Phoebe was aware of Jowan's swift glance. 'He was beyond medical help,' he said tightly.

'What do you mean was?' Rose said. 'He's not...? He's dead?'

The floor started to heave beneath Phoebe's feet and the hall darkened. 'I'm sorry,' she murmured. 'But I–' She heard a clatter and thump as guns and bags dropped to the floor. Knowing she was about to fall she groped for something to hold on to. A strong arm encircled her waist.

'God sakes, miss!' Ellin's warm breath fanned her cheek. 'You is all wet!' Relieved and bereft that it wasn't Jowan who was holding her Phoebe relaxed against Ellin's plump bosom.

'We were caught in a thunderstorm.' Jowan's voice seemed to be coming from a long way off. 'Please ensure Miss Dymond has a bath and something to eat, then put her to bed. I must return to the ship but I'll be back later.'

'Now, miss, you come long-a me,' Ellin coaxed. 'We soon have you feeling better.'

Phoebe made a huge effort. 'Quamin...'

'Give him food as well,' Jowan ordered. 'And somewhere to sleep. He's willing to work so if you want wood chopped or water drawn.' He pulled a small leather drawstring pouch from a pocket inside his breeches and shook out several coins. 'Will this be sufficient?'

'That is most generous, Doctor,' Rose gushed. 'Miss Dymond will have every attention.'

377

Two hours later, freshly bathed, wearing a clean nightgown, her hair smelling of rosewater and loose about her shoulders, Phoebe was in bed in the little tower room. As Ellin's footsteps clattered down the wooden stairs Phoebe raised the cup of hot chocolate unsteadily to her lips.

Providence would be ready to sail in a few days, and Jowan Crossley would leave. *If only* – no. She mustn't look back, only forward. When she left Cornwall she had cut all ties. Jowan had honoured his commitment to ensure she reached Jamaica safely. Though her circumstances had altered with Rupert Quintrell's death – *they had altered long before that. But he would never know* – her future was not his responsibility.

He would return to his career, to Cornwall, and to his family. She would stay here. Thanks to Aunt Sarah she could build a new life, a useful life, independent and self-contained.

She had not sought love. Everyone she had loved had been taken from her. She had vowed never to risk that pain again. But love had come upon her unexpectedly, filling the dark corners of her heart with radiance and warmth. It had imbued her with courage and strength. Through it she had learned and grown. And despite his accusations, his mistaken idea of her, she could not regret anything. Losing his company would be agony. What she had experienced with him could never be repeated and to settle for less was impossible.

Yet she was fortunate. Her knowledge and skills were desperately needed, especially among the refugees of whom there were many hundreds.

She would employ Quamin, if he would stay. During her visit to the apothecary she had seen that a woman out alone on Kingston's streets was considered open to any approach. It had been a salutary warning.

With little money to spare for cabs or carriages, Quamin's presence when she walked to her clients would provide protection. He could carry her medicine chest, or shopping. And later, if he showed interest, she might involve him in the preparation of roots and herbs.

Putting the empty cup on the floor she lay down. Life would go on. One busy day would follow another. Caring for people, treating their ills, healing their wounds, helping babies into the world and easing the pain of those leaving it: that was love of a kind. She would find contentment and be grateful for her memories. But like any recovery it would take time. And while the wound was still raw so too was the pain.

As her breathing slowed and her body relaxed, tears seeped between her closed eyelids.

Chapter Twenty-Three

Back on the packet – after exchanging a brief greeting with the master as they passed on the gangplank – Jowan plunged into work. He went first to the sick bay. There he gave purges, blue pills and James's Powders, sewed up a gash, set a broken finger, and re-dressed wounds sustained during the fight with the privateer. He sat alone in the mess and swallowed the dinner Mossop put in front of him.

After checking the food stores he withdrew to the saloon to update the crew's medical records then make a list of drugs to be purchased. And that brought back memories of accompanying Phoebe to the apothecary. Everywhere he looked as he moved about the ship he was reminded of her.

Shedding his coat and rolling up his shirt-sleeves he drew out a chair and opened his ledger. The ship was noisy with activity. On deck the sailmaker's gang repaired torn canvas. The carpenter and his mates hammered and sawed, turning new spars and replacing splintered planks. Wafting through the open stern windows the acrid reek of hot pitch was accompanied by the *clink* of caulking hammers as oakum was jammed between patched hull timbers.

Up aloft one rigging crew fastened new ratlines to the starboard shrouds of the mainmast while another replaced a damaged forestay. The walking wounded polished brasswork, applied linseed oil and turpentine to the rails, or spliced and whipped frayed ropes.

Resting an elbow on the polished wood, Jowan rubbed his forehead and tried to concentrate. But tension encircled his skull like an iron band. After a minute he flung down the pen, raking his hair with both hands.

While he was busy he was able give his full attention to the job in hand. But as soon as it was finished his thoughts returned to Phoebe. Her stricken face haunted him. Even as the accusing words left his lips he had been consumed with guilt and self-loathing.

But goddamn it he *loved* her. *And accusing her of marrying Quintrell in order to inherit Grove Hill – that was his idea of love?* The sweat of shame oozed from every pore. What he'd done was unforgivable.

The instant attraction that had so shaken him had swiftly developed into respect and admiration as he began to recognize the qualities that made her so different from other young women of his acquaintance. Not that she considered herself remarkable – except perhaps in her healing skills, and those she was always quick to attribute to her aunt's training.

Though her modesty, deflection of praise and desire to be of use indicated a proper upbringing, they were rooted in her character and personality.

But despite her reserve and quiet demeanour she possessed considerable spirit. And, as he knew to his cost, to be the target of her anger was an unsettling experience. Yet when she believed herself unobserved there was about her an air of wistfulness he found profoundly touching.

They had both resented his appointment as her guardian. Yet within twenty-four hours she had been constantly in his thoughts. He had managed to hide his increasing attachment to her by exercising the iron control he had developed to deal respectfully with his father and perfected throughout a demanding medical career.

But yesterday that control had cracked. The strain of knowing what he knew about Rupert Quintrell, and that she had no idea what manner of man her uncle had betrothed her to, had pushed him over the edge. The thought that she would choose to stay with a depraved, corrupt, rakehell unfit even to lick the soles of her shoes was beyond bearing.

So he had accused her of all that Quintrell claimed of women. He had known instantly he was wrong, that he'd made a terrible mistake. The shock on her face – *the shattering distress* – would stay with him forever.

What could he say that would ever be sufficient apology? Should he have told her what he'd learned of Quintrell's history? But how could he have burdened a young woman – even one as remarkable as she – with such information? It went against everything he had ever been taught about protecting women.

Had he described the events and influences that had moulded Quintrell's character, turning an indulged motherless boy into an utterly amoral man, he would certainly have given her a different picture from the one she had received from the sick man's father. But would it have changed anything? No doubt she would have found Quintrell's behaviour repellent. But because of the compassion that informed and enhanced her professional skills, and because it was only too clear that the slaves were wreaking their own revenge, she still might have felt bound to stay. He had not dared take that risk.

Quintrell was a stranger she had not even met. So surely she could feel no grief or sense of loss over his death. And she was free now. But even had he not made those dreadful accusations – he leaned on the table, covering his face with his hands as her voice echoed in his head. *If that is how you view my actions then we have nothing more to say to one another – ever.* She had been white to the lips and trembling like an aspen. But she'd held his gaze, her chin high, while then – as now – he burned with shame.

How could he even think of declaring himself with Quintrell perishing in such horrific circumstances, even though living would have condemned him to a far worse end? Even if – and God help him for thinking it – the man had deserved to die.

She could not remain in Jamaica, that much was clear. He would speak to Burley, ensure a cabin was kept for her. Perhaps during the voyage back to England she would allow him the opportunity to make amends.

A warning shout, a hoarse scream and the thud of a body hitting the deck jerked him out of his reverie. He was already halfway to the companionway when he heard the mate shouting for someone to fetch the doctor.

Her feet silent on the carpeted landing Phoebe stopped outside Rose's door. Taking a deep breath she lifted her chin and knocked twice. She heard movement then Rose opened it, her brows lifting.

'Yes, Miss Dymond?'

'I wondered if I might speak to you.' Seeing Rose's hesitation she added quickly, 'If this is not a convenient time—'

'No, no,' Rose said, stepping back, 'I was just doing my accounts. Come in.'

'Thank you.' Walking into the sunlit bedroom – the bed now concealed behind a folding screen of hand-painted silk – Rose used as her private sitting-room, Phoebe saw a ledger lying on the open lid of a walnut bureau-cabinet.

'I won't keep you long.'

Pushing the mahogany armchair in which she had been sitting closer to the bureau, Rose indicated a small sofa upholstered in yellow damask. 'How are you feeling now?' She clicked her tongue, her forehead puckered in sympathy. 'It must have been dreadful for you. Doctor Crossley told me – about the slaves,' she added, as Phoebe stiffened warily. 'He was right to bring you back at once.' She shuddered. 'I've heard stories of entire families being massacred in their beds. But to have come all this way from England, and for nothing.' Shaking her head she sighed. Her expression reflected sadness and concern but beneath it Phoebe sensed heady relief and recalled Rose's fear of Rupert. 'Poor William will have to be told. I only hope the shock will not prove too much for him.'

'No doubt he will be saddened by the news,' Phoebe said, 'but hardly shocked. After all, it was not entirely unexpected.'

Shock slackened Rose's jaw but she made a quick recovery. 'Why, Miss Dymond, what a strange thing to say. What can you mean?'

Recalling Rose's refusal to warn her, Phoebe strove to remain calm. 'That long before he left for England Mr Quintrell knew well the danger his son was courting.'

'Danger?' Rose blustered.

'His treatment of his slaves, among other things.'

Rose shrugged. 'You are a stranger here, Miss Dymond. You do not understand.'

Phoebe could take no more. The intense strain of the past few days coming on top of her emotional turmoil over Jowan Crossley erupted. Heat enveloped her. She could feel herself shaking and her heart hammered against her ribs. 'You are right, Mrs Stirling, I don't understand. I don't understand the mentality of a wealthy man who would father a child on a thirteen-year-old slave. Nor do I understand that man's son seducing his own twelve-year-old half-sister in order to break the spirit of the child's mother – the mistress he and his father shared. So, it's true, men like William Quintrell and his son are beyond my understanding. And I would not wish it otherwise. If you have sympathy to spare, keep it for the child I delivered of a stillborn babe and

385

could not save. She needs it far more than I.'

Rose's mouth hung open. Closing it with an audible *snap* she swallowed. Her face worked as she pressed her fingertips to her temples and Phoebe sensed her mind racing. *'William?'* She shook her head. 'No, you must be mistaken. Rupert perhaps – but William was *my*–' She covered her mouth with one hand.

'I'm sorry,' Phoebe said, shocked and ashamed at her loss of control, *at her anger.* 'I shouldn't have–'

With a bitter laugh, Rose dabbed her eyes with a scrap of cambric. 'What fools we women are.' She drew herself up. 'Is that why you wanted to speak to me, Miss Dymond?'

'No.' Phoebe folded her hands. 'I do not regret what I said, but it was not intended to cause you pain. I came to ask you if I may stay on here for a while. I will pay for my board and lodging,' she added quickly. 'And Quamin's, for I shall need the protection of a manservant.'

'You're not returning to England?'

Aware of Rose's shrewd scrutiny Phoebe tried to keep her face expressionless as she shook her head. 'As you said, I have come all this way. My skills are needed here, especially among the refugees. But it may be a while before I can find a place of my own so–'

'There's no hurry for that,' Rose said quickly. 'Indeed, it will be very useful to have you here. I confess I have suffered a great deal lately with the headache. Now I come to think of it, the *vicomte* and his family have booked passage to England on the *Providence* packet. They will be gone in a

386

few days. You can have that room. Being larger it will be more convenient' – she gestured with her open palm – 'as both bedroom and private sitting-room. Of course I would have to charge more. But we will come to an arrangement. I have many friends and acquaintances. You won't lack for work. And people like the *vicomte* are willing to pay whatever...'

'I don't plan to profit from others' misery, Mrs Stirling.'

'A noble sentiment I'm sure,' Rose was tart. 'But it takes money to keep a roof over your head, clothes on your back and food on the table.'

The following day Phoebe was in the little tower room. The mid-afternoon air was moist and humid after an earlier shower. Wearing her lightest gown, her hair coiled high on her head, the windows open to catch any breeze, she was warm but not uncomfortably so.

The letter to her uncle had taken almost an hour. The difficulty of deciding what to include and what to omit had resulted in several false starts and the bed cover was littered with screwed-up sheets of paper.

Eventually she had decided simply to relate the basic facts without going into unnecessary detail: Dr Crossley had escorted her to Grove Hill where they had found Rupert Quintrell terminally ill. She was now back in Kingston, residing with Mrs Stirling, and would remain here. Assuring him that she was in good health and spirits she finished by sending her best wishes.

She flexed her shoulders and arched her back,

then bent to add her signature. Next she would write a note of condolence for William Quintrell and enclose with it the miniature of his son.

Placing the completed letter beside the miniature that lay on the white lace runner covering the lid of her trunk she dipped her pen. As she lifted it from the ink-bottle she heard voices outside the door at the bottom of the wooden stairs.

She held her breath, waiting, utterly still, hope battling dread. The voices stopped. At the knock her heart kicked so hard she gasped.

'Miss Dymond?' Jowan's voice.

Her first attempt to speak produced no sound. She cleared her throat and tried again. 'Yes?'

'May I have a word?'

Laying down the pen she set her writing case on the trunk lid. 'I'll come down.'

She heard the door close, his boots on the stairs, and leapt to her feet as his head appeared.

'I beg you will forgive this intrusion. But there are so many people downstairs.'

'I understand the Duclos family is leaving today, and another has arrived to take the room.'

Remaining on the top stair Jowan brushed his hair back, a gesture of nervousness rather than vanity.

'I must apologize for not returning yesterday as I said I would. There was an accident on board. Brennan fell from the rigging and was killed.'

'Oh, I'm so sorry.' Phoebe recalled the able seaman. During the privateer's attack she had sewn up a gash in his skull. 'Did he have family?'

'Fortunately not.' Restless, preoccupied, he

388

shifted from foot to foot. 'I'm delighted to see you so much recovered.'

'I'm very well, thank you.' There was another long pause.

'Phoebe – Miss Dymond.' The words were torn from him, low and intense. 'I – I owe you a profound apology – the things I said – I cannot–'

'Please don't,' Phoebe said quickly, his acute discomfort reminding her too clearly of her own shame after her outburst to Rose. He flinched as if she had struck him.

Bracing herself, for surely now he would go, she waited, watching his gaze flick round the room then linger on the miniature. Even though it was all too late she could not bear it if once again he jumped to the wrong conclusion.

She moistened her lips. 'You find me writing letters. I'm returning the miniature to Mr Quintrell. He might be glad to have it as a memento.'

'You don't want to keep it?'

Phoebe shook her head. 'It wouldn't be appropriate. Nor do I wish to.' She took a breath. He would be leaving tomorrow or the next day. She could tell him now. 'You see, the reason I insisted on going to Grove Hill was to tell Rupert Quintrell that I did not wish to marry him.'

Shock drained the colour from Jowan's face as he stared at her. '*What?*'

'I thought it was the honourable thing to do. In the event, circumstances made it impossible. I never even saw him. And now – well, it's no longer relevant.'

Jowan's voice was hoarse. 'W-why didn't–?'

'I tell you? I did try.' Phoebe saw him wince and

389

knew he was remembering his accusations, *his refusal to let her explain*. A flush darkened his skin and he turned away.

Phoebe forced a polite smile. 'It was very good of you to come, Doctor Crossley. As you see I'm fully recovered. Please excuse me, but I must return to my letters if I'm to have them ready before the packet sails.'

He looked up quickly. 'You can finish them once you are on board. I think I told you, did I not, that one of the non-medical duties required of the ship's doctor is to sort the mail, so–'

'Yes, but I won't be on board. I'm not returning to Cornwall.'

'Not? What do you mean? You cannot stay here.'

'Indeed I can,' Phoebe said calmly, while a pulse fluttered in her throat. 'Doctor Crossley, you have done all that was required of you, and more. Now we must go our separate ways. You need not be anxious on my account. Though my life here will not be as planned it will be no less fulfilling.'

He raked his hair, turning one way then the other. She knew he would have begun pacing had there been space to do so. He resembled an animal in a cage that was too small. 'Where will you live?' he challenged. *'How* will you live?'

'Mrs Stirling has kindly agreed to let me stay here for the time being. As for how–'

'Phoebe, this is no place for–'

'This house, or this town?' She was finding the conversation increasingly difficult. 'I was brought up in a port so I'm aware of the dangers. But I shall have Quamin's protection when I am about the streets.'

'Surely your uncle would not–'

'My uncle has his own life,' Phoebe interrupted. 'It was to pursue it that he agreed to my betrothal. He would not wish me back. Nor would his new wife. I'm sure I shall do very well here. It may take a little getting used to but Cousin Amelia always said I was woefully unsuited to polite society. Still, perhaps the refugees will forgive me that in exchange for my skills and practical help.' She swallowed. 'I will always be grateful to you for – for giving me the opportunity to work with you on the ship, and for your acceptance of my remedies.'

He gestured helplessly. 'How could I do otherwise when so often they proved more effective than anything I could offer.'

'You are very kind.' The strain of talking to him, maintaining her poise, pretending she was fine, was becoming intolerable. She had to make him go, now, quickly. 'We will not meet again, so please accept my very best wishes for your future happiness.' Not daring to offer her hand for fear he would see how it shook, *not daring to touch him*, she made a formal curtsy.

His features taut, he stared at her for a long moment. Then with an abrupt bow he turned and left.

As the door closed on him, Phoebe sank onto her bed, hugging herself, rocking in silent agony.

Jowan stood in the hall. He should leave. *We have nothing more to say to each other.* Why hadn't she told him she wasn't going to marry Quintrell?

Because it wasn't his business. And when she attempted to explain why she had accepted the arrangement in the first place, instead of listening to her, allowing her time to explain in her own way, fear for her safety, *fear of losing her* had made him lash out

He had listened to Rupert Quintrell's poison, yet he had refused to listen to her.

He had tried to apologize, but she did not want to hear. Why should she? He had not listened. He should go. Yet he couldn't make his feet move. Perhaps – perhaps if he went back in and declared himself, told her how deeply he loved and admired her. *Such behaviour would be adding insult to injury. Why should she believe him?*

During the past year she had been moved around like a pawn on a chess-board: powerless: an inconvenience to her uncle and his plans for remarriage, a disappointment and irritant to her cousin, finally disposed of to the depraved Rupert Quintrell.

Now, for the first time since her aunt's death, she was free to decide her own future. And if that future did not include him, could he blame her? What reason had she to trust men? *But he would show her not all men were the same.*

No, if he loved her he must give her what she wanted most – freedom. It would cost him far more than he could ever have imagined. But her happiness must take priority over his own.

The rest of the day and night passed in a blur. There was a physical ache in his chest and his head pounded from the tension knotting his shoulders.

After a night during which her sleep had been punctuated with restless dreams both frightening and wrenchingly poignant, Phoebe had woken with a gasp, her heart beating wildly, her face wet with tears. Unwilling to risk sleep again she got up and went to stand at the window of her little tower, watching dawn break and the sun come up.

Dressing in her spotted muslin she went down to see the *vicomtesse* and her baby son before the family left the house to board the packet. The *vicomte* took her letters and promised to hand them to the master.

Unable to face food, Phoebe swallowed a cup of chocolate simply to stop Ellin scolding then returned to her room for her hat. She would watch the packet leave. Seeing it go would draw a line under the past weeks and put an end to all foolish hope. With Quamin beside her she set off for the waterfront.

But as they reached the quay she saw that *Providence* had already cast off her mooring ropes. With the wind filling her foresail the ship was moving away from the wooden jetty. The deck and rigging swarmed with men as the main was hauled up and the topsails loosed. Phoebe glimpsed the *vicomte* at the rail and guessed his wife and baby were below with Mary who would be bustling around getting them settled into their cabins.

Straining her eyes as she searched, Phoebe recalled her first day aboard the packet and Jowan's offer to escort her up on deck. Terrified of the sea, wondering if she would survive the voyage to reach Jamaica, she had stood frozen at the bottom of the companionway. When he urged her forward she had turned on him in panic-stricken fury. Then their eyes had met. The contact had lasted only moments, but its effect had changed her forever.

Scanning the activity, every nerve and muscle taut as she sought his familiar figure, she wondered whether it might not have been better had their paths never crossed. Denial came instantly, and was absolute. No. She could never wish that.

She could not claim to be losing him: he had never been hers. And though she would miss him more than words could express, knowing him, loving him, had given her so much. Because of him and his friendship she had grown and learned. Not just about medicine and healing, but about herself: about life, about what it meant to love.

But even though she could see the ship leaving and knew it was impossible, she still could not entirely banish the foolish ridiculous dream that maybe, somehow, during the night Jowan had realized he loved her.

And if he had, what difference would it make? He had a job, a responsibility to the packet and her crew. He was on the ship and it was bound for Cornwall. Their time together was over. They had fought and clashed and argued. But they had also discussed and shared and worked together in mutual respect. *She would miss him so much*. Her breath caught unexpectedly and she choked down a sob.

'Miss?' Quamin's face was anxious.

Unable to speak, she shook her head, wiped her eyes and raised her hand in a gesture intended to assure him she was fine. She tried to smile but her lips quivered uncontrollably. Bending her head so that the brim of her hat hid her face she pretended to brush dust from her skirt as her chest heaved painfully. She had experienced loss before, and grief. But not like this. Never ever like this.

Out of sight behind a wall of casks Jowan watched Phoebe's struggle. His own eyes burned and overwhelming relief left him physically weak as he realized that she too had been hiding her feelings. *But why?* Suddenly he understood. She had told him the first time they met that she hadn't wanted him to feel obligated: either to her uncle or to her. So even when her anger at having his guardianship imposed on her had begun to soften, to grow into something warmer than mere friendship, she would have been afraid to reveal it: afraid he might consider her a burden, an additional responsibility, an *obligation*.

He gazed at the slender girl trying so valiantly not to break down. What had it cost her to keep such powerful emotions so tightly controlled?

A great rush of love and admiration engulfed him. He had never expected to meet anyone like her. She was both girl and woman: in so many ways strong and wise beyond her years, yet in others naïve and vulnerable. Her determined independence would cause him anxious days and sleepless nights. But he could not contemplate a future without her.

Picking up his luggage, knowing the next few minutes would be the most important of his life, he drew a deep breath and stepped out from behind the casks. 'Phoebe?'

She spun round, disbelief vivid on her tear-stained face. Her gaze darted from the bags he was holding to the departing ship and back. 'What are you–?'

'I couldn't go.' He set the bags down. 'A surgeon from the naval hospital was only too pleased to take my berth.'

'I d-don't – why?' Shock was making her teeth chatter.

He shrugged awkwardly. 'If you are staying here then so am I. I want you to understand it is entirely my choice.' He had never felt so nervous in his life. 'You are under no obligation whatever to work with me.' He paused, took another breath, and pressed on. 'Or to be my wife. Though I hope with all my heart you can forgive me sufficiently to agree to both.'

Her eyes widened. He saw her face turn pale. As she raised a hand to her throat fear squeezed his heart. Instinctively he reached out, afraid she was about to faint.

'Phoebe? Are you all right?'

'Yes. Oh yes.' Radiant joy lit her face, suffusing it with colour. Then, heedless of the surrounding slaves, wharf-gangs, passengers, and business-men she lifted her arms and walked into his embrace. Holding her close he pulled off her hat and buried his face in her hair, inhaling the sweet fragrance that was uniquely hers.

Quamin examined the ground at his feet, grinning as he darted sidelong glances at them.

Drawing back, Phoebe searched Jowan's face. 'Your family.'

'My parents,' he corrected gently, 'have their life back in Cornwall. Just as your uncle does with his new wife. You will be my family. You and our children.'

A rosy blush bloomed in her cheeks. Her eyes were luminous. 'But your career with the Packet Service. I thought – I mean I was given to understand that you joined because you were seeking challenge and adventure.'

He smiled down at her. 'Really? May I ask where – or rather who – told you so? Was it Mossop or Grigg?'

'Grigg,' she admitted shyly.

Stifling laughter, Jowan shook his head. 'My reason for joining *Providence* was far less romantic.' Remembering the harrowing weeks of grief and frustration his smile faded. 'I could not be what my parents wanted, and they could not understand my need to follow a different path from my brother.' As her gaze softened in sympathy he offered a brief prayer of thanks for the girl in his arms. Then, leaving the past where it belonged, he turned his thoughts to the future.

'As for challenge and adventure' – lifting her hand Jowan pressed his lips to her palm then held it against his cheek – 'dearest Phoebe, life with you will give me all I could desire – or cope with – of both.'